Praise for Author

Tamara Linse

"Linse's gift for fiction lies in her seemingly offhand but richly engaging observations. ... Linse makes each journey relatable and emotionally textured while occasionally injecting her signature literary observations." —IndieReader

"Linse writes as if flexing her own ranch-toned muscles, creating intense, original characters and letting them loose. The result could fill a novel—or two. All bodes well for Linse's future work." —Kirkus

"Linse has created an intimate portrayal of a small family coming to terms with tragedy and strife. ... Linse juggles the hurts of the different characters well, with each suffering from a need to belong and struggling to balance their family and personal lives." —*Publishers Weekly*

"By far, the author's greatest talent is her beautiful eye for detail. She has the remarkable ability to paint a picture with just a few choice words. She does this both in the way she perfectly portrays all four of her narrators, as well as in the way she describes the scenery. It's obvious she loves this land and knows it well." —Books Direct

Also by Tamara Linse

How to Be a Man (stories)
Deep Down Things

Earth's Imagined Corners

Book 1 of the Round Earth Series

Tamara Linse

willow words

Print
ISBN: 0990953327
ISBN-13: 978-0-9909533-2-6
Print (Amazon)
ISBN: 0990953319
ISBN-13: 978-0-9909533-1-9

Epub
ISBN: 0990953335
ISBN-13: 978-0-9909533-3-3
Kindle
ISBN: 0990953300
ISBN-13: 978-0-9909533-0-2

Edition 1.1

For Ma Strong, who loved him despite everything

Holy Sonnet VII

At the round earth's imagined corners blow
Your trumpets, angels, and arise, arise
From death, you numberless infinities
Of souls, and to your scattered bodies go;
All whom the flood did, and fire shall o'erthrow,
All whom war, dearth, age, agues, tyrannies,
Despair, law, chance hath slain, and you, whose eyes
Shall behold God, and never taste death's woe.
But let them sleep, Lord, and me mourn a space;
For, if above all these my sins abound,
'Tis late to ask abundance of Thy grace,
When we are there. Here on this lowly ground
Teach me how to repent; for that's as good
As if Thou hadst seal'd my pardon with Thy blood.

John Donne (1572–1631)

Earth's Imagined Corners

Part 1

Chapter 1

Anamosa, Iowa, 1885

ara Moore should have nothing to fear this week. She had been meticulous in her entering into the ledger the amounts that Minnie the cook requested she spend on groceries. She had remembered, just, to include her brother Ed's purchase of materials to mend sister Maisie's doll house and to subtract the pickling salt that she had purchased for sister Esther but for which Esther's husband Gerald had reimbursed her. She stood at her father's shoulder as he went over the weekly household accounts, and even though her father owned Moore Grocer & Sundries from which she ordered the family's groceries, he still insisted she account for the full price in the ledger. "No daughter of mine," he often said, though sometimes he would finish the thought and sometimes his neatly trimmed eyebrows would merely bristle.

Despite the buttressing of her corset, Sara hunched forward, somewhat reducing her tall frame. She intertwined her fingers so that she would not fiddle with the gathers of soft navy wool in her overskirt, and she tried not to breathe too loudly, so as not to bother him, nor to breathe too deeply, in order to take in little of the cigar smoke curling up from his elephant-ivory ashtray on the hulking plantation desk.

As always, the heavy brocade curtains armored Colonel Moore's study against the Iowa day, so the coal oil lamps flickered in their brackets. Per instructions, Sipsy the maid lit them early every morning, snuffed them when he left for the grocery, lit them again in anticipation of his return at seven, and then snuffed them again after he retired. It was an expense, surely, but one that Sara knew better than to question. The walls of the study were lined with volumes of military history and maps of Virginia and Georgia covered in lines, symbols, and labels carefully inked in Colonel Moore's hand. In its glass case on the bureau rested Colonel Moore's 1851, an intricately engraved pistol awarded to him during the War of Northern Aggression. Sipsy dusted daily, under stern directive that not a speck should gather upon any surface in the room.

Sara's father let out a sound between an outlet of breath and a groan. This was not good. He was not pleased. Sara straightened her shoulders and took a breath and held it but let her shoulders slump forward once more.

"My dear," he said, his drawl at a minimum, "your figures, once again, are disproportionate top to bottom. And there is too much slant, as always, in their curvatures. I urge you to practice your penmanship." His tone was one of indulgence.

Inaudibly, Sara let out her breath. If he was criticizing her chirography, then he had found nothing amiss in the numbers. The accounts were sound for another week. Later, when he checked the numbers against the accounts at the grocery, there was less of a chance that she had missed something.

He closed the ledger, turned his chair, and with both hands held the ledger out to her. She received it palms up and said, "I will do better, Father."

6

"You would not want to disappoint to your mother." His drawl was more pronounced.

So he had regretted his indulgence and was not satisfied to let her go unchecked. His wife, Sara's mother, had been dead these five years, and since then Sara had grown to take her place, running the household, directing the servants, and caring for six year-old Maisie. Ed needed little looking after, as he was older than Sara, though unmarried, and Esther, the oldest, was married with two daughters and farm of her own.

Sara straightened her shoulders again and hugged the ledger to her chest. "Yes, Father," she said and turned and left the room, trying to keep her pace tranquil and unhurried. She went to the kitchen, where Minnie had a cup of coffee doused with cream and sugar awaiting her. Minnie gave her an encouraging smile, and though Sara did not acknowledge what went unsaid between them—one must shun familiarity with the servants—she lifted her shoulders slightly and said, "Thank you, Minnie." Minnie, with the round figure and dark eyes of a Bohemian, understood English well, though she still talked with a pronounced accent, and Sara had only heard her speak the round vowels and chipped consonants of her native tongue once, when a delivery man indigenous to her country of origin walked into the kitchen with mud on his boots. Sara tucked the ledger in its place on a high shelf and then allowed herself five minutes of sipping coffee amid the wonderful smells of Minnie's pompion tart. Then she rose, rinsed her cup, and applied herself to her day.

The driver had Father's horse and gig waiting, as always, at twenty minutes to nine. As Father stretched his fingers into his gloves, pulling them tight by the wrist leather, he told Sara, "When you come at noon, I have something unusual to show you."

"Yes, Father," she said.

It seemed odd that he would concern her with anything to do with business. He left her to the household. He had long tried to coerce Ed into the business, but Ed's abilities trended more toward the physical. He was a skilled carpenter, though Father kept a close rein on where he took jobs and whom he worked for. All talk of renaming the business Moore & Son had been dropped when Father had recently promoted the young man who was his assistant, Chester O'Hanlin, to partner. Mr. O'Hanlin had droopy red muttonchops and a body so long and thin he looked a hand-span taller than he really was, which was actually a bit shorter than Sara. Mr. O'Hanlin didn't talk much, either, and he seemed always to be listening. He held himself oddly, cocking his head to one side, first one way and then the other, his small dark eyes focusing off to the left or right of the speaker. His nose, long and wedge-shaped, seemed to take up half his face. "Chester, the Chinaman," Maisie called him outside of his presence because of the way he stooped and bobbed whenever their father entered the room.

The subject dispatched, Father nodded and then strode out, mounted the gig, and nodded to his driver, who urged the horse to a brisk trot.

The rest of Sara's morning was spent as it always was, planning menus with Mini and ordering the necessaries for them, overseeing Sipsy the maid and the cleaning of the house, double-checking that the laundry was done to satisfaction and sufficiently pressed, planning the construction of new clothing for the family, arranging the at-least weekly supper parties of Father's, and many other things, all the while keeping a watchful eye on Maisie so that Father never felt the need to

8

punish her. This morning, because the nursemaid Clara had her day off, Maisie was in the kitchen attempting to help Minnie, which meant that she picked up tasks, soon became bored with them, and put them aside as quickly as Minnie could invent them, so Sara soon diverted her to a chair near the stove with the thread and needle of her sampler.

At twenty minutes to noon, the groom had Sara's bay mare, Miss Bailey, saddled and waiting for her. Father had suggested to Sara that she use the smaller trap pulled by Old Methuselah, the swayback blue roan gelding, but Sara preferred the singularity of riding sidesaddle on Miss Bailey. Although the elderly groom still prepared the mare and helped Sara to mount, he didn't have to do the heavy work of harnessing, which made Sara feel slightly better about the effort, and once she reached her destination, she didn't have the worry about where to park or Old Methuselah's habit of working his rein from the post and wandering off to find a bit of grass to graze.

Sara checked that Sipsy the maid was looking after Maisie and picked up the packet of Father's lunch from Minnie in the kitchen and tucked it into the saddlebags. She scratched Miss Bailey's withers near the pommel of her saddle, so that the horse leaned toward her a bit. "Feel good, Bails?" she said. With the groom's help, Sara mounted and settled her legs into the pommels, intent on riding the couple of miles down the hill into the heart of Anamosa and to the grocery.

The Moore house sat on a hill overlooking the village of Anamosa, the name of which meant "white fawn," so dubbed for a sweet Indian child. The name had recently been changed from Lexington, to avoid confusion with the plenitude of other post stops so named. The Moore house overlooked the house of Colonel William T. Shaw—Father made sure of that. Colonel

Shaw had been for the North, and the story goes that when Father came to settle he made sure his house, though of plantation style rather than the gothic turreted style of the house of "that scoundrel from Iowa," as Father called him, rested above his. Sara did not remember the move, as she was very young at the time. Nowadays, when Father met the prosperous colonel during the course of his daily business, he would sometimes extol the virtues of southern cooking, as Colonel Shaw preferred the cuisine of New England, having grown up in Maine. Colonel Shaw, in his turn, would sometimes assert the filthiness of the habit of cigar smoking.

As Sara rode into town, the midday heat of the May sunshine was relieved by the breeze down the valley and the fluttering shade of the stately oaks. She could smell the mud of the Wapsipinicon River, named for Indian lovers who leapt to their deaths from the bluffs, and, faintly, the smokestack of the industries at the Additional Penitentiary on the far side of the settlement. The leaves rustled, a faraway train gave a low series of hoots, and birds sang madly and gaily in the trees. Miss Bailey's smooth-but-fast Tennessee Walker gait was as gentle as a drift in a canoe. Sara passed the modest house of the widow who had taught her her letters, next door to a large German family whose garden took up most of their plot and whose plentiful blonde children played in the road and waved to her as she passed. She joined the main road behind the long freight wagon with its team of six, heads bent in duty, and then turned off the side street to her father's store.

Sara rode around to the back alley. The way was partially blocked by a tall cart pulled by mules, which was being unloaded into the grocery by a group of men. Three of the men, including the one obviously the foreman, were brown-skinned and spoke to each other in an undulating language full of stops and starts, but the fourth was a light-skinned man about Sara's height in worn and dusty clothes. Something about him caught Sara's attention and held it. Besides obvious differences of origin and skin tone, something otherwise set him apart from the other three, working alongside them though he was. The man was tall and stout, with a broad chest and barrel legs. Sara couldn't tell how old he was. His shoulders sloped like an old man who had carried heaviness for a long time, but his face was unlined and youthful about the jaw. He had light-colored eyes, a mustache, and brown hair under his hat that was just long enough to curl around his ears, which stuck out a little.

Sara dismounted at the end of the alley—why challenge the fates and have the horse spook at the men's comings and goings—and led Miss Bailey past the cart to the back of the store and wrapped the rein around the hitch rail. Out of habit, though, Sara did not think to knot the rein but rather just flipped it around the pole, as Miss Bailey had never run off once in all the time she'd ridden her. She murmured and patted Miss Bailey and retrieved the packet of lunch from the saddlebag and took it inside, leaving the horse to slump her hind end into resting position, one back leg bent with its hoof resting on tiptoe. When Sara entered her father's office, he was bent to his books, but he immediately stood. His stance, normally ramrod straight at right angles to God's green earth, today canted a bit forward onto the balls of his feet.

"Ah, Sara," he said, "I've been wondering when you would arrive."

Sara glanced at the case clock on the shelf, which read three minutes to twelve. She was even a bit early, just a bit. "I'm here, Father," she said. She hesitated, glanced at her father, and went to the sideboard and began to unpack his lunch, as she always did.

"No, now," he said, "leave that to me. I would like you to search out Chester. He has that commodity we spoke of earlier."

Her father never said, "Leave that to me." He expected her to perform her duties efficiently and up to inspection. Father believed everyone earned their place in this world with an array of duties and few rights. He also took as granted that his place in the world included the unquestioning obedience of his family and staff. With the discipline of a well-run army, they took care of him so that his energies could focus on his ventures.

Despite her surprise, Sara said, "Yes, Father," and left the packet on the sideboard.

"Now go find Chester." He smiled and nodded.

"Oh, yes. Yes sir," she said and turned and left his office. Almost immediately, she met Mr. O'Hanlin, as if he had been listening at the door, though she knew that that was something Father would not have tolerated. Mr. O'Hanlin wore a wine-red cravat and an ornate vest of green under his gray flannel coat. Now, he bowed to her and smiled so widely Sara thought his lips would crack.

"My dear Miss Moore," Mr. O'Hanlin said, his Irish lilt a bit broader than usual. He said it again, as if trying it on: "My dear Miss Moore. What a pleasure it is to see you this fine day."

"It is a fine day, Mister O'Hanlin," was all Sara could think to return. Something bothered her about the way he looked at her. His usual gaze fell to the left or to the right or skittered around the edges, but today he looked under his short red eyelashes right into her face—upwards, as it happened, since he was a bit shorter than she. Well, not exactly into her face, but rather as if he were looking through her, looking at an idea of her instead of the flesh and blood woman that she was. She was tempted to glance behind to see what he was peering at.

"My father said something about a commodity?" Her shortness bordered on rudeness, but she felt the need to find out whatever it was Father wanted from her.

"Ah, yes, the commodity." His focus shifted to the wall. "You will not believe the sumptuousness of it. We recently contracted with a supplier who contracted with a broker out west who contracted with a ship from the ocean isles."

Mr. O'Hanlin stepped back and indicated she should precede him out the back door. As they circled round outside and down the back steps that led to the basement storeroom, Sara caught sight of that man, that dusty light-skinned man from the street, who was hefting a huge carton, his broad back quivering with effort. She glanced from him back to Mr. O'Hanlin, whose lavish clothing contrasted so sharply with that man's tattered coat, its blunt sleeves coming well short of the man's wrists and the shoulder seams yearning to part.

In Sara's mind, the comparison did not bode well in Mr. O'Hanlin's favor. Though she knew nothing of character of the man on the street, she noted his determination at the job of hefting this carton, the contradiction held in the question of his age, his strength, which at this moment seemed pure and unadulterated and uncomplicated. Even the shabbiness of his clothing seemed less disingenuous, more honest and more forthright—dare she say kind?—and even the smell of that man's perspiration, which Sara could only imagine, was sweet in her mind. Mr. O'Hanlin, on the other hand, did not perspire.

13

He was clean and well-kempt. Surely, he was intelligent as well, as Father would not otherwise have taken him on, much less made him partner. Mr. O'Hanlin took pride in his appearance, even though he was slightly pigeon-chested and also shorter than she. He was well off and well provided for, as he was a partner to Father. However, in this spur-of-the-moment comparison, something deep within her tipped the scales in favor of the unknown man. The idea held for a moment. It was as if the clear tone of a bell sounded, separating this moment from the past and the future.

Sara and Mr. O'Hanlin descended the steps and entered the storeroom, and as they steered around a precarious pile of crates, Mr. O'Hanlin put one hand upon her arm and the other around her waist to guide her. She drew back sharply, almost tipping the crates, and left him standing with his arms outstretched, fingers twitching. She felt a strong urge to run back up the steps, away from that moment, and she would have, but there was something that Father wanted from her, so she must see this through. Besides, Mr. O'Hanlin was just looking out for her welfare. The pile of crates was precarious, and he simply was performing the duties required of any man. She tried to smile in his direction, as if it were her clumsiness that led them to that difficult situation. Still, she was grateful when Mr. O'Hanlin dropped his arms and walked to a counter along the wall.

On one corner of the counter was a small crate. With the tips of his long fingers, Mr. O'Hanlin lifted off the crate's top, which had previously been pried up, and set it on the counter. Packed within the crate were large oblong newspaper-wrapped parcels. Up wafted a faint sweetness with an earthy undertone. Mr. O'Hanlin held out his hand, indicating she should inspect them. She took off her gloves, finger by finger, and placed them on the lid. She pulled one of the parcels from the crate and unwrapped the newspaper, a *San Francisco Examiner* dated April 17, 1885. As she did, the ends of the long narrow green leaves sprang from the parcel and pricked her right index finger, drawing blood. She shifted the fruit to her left hand and stuck the pad of her finger in her mouth, sucking the sting from it, tasting the salt of it.

She glanced at Mr. O'Hanlin. He was watching her, his jaw slack. His red tongue darted out of his mouth and wet his top lip. When he saw her glance, he pulled back his tongue, and his jaw shut and clenched.

Inside the newspaper was a strange-looking fruit. The top half bushed into long narrow spiky leaves, and the bottom oblong globe had a roughly textured skin in brown, green, and yellow. The odor was stronger.

"It is a pine-apple," Mr. O'Hanlin said. "It originates in the Kingdom of King Kalakaua, within the expanse of the Pacific."

Sara stroked the golden green diamonds of the patterned skin with her fingertips. Then, using both hands, oozing index finger held straight so as not to touch the fruit, Sara pulled it to her face and inhaled deeply. What had been faint and sweet before now became thick and pungent. The smell reminded Sara of apple cider mash—full and wet and ripe, but with a dark, decaying undertone. It quickly overwhelmed her. It seemed to enter her and make her body quicken and fill her mind with strange yearnings. If only she could … what? She didn't know. But she would settle for a taste to complete the smell. She held the fruit out to Mr. O'Hanlin. "I've never tasted—what is it?—a pine-apple before. Shall we cut a slice from this?"

15

Mr. O'Hanlin froze. "No," he said, "no." He reached out his hands, insistent, until she placed the fruit into them. He began deftly covering the fruit with newspaper and then wrapping it back up. "I mean, your father expects to sell them for a tidy profit. He would be disappointed if we, if you …" He glanced back at the stairway. He then tucked the wrapped fruit back into the crate and scooped up her gloves, which she plucked from his hands, and then he picked up the lid and replaced it. He talked over his shoulder: "What I mean to say is, if we partook of the fruit before it's time, I mean, before all the proper arrangements were made, it would not be right. It would go against, um, all that was proper. We must advertise, we must, must, as it were, tantalize the public, it is an expensive investment, this type of thing, and we must see it through to its proper outcome, in its proper, um, time." He looked at her, his lips pressed together but twitching.

Sara did not know what to think. Was he talking about a piece of fruit? Surely Father would allow her, if she ventured a portion of the household budget, to taste this fruit? Mr. O'Hanlin's reaction was all out of proportion to the thing at hand. What was Father aiming for her to gain from this transaction, this viewing of a fruit that she could not even taste? She shook her head in bewilderment.

Then Mr. O'Hanlin's face opened up. He seemed to calm. He took a step closer to her and put his hands on her shoulders. They were damp and very warm through the cotton of her shirtwaist. He said, "My dear Sara, you will see, in due course, it is for the best." His eyes looked up into her eyes, and then he removed his right hand with its long fingers from her shoulder and lifted it as if to touch her face but then left it suspended so that she could sense the heat of it on her cheek.

At first, all Sara registered was his physicality, the hand that encompassed her shoulder, the heat of him on her face, the shattering of her personal space, but then she registered his familiar usage of her name. He had used her given name, without invitation nor cause. It was her name, hers, not to be passed about like an unembroidered handkerchief. This seemed the worst of all violations. A shock went through her so totally that her mind blanked, and she stumbled back and turned and pushed up the stairs into the open air.

Chapter 2

I t seemed on purpose, the way the backs of the businesses hulked over the narrow alley and blocked the May noonday sun. Each time James Youngblood returned to the cart with that pat-thief Ricci to heft another crate, he focused on the light at the end of the alley, just as he had on the light that came through crisscross of bars at the end of his bed. If he let himself dwell on the enveloping shadows, the walls closed in upon him, and his pulse began to race. Focusing on the light, however, kept those particular wolves at bay.

This alley light was reflected light, much like that that had emanated from the heavens, had streaked gloriously to the earth unimpeded, had touched the open air, the curl of green leaves, the cool of water sliding over rocks, before its misfortune of bouncing through those small panes of glass into that tall dead space near the elevated walkways and then through the riveted iron flats of the cell door. For those irretrievable months, months that had added into years, it had helped James to think about what that light had touched, just as it helped him now.

James pulled his eyes back from the end of the alley to where he was hefting his end of a small barrel that smelled of apples, but he was plunged in darkness as his eyes adjusted.

Still, Ricci pulled on his end of the barrel, and James stumbled, nearly dropping his end. They set the barrel down and breathed. Ricci's mouth was set in a line, and he seemed on the verge of saying something, but then the man glanced down the alley, and his face opened up in surprise as the light dimmed and they were caught in shadow. "The Colonel's daughter," Ricci hissed at James. "Make like beavers." He turned to the other two and bent his head toward the cart, indicating that they should get to work, industriously. And then he bent to pick up his end of the barrel, and so did James.

As they toted the barrel, James glanced toward the end of the alley, and out of the penumbra of light came the figure of a woman leading a horse. At first, the woman loomed large, and James blinked to clear his vision, but then she shrank to human proportion. James's heart gave a leap: it was his mother, there in the street! For that split second, a feeling welled up inside him and closed his throat. It was a conflicted feeling, one of love and relief and joy but also of constriction and gravity and panic. It was the feeling his mother invariably brought forth during their long association, moving about from place to place, just scraping by, never knowing if the next day brought light-headed soul-wrenching hunger or the sting of a step-father's hand.

But, no, this wasn't his mother. That was not possible—his mother was two months' dead, brought down by consumption. Physically, this woman was dissimilar. She was much taller, almost as tall at James. Her dress with its lush green skirts was richly laced and gusseted and tucked, and her heavily embroidered riding cape was of deep brown wool—more expensive than anything his mother had ever worn. This woman's black hair was swept back in the more modern style,

19

with the curls cascading from the back crown of the head instead of around the ears like his mother's. She had a long nose with an ess curve in profile, well-proportioned gray eyes, a small mouth, and a narrow jaw that at present she had set in concentration. Instead of a large bonnet, this woman's hat was small and perched somewhat to the side, and her stride was different than his mother's. His mother's walk had been both proud and sensual, and even as she aged men noticed her entering a room, for which James invariably felt apprehension for what that might bring. This woman, however, even in stride, seemed to be tucking in on herself, her head bobbing low, as if she wanted to make herself smaller. James understood that feeling.

James took in this woman and felt his desire for her rising. It came upon him fast and strong. His limbs weakened and his male member swelled. He wanted to touch her, to see her without her hat, her hair splayed down her shoulders, her bare legs peeking from underneath her chemise. But he turned his eyes away and quelled the thought as best he could. It could only make him feel worse. It had been so long.

The woman led the horse around the cart to the hitching rail and flipped her rein around the wood. The other three men stopped and watched her. James glanced at the expression of hunger on Ricci's face, and suddenly James felt protective over this woman whom he'd never met. He wanted these men to avert their eyes. They had no right. These men were ex-convicts and immigrants without a penny to their names. What right had they to ogle this woman? They should limit their desires—and their eyes—to women of their own race. But, then, he was an ex-convict and penniless too—well, except for the lucky nickel tucked into his left shoe—what right had he?

The thought brought shame rising within him mixing with the strong desire and jealousy of the moment before, and surely he turned red to the ears.

After wrapping the rein, the woman retrieved something from her saddlebags, and before she turned to make her way to the back door of the store, with her free hand she caressed the horse and whispered to the animal. It was such an intimate gesture, so private and tender, that a new feeling arose in James. Though it was desire, it was much larger than mere lust and swept through James and left him unmanned for a moment. This particular brand of feeling was something he had never felt in his twenty-nine years. It made him want both to curl into a ball and to spread his arms, to whisper to someone and to shout to the world.

The woman disappeared into the back of the store, and the walls once again closed in. James took a deep breath and gathered himself. He turned to find Ricci waiting for him. "Cut your lollygagging," Ricci said and then called James something in his native tongue. James could not understand it, but the meaning was clear: Ricci held James in low regard. His body was turned toward the other two men, and he looked over his shoulder at James. The other two nodded with wry smiles. Then they began working again.

Bergamasco and Lottardi were the other men's names. James remembered because names have power. The two men were fresh off the boat and had not spoken a word of English in James's hearing, though Ricci had been in the country long enough to make it from Halifax to Cedar Rapids and get caught with his hand in a gentleman's pocket and thrown in Anamosa for a stretch. James had known Ricci by sight only when they were both incarcerated. Ricci had worked to shape the limestone used in the turrets and bastions of the new penitentiary's buildings, which were steadily transforming from wood to rock, and rumor had it he'd carved one of the lions near the flower beds in front of the administration building. James had had his stint at stonework, too, which left his hands vibrating and his body sore to the bone for months. Fortunately, a crotchety draft horse had illuminated James's equine talents, bringing him to the attention of the man in charge of the farm, and James had spent most of his time among the horses in the barns and in the saddlery. The head man took it at face value and treated James well, even though James's crime was that of horse thievery, something some persons responded to a bit overzealously. Ricci was released months before James, but then James sat across the rooming house breakfast table from him and he had eyed James for a while before offering him a job. Pitiful wages even for an ex-convict, James knew it and Ricci knew it, but there was nothing to be done. It was sustenance for another week. James had no other opportunities in view.

Ricci glanced at Bergamasco and Lottardi and then at James. Then Ricci said, "That's all right." His smile didn't reach his eyes. "You're my half-centesimo man." He said it in English, and then he turned to the other two and said it again in his native tongue. He smiled and they chuckled. Lottardi then said something that made Bergamasco snort and Ricci's broad chest push forward and his head rest higher on his neck. It was all part of that thing men did, something the male of the species had been doing to James his whole life, and James knew that he would have to act in some way. It would continue until something happened, until he was somehow crushed or it came to blows. Ricci needed to prove something to these men.

22

James looked Ricci square in the face and said, "I'll complete this job, but then I believe our contract should be terminated, as I sense it is mutual."

Ricci's eyes narrowed as he looked into James's face. His mind worked behind the eyes. "You gave me the week, and I mean to keep you to it," he said in a loud voice. So he wasn't going to let James off that easily. The hope of a facile solution faded. But then it came to James's mind that he was a free man, no longer a convict. The feeling swelled, as did the anger.

Once before, he'd been trapped in the employ of his uncle, and that is what had led to his incarceration in the first place. Shortly after Mam's last husband died, they had been in desperate straits, hardly making it. A step-uncle, the brother of Mam's last husband, agreed to take James on as a stable hand. He had worked for a month, and come payday, the uncle said he was expecting a large payment the next week and that he would pay him then. James and his mother had a roof over their heads and food on the table, so James had not complained. But then a week turned into a month, and at the next payday, the uncle said again that the payment had not come in but it certainly would soon. James had had his misgivings, but Mam had urged him to stay on. "The man means to pay us, Son," she said. "And by the time he does, we will be owed a small fortune. Be patient." And so he was. Three months turned into four, which turned into six, and James became more and more agitated as the months went on. The uncle if anything became more domineering. Finally, James confronted the man, who said that beggars cannot be choosers and they were lucky to have him. They could leave if they did not like it. Mam was cowed by the man's argument and tried to calm her son, but it so enraged James that he went to the stable, saddled a fine gelding, and took off, leaving his mother behind. He had meant to leave her for good, as she had so obviously chosen against him, and he had long been wanting escape. However, the sheriff and his men caught up with him two days later in a town in the next county, and that's how he ended up in Anamosa Additional Penitentiary.

This was different, though. There was no cause for him to be trapped, no woman hanging on him. Anger rose further. Yes, there were three of them and they were more than willing to take their knuckles to him, but damn it to hell, he'd had enough of it. The nectar coursed through his veins, and it felt good, right.

He stepped forward and said, "My job description did not entail me as your whipping boy, you little tin god on wheels." Then he braced. This breached the line of caution.

The anger built on Ricci's face as he registered James's insult. The other two men did not understand what James had said, but they must have sensed his tone and Ricci's body language, as they began to circle around behind James. James started backing away, slowly at first, but then they quickened their pace, and he scrambled as he tried to protect his back. He had to find a wall, a fence, something to keep them from grabbing him from behind, or he needed a weapon of some kind, a stick, a rock. It was his only hope. Desperately, he pushed backwards, keeping his eye on the three men.

In his haste his shoulder bumped something soft, with a slight give, something warm and alive, and he turned and saw it was the woman's horse, he'd bumped its back haunches, and the surprised horse was curling, tail tucked, bunching under to kick with both back legs—what any horse would do when surprised from behind. James dove to the side as the hooves

24

whipped past him, missing him by less than a handspan. As soon as the hooves landed, the mare pushed off with her front feet, her body listing heavily to the left. She jerked her head, snapping the rein, and bolted down the alley, just as the woman who owned the horse pushed through the door at the back of the store. She ran to the hitching post, skirts held high, and looked up, bewildered by the missing horse. She looked both ways just in time to glimpse it as it disappeared out onto the street at the end of the alley. She looked to the men, who had stopped advancing on James and stood with their hands at their sides.

Ricci took one glance at James and stepped to the woman's side. "This man," he said, "this man just spooked your horse. He ran her off. He's the one."

James shook his head but then nodded and gave a short bow. "I did, ma'am," he said. "My deepest apologies. I did not mean to. Let me assure you, it was accidental. Let me corral her for you." Before she could respond, he turned and trotted down the alley after the horse. He glanced back to make sure the men weren't following him. They weren't—for now.

He had seen which way the mare had turned, so he followed her onto the street. A horse's first instinct is for the herd, but if the woman had gone to the trouble to ride, rather than walk, this mare's herd most likely would not be too close. James hoped, though, with nought chasing her and such a gentle nature, the mare's panic would ease quickly and she had not gone far. The street he turned on was bordered by small houses with yards enclosed by fences. Nothing to draw a horse to stop there. She would be looking for a spot of green—and there it was. An undeveloped lot with trees and grass. Sure enough, there was the bay mare, head down and grazing,

25

calming herself, one long rein trailing. From a distance, he inspected her nose to tail to make sure she hadn't hurt herself in her panic. No signs of injury. That was good.

James walked up and stopped, not too close, giving her room, and turning his body to the side so he wasn't confronting her, and then began murmuring low. "That's a girl. You're a good girl, aren't you? Not a wild bone in your body. Tame as an old kitty cat, aren't you? Nothing to be frightened of here. Just little old me, and all I want is to scratch your withers a bit, now don't I? Won't that feel good?" He kept on murmuring as he worked his way closer. The mare ignored him at first and kept grazing but then raise her head and eyed him. When he got close enough, he stopped and held out his hand. Horses were curious creatures and social by nature, but they were also looking after their safety. If they were decently broke and hadn't been ruined and you approach them quietly and with respect, they most likely would take you up on an offer of friendship. That's one of the many things James loved about horses. They were understandable, and unless they'd been maltreated their hearts were as good as gold.

Sure enough, the mare took a tentative step forward. James waited with his hand out. She took another step. He had nothing to offer her, but that didn't matter. She sniffed his hand and then his face, doing that thing that horses do in greeting, exchanging breath. James blew in and out, letting the horse smell his breath and taking in the warm green grass scent of hers, all the while slowly reaching and gathering in her rein. Then she relaxed. "Whew," she was saying, "it was scary out here all by myself. I'm sure glad you happened along." He didn't reach for her head—a mistake many people made—but instead sidled along to reach her withers and scratched them a bit, not too much. Then her patted her gently on the shoulder and turned back toward the store. "You're a good girl, aren't you?" he said and sighed. Just standing next to the horse made him feel better.

Chapter 3

ara's mind worked as she strode along the street and ground her teeth. What would make Mr. O'Hanlin believe he had the right to touch her shoulder, to use her given name? She would tell her father and he would immediately be sacked. How dare he? Then a thought came to her that halted her in her tracks. Her father had arranged it. The two of them had come to an agreement: she was to be married to Chester O'Hanlin. Oh my God, oh my God in heaven. What was to become of her?

But wait. Would that be so bad? She tried to imagine a life together. Mr. O'Hanlin—Chester—seated across from her at the dinner table, his habit of holding the knife in his left hand while eating, never switching the knife and fork from hand to hand and maintaining the knife throughout his efforts, never placing it on the edge of his plate. They would dance together, his left hand holding her right and his right in the small of her back, his cheek close to hers. Wait, no. He would have the right to touch her. The thought was repulsive, very repulsive. And that was not all. There were things required of a wife by a husband, and the thought of Mr. O'Hanlin doing these things was so repellant to Sara that a shiver crawled up her arm and then down her back. How could she submit to that? His physical person was nothing less than disgusting to her.

She shut her eyes and took as deep a breath as her corset would allow and let it seep out between her lips. She opened her eyes. In the distance, a couple, a man and a woman, walked away from her toward the countryside. The sun had slipped from its noon peak and started its descent toward evening. She felt it on her shoulders. The flat light had softened a bit, as had the heat. There was the sound of children playing in a backyard, and someone practiced piano scales. A dog barked once, twice. Someone yelled, "High-up," to a team. Far off, she heard the hoot of a train. The air smelled strongly of the lilacs in the yard next to her, blooming gloriously, and of horse manure.

Her horse. She glanced up to see that man from the alley walking toward her leading Miss Bailey. Before, he had seemed strained, as if the work of shifting the crates took more than the usual toll upon him, but now his shoulders were relaxed and his face was open and his head was turned toward the horse as he spoke to it. His face was broad and square with flat cheeks and a wide forehead, his nose was short but not stubbed, and his eyes were somewhat narrowly set but a surprising shade of blue. He looked happy, and Sara wondered what he was thinking. He glanced up and saw her and smiled, but it was a smile that was meant for the horse because he glanced to the horse and then back again and then his eyes widened a bit, his shoulders squared, and his expression flattened out. His body was stiff as he walked up to her and stopped.

"We have not been introduced," Sara said, conscious suddenly of the eyes behind the windows of the houses.

"Indeed, we have not," the man said, "but your horse

cannot help that." He glanced over at the horse and his face softened again. Then he gave Sara a short bow. "First, let me apologize profusely for the maltreatment of your horse. I was … I mean, it was an unavoidable accident, spooking her like that. Let me assure you that I would never harm this horse." As he said it, she believed it immediately. It was in his look. He glanced around. "Since there are no parties handy to do introductions, I fear we must do them ourselves, if you'll permit me." He pulled his hat from his head and held out the hand with the rein. "James Youngblood, at your service."

It was not proper, this introduction, and eyebrows would raise. She hesitated to extend her hand, but then she looked into his face and he was looking at her and really seeing her. He wasn't dismissively looking past her. Sensing the open perceptiveness of his look made her suddenly resent Mr. O'Hanlin's earlier possessiveness all the more. Almost without thinking she extended her hand. However, instead of him taking it and kissing it or shaking it and even taking it in both of his, as some men did, he simply extended the rein to her, which she took without touching him.

"It isn't a proper introduction, either," he continued, "until you tell me your name."

"Oh! I am sorry," Sara said. "I am Sara Moore. Pleased to meet you." She tipped her head. His hat held in both hands, Mr. Youngblood bobbed his head too and then stood there, not speaking, eyes askance but attentive at the same time. It bespoke more than polite interest but also a respect for propriety and space. As the silence grew, Sara became uncomfortable, as she searched her mind for something to say, but Mr. Youngblood seemed to sense it and came to her rescue.

"Here, let me fix that rein," Mr. Youngblood said. "Just

enough to get you home so that someone can mend it properly." He placed his hat back on his head and pulled a Barlow knife from his belt and flicked open a blade. He held out his hand and waited for her to place the rein in it. Once she had, he used the knife to split the end of the leather into two thongs. Then he took the short piece of rein that had been broken and hung from the bit and cut a slit in it. Then he pulled the reins through his hands to make sure they weren't twisted and then threaded the thongs through the slit, wrapped them around the rein, and tied them in a square knot. So, instead of two long loose reins, there was one rein that circled from one side of the bit to the other that would have to be hoisted over the mare's ears. "A bit short, but it'll do," he said and held it out to her. She reached for it.

Standing next to him, she felt petite and small-waisted, which was a good feeling. She glanced at his shoulders and remembered their quiver and strain as he hefted the crates. Something about the thought prompted within her a longing, an ache. She felt her body leaning toward him and then realized that she wanted his body near hers. She took a deep breath and with it came his scent. Although his clothes needed spruced, he smelled clean, newly bathed, and his sweat was fresh and pleasant, not rancid from days of accumulation.

As Miss Moore took the rein from James, her gloved hand touched his, which jolted James to his toes. A quick intake of breath. Had the touch been on purpose? He searched her face but it showed nothing. Could he dare to hope? Because now, standing next to her, he wanted to hope that it had been on purpose. He wanted her to want to touch him. He just wanted her—to be next to her, to hear her voice, to smell her perfumed scent with its earthy undertone, to touch her. Oh God, to touch her. It bowled him over, this feeling. He took a long shaky breath.

"May I walk you back to the store?" he asked. Please, oh please, he added silently.

A look of panic crossed her eyes as she turned her head and glanced the way they had come. "Heavens, no," she said.

A flat rejection. All the air that had seemingly pumped him up the moment before escaped in a rush, and he cringed inwardly. "Oh, I am so sorry, Miss Moore. So so sorry. I did not mean to presume. Forgive my hast, my ..." He turned toward the horse and breathed, trying to comfort himself with the mare's smell. As he'd feared, he was beneath her consideration.

"Oh, no! Mister ... what was your name?" she said.

He looked at her face. Instead of the revulsion he had expected, her eyes were wide in alarm and her hands reached toward him, one hand cupped and beseeching while the other was flat, palm forward, fixing him in place.

"Youngblood, is the name," he almost whispered.

"Mister Youngblood," she said. "I did not in any way mean to refuse you." Red crept up from her collar and into her cheeks. "I won't go back there. I mean, what I meant to say was, I won't be returning to the store. I mean to return to my home."

And then she waited, as if she were prompting him to say something. Did she want him to offer to escort her? After the crush of the moment before, he did not know whether he could, but one look at her face, head thrust forward, eyes open, trying to get him to say something, he did say it: "You ... would you like me ... I mean, would you be needing an escort? Home, I mean."

Almost before he finished his question, she said, "Yes. I would be honored to accept your escort."

Jubilation! It was not a rejection of him. What it had been, he did not know—there was something there—but it was not meant for him. "Allow me," he said and plucked the rein back to lead the mare. He almost offered his arm but then thought better of it. Instead, he held out his hand to indicate she should lead. They started walking first toward the store, but then she turned east at the first available intersection.

"You like horses," she said.

He did. It was the one thing in this world that felt good, felt right. "I do," he said. "They just make sense."

"Make sense? In what way?"

James shrugged. "Just make sense. People are hard to read, but a horse will indicate what he's feeling. When he is happy, he will nudge you. He will roll in the dirt and shake, or he will take off across the pasture kicking his heels." He smiled at the thought. "If he is angry, he will lower his ears and take a bite out of the gentleman next to him. You know what a horse is feeling. And a horse knows what you are feeling too. You cannot lie to a horse. He sees through it."

They did not demand a pound of flesh. This was a new thought, a realization about James's place in the world and the nature of the world itself. Horses were inherently social and banded together in herds. Sure, the stallions fought one another, but not with the viciousness nor deceit of men. There were well-established rules, and the fight was not to the death, a world of decency and cooperation.

"I am fond of Miss Bailey," Miss Moore said and smiled toward the horse. They were walking uphill under the cool shade of a row of elms that skirted the drainage on one side of the road.

James's belly growled loudly. He clamped down with his diaphragm to try to stop it, but still it ground on. It reminded him of how hungry his was. There was the apple dumpling in his pocket from the rooming house. Maybe he should offer some to the lady. "Have you eaten?" he asked. "Missus Smit, at the boarding house where I'm staying, makes the best apple dumplings."

"Oh, I know Missus Smit," Miss Moore said. "She runs a good establishment, so I hear."

"Indeed she does," Mr. Youngblood said. "She takes in … Let's just say she's charitable toward the not-so-fortunate, but she also insists upon propriety within her premises. And she's a great cook." He retrieved the cloth bundle from his pocket, unknotted it, and flipped it open for Sara to see. The small golden pie was only slightly crumpled. "This won't tide you over for long, unfortunately," he said and then gave a nervous laugh.

Sara laughed too. In truth, it was a sad looking thing, having ridden in a pocket all morning, but the smell of the cinnamon and apple reached her nose, and she saw the brown ooze of the filling and she became aware of her hunger. Did she trust this man? It only took a moment—yes, she thought she did. "I would be honored, Mr. Youngblood, to share your pie." The formality of it struck them both as funny and they laughed again.

Grasping the pie through the cloth, Mr. Youngblood pulled it apart and held the cloth out to Sara. Sara pulled off her gloves and tucked them under her arm and then scooped the half of pie from the cup of his hands and brought it to her face. It smelled heavenly, and she was ravenous. Trying to be dainty, she took a bite. It tasted heavenly too. She closed her eyes and felt the soft sweet texture of the cooked apple and the salty crisp of the crust. She swallowed. It was all she could do not to wolf down the rest. After she had finished, she brushed her hands against her skirt to remove the crumbs and pulled her gloves back on.

"Thank you, Mister Youngblood," she said. "That was delicious. As you said."

"That's what I call bachelor cooking," he said and smiled. "Now if only there were thirty or so more around here." He made a show of digging in his pockets and opening his coat and peering into it and then glancing at her under his brows. The silliness brought an amused laugh from Sara, and he smiled back. It was dazzling. The crinkles at the corners of his eyes and the creases down his cheeks and the broad open mouth with teeth that were pleasantly crooked. An unreasoned happiness flushed through her.

He continued, "And who is Miss Moore, if I may be so presumptuous as to ask. What do you do when you're not, not …?" He didn't finish the thought.

Who was she? What did she do? Sara tried to think—what to tell this man? She was a middle daughter of four, and she kept house for her father, which was just what women did, nothing out of the ordinary. She was an old maid—"I'm not married," she blurted out. Not yet, thank God, she added silently. "Of course I'm not married. If I were, I wouldn't be here with you." She continued the thought to its natural conclusion but then realized the implications of what she had said and color rose in her cheeks. "What I mean is—" she said in a panic.

"It's all right," he interrupted, a bright look on his face, and somehow it was. This man relaxed her, made her feel safe from all the different ways one can feel threatened through the course of a day. She trusted him.

He smiled at her but did not say anything and seemed comfortable in the ensuing silence. They were walking along the slope of the hills on a road that wound around before eventually meeting the driveway to the Moore home. They had made good progress. The thought made Sara slow her step.

"I don't know what to say," Sara continued. "I am truly unremarkable. My father is Colonel Moore—I don't if you know who he is. He owns the grocery and other ventures. He was an officer in the War." She decided not to mention that he was for the Confederacy. "And we moved here when I was but a child. Let me see, what else? My mother, well, my mother …"

Her mother was dead and had been for five long years. How does one express something like that? To this day, it rent her world. Words did not suffice. How do you encompass the horror of months of bed rest and wasting away? Watching your beautiful and lively and kind mother as she diminished, as her thoughts turned inward and then evaporated, leaving behind the living husk? Those final hours when the death rattle shook the house to its very foundations, and Ed fled to the stables or on horseback. Esther, the no-nonsense caretaker, efficiently focused on Mother. Maisie, just a babe and unknowing. How do you explain your realization that Mother was the complement to Father, that she was the soft to his hard, the empathy to his businesslike objectivity, and without her all that was good and kind seemed to go out of the world?

Despite her best efforts, Sara choked a little as she sad, "My mother has passed on."

"So has mine," came his reply. "Just. I mean, she was laid to rest in March."

Sara look at his face but could not read his expression. He was somber—aggrieved, of course—but there was more to it than that. James then explained that his mother had had five husbands, an extraordinary thing. The first husband she had married quite young, and Mr. Youngblood's father had been her second. He was a gambler who ran off shortly after Mr. Youngblood was born. Her third husband was a man named Jacob Vincenti. He had been around for most of Mr. Youngblood's growing years, and he had been a good man but with little means. "That was when we were in New York City," Mr. Youngblood said and smiled. "He was always bringing Mam flowers. There he was working as a knacker all hours of the day and night. Dead tired, he'd be. But he'd remember to pick maybe some lilacs or marigolds to give to Mam. 'Eh, my little lady,' he'd say. She preened like a swan, she did." His smiled at the thought. "Sometimes he'd bring me candy. Lemon drops. Horehound. But he was killed in the War." When he said that, Sara was glad she hadn't mentioned her father's part in that war—if the step-father was from New York City, he would of course have been for the North. Mr. Youngblood's mother had two more husbands after that—an intemperate wastrel who ran off and an old man who lost his money and died and left them poorer than ever. "I was old enough to support her by then, so's she did not have to marry again," Mr. Youngblood said, his voice small.

"What was your mother like?" Sara asked. While losing a spouse and remarrying was not uncommon, five was a large number for anyone. What sort of woman had five husbands?

"She loved to dress up, and she loved bright colors," James

said as an impression of Mam came into his mind. She often smelled of the peppermints she loved, and when she could not get them she drank a tea made from wild peppermint. Her stature was short and small, but her presence loomed large. When she could, she wore the latest fashions, often remaking a dress into a new cut. Her dark hair she parted in the middle and, on days she stayed in, pulled back along the sides of her head or, on days she went out, curled around her ears. The sound of her voice, deep for a woman and for someone of her size. And then that cough that began shortly before his incarceration, the beginnings of the illness that would take her life.

"She danced for kings and presidents, you know, and at Tom Thumb's wedding," James continued. "At least, that's what she said. She told me once that she was part gypsy. 'Get your ears pierced, you're a member of the tribe,' she told me." He chuckled at the thought but then shook his head. "You'd think with all those marriages she'd have acquired enough money to keep herself." Maybe he shouldn't have said it aloud, but it was a thing that vexed him. How could she sell her person over and over to these men yet receive so little in return? She was a hopeless romantic absent a healthy and practical sense of self-preservation. That had been his purpose.

"Well, she sounds delightful," Miss Moore said. "You've a way with horses and you lived in the East, but I know nothing else about you. What do you do?"

"Me? Oh …" he said. What could he say? "I've worked a lot of odd jobs here and there. Some with horses. Moved around a lot." He did not want to lie but there was no way revealing his past would help him in this situation. He desired her approval in the worst way. He would tell her—he would—

if there came an appropriate moment.

"Really? I've never been out of Anamosa. Where've you been? What was it like?" Miss Moore asked.

"Oh, you know, all over. New York, Philadelphia, Pittsburgh, Chicago, points in between. Mam liked to move. The longest was in New York City, or maybe Chicago." He was silent again. The thought cast a pall over his mood, but he had to say something, so he changed the subject. "You know what? Some day, I'm going to own a team of horses and I'm going to hire them out out West." The Homestead Act meant that James could lay claim to an amazing 160 acres of land—him, with hardly a cent to his name, a landowner—and all he had to do was prove up on it. He didn't have to pay for it, but he had to live on it for five years and to make improvements, which was something he would have done anyway. Then it was his and no man could take it from him. He wouldn't have to go begging for menial jobs that barely fed and clothed him. He could raise his own vegetables and if luck was with him, he could build up a herd of fine mares and train each crop of colts himself. He could support a family on such a dream.

They had been ambling through a wealthy section of town up on the hills overlooking the business section of Anamosa. James had not been to this area. Miss Moore stopped, glanced up at the huge house above them, and put her hand on the gatepost. "Well, here we are," she said, a look of familiarity and fondness in her eyes.

James looked in awe. The home was grand—plantation style, with columns supporting two stories surrounded by broad porches on both levels and dormers and a widow's walk on the roof. The grounds encompassed at least five acres, if not more. Tall stately trees offered plenty of shade, and flowers lined the house and the walks. Tucked behind were a large stable, a small horse pasture, and lots of outbuildings. A formidable fence surrounded the property, white pickets in front, heavier log construction behind. The grounds and the house were in excellent repair and immaculate, all freshly whitewashed.

All this from her father's grocery. He was a man of means and influence. James had sensed that she was well-off but he had had no idea of the income at her disposal. It was a testament to her character that she remained so modest. James's admiration for her grew. But what was he thinking? How could he consider her appropriate for him when he had nothing whatsoever to offer, not even a good name? And how could a man of Colonel Moore's stature even consider someone in his station of life as a mate for his daughter? It was all so hopeless. He had to steel himself for the inevitable. This would simply be a pleasant memory for him to stow away and to take out when he was feeling low, nothing more.

"Arrived safe and sound," James said, trying to keep the melancholy from his voice, and handed back her rein.

"Indeed I have," Miss Moore said. "There was never a doubt in my mind, Mister Youngblood." Her voice was warm and confidential. And then she laid her gloved hand on his arm, which sent a shock through him and all sense of propriety and restraint fled.

If he simply said goodbye now, he might never see her again, and he desperately wanted to see her again. What could be done? In response to her encouragement, he ventured, "I am so glad to hear you say that, Miss Moore, because I, I …" Was there nothing to come to his rescue, no excuse he could offer, no inducement? "I am a fine man with a horse—"

"I can tell," she interjected quietly.

"—and if you were needing any sort of help in that department, I would be more than willing."

"I will mention it to Father," she said and then added, "he's always looking for skilled men."

Did this mean the colonel also was a man who rose above his station and judged other men by their characters rather than the contents of their wallets? Maybe, just possibly, there was hope. What could he do or say in furtherance of this cause? There had to be something. His feelings ran deep, and he had to express them. That was it. He would try to convey the depth of his feeling to her.

"Miss Moore," he said, watching her face, "you will forgive me my forwardness, I hope. You are an extraordinary woman. You are the most agreeable, er, I mean to say, I find you the most intriguing woman I have ever met. Let me speak plainly: If you found yourself the least bit fond of me, would you consider—" What? What could he say? They had just met. Could he propose such a thing? "Would you consider me in your heart? By that I mean to say would you consider extending our relationship for a longer term?" How could he in good conscience be asking this of her? But, if he were totally honest with himself, which he was not—how could he be, the state he was in—he would have admitted that somewhere, deep down inside, he had also noted her father's wealth and a small bit of hope had gleamed inside him. There were prospects there for which he had never dreamed.

In response, Miss Moore's eyes narrowed, but before she could speak he blurted in a panic, "With the utmost respect for your person. In no way to devalue your womanhood." It came out all wrong, every bit of it, but he could not regret saying it. If he had let this moment lapse without a word, he never would have forgiven himself.

Sara could not believe her ears. "Mister Youngblood!" she said. They had just met. What right had he to be saying these things to her. She knew not the first thing about him, they had not been formally introduced. He could be an ex-convict from the penitentiary for all she knew. Maybe she had encouraged him, but that still did not give him the right. In essence he had presumed in the same way Mr. O'Hanlin had presumed. This thought should have made her even more angry, and she tried to muster it, but instead the idea swept through her, and she found she liked it. What was so repulsive in Mr. O'Hanlin—his hands, his person—she longed for in Mr. Youngblood. She imagined them on the dance floor, his left hand in hers, his right hand on the small of her back, the heat of his body seeping through his clothes and into hers. This thought caught her breath up short, made her quicken in unimaginable ways, and she clutched at the gatepost. Could such a thing be possible? Could she spend the rest of her life with this man? She flushed at the admission. But, like Mr. Youngblood, she too was denying a deeper truth: Mr. Youngblood offered an alternative. He represented hope for a life of self-determination, a life in which she was able to make her own destiny. It lay deep within her like pirate treasure at the bottom of an ocean, undiscovered as yet, but all the more compelling for the phantasm it offered.

But of course nothing was simple. Sara was not officially betrothed, but what of that? If her father lobbied for it and Mr. O'Hanlin agreed, it was all but done. Within this transaction, her wishes did not matter.

She squeezed her eyes shut to try to dam the wetness. Finally she managed, "You see. I ... It's not possible. You see,

I'm …" Her throat closed on the words, and she couldn't complete the thought. Shaking her head violently, she turned and pulled open the gate and yanked Miss Bailey through. Without bothering to shut it, she made haste up the walk and around the house toward the barn.

James was crushed. He pulled the gate shut and latched it. So that was that. How could he have hoped for such a thing in the first place? It was preposterous, really. But he had had to ask. He had the memory of their walk together and her hand upon his arm to take with him. That was all.

What could he do now? He couldn't go back to work for Ricci. In fact, he would need to carefully avoid Ricci, if at all possible. Ricci would be laying for him now, and James would be lucky to avoid that confrontation. Yet he did not want to up and leave the town. Sara Moore was here. The unreasonable thought rose yet again: Perhaps if he plied his suit a bit longer, he would make some headway. Certainly her body language belied her words. Perhaps her mind would come round to her body's viewpoint. On the other hand, he had no money and no prospects for a job. Heaven forbid he get thrown back in Anamosa for a vagrant. Should he pack up immediately?

He stared at the house for a long while. So it came to this. If no other opportunities presented themselves, it was time to move on. Perhaps he would go to Kansas City. He'd heard there were lots of opportunities there. Leave tomorrow, he thought, or the day after for sure. In the meantime, he would lay low, try to avoid the run-in with Ricci and his gang.

Chapter 4

I t was still early when James returned from walking Sara home. He stuck his head into the kitchen to find the cook who came in to spell Mrs. Smit sitting at the kitchen counter, her stout ankles on either side of the stool, eating a large slice of buttermilk pie and reading *Ladies Home Journal*. She was a middling woman of middling culinary talent, and when she saw him, she ducked her head and appeared guilty of some misdemeanor or other. This permitted James to boldly walk in and suggest that maybe, quite possibly, he might avoid the communal dinner table and have a roast beef sandwich to take to his room—he did not feel up to tackling Ricci this evening but did not mention that, of course. Taking food to your room was not allowed, according to the rules posted on James's wall. "We're here for the constitution, not the fine palate," Mrs. Smit had said on a number of occasions, though in truth, her talents would have satisfied even the daintiest of appetites. The spell cook hesitated a moment, but James made a deep bow and said, "I would be forever indebted for your infinite kindness," and stood patiently. He did not let his eyes rest upon the pie or otherwise insinuate anything but the best of intentions. She considered for a moment, glanced at the half-eaten pie, and ventured that there might be a bit of mutton left that she could throw between last week's bread. When she delivered it, along with a draft of beer, James thanked her effusively.

Once he retired to his room, he put his sandwich and cup on the small table and then kicked off his boots. He sat in the chair and then stretched his toes up and then down and sighed. He held the sandwich with both hands and took a big bite. The crust of bread slathered in butter was the best part of the assemblage, unfortunately, as the meat was a touch old and overcooked and emitted the slightly footish odor characteristic of some mutton. He sniffed down toward his feet to make sure. Yep, the odor of his feet was strong but distinctly different from that of the sandwich. He took a swig of the beer to wash it down.

As he ate, he turned the day over in his mind. One thing was for sure: Miss Moore was like no other woman James had ever met. So unlike his mother. Mother's emotional life had been there for James to see, and with it came demands on his sympathies. Often these demands were only hinted at, but it was a game he and Mam had played at their whole shared lives, the steps well choreographed, so when she said, "What a day," or "Oh, the day I've had," he was supposed to insist she take to the settee or to her bed and he would scrounge together something to tide them over until the next day when Mam felt better. "My womanly countenance, how it fades," was her prompt for him to protest how beautiful and young she looked. "Don't worry about it, James, I'll take care of it," was her cue for him to insist that he take care of it, but "I think I'll manage," was her cue for him to let her alone.

The last time James had laid eyes on Mam, she had made the trip down from Oelwein. Before, when James had been placed in the penitentiary, she had moved to Anamosa but, without James's help, she had had no luck finding a way to keep herself. She had then moved to Oelwein to be a lady's companion, an employment James knew she chafed at. In her letters, she reported the lady to be miserly and demanding, which James lent only the minimum of credibility. Maintenance of Mam in all its forms was high as she could command. When she presented herself to James at the prison, she had taken special care at her appearance. Her hair was curled and her dress was newly pressed. However, the dress was patched at the elbows and had worn so thin in other places he feared the cloth would part. His first impression, though, was that she had aged considerably. Her walk was slow and slightly bent and her hands shook ever so much. She was also so slender that her cheekbones jutted alarmingly over her jaw. Her hand felt hot as he held it, and periodically she coughed deep in her chest and produced phlegm, which she discretely spit into a handkerchief, pretending to be covering her mouth for the cough. This was the affliction that would eventually claim her life.

He had not known, of course, that that would be the last time he would see her—her thin shoulders disappearing around the corner of his cell door, the guard looking away with deference to the lady's feelings. After that, her weekly letters became more erratic until they stopped altogether, and then he received a letter in a hand he did not recognize. It was his mother's employer informing him that Mam had gone to glory and was buried in a cemetery near Oelwein, if he cared to visit. If he were truthful to himself, he would admit that his first reaction had been immense relief, the lifting of an enormous but unrecognized burden, but guilt for that emotion immediately overtook him, and for the first time in his life he felt truly alone, that there was not another soul in the world who cared for him. The feeling was so deep and all-encompassing that he fell physically ill with what the doctor diagnosed as malaise and spent a number of days in the hospital wing.

During his walk with Miss Moore, she had not been at all like his mother. She had a self-contained confidence, a strength, that had been missing in James's mother. Miss Moore seemed to be able to care for herself, her emotions well in check, and yet she had also seemed pleased with their conversations and had prompted him to continue and had consented to his escort. Yet she had rejected him. With that hopelessness closing about him, he turned in for the night. He thought he would not be able to sleep, but the physical exertions of the morning had taken their toll on him, and the potent beer had been just enough that he was asleep almost before his head hit the pillow.

After he awoke the next morning, he dressed quickly, intent upon eating before Ricci made the breakfast table. Though he did not want to try the cook's generosity, he hoped to coax her to produce a fried egg sandwich and perhaps a cup of cold buttermilk, if there were one to be had. He checked the hallway outside his door, which was empty, and stepped quickly down the stairs. James was about to enter the dining room where an old man with an ivory-tipped cane sat with his coffee cup when he heard a door close firmly upstairs. Afraid that it was Ricci, James ducked quickly into the kitchen.

"Ssss!" the spell cook said. "You ain't supposed to be in here." She looked intently at him and then glanced away, once again with guilt in her eyes.

"I know, I am sorry," he said but stayed where he was out

of the sightline of the doorway.

"You get on out of here," she said. "You owe me that, at least, for …"

"I do, I know that," James said. "I was—"

She didn't let him finish, and her eyebrows raised as a thought came to her. "Say, you have to do something for me."

"I, well, sure."

She lowered her head on her neck and thrust it forward. "I find myself an egg or two short today." She paused and then continued. "You know how it is, one extra for pudding and then another extra for the, say, …" She searched her mind for something to add but apparently could find nothing. "You know," she said and shrugged, a sly smile across her face. "You run along to Missus Weiss's and get me two dozen eggs. She charges half of what that shyster Moore exacts."

"I can do that," he said. He had nothing else on his roster, and if he expected special treatment, he might expect to pay back the favor.

"Well, off you go then." She turned back to her breakfast preparations.

She must expect that he would pay for it. Had he been in command of more than a buffalo nickel, he might even have agreed, but he did not have the luxury. "Missus"—he could not remember her name—"well, I am more than happy to fetch them for you. However, I have not the means to purchase them, if that is what you were requiring."

"Sure you do," she said. "You think you can take advantage of a poor women simply trying to make the best of a bad situation." Her voice registered righteous indignation.

"No, in actuality I do not, I am sorry to say." He held out both palms. "Really."

48

She narrowed her eyes and shifted her face sideways but kept her eyes on him. "I think your mendacity will come back to haint you. Don't say I didn't tell you so." She focused on him for a minute before fishing in her apron pocket and retrieving a handful of pennies. She hesitated again before handing them over. "Two dozen. That's eighteen cents to Moore's forty. See that you come back with them, or you might find something *unexpected* in your stew."

James was now sorry to have prevailed upon her, but good to his word he received the tin pail to carry them and then listened to her directions to Mrs. Weiss's farm and then snuck out the kitchen door and was on his way.

Chapter 5

he evening of Sara's walk with Mr.
Youngblood, Colonel Moore was hosting a
supper party, so the rest of Sara's day was
ruled by preparations. Although her mind
returned to Mr. Youngblood and to Mr.
O'Hanlin and her father, she had neither the
time nor the inclination to ponder the situation. As always,
nursemaid Clara fed Maisie an early supper and would
entertained her in the upstairs nursery until bedtime, soon to be
joined by sister Esther's two girls, Charlotte and Lizzie, when
they arrived. Sara was changing for supper when Father arrived
home, so she did not see him until the guests arrived, and
though he gave her a meaningful look down the table when Mr.
O'Hanlin's name was raised, she let nothing register in her
demeanor and struck up a conversation with the elderly widow
sitting next to her. Luckily, thankfully, Mr. O'Hanlin was
unable to attend, as he maintained a strict schedule of Catholic
services some evenings during the week.

Though always subdued, brother Ed was unusually quiet
during supper, but he did smile up at her when Sara stood
behind his chair and rested her hands on his solid and fleshy
shoulders. She raised her eyebrows and then glanced at Father
and then back to Ed—is it something Father's done? she was

asking—but Ed just shrugged. During dinner, true to her keen and forthright character, sister Esther raised the topic of President Cleveland's mistress—she had strong feelings on the subject—while her husband Gerald steered the conversation to the merits of the William Deering twine binder versus the tried-and-true wire binder. Finally, supper completed, the men retired to the library to smoke cigars, while the women took coffee in the sitting room. Esther and Gerald gathered the girls and exchanged kisses before mounting their carriage home, and Sara retired, Father still closeted in the library with a business associate.

When the Sara entered Maisie's room for the night, it was way past Maisie's bedtime, but there she sat on the bed with one stockinged foot curled up under her lacey night dress and holding her life-sized China-head doll in her lap. Sara was pleased to see that Clara the nursemaid had brushed and braided Maisie's unusually long brown hair and made sure that her freckled face was scrubbed clean, as she was supposed to. Usually, on nights when there weren't supper parties, Sara did that task before tucking Maisie in. Evening chill had entered the room and Maisie had on one of her warmer nightcaps, Sara was glad to see.

"Maisie May," Sara said and flopped next to her on the bed and extended her palms behind her, leaning back and comfortably bracing herself and crossing her ankles. "Where's Clara? Where are you supposed to be?" She let her voice carry the amusement she felt. "Don't let Father catch you."

Maisie mimicked Sara's movements, letting the doll rest on her lap while she extended her arms behind her and crossed her wool-stockinged ankles. Her brow wrinkled as she said, "I just don't want to go to bed."

"You know better than that," Sara said. "Father will have something to say." As Sara said it she heard a noise and stopped to listen to make sure it wasn't Father. Just as she didn't want him to catch Maisie out of bed, she also did not want him to find her awake and have the urge to discuss things. She hadn't absorbed everything yet, and she had no idea what to say to him.

"It's not that I don't want to go to bed," Maisie said. "It's that I don't want to dream."

"Are you having nightmares again?"

"Uh huh," Maisie said and leaned forward and put her arms back around the doll. "I was dreaming about Momma."

"Oh, Little Sister," Sara said and leaned forward and put her arms around Maisie. "I didn't think you were old enough to remember her. How can you dream about her?"

Maisie considered for a moment and then said, "I don't think it's Momma I remember, but I remember ..." She tilted her head and played with the ribbons on the doll's bonnet. After a bit, she continued, "Why do things have to change?"

Why indeed? Sara was happy in her life. Why did the world—or, more specifically, her father—feel the need to ruin everything.

"Not everything changes," Sara said and sat forward and took Maisie's face in both her palms and looked into her eyes. "For example, I will always love you, my Maisie May. I'll always be there for you. And if Mother had had anything to say about it, she would be there for you too. And she always loves you. You can bet the farm on that. God just had other plans."

"I don't believe you," Maisie said, pulling her face away. "You say Momma wouldn't go but she did. God could take you away, too, at any time."

"God won't take me away, at least not for a long long time," Sara said. "Tell you what. Let me get into my nightdress and then you can brush my hair. Would you like that? Then I'll tuck you in and sing you a song." However, at long last, after Sara led Maisie to her room and Sara's lengthy process of undressing and preparing for bed, Maisie nodded where she sat. "Well, well, looks like the Sandman has come and gone," Sara said. "Here, let me put you to bed. We'll brush my hair another night." She led Maisie down the hall to her room and tucked her in and gave her a kiss. "No bad dreams, you hear?" she whispered. She went back down the hall and sat on her bed and gave her hair one hundred strokes, first flipping her head upside down and then right side up. She knelt by the bed, said her prayers, and got under the covers.

Sleep would not come, however, no matter how hard she tried. She counted backwards from one hundred, she told herself a fairytale, she focused on the sound of crickets out her window, but none of it worked. Her mind returned to the incidents of the day and played them over and over in her mind. Finally, in desperation, she got up in the darkness, slipped on her robe, and made her way to the kitchen and filled a glass with water from the pump in the kitchen. She padded into the dining room, set down her glass, pulled out a chair, and sat, listening to the quiet gloom. She was tired, and finally her mind began to unwind, and she felt only her body. The chair was firm and supportive underneath her, and the glass of water was cool in her hand. The air was chilly where her skin was bare. She heard the tick-tick of the grandfather clock and a breeze stirring the trees outside and the chirp of crickets.

She felt a hand on her shoulder and jumped. She craned to look but could only see an outline but then she smelled the shaving soap. It was Ed. Of course it was Ed. His outline was much bigger than Father's.

"Hey, Sister," he said as he pulled out the chair catty-corner to hers and sat down. "Couldn't sleep either, eh?"

She nodded but then realized he probably couldn't see that, so she said, "Yes." They both fell silent. She thought about Ed. A master carpenter, he was the one who fixed things. He didn't make a big show of his efforts like Father did but quietly tried to make things right. He had been the one, after Mother's death, to give her unobtrusive encouragement as she tried to figure her place in that new world. Through the darkness, Sara asked, "What so vexed you at dinner?"

"Oh, you know," Ed's voice came, deep and resonant. "The usual. I got that job over in Fairview. Good work, good money. A spiral staircase of Douglas fir. Ingenious design, really, the way the treads attached to the center post, almost free-floating, really, entering the upper story through a circle in the ceiling. An architect out of Boston, I believe." This was just Ed's thing. A giant puzzle of wood, beautiful and intricate. Sara could hear the fascination in his voice, and even though she could not see his face, she knew his auburn eyes would be focused in the middle distance, his mind working behind them. Ed continued, "Then *he* pulled me to work on simple buck-and-rail fencing, a favor to a business associate."

Not the first time Father had directed Ed's employment efforts. Ed had once had the opportunity to apprentice with a well-known builder of expensive homes, back when Father still harbored dreams of Ed inheriting the business, so Father had nixed the idea immediately. It was what Father had always done with Ed. But then it came to Sara that her situation was exactly the same as Ed's. Father had decided Ed's fate early on and steered Ed's course without consultation nor consideration of Ed's proclivities and talents, just as he did hers. This realization made what had been a pleasant retrospective of her life transform into something more sinister. Her muscles tensed. How dare he?

"How do you stand it, Ed?" Sara said. "His charting your path before you can even imagine there is one?"

"There will be no deserters in this man's army," Ed said, his voice taking on a bit of the drawl that permeated Father's speech.

Sara wished she could laugh. Yesterday, she would have. "But how do you simply take it?"

"You can get used to hanging if you hang long enough," came his reply. It was a line he often used. It came from one of the Wild West dime novels he read avidly as a youth and still picked up on occasion.

She sighed.

Ed got up and moved behind her chair and massaged her shoulders for a few minutes, his big hands encompassing them, moving gently and with precision. It was such a comfort. She leaned forward so the back of the chair did not interfere. After a bit, Ed pulled her back upright and kissed the top of her head. "Another day will dawn, Sister, come hell or high water." He yawned through saying, "Good night," and went up to bed. She listened to his tread on the carpet in the hall and then up the stairs. Perhaps now she could fall asleep.

Sure enough. She could, and did.

When Sara woke, she did not immediately remember the events of the day before and thought instead of the coming day to be spent with her precious friend since childhood, who was named Lily, and with the other women of their circle. She hummed as she poured water from the pitcher on her dressing table into the basin, washed her face, and pinned up her hair. It was after she had dressed that it all came back, darkening her mood considerably. Clara met Sara on the stairs to inform her that Maisie had woken with a bit of a fever, complaining of a headache and a sore throat, so Sara went to the kitchen to make some hot lemonade and for a washcloth and a basin of cool water. She let Minnie know that Maisie would not be down and most likely that Sara would not be down until after breakfast. Sara and Clara did their best to make Maisie comfortable, and soon she was again fast asleep. Sara went downstairs, to find her father and Ed finishing their coffee. Ed nodded to her, and she smiled back.

"Good morning," Father said. "A full day ahead, I trust?"

She said, "Esther and I will be all day over at Mrs. Weiss's to quilt for Lily's coming blessing." Mrs. Weiss was Lily's mother, and she, Lily, and Lily's husband Cornel Van Tassel lived on a modest farm a couple of miles out in the country. Sara sat down at her place to eat her breakfast of poached egg and toast and coffee. She kept her head down and focused on her food.

"Ah, yes, yes. Indeed a full day," Father said and glanced at Ed. Whatever he had been going to say he let drop. He wiped his mustache with his napkin, rose, and said, "Well, good day, then," and strode out. He was off to tend to his affairs.

Sara was relieved. She quickly finished her breakfast, and with a nod to Ed she had Miss Bailey saddled and was soon on her way. She loaded her saddlebags with carefully wrapped packages of Minnie's Amish sugar cookies, ladyfingers, crybabies, and sweet saleratus bread. Cool temperatures and an overcast sky portended a heavy drizzle later in the day. As it could not be helped, Sara pulled on her heavier blue traveling coat, and she hoped that the rain would not be so much as to ruin the day.

When Sara arrived at Lily's house, Lily's mother Mrs. Weiss was toiling in the side vegetable garden. Theirs was a much more modest operation than Colonel Moore's, and they only hired help or traded services with their neighbors during the harvest. Sara held much affection for Mrs. Weiss. She was an outgoing woman with a bountiful figure who cared not a whit for the latest fashions. She favored the ruffles, empire waists, and leg-of-mutton sleeves of her youth, and her hair was pulled back in the antiquated style—smoothly over her ears into a tight gray bun at the top of her neck. Mrs. Weiss was industrious and generous but shrewd, having made her own way after Lily's father was killed in the War. She never remarried and moved herself and Lily, not more than eight at the time, to Iowa to be near a dear but distant cousin by the surname of Van Tassel, who happened to be Cornel's mother. When Lily and Cornel married, Mrs. Weiss moved in with them, to everyone's satisfaction.

Mrs. Weiss waved and straightened and began walking toward Sara as Sara unloaded the saddlebags and handed Miss Bailey's reins to the neighbor boy who had been hired to help for the day.

"I don't see Miss Maisie," Mrs. Weiss said in a loud voice, as was her manner.

"She had to be put to bed, I'm afraid," Sara said, balancing the packages in her arms. "A bit of a cold. She's disappointed not to be here, I assure you."

"Nothing serious, I hope." Mrs. Weiss looked concerned.

"Not at all, not at all," Sara said. "How's our Lily?"

57

"A bit immobilized by her advanced condition, but other than that as chipper as pig in slops. Does not slow her much."

"I am so glad. Well, I think I will slip in and see if I can lend a hand to the preparations."

Sara turned toward the house, and who should exit from the door than one Mr. Youngblood. Sara's arms dropped in shock, and she had to scramble to catch her packages before they tumbled to the ground. A warm glow mounted from her chest into her cheeks as she watched him catch sight of her and then stop abruptly and stand there, shoulders erect.

"Oh, child," Mrs. Weiss said, "let me perform the introductions." She grasped Sara's elbow and led her toward where Mr. Youngblood stood. "Here's a young man of promise, let me tell you. I spoke with him not ten minutes and already I'm convinced of his upstanding character and bright future. Did you know that he once tended Henry Pettit's horses?" When Sara looked at her blankly, Mrs. Weiss continued, "You know, the architect? The World's Fair what was held in Philadelphia. The largest building in the world? Surely you remember?"

Sara only half registered Mrs. Weiss's words. Here was this man again. Why was it so unsettling? He was a mere stranger, someone who had yesterday presumed upon her company for a time. It aroused such conflicted feelings within her, she was quite beside herself.

They reached the spot where Mr. Youngblood stood, and his eyes were intent on Sara's face. "Mister Youngblood, let me introduce one of the most capable and level-headed girls in the world. She is the apple of her father's eye, and the closest to my heart, after my own dear progeny. Sara Moore, meet Mister, er, Youngblood." She paused a second before charging ahead. "Mister Youngblood, meet Miss Moore." She then glanced expectantly between them.

His eyes not leaving her face, Mr. Youngblood shifted the tin pail to his left hand and then extended his right to her. Not knowing what else to do, Sara extended hers, and he grasped it firmly. He miscalculated and caught only her gloved fingers, so he stutter-gripped to receive her whole hand including thumb, which he held tightly. His hand was so large and warm, hers was lost within it. He did not shake but merely pressed her hand tightly, as if the connection established were irrevocable. At first it felt assured, supportive and comforting, and then it became more intimate, as if his body had slipped closer when in fact he had not moved. Sara was mildly shocked to find herself leaning forward ever so slightly, as if to cut the distance between them. An impulse came upon her—had her other had been free, she would have laid it upon their clasp.

Mrs. Weiss grinned. "Mayhap you young people can get to know one another better in the future?"

Sara looked from Mr. Youngblood's face to Mrs. Weiss's and nodded and then tracked back to Mr. Youngblood and continued nodding. He was not letting go of her hand, and she realized that she did not want him to.

The neighbor boy who was tending to the horses came over and demanded Mrs. Weiss's attention. As she turned and bent to address the child, Mr. Youngblood gripped Sara's hand fiercely and leaned in, which pulled Sara forward off balance and onto her toes. "Miss Moore," Mr. Youngblood whispered desperately, his face inches from hers. She could see smell his shaving soap and see the delicate blue veins of his forehead. "Miss Moore—" he repeated if anything with more intensity, but then Mrs. Weiss was turning back around and so he

59

released his grip and Sara fell back and had to step to catch herself. The image of his face, eyes pushed wide, brows raised, and his intense tone was fixed in her memory.

Mrs. Weiss then waved her hand in a general way. "Right, then." She nodded to Mr. Youngblood, who held Sara's gaze a half-second longer, nodded once to both of them, and then stepped around them and walked down the path. Sara turned to watch his retreating back. He too glanced back at them. A smile in her voice, Mrs. Weiss said, "Hey, when you go inside, see if you can get my girl to sit for a spell. She should not be pushing herself so much."

"Will do, I assure you," Sara said.

Mrs. Weiss turned back to her garden. "I'll be in soon as I gather the necessaries."

Sara stood for a moment before shaking her head and then mounting the side porch. What had just happened? What had he been going to say? She did not know. However, it left in its wake an indescribable longing. After a moment's thought, she put it behind her and pushed through the door into the kitchen without knocking, saying, "Hallo, hallo," to announce her arrival. Inside, busy with preparations for the day, were Lily and Lily's mother-in-law Mrs. Van Tassel.

Though at present swollen with child, Lily was thin and tiny but she always looked more imposing because she held her back straight and her shoulders firm and because she was always in enthusiastic motion. Her round pale face surrounded by pale hair was mobile like a puddle in the rain. Sara and Lily had known each other since they were girls. They had met at Sunday services where, over the pews, Lily had peered at Sara, pinched her cheeks, pulled her eyelids downward and her lips up, and stuck her tongue. The next Sunday, after making sure

Father was not looking, Sara had timidly returned the favor. They had been fast friends ever since. Truth be told, Sara envied what she saw as Lily's idyllic life. Sure, it entailed much hard work and drudgery—cooking, raising vegetables and chickens and pigs, milking their cow morning and night, bringing in mending and laundry and fancywork when they could—and an amount of uncertainty, as they did not have the financial resources that Sara had at her disposal. But, as Sara had never had to concern herself with such things, she counted them near insignificant.

Lily had known her intended almost her whole life, and their relationship had flowered from a child's affection to adult passion. Cornell, also short in stature but broad in the chest and hands and ears, was the perfect friend and the hardworking husband, and his coming of age had eased their existence to a great extent and brought them back from the brink of poverty. Their future was in glorious ascension. Sara did not know Cornell's mother Mrs. Van Tassel well. Hesitant in her speech, she was a round brown-haired woman whose left eye listed down and away. She had an air of disarray about her, though she seemed a determined worker. She had always seemed pleasant enough, and Lily spoke well of her.

In honor of the gathering this day, Lily wore a cheerful pastel peach gown that fit closely to her small shoulders with a high waste and skirts that cascaded loosely over her bulging stomach, which was covered with an oversized apron. Lily was rolling pie dough and lining tartlet tins, her butt sticking out as she worked around her protruding belly. Mrs. Van Tassel stirred a large pot of what smelled like caramel candies.

"Hello," Sara repeated as she smiled broadly and sniffed. "Missus Van Tassel, is that what I think it is? I've never seen anyone make caramels at home. If you know how to make them, I would be forever indebted for the receipt. Minnie would make short work of it."

Lily smiled, a bit of the devil in her eye. "I think *you* should give it a go, Sara. That would be quite an interesting experience." It was a joke between them. Putting water on for tea was the extent of Sara's cooking abilities. Most certainly, she could plan a dinner party to suit the wife of a railroad baron but could only bring it to fruition with Minnie's able assistance. Lily's alimentary accomplishments were second only to Mrs. Weiss's. Invariably, her roasts were done to a turn, her cakes never fell, and her bread was crusty on the outside and soft and moist on the inside.

Sara smiled back and placed the packages on the counter, removed her gloves and coat, and hung them on the coat tree. As she went to the linen drawer and retrieved an apron, she said, "Indeed. Missus Van Tassel, do you not think Lily's pie dough looks a bit off? In my expert opinion, it'll turn out tough, mark my words."

Lily laughed, warm and enfolding as a comforter, and Mrs. Van Tassel shook her head pleasantly. Lily said, "Truly. Not that you would know pie dough from a cow flop."

Sara agreed and began unwrapping the packets of cookies. "My—er, Minnie's—offering," she said. She retrieved serving plates from the cupboards and laid the cookies out as artfully as she could, slicing the bread and placing it as well. She covered the plates with towels. As they worked they gossiped about the ladies who would soon be arriving and about the coming baby. Lily finished the linings of the tartlets and started on the filling while Mrs. Van Tassel poured out the caramels to cool and Sara transferred butter from a tub, preserves from jars, and small pickles into serving dishes. Then Mrs. Van Tassel drew on a wrap, nodded their way, and left by the side door to help Mrs. Weiss.

"Oh, Lily, you'll never guess what happened to me yesterday," Sara almost whispered after Mrs. Van Tassel had closed the door.

"Something by way of adventure?" Lily said. "I do not believe you have had an adventure in your whole life." Lily was a great reader of newspapers and was particularly fond of sensationalized news reporting and salacious personal ads.

"Oh, I so wish you were right," Sara said. "I think Father has arranged that I am to marry Mister O'Hanlin."

Lily plunked down in a chair. "Seriously?" she said.

"I'm convinced of it."

"Really? Chester the Chinaman? Oh, my God in heaven, Sara, I am so sorry."

"I know, yes?" Having said it out loud and had her initial reaction affirmed by her dear friend made her feel both better and worse—better because she was not the only one with that reaction but worse because what was there to do?

Sara launched into a retelling of the events of the day before. When she reached the part about the man from the street, she hesitated. Lily was her dearest friend and she so wanted to confide in someone. It was not proper, what had happened, and what did she know about this man Mr. Youngblood anyway? What account could she give of him? The glow she felt at her remembrance of him was countered by a sense of shame.

"Yes?" Lily said, her eyes keen.

"Oh, it's just that, you know, in the street I could hardly contain myself. On the way home, I mean. All those eyes in the windows, and me, um, hardly presentable." It sounded lame but what else could she say?

"Oh, I bet," Lily said. "I would have been in total hysterics. Mister O'Hanlin actually touched you. I could not imagine it, Sara. Mister O'Hanlin is so, so, well, he is no warmer than a catfish. And he's so, well … Irish." Lily fingered the locket at her neck. Sara knew what was in that locket. Lily had shown her the tight dark coil of Cornel's hair.

"What am I going to do?" Sara said.

They both understood that, if Colonel Moore had decided Sara was to marry Mr. O'Hanlin, there was little to be done about it.

"Do you like Mister O'Hanlin at all?" Lily said, her face peering in sympathy. "Maybe being married to him would be all right. Honestly, what is the point of being married anyway if it is not to be all right?"

Lily and Cornell were all right. They were more than all right. They were meant for each other. But not everyone could hope for Lily's good fortune. Sometimes one had to make due with one's lot in life. Sara's throat closed just a little. "Help me think of options."

"Besides Mister O'Hanlin, whom would you like to marry? Is there not anyone of whom your father would approve?"

Whom, indeed? Certainly not Mr. Youngblood. What was it about Mr. O'Hanlin that Father favored? Then it came to Sara: Perhaps some of the qualities she sensed but did not like in Mr. O'Hanlin—an ambitiousness, a calculating grasping quality—might also belong to her father, and conversely, her father's qualities might not be so far afield from Mr. O'Hanlin's. There had been murmurs about what Father had done at the end of the War, an off-colored remark here, a

64

silence there. Such a self-professed lover of the South, Father had suddenly decided to move west to Iowa? And why had Mother never spoken of the reasons for their move?

Sara mumbled in reply, "I don't know ... there was Jeremiah what's-his-name." He was a young man with long limbs and a well-to-do family from Waterloo who had plied his suit shortly after Mother had passed.

"He married last summer to a fancy woman from the East. Had you not heard? Honestly, Sara, you do not pay attention at all."

"Oh. Well, I could ... I could ..." Sara tried to think of options. There really weren't many for a woman. As her maintenance came from her father, she was bound by his will. Certainly there had to be something. But what? Could she follow Mrs. Weiss's example? No. Father's wrath would come down upon them. It came to this: If she defied her father, he might go to the length of expelling her, and then her options were so limited as to be nonexistent. Sara knew what happened to women who defied their fathers. There was the woman who followed a man to Cedar Rapids who a few years later was scandalously arrested as a lady of the fair but frail order. Sara had read popular women's novels like *Charlotte Temple* and *The Coquette*. *Charlotte Temple* was about a girl who was seduced by a soldier, and once she was with child he abandoned her. After giving birth, she died a pauper, stricken by consumption. *The Coquette* was based on a true story about a woman who was courted by two men, a staid clergyman and a more appealing libertine. She could not decide between them, though, so they both married other women, but then the libertine returned and seduced her. Her end was to die in childbirth among strangers at a wayside inn. These thoughts so unsettled Sara that she put down the napkins she had been placing in rings and hung her head.

Lily hoisted herself up and came around the table. She put her arms around Sara and held her tightly. Sara could feel the press and heat of Lily's belly next to her shoulder, and she gratefully hugged Lily's arms.

"I will talk to my father." Sara said. "It's all there is to do. Maybe he can be persuaded. And if not, Mister O'Hanlin is the only option."

"Yes. Your father can be reasoned with. Truly." Lily's voice cracked.

They were both quiet for a minute, and then Lily released her.

"I know," Lily said, a bit of the imp in her eyes. "Maybe ol' Chester will soon discover his calling as a circus performer and be compelled to follow his dearest ambitions."

"Yes," Sara said, almost under her breath, "and during his travels, a nasty foreign beetle could nip him in the toe and swell him up like a purple and green balloon." They began to chuckle.

"I know, I know, a herd of elephants," Lily said. "Jumbo could just happen to run over him." She threw up her hands. "Whoops." They were laughing now.

"So much for following the elephant," Sara said. This brought forth further peals of laughter from both of them.

Just then, Mrs. Weiss and Mrs. Van Tassel came through the door lugging baskets of garden vegetables. "What the devil's so funny?" Mrs. Weiss asked.

Sara and Lily stopped laughing and then burst out again. Lily said, trying to contain herself, "We were laughing at you, Momma, of course."

Mrs. Weiss hoisted her basket onto the table and retrieved two stalks of pie plant. She put a large green leaf over each ear, crossed her eyes, and stuck out her teeth. "It'fff not because of my lookffff, ifff it?" This even brought a smile from steadfast Mrs. Van Tassel.

Soon the other women began arriving. A quilting bee was a necessary thing, but in many women's minds it was incidental to the opportunity to socialize, and everyone knew that Mrs. Weiss's home was open to all and that her events were invariably the most successful, so there was a good turnout. The Moore's sewing machine had been transported over for the day, and Esther and her two little girls, Charlotte and Lizzie, were there, as were many other women of Anamosa. They talked as Esther pumped the treadle of the machine and sewed together quilt blocks. The quilting frame was set up and the various elements of fabric were assembled. Soon they began quilting. The conversation ranged far and wide. At noon, they adjourned for a lunch of sweet lemonade and cucumber sandwiches, but everyone knew that the real event was dessert. In addition to those delicacies that Sara had brought and Mrs. Van Tassel had made, other women had brought things, and it was a friendly competition to see whose goods were the tastiest. Mrs. Van Tassel's caramels were a hit, and after much refilling of plates and dithering over the merits of each confection, the overstuffed women returned to the quilting frame.

A while later, Lily stuck her needle in the quilt and leaned back. "My back has just been aching," she announced. "You would think I was carrying cannonballs instead of a wee precious one."

A number of the women agreed: Being with child was the

most tiring thing in this world of weariness, and Mrs. Weiss said that the midwife thought it could be any day now. "You had it coming, child," she added. "When you were in me, my ankles felt like overstuffed sausages, about ready to burst. Lord, that was a hot summer!"

"So it's your fault," Lily said, laughing. "Mother's curse. I should have known." She stuck her tongue out at her mother. This elicited chuckles from the assembled women.

Mrs. Weiss turned to the rest of them. "Really, I don't know what she is complaining about. She's had a wonderfully easy time of it. Hardly sick in the morning at all, eats like a horse, and she complains of a backache."

"Ouch," Sara said quietly and put her finger in her mouth. More loudly, she said, "You're sitting over there feet up and lollygagging, and I just pricked my finger—on your quilt. See, we're all slaving for you, and all you have to do is carry the precious bundle."

"Well, since you're all so good-natured about it," Lily said, "Bonbons! I want bonbons."

Another woman ventured, "You did not have enough at lunchtime?"

"She's craving sweets," Esther said. "That means she is going to have a boy."

"Naw," Mrs. Weiss said, "the only real test is the wedding ring. Hand it over, girl." She reached down for a spool of thread and pulled out a long piece.

Lily pulled at her ring but it would not move past the knuckle. "My fingers are swollen. I do not think I can get it off."

Sara hooked her needle through the quilt and got up. "Here, let me have a try." She looked at Lily's finger. "Does look fairly swollen, but a little pain for a lot of knowing. Here, give me your hand." Sara wet Lily's finger with her tongue and then twisted the ring back and forth until it slipped off the knuckle. Lily's finger tasted salty. "That didn't hurt, did it?" Sara asked Lily quietly.

"Oh, the pain!" Lily whispered but then smiled. "Just kidding." Mrs. Weiss directed Lily to lie on her back on the floor, which she did, saying, "I may never rise again, you know."

Mrs. Weiss handed Sara the thread. Sara tied the ring to it and then held it suspended over Lily's belly.

"And it is going to be ..." Sara said dramatically.

The ring did not move at all at first, and all the women hushed. Neither a boy nor a girl—there was only one other option: no baby at all, a horrible thought, and there was a protracted silence as the ladies held their breaths, but then the ring moved, a little this way and a little that until it began swaying back and forth.

"A boy! A boy!" Mrs. Weiss whooped. "Cornel will be thrilled. He has been convinced it will be a boy." Everybody laughed with relief and congratulations. Sara and another woman helped Lily up off the floor.

From the corner where she and Lizzie were making doll dresses, Charlotte announced, "I'm going to have a boy, too, but I am not going to get married." It was a lull in the conversation, so everyone heard it, which elicited a burst of nervous laughter from the women.

"But, Lottie, honey," Esther said, "you have got to be married to have a baby."

Charlotte shook her head. "Nope. Missus Brown isn't married and she has a baby every year." Esther explained that

Mrs. Brown was their milk cow. That brought peals of laughter. Sara laughed till her sides ached.

Then Esther turned to Lily and said, her voice animated, "So, Lily, less than a year. What do you think of this being married?"

Lily's voice was rapturous in her praise of how wonderful it all was, and no one could deny the infinite good care that Cornell offered his bride. "And ever since I have been with child, he falls over himself to take care of me."

"It's true. He is a huckleberry above a persimmon," Mrs. Weiss said. "He treats her as if she were made of fine china."

Someone offered marriage advice, and others chimed in. Esther, of course, had her own opinions. She had enough confidence to fill a trough. "Now, you look ahere. After the baby's born, do not let him slack off. You need to let a husband know who is boss right away and keep after it. If you let him get away with it, he will have you stepping and fetching before you know it." Esther was undisputedly the head of her household, and Gerald held her in high regard.

"Oh, Esther," Lily laughed. "Cornel is not like that. I would never dream of doing that. We, we share everything." Her face had reddened.

Mrs. Weiss looked over her glasses at her daughter. "Child. You are talking dreams. I know you did not know your father, but he wasn't perfect, and shame on me if I led you to believe that he was. Having a husband is no different than anything else—there are good times and then there are times when you'd like to run him off with a broom."

Esther nodded her head. "You listen to her, Lily."

Sara was listening, too—listening hard.

Mrs. Weiss continued. "There will be days when you think

70

your man was put on this earth to make your life a heaven. You will glory in those days. Remember them, because there will also be days when he was put here to make your life a living hell."

Lily shook her head. "Not my Cornel."

"Yes, your Cornel and every other man put on God's green earth. Now, don't get me wrong—Cornel is a good man, and you are right happy now, but there will come a time when he's tired and you're tired and the baby's crying when you will find out what you both are really made of."

Sara thought this made sense. So what was Mr. O'Hanlin made of? Money, she supposed, especially since he worked with Father. But what else?

"Yeah," Esther said to Lily. "You chose well."

"The most important thing," Mrs. Weiss continued, "is to have him treat you well. Is that not right, Esther?" All the women smiled, as they all knew how well Esther was treated. "If he does not treat you well now, it will only get worse."

Sara felt herself pale and turned her face down to the quilt. It came to her that she did not in fact know how Mr. O'Hanlin might treat her in private. They had spent little time alone. What would he be like in a year? In ten years? Possibilities came to mind she had not yet imagined. Him ignoring her. Him yelling at her for slights real or imagined. Him locking her in a room. Beating her? She knew of women who periodically appeared in church with bruising about their eyes, and there were whispers about what went on. The papers were full of such stories. Or worse. Were there worse things? What was Mr. O'Hanlin capable of? He had shown no indication toward these proclivities, but Sara's gut told her that these things might just be possible, and the more she thought about it, the more possible it seemed. She felt the vice of the situation tighten about her but tried not to let her feelings of increasing desperation show on her countenance.

Chapter 6

ames awoke late the next morning, well past time for breakfast but well-rested and with a renewed sense of hope. Sure, he did not have money, but he was a free agent, able to come and go as he pleased. His second meeting with Miss Moore had reaffirmed his feelings toward her but had also confirmed her indifference toward him. God in heaven, the tangled feelings that women invariably produced. He must choose another path. He had a place to stay, meals provided, for a bit longer. The world in all its possibilities lay open before him, and there was nothing to hold him back. Kansas City or California.

The memory of a city in the Midwest—Pittsburgh, maybe—came unbidden. He might've been nine. He played an afternoon game of baseball with some boys on a city street, the thwack of the stone wrapped in cloth against the tree branch bat, and for a moment a sense of camaraderie as he made home base. The tall boy threw an arm over his shoulders and shook him good-naturedly. Darkness closed in, but he and his newfound friends continued to play until the yellow light slanted in from the horizon. He had not wanted it to end, as he so rarely happened upon these situations, but then Mam came looking for him. She wore a dress of her favorite color, red, close and low-cut in the bodice with a plain skirt, but it had been washed so many times it had faded to orange and it had been mended so that it hung unevenly on her body. He had thought of her as old at the time, but she might still have been in her twenties. She was vain and had the habit of lightly powdering her face, though it was improper, but in daylight it made her appear ghostly and unnatural. The tall boy who had thrown his arm around James's shoulders sniggered and whispered loudly, "Look at that old hag. I bet I could have her for two bits." The boys had all laughed and then went back to their game. Most of them were probably too young to even know what the boy meant, but they laughed anyway.

Shame had flamed through James's body, along with a hatred so intense he felt it could destroy him and his mother. He hated her then with every fiber of his being. He fled from the street, hiding behind the corner of a building as his mother walked on. She looked so worried and frail as she called out his name. When the boys asked, "Are you her James?" he had denied it. He had deliberately stayed out late, and when he came in she asked him where he had been, she had been worried. He had replied with something nasty, and she had looked stricken.

James twisted his head at the memory. He got out of bed late and poured water from the pitcher into the basin and splashed his face and dressed. As there was no Ricci to be found, he went downstairs and loitered in the dining room, reading until dinnertime the Anamosa *Eureka* that someone had abandoned. Dinner was a thick stew of beef and root vegetables, a side of beans, crusty bread with butter and mulberry jam, and coffee. He took his time, savoring his meal and asking for seconds, though he did keep an eye out. He stayed at the table, sipping coffee and dipping further into the newspaper until midafternoon. Once the paper was finished, though, all contentment abandoned him, and in his restlessness, he went for a walk. It was chilly and overcast. James buttoned his coat and put his hands in his pockets. First he made his way south along the streets to the Wapsipinicon River and followed a trail that skirted it. The trees along the bank hung out over the turbid high water. It was soothing to watch it stream by, with its calm surface barely hinting at the strength of the currents underneath. Eventually, James left the riverbank and circled back around to the north toward the hills. He told himself he was not, but all along he knew exactly where he was going. I should not, he told himself. I should just stay away. No use torturing myself, he said as he turned along the road that led past Miss Moore's house. This is silly. Why would I do such a thing, he said as he found a copse of trees along the road with a good view of the Moore front door. I should just keep walking—there's no harm in just walking by, he told himself as he sat down so that his profile blended in with the bushes. Perhaps I'll just rest here a minute, he told himself as he got comfortable. No harm in that.

Nothing was happening at the house that he could see. No one coming or going. He glanced around. He had a good vista there where he sat on the side of the hill. Through a gap in the trees, he could see the distant crowns of tree groves, which look like soft green mounds, puffy, almost cloudlike. He could also see light green fields of young corn and the pale tan of the fallow fields. The gray overcast sky washed out and darkened the colors. The longer he sat there, the more distinct and discrete the clouds became, and the more threatening.

He heard the wheels of a cart approaching back the way he

had come, which made him aware of how odd it would seem for a lone man to be sitting beside the road staring at a rich man's house—odd enough that someone might try to contact the authorities, and then where would he be? He quickly pushed himself back into the bushes where he could not be seen. The cart breasted the rise and passed in front of him. It was an open cart with sacks of grain or meal, driven by an older man, with another younger man sitting beside him. They went through the Moore gate, delivered the goods, and returned the way they had come. A while later, a man on a horse road by, and then James spotted two young boys in the distance playing kick the can. He feared that if they came by they would spot him, as children have keen eyes and generally no sense of forward purpose that blinds adults to their surroundings, but they did not pass by but instead cut across a field before they reached him on the road. After a while, it began to drizzle. James was protected from the steadiness of the rain by the trees above him, but that did not stop accumulated drops from plopping down upon him from the leaves above. Two young men walked by, wet to the bone but unconcerned, talking about last night's drinking.

Evening came on and James was about ready to give up and go home when at long last he caught sight of Miss Moore. His breath caught and he held it without realizing. She rode sidesaddle up the road toward the house on the mare he had rescued. She was wrapped in a long heavy coat and a large floppy hat covered her head, and he wasn't sure it was her until he recognized the mare. She did not appear in a hurry, possibly because she seemed so tired in the way she let herself move limply in the saddle. At the gate, she slid off her horse, opened the gate, led the horse through, and then closed it behind her.

She then led the horse to the barn, where a man came out and took it from her. She then returned back to the house, where he could just see that she paused for a moment, looking back over her shoulder, before she entered the door and was gone.

This was what he had come for, and the experience left him with such a sense of exhilaration, of fortification. It was as if he were an avid ornithologist and he had just spotted an exceedingly rare and valuable species. He did not need to possess the bird. He did not even need its likeness in the form of a photograph or painting. No, the mere memory of it was enough to sustain him. He sat for a while savoring it. Then he pushed himself to standing and began his walk back to the boarding house. It was the much shorter route to go directly past the Moore home. Night had fallen so he had no fear of being seen through the windows, so that was the way he took. He had missed the supper provided by his board—he knew that—so he did not hurry his pace. As the rain was light, the mud was not deep and he was able to make his way easily. He even whistled a bit to the tune to "John Brown's Body" as he walked along. The wind picked up and prompted the trees to sway and rush and the rain spat against his hat and coat. Still, he did not mind.

He had such a sense of peace and well-being as to leave him helpless and unaware. As he approached the boarding house, he was thinking about a girl he had once glimpsed through a parlor window, nothing more than a flash of black curls and cream-colored fabric. He did not perceive the three figures loitering along a side street, only becoming aware of them as presences rapidly overtaking him. When he felt them, vigor rushed through him, but not in time. He spun and threw his hands up to protect his face before they were on him. The blows came from all sides into his ribs, his kidneys, his arms, the side of his skull. One landed next to his groin but lucky for him missed the more vital areas. Pain bloomed in one portion of his body and then another. It seemed to go on and on and on, his body contorting in response. Soon he was unable to differentiate where the blows hit, and he was enveloped in a cocoon of pain. Then he was grabbed from either side and his arms were pinned. The man in front, whom he knew by voice to be Ricci, punched his belly and then his face, hard. Little blue twinkle lights like fireflies flitted across James's vision, though his eyes were closed. Ricci said something in his own tongue, something pointed and vituperative, but did not bother to translate. Then James was let to fall to the ground and given a few hefty kicks in the side that stole the air from him.

He lay trying with all his might to gain a breath as the three men walked away. He rolled off his stomach to his side and gasped and pulled with his belly, trying to breathe. Finally, a trace of air seeped into his lungs, then a partial breath, and then he could breathe. He gasped again, pulling it in, but it sent a shock wave of pain through him that originated in his ribs. He had to breathe but it hurt. He settled on quick shallow breathing and tried to move his body as little as possible. He lay in the mud assessing the damage and trying to gather himself. He could not tell whether the substance on his face was mud or blood, and one eye would not open enough to see the light from the oil lamps emanating from the windows of the boarding house. He was beaten up and down his face and torso, but his arms, though sore, seemed to be unbroken. He pushed himself to standing as best he could, coughed, which he immediately regretted, and then stumbled and propped his way along the fence. It took a good twenty minutes to make it to the porch. He stopped and swayed after every step, leaning heavily on the pickets. He pushed through the gate, which sprung closed behind him. He took the walk in a rush and fell against the sharp edges of the steps. Pain once again bloomed through his body and he almost passed out from the renewed sense of it, his head fuzzing over and his senses rolling toward it. He lay there gasping, the steps pushing painfully into him.

First the door and then the screen door creaked open and he heard the voice of Mrs. Smit, saying, "Who's fussing on my porch? You'd think the Devil himself—" He heard her pause and then rush down the steps. Light from her lantern seeped through his eyelids, and she said, "Oh my God in heaven." Whether she recognized him, he did not know. She yelled back toward the house, and then he felt her strong arms wrap around him and pull him upright, and then another pair of strong arms supporting him. It made him wince. He was pulled and hoisted for what seemed like a long time and then released into the soft embracement of what must have been a bed. His shoes and jacket were pulled from him and a warm cloth was gently rubbed against his face. Soon, there was another voice in the room, a man's, and it sent a panic through him. Were they sending him back to the penitentiary? Had the man come for him? He struggled to rise but was held down. The man repeated a word several times until James understood it as "doctor," this man was a doctor. He relaxed. The rest of his clothing was painfully pulled from his limbs, and then someone held a cup to his lips and forced a bitter liquid into his mouth, which he convulsively swallowed. Soon the pain floated away from him and he didn't know if he were awake or asleep and it felt so good and then the world faded and was dark.

Chapter 7

he next day after an errand to a neighbor's, Sara rode home in the rain. It was after dark by the time she stumped bone-weary through the front door. She changed out of her wet things and bundled into a warm nightdress and socks and a wrap and went to check on Maisie. Maisie was sleeping, but Clara reported that the girl had felt better in the afternoon, and Clara had had to be stern with her to keep her in bed. After that, Sara went to the kitchen, where Minnie had kept some soup warm for her, which she ate in the kitchen next to the ticking stove. She went to bed soon after to the sound of rain beating against the windows.

It was midafternoon of the next day that Sipsy came into the sitting room where Sara sat mending one of Father's shirts and told her that Ed was waiting for her out in the covered trap. "Miss, he says to tell you Missus Weiss's sent word for you, it being the young Missus Van Tassel's time."

Lily was going to be a mother! Her best friend. Sara wondered how this birthing would compare, as it was not the first Sara had attended. She hadn't seen Maisie born, as almost everyone had been kept from the sick room because of Mother's health, but Sara had helped with both of Esther's girls. Esther had been attended by the midwife, which had been against Father's wishes—he had ordered her to be attended by his doctor, but Esther had flatly refused, responding, who better to know a woman's concerns than another woman? There was not much Father could do about it, as Gerald sided with Esther, though Father fumed about it for days. When Esther's time came, she had paced the floor in a long and loose nightgown until it was time and then she had climbed up onto the bed and squatted. Sara could tell that Esther was in pain, but with characteristic stoicism, Esther said not a word, just grunted a bit. Sara had supported her on one side while another woman friend held the other, and the midwife had encouraged her, guiding the baby out and cleaning it off and awaiting the afterbirth. Both births had gone smoothly and were over fairly soon. Sara's first impressions of the newborns had been of a dark wet odd-shaped head, a fat but floppy body, and waxy greenish effluvient covering angry red skin. Each baby had cried in that anguished new baby way while being bathed and then quieted when she was put to Esther's breast.

Sara hurriedly laid the mending aside and put on her coat and gloves and pinned on her hat and joined Ed in the trap. The rain had abated, but the sky remained overcast and ominous. Off they went at a brisk trot. When they reached Lily's house, the physician's buggy stood unhitched by the barn, which meant that he had been there for a while. Lily had been going to use the same midwife Esther had used, so Sara was surprised to see that the doctor had been called. Sara's chest tightened at the thought. As she dismounted the trap, she told Ed she would send for him but not to expect the call any time soon.

She let herself into the house by the front door. After taking off her outerwear, she went to the main room, where Cornel stood holding a bundle tightly wrapped in blankets and staring soft-faced down upon it, with Mrs. Van Tassel at his side, hand on his arm. Sara had missed the birthing. She tried not to let the disappointment show on her face. She had not been able to witness it, but, more importantly, she had not been there for Lily at this moment of such consequence in a woman's life. How had it happened so quickly? For some women, it took days. Ah well, it was something Lily could tease Sara about for the rest of their lives. Sara could just hear Lily's good-natured ribbing: "Such a best friend. Dawdling along the way like the Anderson child with a scarlet hood. Least you could have done is brought me flowers." At that thought, Sara wished she had brought flowers. Next time Lily was with child, she would urge Mrs. Weiss to send a message earlier, so that she could be there, now that they all knew Lily was one of the fleet ones.

The midwife stood whispering beside Cornell and Mrs. Van Tassel. Cornel glanced up and saw Sara and gave her a broad smile. "It's a boy, a fine boy," he said, lifting the bundle in his arms. Mrs. Van Tassel smiled at her too.

"Oh, congratulations! I'm so happy for you," Sara said and glanced at the midwife. The midwife's face was pleasant but a bit tight about the jaw. "How's Lily?" She asked but then immediately regretted it when both Cornel and Mrs. Van Tassel glanced at the midwife.

The midwife said, "She's had a bit of a rough go. The doctor's attending to her now."

Sara stepped forward and peeked in at the baby. He was smaller and thinner than Esther's babies had been. He was blinking around with a concerned look on his face, his brows wrinkling. He had every right to be concerned, Sara thought. The world is an unpredictable place, and all it took was one thing to change it all forever.

At that moment Mrs. Weiss poked her head through the door of the bedroom. She called the midwife to come back in. Sara followed the midwife over and offered a questioning look to Mrs. Weiss, hoping to be able to see Lily, to berate her good-naturedly for her speed, and after some hesitation Mrs. Weiss nodded, held the door as Sara went through, and shut it behind her.

As Sara stood next to the door, time seemed to leap ahead with the willy-nilly jerk of a spooked horse. The midwife rushed over to the bed, where the doctor was leaning over Lily. Mrs. Weiss stepped to Lily's head. Sara moved toward the bed too, but her body seemed held back, bobbing in a side stream of the passage of time, while the events on the bed had caught the rapid and powerful current. What she saw was too horrendous to contemplate. A sudden bloom of frightful red that emanated from Lily spread quickly across the starched and sun-bleached white of the bed linens and wicked up into the delicate lace of Lily's nightshirt. When the midwife turned frantically to reach for linens stacked nearby on a table, her hands dripped with the bright liquid. Sara approached the bed on the opposite side as Mrs. Weiss, staying back out of everyone's way, and as she did she glimpsed Lily's face. It was pale and seemed more broad and flat than usual. Lily's eyes held a shocked but fixed and inward-looking expression. With grunting efforts, the doctor pressed handfuls of cloth underneath the sheet where it sank between Lily's legs. As these rags became soaked, he tossed them to the side as the midwife fed more into his hands.

Sara glanced across the bed at Mrs. Weiss. Mrs. Weiss in all her bulk had knelt and grasped Lily's hand in both of hers. She was whispering Lily's name over and over again, almost chanting it, until all the syllables sounded the same. Lily's eyes searched for the source of the sound, but they never seemed to fasten upon any one thing. Mrs. Weiss let go of Lily's hand and put her palms on both of Lily's cheeks and turned Lily's head toward her: "Here, I'm here. Don't you see?" Lily's eyes kept searching, and though Mrs. Weiss's hands directed her face firmly toward her, Lily could not seem to fasten on her mother's face, but she seemed still to be listening to the sound of the voice. Sara glanced to the doctor and midwife. The midwife whispered something at the doctor's shoulder, to which the doctor responded with a slight shake of his head. He still held the linens to Lily, but he did not seem to be pressing as ferociously.

Sara wanted to do something. There must be something she could do. Lily's mother was doing her best to hold Lily's attention and the doctor was ably assisted by the midwife. All there was left for Sara to do was to frantically offer a prayer. She pressed the fingers of both hands on Lily's clothed arm where it lay above the cover and closed her eyes. Sara did not know whether she should pray to save Lily's life here on earth or to pray for the best of outcomes—as it was God's will how this would develop and resolve. It seemed selfish to presume to keep Lily on the firmament if God had plans for her elsewhere, but there was nothing for it and Sara prayed with all her might. Lily was needed here. Mrs. Weiss needed her and Cornell needed her and Sara needed her—God help my selfishness, she thought—and that little babe most of all needed her, for what was a life without a mother? She knew from her own experience that life without a mother was a wander in the wastelands, and so Sara prayed and prayed hard.

"Doctor?" Mrs. Weiss said, urgency in her voice. Sara

opened her eyes. "Doctor?" Mrs. Weiss said.

"The tide is stemming somewhat," the doctor said, "but I'm afraid such a shock to her system may be irreversible. It may be a thing from which she cannot recover." The midwife stood next to him with a slightly changed expression, an outwardly concerned but professionally distant expression. This look sent a chill through Sara—what did the midwife know that caused this slight withdrawal? Sara looked back at Lily's face. Lily's eyes were still open, but they were no longer trying to focus nor to see. If it were at all possible, her face was whiter than before, and her lips were gray. Sara made a small whimpering outrush of breath.

The midwife turned and went to the door and went through, leaving it open.

"Lily, now," Mrs. Weiss said, still grasping Lily's hand, her voice taking on a tone of reasonableness, "now you listen to me. You'll live another day if you keep after it. You know better than to give up when something's difficult. You know. You're a squabbler, like me. You know you are. Let's see some of that puckish determination, now. Lily? Lily?" Mrs. Weiss pulled Lily's hand to her breast and held it crushed there. In a small voice, almost as an afterthought, Mrs. Weiss said, "Lily?" No response. Lily's face was as slack and empty as a glove left behind on a pew, and her eyes were fixed. That was all. The essence that was Lily had vacated its mortal shell and what was left was a poor duplicate. The sharpness in Sara's mind flattened, and Sara's senses fuzzed over as if cushioned by heavy pillows. Mrs. Weiss's head slumped down between her arms onto Lily's chest. Then a small mewling noise. It grew and grew to be continuous, and Lily realized—and was surprised not at the fact but at the realization—that it was Mrs.

Weiss weeping. Sara couldn't breathe. She pushed her diaphragm against her corset, but the canvas and whale bone would not give. She couldn't get enough air, and she tried again, her breath coming quick and short.

An animalistic bellow came from the next room, followed by the high-pitched *ee-aw* of a startled infant, and then Cornel appeared in the room, which seemed suddenly overwhelmed with his presence. Mrs. Weiss pushed up and stared at him, her eyes melting down her face. "Our Lily of the Valley," she said, her voice stretched thin. "No," he said, shaking his head. "No-no-no-no-no-no-no." Sara backed out of the way as Cornell rushed past her to the bed and scooped Lily's body up in his arms. He looked around as if trying to figure out which way to go, as if there were something there that would tell him what to do, how to fix this thing. He let out a groan that held anger and frustration and anguish, a creature in a trap. He glanced down at Lily's face and then down her body and then focused on the bloody drape and held her out from his body and craned his head to look underneath, as if there lay an answer. He let her drop back against him and then pulled her to his chest and buried his head against her. Mrs. Weiss pushed herself to standing and made her way around the bed. She put a hand on Cornell's shoulder and bowed her head and was still as Cornell rocked back and forth, his face still buried.

Standing back to the wall, Sara's head was enveloped in felt. She moved it side to side, trying to shake the feeling, but this only served to unbalance her, and in slow motion, her feet pressed against the floorboards, she slid at a slant down the wall and came to rest on her shoulder. It felt as if she had remained fixed and the earth had moved around her, and she lay stiff for a long moment, gravity pulling against the side of her head, until she let it drop slowly to the floorboards and relaxed her body. It cushioned her fall in more ways than a simple knock against the ground. She had no awareness of time, but people behind the haze rushed about the room and at some point someone righted her and gave her a handkerchief doused liberally with a pungent perfume to hold to her nose. Slowly, the fuzziness receded and her normal perspective on the world reasserted itself. When she felt able, she pushed herself up and went to help the shattered household.

Late into the evening, Sara, Mrs. Weiss, and Mrs. Van Tassel laid out Lily's body. Ed came over to help build the coffin, and the reverberating *rap rap rap* of Ed's and Cornell's hammers imposed itself on everyone's ears. Someone knew someone who had a nursing toddler who might be willing to put a baby to breast. The woman was contacted and was willing, so the last Sara saw of her best friend's infant boy was the glimpse of a swaddling blanket as a woman she hardly knew toted him out the door. In the days and years to come, she would regret not holding him in her arms, and she would periodically wonder what he looked like and how he was doing. Had he survived the traumas of his childhood? Had he grown into a handsome young gentleman? He would be short in stature like his parents, but would he be slender like his mother or broad like his father? Would he have his mother's pale hair or his father sturdy brown locks? How had that tiny infant face with its upturned nose stretched onto an adult skull? Did he have a sweetheart, a family of his own?

The women covered the dining room table with oilcloth and, heaving and grunting, lay Lily's body upon it. The small form was surprisingly heavy, awkward, and hard to handle. It took the three of them, one on each end and one supporting the middle. Sara had to remind herself to grip tightly, that it wouldn't hurt Lily a bit. Once the body was on the table, they removed the stiff blood-soaked nightgown and placed it the pile of linen to be burned later.

Sara only glimpsed the body before Mrs. Van Tassel thrust a sheet into the air, which billowed out and slowly settled over the form. Tucking and folding the top, Mrs. Van Tassel adjusted it so only the head was uncovered, as if shielding Lily from a draft. But before the sheet settled, Sara glimpsed Lily's body so small and pale on the table—like a child's, but for the curling pubic hair and gravity-flattened breasts. Though the table was not expansive, neither her head nor her feet, which had turned somewhat blue, reached the ends of it. Her belly was distended, as if a baby still curled within it. Muscles sagged on bones. Her long pale hair lay in gnarled matted strands, and her face was cast blue-gray, the skull standing out sharply under the skin, the eyes deep in their sockets. Someone had pulled her eyelids closed, but the left one remained half-lidded, as if Lily were only pretending and at a moment's notice would leap to her feet and shout, "Boo!" Sara bent to peer into that impassive eye, and as she did she caught the distinctive odor of Lily's hair—Lily's preference for a particular sweet-scented soap combined with the natural smell of her scalp, like sun-warmed grass. This smell was soon overwhelmed by that of the body's adrenaline-laced sweat and of urine. It was all too close. Sara straightened and turned to her work.

Mrs. Weiss and Mrs. Van Tassel washed the body, and Sara washed Lily's face and hair. Wet, Lily's hair was a heavy brown, but it dried to its former lightness. Sara went to the sitting room to locate a pair of scissors. On top of Lily's sewing basket—a square wicker box decorated with blue- and yellow-embroidered tea roses—lay a small linen baby gown, one puffed sleeve attached, the other open and half-sewn, the needle with its thread secured through the fabric. Sara paused and stroked the cloth for a moment before she lifted it off the box, opened the lid, and retrieved the scissors and a coil of thin copper wire. As she turned, she spied a bit of threadlike blue ribbon, so she snipped a bit of it as well.

She returned to the dining room and then snipped off a long piece of the wire and set it aside with the ribbon. From the top of Lily's head, where the hair was bleached white from the sun, she gathered together a long thin bundle of strands and snipped them close to the head. She added the wire and the ribbon and then plaited the strands. From this slender plait, she made three rings, carefully measuring her finger and those of the other two women. She tied them off with bits of wire. She gave the other two women theirs and slipped her ring over the middle finger of her left hand, rubbing her digits together for a moment to get used to the feel of it. The remaining plait she coiled into a tight circle. She went to Lily's jewelry box in the bedroom and found the locket that held the dark coil of Cornel's hair. To it, she added Lily's white and blue plait. She snapped it shut and put it back into the box for Cornel. Then she went back and carefully pinned up Lily's hair. Meanwhile, Mrs. Weiss and Mrs. Van Tassel had washed the body and put on underthings. They topped it with Lily's favorite sunflower yellow dress. They strung a cameo from a black velvet ribbon and tied it loosely around her neck. They didn't put on shoes but instead wrapped her blue feet in thick woolen socks. Then they carried her into the bedroom to rest there until the coffin was complete.

Sara did not make it home until the dark early morning

hours and fell into bed exhausted. She was up early the next day and, in anticipation of the day's events, she dressed in a practical frock of dark wool. When she checked on Maisie, Clara reported that Maisie had taken a turn for the worse. Nothing to be too alarmed about, but her coughing was constant. Sara told Clara to send for the doctor and then made hot tea with honey to sooth Maisie's throat, noting to herself to stop at the grocery on the way home to replenish the low honey pot and, while she was thinking of it, some horehound drops might help. Then, leaving instructions to have a more-formal black gown delivered, Sara was out the door again over to Lily's—it's no longer Lily's, she thought and took a shuddering breath—to help the women as they bent to the task of funeral preparations. The sun shone brightly and the birds sang loudly in the trees and cicadas buzzed in the background. The air was fresh from yesterday's rain. It served only to remind Sara how unusual the day was.

Sara's first job was to transfer the still-suitable pastries and sweets left over from the women's gathering to platters and to cover them with towels. Then, as neighbor women brought their contributions of food, she met them at the kitchen door, ushered them in, received their offerings, and thanked them. Soon Esther arrived too, minus the girls, and pitched in in the kitchen. With Mrs. Weiss's guidance Sara located a black floral wreath in a trunk, dusted it, and hung it on the front door. Going from room to room, she draped clothes over all the mirrors. In Lily and Cornell's room, the case clock had been stopped at about 4:40, the time of Lily's death. They removed the furniture from the living room to make space, and Ed and Cornell brought in the casket and placed it in a corner. It showed Ed's fine handiwork, with a muslin lining, a smooth top, and dovetailed corners. The women arranged Lily's body in the coffin, pulled the curtains, and lit the oil lamps. Mrs. Van Tassel carefully folded the lace pall—white instead of black, as was traditional when a woman died in childbirth—and hung it over the bottom of the casket, to be draped after the casket was closed. Sara helped decorate the room with the flowers and dried arrangements that were sent over. She ushered in the photographer when he came to take an image of Lily in her coffin and then shut the curtains again after he left. Then she changed into her formal gown.

By late morning, women in black mourning hats and leghorn bonnets and men in black beavers and derbies began to arrive. Children were held firmly by hand and quickly hushed whenever they forgot where they were. People mingled on the porch and in kitchen and dining room, talking in low voices. They took turns filing past the coffin, emerging with solemn or stricken faces. Sara took her turn among the mourners. She began walking toward the coffin purposefully but then slowed as she approached. She did not want to look, to see what death had done to this person she loved so dearly, so she stood there with her eyes closed. The smell of death had begun to rise and closed Sara's windpipe and prompted her to discretely clear her throat. When she got the courage, she glanced into Lily's face. In such little time, it was unrecognizable as her friend. It retained its greenish cast, and the flesh was slack across the bones of the cheeks. The left eye had relaxed closed. It wasn't as if she were sleeping. The taunt and concentrated feeling of a live person in repose was absent. It was as if someone of little artistic ability had formed a poor lifeless replica of Lily from memory. Tears began to flow freely down Sara's face.

It was Mother all over again but then again it wasn't. They

had had months to prepare themselves for Mother's death. She had lingered, and the death rasp had rattled the house for what seemed like weeks. She had been in such pain, her brow beetled, her hands grasping at the covers, her body small and bony and but a shadow of her former robust figure. It had been such a relief to see the pain leave the body, something no one would say, though they exchanged streaming open-faced glances. There was a grand beautiful funeral, with the town in attendance. Mother had been a generous woman who believed in kindness and charity and doing good works. She had been pious but not pitilessly so—she believed in all the compassionate parts of the Bible and left the Old Testament fire and brimstone to Father. There had been a viewing with a full-course meal eaten while standing, and then the funeral was held in the church, and the attendees stood in the aisles and against the walls and spilled out of the doorway and craned their necks to hear what was spoken. At the cemetery, men young and old took turns at the shovel, and people wept openly.

No, that had been very different from this, Lily's death. It was so sudden. Surely, that's what people always said, but it was the truth, the God-awful truth. It made her feel like that child at the adult table where the conversation went in places she had no idea the meaning of. What was she to take away from this? What had God envisioned? How could He be so cruel as to take someone so undeserving, someone so needed here on Earth, someone who did nothing but good in the world? Just like her mother. Rage rose and balled her stomach and prompted bile to rise in her throat. Why? She glanced down at the body again, and quickly as it came the rage drained from her. Suddenly, the smell of Lily's body did not matter, nor did the fact that this earthly vessel looked nothing like the Lily Sara had known. Sara kneeled down by the coffin and bowed her head. She gave in and let it all come pouring out in hiccupping sobs. There were others waiting, however, so she pulled herself back, took a long shuddering breath, and stood.

Father soon arrived with Ed, who had changed to a new suit, followed shortly after by the Colonel Shaw family, and then the pastor conducted the funeral to everyone packed into the room. The casket was closed, the pall hung over it, and flowers placed upon it. Sara did not hear his words to understand them. She tried to seem attentive, but inside she again felt fuzzed over, covered in felt, numbed. An openly weeping Cornel and Ed and some other men hoisted the casket and carried it to the wagon, and with flowers gathered in hands they all walked in procession to the cemetery, where the casket was lowered in and covered with earth. Men took turns at the shovel, the earth mounding up and over the hole as if what Lily was took up more space than it would seem, and the bouquets were laid upon the grave. It was all too much. Sara had to get away from all these people who embodied the grief she felt so keenly. She said her goodbyes and took her leave.

Chapter 8

here was nothing, but then James became aware of himself as the bitter liquid was forced through his lips, and again his senses were taken from him. Out of the darkness again he was disturbed, hoisted and propped, and a man's voice, raspy but relatively high, in his ear said, "If'n you got to widdle, now's the time to let loose." He did not understand, and he shook his head and tried to pull away, back into the darkness. Came the voice, "You've long been in the pleasure domes of Xanadu, my friend, you've got to have to relieve yourself. Micturate. Pee, for God's sake. Let your bladder go." Then he understood and realized the pressure on his bladder was intense and he let it go and a sound of water against metal came to his ears. "Good man," the voice said and let him fall back into the darkness.

Again, he became aware of himself. Just a little at first. The soft sound of a door closing. The sense of light through his eyelids. The pressure of the bed against his body as he rolled onto his back. A twinge of pain from the barrel of his chest. There was someone in the room, a man's voice coming to him. "Mister Youngblood, pleased to see you awake."

James opened his eyes and blinked and shook his head, which threw him off balance, though he was lying down. He shut his eyes again and felt the world tilt a bit and then right itself. He opened them again and let them adjust. There was a dull pain in his skull. He planted his palms and pushed against the flat of the bed and scooted himself back in order to sit more upright. It all tilted again, and pain throbbed through his temples and a rush of nausea caused bitter bile to rise in his throat. He swallowed and winced.

"You took quite a beating," came the voice. "And you'll be woozy for a while. You've been under a couple of days, as I've kept you sedated to give your body a chance to recover."

The pain in his head receded. He let his head fall back against the hard surface behind it and opened his eyes again. There was something around his pate, something snug against his forehead and looped over his left ear and around to the base of his skull. He reached to touch it and found it to be soft cloth, which stiffened near his eyebrow and was painful underneath. He let it alone. Once his eyes adjusted, he took in his surroundings. He wasn't in his old room. This was a bigger room with a generous bank of windows and a larger bed and more light filtering in. His first impression was that it was feminine—pale colors, lace curtains, tatted doilies—but also that it was old because of the outmoded style of prints and silhouette portraits on the walls and the last-century manner of decoration.

The man, the source of the voice, sat down beside the bed. He wore glasses and a rumpled black suit over his dumpy frame, and a stethoscope hung from his neck. Short limbs and a lumpy but pleasant face. When the man leaned in, James caught the smell of onions and of shaving soap. Something about him gave James confidence, and he immediately liked him. His small hands reached for James's face. "Time to take another look there," he said. With a deft but gentle touch, the man untied a knot near James's ear and peeled the cloth away from James's forehead. James pulled away in anticipation of the pain, but it caught only a little. "Fine, fine," the man said. "Looks ugly, but coming along well." He wrapped it back up and tied it, pulling a little at James's head as he knotted it. "Now let's look at those ribs." The doctor gestured with his hand, fingers flapping, for James to sit forward. James threw back the covers and was relieved to see he wore clean underdrawers, and he also had cloth wrapped tightly around his chest. Red and purple bruises bloomed under the skin of his arms. Slowly in order to put off the dizziness, he sat forward and swung his legs one at a time over the side of the bed. The dizziness came and he felt himself falling backwards, but the doctor caught his shoulders and held him until it passed. The dull roar of pain swelled, peaked, and ebbed. The doctor unknotted the bandage around his chest, James holding his elbows out of the way, and the doctor unwrapped it, repeatedly mock-hugging James while transferring the tag end of the cloth from one hand to another behind James's back. As soon as the cloth was free, James felt how tightly it had been wrapped and obeyed the urge to take a deep breath. He immediately regretted it, as pain shot through him.

The doctor gave him a sympathetic smile. "Yep. That's going to hurt for a while. You'll want to breathe shallowly because of the pain, and that's good, but you'll also want to take a deep breath every now and then. If you don't you'll be visited upon by a much nastier resident, lung fever." He put his stethoscope in his ears and held the cold metal cone up to James's chest and rib cage. After a minute, the metal warmed. The doctor tilted his head as he listened, moving the cone here and there, and then dropped it to his chest and pulled the instrument out of his ears. "Well," he said, "you've had a bit of luck. A rib or two cracked, but not broken. Lungs and internals all sound fine. I stitched up that cut over your eye, and we'll take the stitches out in a week or two. You'll get a nice scar out of it. You're pretty banged up, and you'll be in pain from the ribs and bruises, but nothing serious." He paused and looked at James's face, his eyebrows lifted, soliciting any questions. James couldn't think of a question, so he just nodded slightly. The doctor nodded back and then wrapped him up again. "You'll want to change those when they get dirty. A good tight wrap will help the pain, but don't get carried away with it." James lay back against the pillow, the doctor helping him put his legs back onto the bed and pulling the covers back over him.

"Thank you, Doctor," James said, his unused voice rusty. He coughed gently, wincing in anticipation, though it didn't hurt this time, and said more loudly, "Thank you."

The doctor smiled, patted him on the arm, and stood there on his tiptoes, ready to leave. "I'll be back tomorrow to check on you," he said. "And, so you can anticipate, you can recompense me then." He named a price.

James stiffened. He had no money to pay the doctor. "But I—" he said. Would it be wise to tell this man his plight? As evident by Ricci and so many others, trusting a man was commensurate with allowing him power over you, and James had made that mistake before. But, when the good doctor returned the next day, he would have nothing to offer, and he knew he would cogitate on it all night. Could he trust this man? He looked at the round pleasant face and decided that maybe he could, that it was his only option, really. "I apologize,

Doctor," he began, "but you see, I've come up a bit short. Lady Luck's been turning her back, so to speak." She had, for a long long long time, he thought to himself. "I have nothing from which to pay you. I didn't plan …" He looked away. "I—" he began again. Should he tell him about prison? He looked at the doctor, who sat with a wide-open expression on his face, a pleasant I-mean-you-well expression. Could he trust him? Well, in for a penny, in for a pound. What else was there to do? "I have just been released from the Additional Penitentiary, you see, and what little they provided by way of wages has been passed along to the good Missus Smit." There, it was done. Let's hope good sense prevailed.

The doctor's expression did not change. "Oh, I do understand," he said and sat back down and put his hand on James's arm. James flooded with relief. The doctor truly was a good man and could be trusted. James felt a spark of hope. "I do understand," the doctor continued. "It will be all right." He nodded and smiled. "It will, as you see, I am under the impression that you are in the employ of Mister Ricci"—panic flooded James at the sound of the name—"who, as he expressed it, has shown himself an industrious and useful member of the community. Mister Ricci, who has recently made himself known to me—sought me out this very morning in fact—to assure me that he would be a responsible party in the event you were, shall we say, caught short. He said he would deduct it from future wages, once you were able to once again perform your duties." James tried not to let the fear that shot through him register on his face. "He asked after your health," the doctor added. "I told him you'd be at least a week in bed. He seemed very concerned about your welfare. He said to tell you there was a job waiting for you as long as was necessary." The doctor's countenance shone with certainty in the good will of his fellow man.

So Ricci would not let him off so easily. He showed remarkable resourcefulness at the dispensation of his particular brand of domination. Ricci would be waiting for him, and he would use all his powers of deviousness to keep James captive. He was the type of petty tyrant that James most feared, the smart one, the tenacious one, the unforgiving one. It was much worse than James could possibly have imagined.

The doctor interpreted James's blank look as one of gratefulness, and as he stood again, he said, "Life comes with many blessings." He gathered his things and with a pleasant nod was out the door.

James had to leave immediately. He had to take advantage of Ricci's expectation that he would be incapacitated, recuperating for a period of a week. He hated to skip out on the good doctor's bill, but there was nothing to be done about it. All he could hope to do was to send the money once he achieved better circumstances. As soon as the doctor left the room and James heard the sound of his footsteps dissipate down the hall, he pushed off the bedcovers. He searched about the room for his belongings. They were there, to his relief. A worn carpetbag, a few toiletries, a change of underthings, a package that contained a small tintype and other mementos of his mother, a small Bible rolled and held together with a string that he didn't read but that had been given to him by the stepfather who had raised him. He was relieved to see his clothes washed and neatly stacked on the sideboard, his shoes cleaned of mud and resting underneath.

No one must know of his departure till the last possible moment. No one, not even Miss Moore. The thought caught him and spun him. Instead of wistfulness, he felt a loss much deeper than what would seem owed to their brief time together. But such thoughts were for people of means and leisure. He must press on. He must survive. There was nothing for it.

Slowly, James swung his legs over the side of the bed. Less dizziness this time, and no pain. He was able to stay upright. Perhaps it was receding. He sat on the edge of the bed and breathed for a minute, letting the dizziness pass, gathering himself to rise. Then he pushed off with his palms and let his weight carry him to his feet. It was a precise move, momentum pushing against the bones of his legs, to prop him upright, and then muscles pulling against other muscles to hold him in place, to maintain balance. It was all so easy, normally, something to be taken for granted, but not this time. The motion set his head spinning and pain bloomed again, and like a bad-tempered horse the world bucked James off. He found himself sprawled on the floor and shot through with throbbing anguish. The stool upon which the doctor had been sitting had broken his fall and was crushed in pieces underneath him. He lay there breathing heavily and trying to keep his senses from receding. As soon as it had abated a bit once again, he tilted his ear to listen for any sign that someone had heard. Nothing. His collapse had not alerted the household.

He dared not try to rise again, not yet, so he raised himself so that his ribs did not touch the floor, halfway to his hands and knees, and pulled himself along to the dresser. He propped himself up, back against the drawers, and worked his way through dressing. It was a long process, and he kept his ears open as he did it, silently praying that the good Mrs. Smit would not decide to come check on him. It seemed to take much more strength than usual just to pull on his boots, and when the task was complete, he lay there resting.

This would not do, not do at all. He had to find something to fortify himself. Even a mouthful of water would help. He reached high on the dresser to the pitcher that rested next to the basin and carefully jiggled it, testing to see if it had any water but keeping it in control so that it would not come crashing to the floor. It was empty. He glanced around for a scrap of bread or something, anything, to calm his stomach and his head. He noted a glint in shadows behind the leg of the bed. He pulled himself over to it and saw that it was a bottle of patent medicine labeled "Dr. Parker's Tonic, the Great Health and Strength Restorer." It had an image of a miserable shrunken old man on one side and a smiling double-chinned man on the other. God bless little old ladies with secret habits, James thought. He pulled the cork out and tipped the bottle to his lips and let a generous portion decant into his mouth. At first it tasted a bit like syrupy sweet root beer, but then the spirits hit him and numbed his lips and tongue and rose into his sinuses and he swallowed convulsively. He let that sit for a minute or two, steeled himself, took one more swig, recorked the bottle, and replaced it behind the bed's leg. He probably would need another leg-straightener later, but the bottle was not his to take. He sat back to the wall and in not but a wink he did actually start to feel better. He relaxed and his extremities melted away, and soon his nose and all those parts of his body that hurt were numbed.

He decided it was now or never. He brought his feet around and propped himself onto his knees and then slowly and carefully propped himself to a standing position. He stood for minute to gain his bearings. He buckled the carpetbag and tried to lift it but its weight unbalanced him, so he retrieved the package of mementos of his mother and slipped it into his coat. He retrieved a few toiletries. He fingered the Bible for a long minute but left it resting there in the suitcase. He would let it go. He was ready. Gone were the nausea and dizziness and stabbing pain in the skull, to be replaced by a sense of well-being, of calm and oneness with the world. Granted, he stumbled a bit and mobility was a challenge as he did not seem to have full command of his limbs, but he was walking and he was not in pain, and that was something. It was enough to get him to the depot and fall into an empty box car, should he come across one. That was his goal, his aim in life—to make it through the next hour, to avoid the rail's Pinkerton agent, and somehow to place himself on a train moving him from this part of his life to the next.

Chapter 9

n the slanting afternoon light, the neighbor boy at Lily's saddled Sara's horse for her and helped her to mount. She was almost home before she remembered Maisie's cough and her vow to purchase honey and horehound candies at the grocery, so she backtracked. She did not relish seeing Mr. O'Hanlin, especially not today, when she had but a modicum of reserve left to her, but Maisie needed her, needed this, and so it was.

Mr. O'Hanlin stood by the cash drawer as Sara came through the door, bell tinkling. There were no other shoppers, and the store smelled as it always did of licorice and camphor and coffee and dust. Emotion flicked across Mr. O'Hanlin's face when he saw her—first surprise, then a narrowness, then blank. As she approached, he did not smile, just looked at her under hooded lids. Sara did not know what to make of it. She had expected him to be over-solicitous, perhaps coming to her and taking her arm, and so to be met with the opposite reaction was disconcerting.

"Good day, Mister O'Hanlin," she said, trying to ease whatever it was.

There was no response for a long minute, as he considered her. Then he glanced away toward the back of the store and said, "Miss Moore."

Sara sighed. She couldn't help herself. She wasn't sure she could manage this, whatever it was, plus everything else that weighed upon her. She just did not have the vital energy for it. She would be formal, she decided. She would transact her business and have it done and the contract between Mr. O'Hanlin and her father would have to wait. They certainly could not take their plan forward without some say from her, and that they would not get this day of all days.

At her sigh, Mr. O'Hanlin's shoulders straightened significantly. He seemed about to say something, but then held it back between his teeth.

"I stopped by to pick up a pint of honey and some horehound," Sara said, looking away. "Maisie has a cough, you see."

"Is the girl all right?" he said, with what sounded like genuine concern.

"Just a spring cold. She should be fine." As Sara said it, though, it came to her that that was exactly what she had thought about Lily a week ago. The thought chilled Sara in an instant, and she determined she would get her purchases and asquickly as possible go home and minister to Maisie.

The brown horehound candies in the jar on the counter were coated in white sugar to keep them from sticking together. Trying to keep the sugar granules contained, Mr. O'Hanlin scooped the candy onto the brown paper-lined scale, noted the weight, and wrapped the parcel deftly with a cotton string and slid it across the counter. "Your jar, please," he said, his voice formal, "for the honey." He held out his hand.

"Oh, I did not bring it," Sara said. "I, well, I'll just pay the deposit on another"—Father would certainly not let her take advantage of her position as his daughter to bypass the deposit—"and return it tomorrow."

Sara was shocked at how quickly the rage spread through Mr. O'Hanlin's body. It pumped him up, his chest filling out, his eyes widening. He moved around to the side of the counter and leaned toward her, his face tilted upward. There was no hesitation as he said through clenched jaw, "You useless twit of a girl. When we are wed, you'll conduct yourself with more intelligence and prudence." It took a second for the words to sink into her consciousness. When they did, her whole body flushed.

Sara stepped back. "Mister O'Hanlin!"

She could not believe her ears, that he had actually said such vile things to her. If he took such license now, before a wedding, if he felt he had the right to beat at her with his words in such a brutal manner, no telling what would happen once they were alone in a room and she was his and his alone.

"I have not agreed that you are to be my husband," she said.

"Aah, but you will. You will. Your father wants it so."

"There is no way on God's green earth," Sara said, her hands shaking with fury. "What Father wants means nothing." She couldn't hardly believe that these were her words. She never before would have thought them, much less uttered them. "I must also give my consent, and that I will not do. I'm handing you my mitten, *Mister* O'Hanlin."

"You will marry me," Chester spit. "I've not spent these many years …" He did not finish the thought. He stepped forward, forcing her to back up until she was against the glass case on the opposite side of the room. Still, he stepped forward, gripping her arms and making her wince, forcing his body up

105

against hers, his lips next to her right ear. She could smell the fetid odor of coffee and cigars on his breath, and she could feel the scratch of his cheek bristles.

"You will, you little harlot," he said, "and you'll stop gallivanting around town with delivery boys. I'll make sure of that."

So that was it. He had spied her on her walk with the kind and perplexing Mr. Youngblood, which had occurred after she had rejected his tender advances. At that moment, the bell on the door tinkled and two elderly matrons walked in. They glanced at Sara and Mr. O'Hanlin and then turned toward a shelf and talked between themselves, acting as if they had seen nothing. Their actions chilled Sara further. That's how the whole town would act, just as it did with those poor women who came to church with black eyes. They would not intervene and they would pretend that they did not notice. She would be totally and irrevocably trapped in a hellish situation for which there was no recourse and from which there was no escape.

With narrowed eyes, Mr. O'Hanlin pulled away from Sara and turned to wait on the two women. As quickly as she could without seeming to hurry, Sara scooted out the door, without the honey nor the horehound.

Miss Bailey stood patiently at the hitching rail, but there was no one to help Sara mount the saddle. All she could think was that she needed to get away as quickly as she could, so she pulled the rein from the post and began striding toward home. After a bit, the adrenalin wore off, and she realized how bone-weary she was, how just the idea of the walk home made tears smart in her eyes. She let herself wander to a stop, the emotion overwhelming her. Miss Bailey stumbled to a stop behind her and then nudged her back with the flat of her head, causing

Sara to stumble forward. This brought Sara out of herself. She patted Miss Bailey on the neck and said, "You are surely right, Miss Bailey. There is nothing for it. We must soldier on." Miss Bailey's companionable swaying gait next to her buoyed her mood somewhat, and with purposeful stride she made her way home.

That was that. She would not marry Mr. O'Hanlin. The choice had been made. Come what may, it was her life, and she would not subject herself to what surely would be a living hell. If she did not resist now, she would never again have a chance. But, then, Father would surely oppose her decision, and he would not take kindly to such a thing. Well, she must try to persuade him now. Her very life depended upon it.

The decision made, Sara felt better. She realized that she was hungry, as she had not eaten since breakfast, and then only a slice of toast, due to the call to duty of the day. She would go home, serve a sumptuous dinner to her father to put him in a good mood, and then she would ply what wiles she had—her own initial sally in what might develop into a war. The thought sobered her. Her father knew all about war, and she knew nothing.

When she reached home, the sun had just sank below the horizon, and she gave Miss Bailey over to the groom and immediately went to check on Maisie. Clara reported that Maisie was doing okay, holding her own, but that she was not any better. When Sara held her hand to Maisie's forehead, which was hot, Maisie said, "I don't feel good," and tucked in her chin the way children do.

"I know you don't, sweetheart," Sara said. It was nothing but a spring cold, she told herself, nothing to be too concerned about. All Maisie needed was a little rest and a little time, and she would be as right as rain. Still, Sara ordered an extra hot water bottle to be brought up and tucked next to Maisie's chest, tea with honey to be brought, and a cold rag to be placed on her head to stave off the headache.

As Sara rose to help with preparations for dinner, Sipsy burst into the room, her eyes wide. "Miss Sara, the Colonel is home and he would like to see you in his study." She added, nodding, "Now, in his study."

"What did he say?" Sara asked. "Is there something wrong?"

Sipsy glanced back the way she had come and shook her head. "I've no idea. He did not say. But he's madder than the Mad Hatter, I can tell you that."

This was not good, not good at all. As she went down the stairs, she prayed that it was something Colonel Shaw had said or done, or a bad-tempered horse, or some other matter, and not that he had stopped at the grocery on the way home and spoken with Mr. O'Hanlin. If that was the origin of his discontent, all was lost.

Father sat at his desk, his head sunk into his shoulders, his body deceptively relaxed, but he rose immediately as she entered and came around the desk, his eyes never leaving her. He indicated that she should sit, and she quickly sat on the edge of the leather-upholstered chair opposite the desk and leaned forward, her hands folded in her lap. He went back around the desk as if to sit down but then stopped, turned, and walked back to where she sat and stood over her, heels together, shoulders set, looking down upon her. He didn't say anything for a long minute, just peered at her with jaw set.

He shook his head and said loudly, "You *will* marry Chester." She had not said anything, but his first words were as in the midst of an argument. There was no couching of it to try to win her over, as he might have done.

"Father," she began, her voice high and quiet. What could she say? Should she directly oppose him? Was it too late for mollification? Would it gain his regard or just enrage him further? After a second, she decided the indirect approach was best. It was the only thing she had. "Father," she began again, "I know this decision means a lot to you. You took Mister O'Hanlin on as a partner because you trust his business sense. You think he will help build on what you have made." She knew it was true as she said it. He had given up hope on Ed, but what he truly wanted was someone to help further this business that he had been working on so determinedly, and he saw Mr. O'Hanlin as the one to do it.

Why Mr. O'Hanlin? It came to her again that perhaps he thought of Mr. O'Hanlin as a younger version of himself. The thought was repugnant. Wait. Had Father acted toward Mother as Mr. O'Hanlin had acted toward her? The thought caused her to search her mind, to reevaluate all the memories she had of her father and her mother together. Her mother deferred to her father in all things, no matter what. Was it because she was afraid of him? And it came to her then that her mother was the heroic one, not her father. She pushed herself to standing, causing Father to take a step back. She was as tall as her father, and when she held her shoulders up, she looked him in the eye. She let the feeling of anger course through her and lend her strength. This was not right. He was not in the right. His jaw clenched once again.

"I *will not* marry Mister O'Hanlin," Sara said.

"You will," he said. "You are my daughter and you will do as I say. You will marry Mister O'Hanlin, or you will leave this house."

She had never seen him this angry before. His whole body spoke of a seething rage barely contained. It was puffed and took up as much space in the room as possible, trying to tower over her, his eyes boring into her. Sara took a step backward but kept her widened eyes on his. Her body was shaking and she felt light-headed—she was not sure now what he was capable of—but she did not lower her eyes.

Her voice came out a whisper: "I will not, Father."

He took in her words and then stepped forward, raising his right hand across his body and over his shoulder and brought the back of his hand into the side of her head with such force she fell sideways to the ground, her ears ringing, unable to get her bearings. She lay and the world swayed and twirled around her and then slowed and clicked back into place. She looked up at him as he stood over her in righteous anger. This was the first time he had struck her, but it was not the first time he had done this, she realized. He had in fact hit her mother. A man who hit an intimate friend for the first time would surely show some sign of remorse, some indication that he felt he had crossed some border into another country. Father showed nothing, that he was in familiar territory, that he felt assured that this would get him what he wanted.

First with her hands and then with the assistance of the arm of the settee, she pushed herself back to standing. Father stood there, doing nothing to assist, leaning forward aggressively. He did not say anything. Once she settled back on her feet, she looked into his face once again and said, "No, Father, I will not," and then she closed her eyes and braced for what was to come. He smacked her again, and again she fell down. Her head pounded in pain, and her vision blurred. It took her longer to recover, but she once again pulled herself to standing. How much of this could she take? Would he continue to beat her unto death?

Again she rose. As she stood swaying in front of her father, what came to mind was the kind solicitude of Mr. Youngblood. If only it were Mr. Youngblood that Father wished her to marry. "Father," she began, realizing that her speech was slurred. "Father," she said again more clearly. She could see on his face that he was expecting her to capitulate, to accept his demands. "If marriage it is you want from me," she continued, "then there is a man, a kind hard-working man, to whom I would wed. He is …" She watched his expression as she said these words and she knew that is was exactly the wrong thing to say. Understanding and then accusation spread across his features.

She shrunk back, expecting him to strike her again, but instead came the words: "Chester informed me of your disgraceful conduct, your utter betrayal. I did not believe it was true, but now I see that you inherited the deceitful tendencies of your mother. You are to leave this house, now." He stepped forward and grabbed her by the arm. "You own nothing here, from this day forth, you are not my daughter, leave immediately, this instant." He dragged her across the room as she scrambled, trying to keep her feet underneath her. He exited the study, and there stood wide-eyed Sipsy and Minnie who scrambled backwards and scurried away. He dragged her down the hall and to the front door, which he pulled open and thrust her through and out into the darkness of the lamplit porch. He threw her forward and let her go, and she just regained her balance in time to keep from tumbling down the porch steps. He stood and looked at her, the sides of his face lit by the orange-red glow of the lamps, and then he turned his back on her, walked back into the house, and slammed the door.

What just happened? Sara shook her head. She had just been kicked out of her own house, the house she had lived in since she was a little girl. She had no food, no money, not even a coat, just the clothes on her back and what she was sure were brutish marks on her face. Her ability to see out of one eye was narrowing and she reached up and touched it and realized it was swelling shut. Her head was pounding, and she was suddenly so tired she could hardly stand. What was she going to do?

"Psst," came a whisper, "Miss Sara." She looked around but could not see anything in the dark. "Down here by the porch," came the voice. Sara turned and carefully walked down the steps, holding tightly to the railing in case dizziness set upon her. There was the shape of Sipsy, crouched down so that she could not be seen from the windows of the house, even though it was dark. She straightened when Sara came near, and Sara could just make out her facial features. She held some things in her hands. Sipsy glanced at Sara's face, and a look of shock came over hers. "Oh, Miss Sara," she said and looked away. "Minnie said it would be a good idea for you to go to Miss Esther's for a while," she continued. "Here's your coat and hat, and she wrapped up a bit of bread and cheese for you." As soon as Sara took the things from her, Sipsy gave her a meaningful look and, crouching, made her way back around the porch to the side of the house. Sara set the parcel and the hat on the edge of the porch, put on her coat and buttoned it, pinned her hat to her head, pulled on her gloves, and gathered the parcel.

She would go to Esther's—good advice on Minnie's part. That was the only logical thing to do. Sara walked out into the dark and down the hill and let herself out the gate. As she did, she glanced back at the house. There were lights in the windows, and the house looked beautiful and welcoming in the dark. There were lights in the kitchen, the dining room, her father's study, and in the second story in Maisie's room— Maisie! She had forgotten all about Maisie. Who was going to take care of her? The thought made her reach for the gate to go back to the house, but then she thought of her father. He put his own needs before that of his children to be sure. How could he be indifferent toward young Maisie? How could he? Anger rose within her and she clenched and unclenched the hand not holding the bundle. How dare he? She wanted to return to the house and scream at him, you irrevocable reprobate! How could he? She shook her head looking for something, anything she could do to ameliorate the effects of evening's developments upon Maisie. Something, there had to be something. But there was nothing. The anger evaporated into the cool night air, leaving in its wake a feeling of intense hopelessness. Could she? She almost felt that she could bear Father's wrath for the sake of Maisie, but then what? If she went back, she would have to agree to marry Mr. O'Hanlin— there was no doubt about it—and unless she was prepared for a repeat of what happened today for the rest of her life, she couldn't do that. She just couldn't. There was no way she could go back.

She turned to walk down the road. As she walked, she realized that her belly was still empty, as she had not yet eaten, so she flipped open the package and found bread and tore off bits and ate them as she walked. It calmed her, the rhythmic motion of her feet against the road in the dark and the dissipation of growling hunger. Around her through the trees and on the hills, she could see lamplight from windows where people were enjoying their dinners with their families. She heard the on-and-off-again mournful call of a night bird and the low of a cow. There, the yip of a dog or a fox. The air smelled of wood smoke and growing things. She finished the bread and nibbled on some cheese. She made it down the slope of the hills, bypassed the main part of town, weaved along a side road, and was once again back in the countryside. She could see the darker shapes of trees. She glanced up, and the sky was filled to the brim with stars, and the thoroughfare that was the Milky Way blazed a trail through the middle. She tilted her head back and looked more closely. She was reminded of how very many stars there were. The sky was stuffed with them, and they twinkled, keeping her company. She took a sigh and breathed in the cool air.

Then what looked like the greenish yellowish light of a train pierced the sky from the north for a second and was gone. That wasn't possible, as the rail line was south of town and ran east/west. Sara stopped and listened. Nothing, no clattering of rails. But then, again, the searchlight pierced the sky. What was it? There was no sound. She watched carefully. It came again, more green this time, and this time it climbed slantwise up the northern sky and then pinched out. No, it wasn't a train. Its source was not earthly at all, but instead the heavens. It was the luminations of the aurora borealis. Sara had heard of it in adventure tales of the north, but she never seen it before. In fact, few people she knew had seen it. A singular experience. It began again and climbed the sky, distinctly green, striving to reach the zenith, overweening the stars behind. She stopped and watched it for a while before walking on.

Chapter 10

y the time Sara reached Esther's, it was deep in the night. The stars had wheeled and turned. She pounded on the door a long time before Gerald opened it and held the lamp high to see whom it was. He saw her and yelled back over his shoulder, "Esther, dear, it's your sister." Then he gestured for her to come in. She did and removed her hat and coat and gloves and put them on one of the hooks in the hall. She glanced at Gerald and he was looking at her face. By the pressure she felt in her eye socket, she was sure it was still swollen, and it had to be bruised. He put his hand on her shoulder and squeezed, his face open and full of empathy.

Esther soon came down the stairs in her nightgown. "Oh my God, what happened to you?" she asked. Should Sara tell Esther about Father's beating her? Well, truly, Esther was owed the truth, as she would be in it up to her eyebrows if Sara were to stay with her. There was no getting around that. But it was late, and she wasn't sure how to couch it, and she did not want to keep them up, so she said, "I'm all right, Esther. Can we discuss it in the morning?" As she said it, she realized how very bone-weary she was. The morning seemed a continent and a century away. "May I sleep here?"

"Certainly," Esther said. "Need you ask?" She looked at Sara but put her hand on Gerald's arm. "What happened? Shall we call the doctor? Did you have a fall from a horse after the funeral? Down a flight of stairs? Did someone hit you? Certainly we need to apprehend this ruffian. Did he ..." She considered her words. "Did he molest your person otherwise?"

"No, no, not at all, nothing like that," Sara said. "I don't need the doctor. It's not like that at all. And anyway the personage at fault is not going anywhere."

"So it was a person. Who was it?" Esther said.

"Please, dear Esther." Sara became convinced if she told Esther about it now, it would go for the worse. Esther was intent on blaming someone, and that someone very well could turn out to be Sara. Or worse, Esther would feel that she needed to do something about it immediately, and that could not be good.

Esther raised her eyebrows, reluctant to let it rest. "There's nothing that need be done tonight?"

"No, nothing that can't wait till morning."

Esther nodded, though she still appeared skeptical, and Gerald went back up to bed. Esther took Sara to the guest room behind the kitchen. She ladled some warm water off the wood stove into a basin and brought it in and gently cleaned Sara's face. She tossed the water out the window and filled the pitcher with cool water from the pump in the kitchen and set it on the bureau. "Wet this cloth and put it over your eye. It'll take the swelling down. And help your head." She retrieved a nightdress from the bureau and put it on the bed for Sara and turned to go but then turned back. "Oh! Have you eaten? Are you hungry?" Sara had not in fact had dinner, but she did not want to keep her sister up any longer and the bread and the cheese were enough to fill her empty belly, so she said she had and thanked Esther again. Esther came over to where she sat on the bed and wrapped her arms around her and gave her a firm squeeze and then was off to bed herself. Sara went to the kitchen and retrieved a tin cup and poured water into it and drank long and deep. The water was cool and made her realize how thirsty she was so she had a second cup. Then she undressed and put on the night dress and unpinned, combed, and braided her hair and was soon asleep.

The sun streamed in the windows by the time Sara rose the next day. Her head ached dully. As she got dressed, she had a chance to see herself in a mirror. Her right forehead down past her cheekbone was one large bruise grading from purple to red to blue to green. It was a shock to see the extent of it. It brought to mind the force of both blows and made her wince. Her right eyelid puffed a bit, but it must not be as bad as the night before, as she could open it all the way without pressure.

In the kitchen, Esther was making a breakfast of flap jacks. Sara could smell them before she entered the room, and they prompted her stomach to growl. Esther's two girls, Charlotte and Lizzie, sat at the table in their nightdresses. Lizzie's eyes were level with the table top. "Auntie Sara!" they yelled in delight and surprise when she entered the room.

"Lizzie," Sara said, "Do you need your blanket to sit on?" The girl nodded. They kept an old quilt folded for just that purpose on a shelf nearby, and Sara placed it on the chair and helped her get up onto it. As she did it, Charlotte's eyes fastened on her face, and Charlotte said, "Auntie Sara, what's wrong with your face?" She got up out of her chair, came over to where Sara was leaned over, and touched her face, which made Sara wince, and then Charlotte gave her a hug, and

118

Lizzie slipped down from her chair and followed suit. Sara knelt and hugged them both and inhaled deeply the little girl sleep smell. Then she helped Lizzie back into her seat and scooted an extra chair at the corner between the girls.

"Your Aunt Sara came in late last night, girls, and we don't know what's happened," Esther said. "Maybe she was kidnapped by gallefalumps? What do you think? Was it gallefalumps?" The girls looked from their mother to Sara and back. Charlotte smiled at Esther's words, but Lizzie's face was solemn. "Maybe they were herfaloes? Lizzie, do you think they were herfaloes?" Esther put the spatula down and came over and put her arm around Sara. "Well, we'll just have to be extra nice to her to make her feel better, won't we?"

"I already gave her a hug," Charlotte said, proud of herself.

"Get started on breakfast," Esther said, gesturing to the plate of cakes and then returning to the stove. "I'll join you as soon as I make Gerald's eggs. I see he's on the way in." Esther cracked five eggs into a waiting fry pan and salted and peppered them. Sara helped the girls with their pancakes. She put butter and home-canned chokecherry syrup on them and cut them into bite-sized pieces. The girls bent their heads and said their prayers of thankfulness, Sara holding their hands. Then she made herself a plate and dug in. The syrup was tart but sweet and the butter tasted heavenly on the light and crisp cakes. Sara was really hungry.

Gerald came in through the kitchen door carrying a small tin bucket of eggs, which he set on the counter. "Morning, hon," he said to Esther, and they kissed each other warmly on the lips. He turned. "Morning, Sara," he said and nodded her direction. He smiled at the girls: "How're my little gallnippers?" He walked around the back of the table and kissed the tops of their heads.

"Morning, Gerald. How's the pigs?" Sara said and smiled at Esther. Gerald was particular about his pigs. He was a born hog farmer, and he ordered all the government pamphlets on the latest scientific developments. "Pigs is the cornucopia of animals," he often said. "You'll see. Them refrigerated cars are going to revolutionize the pig business." He had big plans.

"Fat as mayors," Gerald said as he worked the pump handle to wash his hands.

Esther flipped flap jacks onto a plate, topped them with the sunnyside eggs, and set them in front of Gerald's place. Gerald sat down and began to eat, and Esther joined them too.

Because they lived so close, it was convenient for Sara to return home when she spent the day at Esther's, so she was rarely there at breakfast. On this day she was alert to their rhythms. Theirs was a family built on common devotion, which was revealed in the smallest of motions. It contrasted so steeply with the formality and tenseness of meals in her father's house. If someone were to spill their cup, the household was in an uproar for an hour, and Sara often left the table with an upset stomach. So this was what a family could be, and it all depended on the husband and wife. If they had a good relationship, then all that flowed from it was good. By marrying Mr. O'Hanlin, she not only would be damning herself but also her children.

She had but one slight of a hope, and his name was James Youngblood. What had he said? Had he indicated anything beyond mere flirtation? She remembered the warmth in Mr. Youngblood's face as he spoke and his solicitous body language, the desperate grasp of his hand, and she knew it had meant more. She knew it deep down the way you just know things, and she trusted that feeling. Mr. Youngblood had all but asked her to marry him, she was sure of it. She would go to him, today, first thing, and profess her desire for the future of their relationship. The decision made, Sara felt better.

When breakfast was finished, Esther sent the girls to their room to change and then to play outside. "We adults need to confab," she said, more to Sara than to the girls. Once they left, Esther filled Sara's, Gerald's, and her own coffee cup and then sat down and looked at Sara, prompting her to speak. Now Sara would have to reveal what had happened, and while she trusted Esther to continue to hold her in high esteem, Esther's reactions were sometimes unpredictable.

"There's no putting it any other way," Sara said. "Father did this to me."

She looked into Esther's face and expected to see shock and disbelief. How the confession was received, instead, was quite different. Esther and Gerald glanced at each other, exchanging affirmation, and Esther nodded her head. The surprise on Sara's face must have been evident, because Esther said, "You were too young to remember Virginia." Sara nodded—she could not remember their time in Virginia. "It was quite different there," Esther continued. "Mother was a different person. She was surrounded by friends and loved ones. She felt strong. It caused tension between them. And then there was that business about running supplies, guns maybe, during the War. Neither side took kindly to it. And then we had to move. He was—we were—run out of town, basically. She blamed him for it—rightly so, in my mind. She wanted to stay where her family was. It got pretty bad." Gerald put his hand on her arm as she spoke. Esther must've previously relayed the whole story to him. "There was a time when Mother would not leave the house for the evidence of his hand. And then we moved and Mother was a different person, a shadow of who she had been."

So it was true. This was not the first time Father had taken his wrath out on the women in his life. It made Sara feel so bad for the kind person she knew that her mother had been.

"So what happened?" Esther asked.

Sara told her. She talked about Mr. O'Hanlin and his conduct and her fears for their shared future. She talked about their father and what he had done. She did not yet mention Mr. Youngblood though. Again, Esther was a pious woman, and she had strong feelings about marriage and adultery or anything perceived as untoward.

"Quite a quandary, Sister," Esther said. "What do you plan to do? Staying with us is most likely a short-term solution, as you know Father as well as I do." Esther glanced at Gerald as she said this. Sara knew that the repercussions could be extended to them, and she definitely did not want that. "Though you're very welcome," Esther added quickly.

Should she tell them? Well, if she were going to act on her impulses yet still be living under their roof, she could not very well sneak around behind their backs, especially with Esther's firm marital beliefs. She must tell them. She must trust them with this.

"Well, there is one thing I might do," Sara said. How should she couch this? "There is another gentleman—" She cut herself off but then quickly added, "I'm not saying he is someone Father would, shall we say, well, you know, once Father gets his sights set on one thing, all other options are out the door."

"Who is he?" Esther said.

She took a deep breath. "His name is James Youngblood. He works with horses." She searched for something more to say and found that that was almost everything she knew about him. "And he's from back East."

At the name, Gerald's face changed, as if he knew something. Sara wanted to ask, but she felt sure he would not say anything unless it were really awful, and if it were really awful, he would say something without asking. Also, she did not want in any way to express doubt. Esther's face changed too, once she saw the look on Gerald's. "And he's asked you to marry him?" Esther said.

"Well, not exactly," Sara said, "but he will." I think he will, she added silently to herself.

Esther was quiet for a minute—they all knew it was Esther's impetus, what would happen next—and then she came to a decision. She said, "Well, Sister, the only way this is going to work is if Father is also on board—as much as I hate to say it and as hard as I realize that is. Of course Gerald and I won't leave our sister out in the world to fend for herself, but it cannot be a thing that is done behind Father's back. He must know about it, and at least not oppose, whether or not he gives his consent." Esther looked into Sara's face and nodded in sympathy with the expression she found there. "I know, I know, but that's the only way it can happen." Gerald also nodded in agreement.

That meant that Sara could continue living at Esther's as long as she remained an old maid. There was just no good solution. But even hazarding Esther's disapproval, Sara had to see Mr. Youngblood. She could not let the sun set upon this day without at least either confirming what she felt his intentions had been or dismissing them in her mind. There had to be closure. Only then she could resign herself to maidenhood.

It was late morning by the time Sara helped Esther with the dishes and then carefully washed her face and did up her hair. There was nothing to be done about the horrible bruise, and it caused her some worry as to how Mr. Youngblood would receive her. As Sara let herself out the kitchen door, Esther did not ask where she went, and she did not offer a reason. It was bright but overcast, with promise that the haze would burn off later in the day, and the rising heat and humidity made it somewhat oppressive. As she walked, she tried to think how she would explain the bruise, and she decided that honesty, as much as possible, was the best policy. She also tried to figure out what she would say. She couldn't flat out ask him, did you intend to ask me to marry you? Doubts plagued her, and the closer she got to town, the sillier it all seemed, yet she remained steadfast. It was in reality her only hope.

As she approached Mrs. Smit's from the back way, she spied a man reeling down the road, using a ladies' parasol to prop himself up. He seemed hardly to be able to stand, he was so incapacitated—drunk, evidently. As she came upon him, she crossed the road so as not to intercept his path. As she passed by, she heard him say, "Miss Moore, Miss Moore," but it was slurred. It shocked her that a drunkard would accost her on the street, much less know her name, and she hurried on, but when she glanced back, there was something beseeching in his stance, something that sparked a memory. She knew this man from somewhere. She turned and walked back toward him, tilting her head to try to see his face as she approached. She saw then that there was a bandage slantwise across the man's forehead, and that he held his side with one arm, as if to stabilize it, while his other arm propped on the parasol. The man was not drunk. He was injured. And then she recognized the black corduroy suit as the same as the one Mr. Youngblood had worn, and she looked deeply into his face and realized who he was. "Mister Youngblood!" she said.

In turn, Mr. Youngblood looked into her face, and his eyes came to rest on the bruising and he tilted his head, brow wrinkled. He was asking what had happened to her. She shrugged and looked him up and down in an obvious manner, asking the same question. He shrugged and then winced and held his side, and then he shook his head and chuckled a bit and she too began to chuckle. Soon they were laughing. Sara laughed quietly at first and then she couldn't help herself—she laughed and laughed and soon her sides hurt. Mr. Youngblood laughed quietly and reservedly throughout as he held his side and tried to suppress it, which only made him laugh more. It continued on. She took his arm to help support him as he teetered, and they laughed some more. It felt good to laugh.

Chapter 11

A s their laughter ebbed, Sara said, "I'm sorry. You were going?" asking him if he needed to go his way.

"Nowhere particular," Mr. Youngblood said. "Just out for a walk."

Sara nodded and then turned to walk and again offered her arm for his support. He seemed about to pull away but then continued to rest his hand on her arm. As they walked, it was apparent he did not actually need her support, though the parasol gave him a bit more balance, and soon they switched and she politely held his arm. It felt so natural, and this time it did not occur to Sara to consider onlookers' disapproval and to pull away. Sara led Mr. Youngblood back the way she had come to the outskirts of the settlement. It was opposite from her father's house and away from the grocery in the center of town. Mr. Youngblood seemed more than willing to accompany her. For this, Sara was grateful and encouraged. He confessed as they walked that he did in fact have a bit of a brick in his hat, as the concoction the doctor had given him left him unstable. "I am not a drunkard," he added. For the most part, they did not talk, and it was a nervous silence. They wandered off the road and took a deer path through the bushes. The path was overgrown with trees and brambles, and they had to walk single file as the brush scraped against their jackets. The burr clover snagged at Sara's skirt, and she tried not to think of the sheep ticks crouching in the surrounding foliage, ready to pounce upon her and crawl into her hair. The path dipped down and then came out of the brush onto a branch of the river, just as Sara had expected, and they found a small open area right on the water. Sara invited James to sit with his back against a tree and she sat down the slight slope at his feet as nearly as she dared.

"What a sight am I," Mr. Youngblood said as he settled. It was not a light comment. It contained a sense of deep sorrow and regret.

Sara looked up at him. In truth, he was a bit of a fright. It was as if he had just returned from war, his bandaged and bruised pate, the stiff way he held his upper body, the way he balanced himself with the parasol. She could only imagine the bruising that prompted the way he held his arms tight against his ribs. But for all that, he was still a handsome man, with his bright blue eyes and broad shoulders and large hands. At that thought, Sara felt her body respond. It was a deepening, a quickening. It welled up within her and made her restless, but she liked the feeling.

"You are truly a sight for sore eyes," Sara said, the feeling of the moment before imbuing her words. No sooner had the words escaped her lips than she realized their meaning and she felt the pressure of a hot blush rise from her neck. Yet, she did not wish to pull the words back, and, even, she hoped that he would interpret them with the intensity that they contained.

He did not speak for a moment—or was it that he could not? He moved his lips to say something but then shook his head, his eyes wide and focused on her face. "Miss Moore," he said finally, simply. And then, "Do you truly mean that?"

"I do," Sara said. "I truly do. I ..." Should she go further? What were the limits of propriety? But then she thought, I am much past the bounds of propriety. It does not feel wrong. Does that make it wrong, just that thought? And is that the pretext with which every ne'er-do-well excuses himself? But, it did not matter, suddenly. It was enough that it was what she deeply wanted. Not only that, but Father had far exceeded the limits of propriety. Sara did not care if society excused or ignored such things men did. Such violence against those you purported to love was inexcusable. This thought caused anger to rise within her, so she peered at Mr. Youngblood and plunged ahead. "Truly, Mister Youngblood, did you mean what you said at our first meeting? Did you truly want, er, a longer term relationship?" There, she had said it.

"I did," he replied, "but I did not think the proposition, er, proposal, um—you know what I mean—that it would be well-received, coming from the blue like that."

At those words, Sara felt her mood lift and soar, and suddenly all things were possible. It had not been her imagination, and there was in fact a future of her own choosing. She felt a joyful sound rise from within her and she wanted to squeal her exuberance as young girls did when they were excited. She settled for clenching her fists and leaning forward straight-backed. What could she say next? She searched her mind. There was nothing. It was not her place to make the next move. She looked into his face, leaning forward and with her whole being willing him to speak.

Their gazes linked and held.

James couldn't clear his head. Her words had caused emotion to rise so strongly within him that it stopped his nose, and he blinked to keep back the moisture in his eyes. The patent medicine left him in a fog yet also bare and defenseless, his emotions raw and uncontainable. Had this object of such beauty and grace really just invited him to, to, to what? He focused on her face. The bruise up and down the side of her face was disconcerting. It made him angry. He wanted the perpetrator to be punished for such abuses of her person, of that tender skin, of the delicate bulb of that eye. He swallowed hard. Was she asking what he thought she was asking? He looked for any sign on her person that she was disingenuous, but her whole countenance spoke of openness—to him!— and willingness to hear whatever words he spoke.

"I think you mean ..." he finally said and took a breath. "I mean to say"—unbelievable as it is, he thought to himself—"that we are of like minds"—she was nodding—"and I desire of you and you desire of me, to be joined in wedlock?" The last word came out small and high-pitched, but, there, he had said it.

She did not make him wait. Almost before the words were out of his mouth, she said, "Yes, I desire that. Truly, I desire it." She was nodding vigorously.

And then they both sat in stunned silence, just looking at each other, shaking their heads. It was unbelievable. They had dared the wild briar thickets of this outlandish possibility, they had forged ahead despite the prickers and the doubt and the shame and their own weaknesses, and they had reached their mutually desired destination. She scooted closer to him so that her seat was not far from his knees and she extended her right hand, keeping her eyes on his face. He reached to extend his right hand, then winced and pulled it back, but then quickly extended his left hand. They grasped each other's fingers and held tightly, grasping again for a better grip, squeezing, and then just holding. His single hand was as large as both of hers together, and he could feel the soft pliance of hers through her gloves.

"I thought—" he said with animation.

"*I* thought—" she replied.

"Well," he said.

"Yes. Well," she said. And then they were quiet, and he looked at her and then out over the river, and she followed his gaze and looked out over the river too. It was narrower here, with the promise of snags underneath from the trees felled into it. Lots of deep holes that would be good for catfish and other water creatures. They sat and listened to the buzz of the cicadas and the lazy chirp of a single bird and smelled the earthy odor of the river, and they rested. The air was warm. The sky had cleared off, leaving it a hazy blue, and way off over the trees, clouds were gathering. They were mounding, dark and pregnant with rain, and they were moving this way. There would be a storm later.

"Well, where do we go from here, Mister Youngblood?" Sara asked after a time.

"Well, first, I suppose you should call me James, considering," Mr. Youngblood said. "If you want to," he added and looked down at his lap.

"Where do we go from here, James?" She let his name rest and elongate on her tongue.

"To be honest, I am not sure."

"I am not sure, *Sara*. Call me Sara."

"All right, Sara." He too seemed to take pleasure in saying her name. "You see, there is a little trouble with—" he tilted his head and lifted his shoulders, indicating his injuries. "The man who did this will not be easily placated."

The statement made Sara stiffen. What if James were involved in some shady business? No. She trusted what she sensed about him. Just in case, though, she asked, "You're not in trouble with the law, are you?"

"No-oo," he answered. "I got this from a man I worked for who believes he can abuse me yet expect me to continue in his employ. That I won't do."

"I can't hold you to blame, there. I wouldn't either." Of course she wouldn't. Wasn't that another version of what she was doing? She was extracting herself from a difficult situation, a violent situation. "In truth, I also find myself in a bit of sticky situation."

They looked again at each other's faces and gave each other a smile of understanding and gallows good humor. It wasn't funny, but there it was.

James seemed to come to a decision. "Well," he said, "I don't know what that situation is and how set you are to stay in Anamosa—as I do not have much to offer but my certainty that we could make a good life—but I was now, this very minute, on my way to the train station to catch a train to Kansas City. I've heard rumor of a good wage for good work there. Jobs aplenty."

Her thoughts immediately brightened at the proposition, and she tilted her head and mulled it over for a time. Yes, that might work. Then the man who was after James would be foiled and her father could not hold her under his thumb. Esther would be placated and not affected by Father's wrath. Sara—they—would be free to start a new life, to start over. The perfect solution. "That might be just the thing," she said, nodding. "Just the thing. The solution to both our problems."

James nodded and then reached out and touched the bruised side of her face so gently Sara could just feel the wisp of it. She leaned into it, so that his hand was in full contact with her cheek. "How came you upon such an offensive mark upon your person?" he said. "I could not imagine ..." He let whatever he was imagining go unsaid and dropped his hand.

"That's why going to Kansas City would be a solution for us both," Sara said. "Just as you would like to escape the clutches of an unscrupulous man, so would I." She hesitated and then said, "You see, my father is also such a man." He might as well know. It was not her shame that her father was a violent man, and James of all people would seem to understand. She turned her head and tilted it, showing the bruised side of her face, indicating that her father was the responsible party.

The admission hung in the air between them.

James said, "Your father did this?" He thought, I must revise my opinion of this man. What was he getting himself into? Maybe he could make his excuses and still make it to the train, out from under the power of an unscrupulous bastard. But, no, asked and answered. It was what she wanted and what he wanted too. No. She was such a rare creature, and she had actually agreed to marry him!

"Yes," she answered, "and that is why Kansas City would be the perfect solution." She considered for a time, her eyes darting back and forth as her mind worked. "Not only that, but, as you really are planning to marry me, yes?"—she tilted her chin down and looked under her eyelids at him, and he nodded and smiled—"let's not have the wedding here. Let's elope." She smiled like a naughty child and nodded her head. "There's no way I can see that we can have a church wedding in

Anamosa, what with the … well, with my father's, shall we say, determination. We can get married in Kansas City, or along the way. Yes, let's. Shall we?"

James began nodding slowly, thinking upon it. That would in fact serve his purposes well, but the fact that she would want it, would suggest it, spoke to the desperation of her plight. There was much more to this woman than met the eye. She had grit and nerve.

"Agreed, then," she said. "We will elope to Kansas City. Oh, it sounds a bit romantic."

He hoped it would be. The practicalities of it were daunting, however. He had not the fare for himself much less her, and how could he admit that to her? How could he get the funds so that he would not have to admit it? It shot a feeling of desperation through him, a familiar feeling of responsibility coupled with lack of options. But it felt different, too, because he had just won biggest prize of his life. This beautiful funny wonderful woman was to be his wife.

"I need to walk back to my sister's and gather my things," Sara said. She pushed herself to standing and held his hand as he stood. But, Sara thought, really, what things do I have to gather? She had not a single toiletry, much less clothing or anything else she might need. She would have to ask Esther. They could purchase what they needed when they reached Kansas City. Sara had never up unto this point had the necessity to question the availability of finances. "And you can go and retrieve yours," Sara added.

James looked at her and shrugged.

"Don't you have any luggage?" Sara asked.

"Not really," James said.

This caused Sara a bit of consternation. How did one make

it in life with so few possessions? But, apparently, he had and did, and that was enough at the moment for her. What freedom. He was able to do as he willed, and now, because she was marrying him, so could she.

"So I shall gather my things," she continued, "and meet you at the train station at, say four o'clock, four thirty at the latest?" She brought out the watch she had inherited from her mother, which she wound every morning and kept tucked into her skirt pocket. "There is a train going west shortly after five, I believe. I hear it every day as I teach Maisie her letters." She tucked the watch back in.

"Maisie?" he prompted.

"My sister Maisie," Sara said. "She's six. Oh, I didn't tell you, I have an older sister Esther, who's married with two girls, and an older brother Ed who's a carpenter, and then a younger sister Maisie. Do you have any siblings?"

"No, I am my mother's only child."

"We know so little about one another, yet I feel we've known each other a long time." It was comfortingly true.

He nodded in response and smiled.

"But I should go," Sara continued, "if I am to make it back in time. You'll be all right, I mean, you're not too … incapacitated?"

"Not at all. I feel quite well, actually." He tossed the parasol into the bushes to demonstrate. Sara watched it fall, looked at James, and then laughed. "Quite well," he added and puffed out his body, indicating his supreme understatement. Then he took a few steps one direction and then back without a wobble.

"Well," she said, "then I'm off." Hesitating to part, they stood and looked at each other for a long moment, and after a bit Sara nodded, saying, "Well then," and turned to go, but James put his hand on her arm. She turned back to him, waiting, and he slowly leaned forward and bent his head. She leaned toward him in response and their lips touched, just. It sent shocks through them both, and they held for a long moment, neither moving their head, and breathed each other in, wanting to go further, to touch each other more fully, but then they released. The thrum still coursed through them as he looked at her and smiled broadly, and she looked at him and smiled and nodded, and then they turned and went their separate ways, glancing back at each other as they went.

Sara was so energized that the walk back to Esther's took no time at all. She caught herself singing at least three times, and her mind flitted from topic to topic. Kansas City. Big city life, the high fashion of the ladies, the quantities of cattle that moved through every day to be converted to cuts for the table. It was truly the beginning of the Wild West, as it wasn't but a year or two ago she had read in the Anamosa *Eureka* of that notorious outlaw Jesse James shot and killed not far from that city by one of his own gang. Then, her father. It gratified her to think that Father would hear second-hand of her decision to wed and to relocate to Kansas City, that he would fret and perhaps even grieve, and that he would be powerless to stop her.

Thus invigorated, cheeks red from the walk, Sara returned to Esther's. Esther was at the table shelling early peas when Sara entered. On an extra chair to the right of Esther was a large tin pail full of ripe peapods, the bright green bumps of shelled peas were piled in an earthenware bowl in her lap, and a pile of husks lay on the table. Sara danced past and leaned in and kissed Esther on the cheek, almost upsetting the pail of peas. Sara did not apologize but instead began to sing.

"Shh!" Esther said, nodding her head to the inside doorway, indicating that the girls were in the midst of their afternoon nap. Sara quit singing but pirouetted and glided back to the table and flopped into a chair. She reached into the shelled peas and gathered a small handful, and with Esther swatting at her hand she pulled back and popped them into her mouth. "What in the darnation's gotten into you?" Esther asked. "You left as dark as blood pudding, and you return as light as victory cake."

"Oh, I am, I am. It is true," Sara said. "Oh, Esther dear. I am to be married." She hadn't meant to just say it like that, but there it was, irrevocably, irrepressibly. She wanted someone and he wanted her and there was no other worth nor meaning in the world.

Esther stopped shelling peas and stiffened, her face fixed. "Have you spoken to Father?" she said, finally.

It came back to Sara Esther's prohibition on going forward without Father's permission. She sat forward in her seat. "No, I have not." She said it openly, a denial but without guilt. "That's the beauty of it," Sara said, "don't you see? I am not going courting. I am to be wed. I do not need Father's permission because it is not Father's decision to make. It is mine, and I've made it. And it's not yours, now, either, as I won't be imposing upon you further, as we are to elope to Kansas City." Her voice held conviction, but she watched Esther's face closely.

Esther grew more still. "You what?" There wasn't anger in it, as Sara expected, but a wounded quality.

Sara tried to guard her heart against it. She said, "I am to be wed, Esther. Please let that be enough. Like you, it is a mate of my own choosing, and we will be happy, just as you and Gerald are happy." She leaned in and put her hand over Esther's, there in her lap. "Oh, please, be happy for me, Sister Mine," she said, her eyebrows raised in suit.

Esther, for her part, did not immediately take up opposition, as was her way. She sat transfixed for a long moment and then said, "But what do you know of this man, Sara?" Esther asked. "Gerald's heard, well, nothing that he liked."

"What? What did he hear?" Sara hoped it was nothing. She trusted Gerald implicitly, as a brother, and she trusted his word, but Esther knew that too.

"He could not say," Esther said. "Or, rather, there was nothing specific but that he thought he'd heard of man recently in town whose past was questionable. However, he did not know if this man, your man, was the one referred to."

"It would not be James," Sara said.

"Do you realize," Esther continued, "that you are hooking your wagon to what may well be a runaway train? Or a slowcoach? Or the pathway to hell, for all you know. What do you know about this man? Sara, don't you see?" Esther was maintaining her reasonableness, but she was shaken, Sara could tell.

"I may not know in concrete terms, but I know in my heart," Sara said. "I trust him completely."

Esther snorted. "You'll starve, if'n you trust nothing but your heart. Listen to your head, girl."

"I am," Sara said. "Now you listen to it too." It suddenly felt imperative to get Esther on her side, if only to justify her confidence in the decision. "Don't you see, Sister? It solves all our problems. You no longer have to worry about propriety and about Father's recriminations. And I don't have to marry that horrid Chester. I am free to have a happy life." When Esther still hesitated, Sara said, with more force in her voice, trying to make her understand the reality of it, "You see what he did to me, don't you, Esther? This bruise is but a beginning." She turned her head so her sister could get a full view. "And it will not stop. Mister O'Hanlin is just such a man as Father. He will not stop his hand either, and you will have to stand by and watch as I come to your door time and again, broken and bleeding. You know that, don't you?" Esther looked down at her hands in her lap. She was softening. Sara pursued her advantage. "Please, be happy for me, Dear Sister, please."

Esther stayed with her head bent, and Sara thought at first she was about to become angry, but then she realized by the pursing of Esther's lips that Esther was overcome with emotion and dare not say anything. Sara rose from her chair and leaned over and wrapped her arms around her, and Esther wrapped an arm around Sara's arms.

"Well, I can see you've made up your own mind," Esther said. "My little sister, married to a stranger."

Just then, Charlotte came in, trailed by Lizzie. Charlotte's hair stuck up like a cockscomb, and Lizzie held her blanket wrapped into a ball in her arms. Charlotte looked at them and said, "What's the matter, Mother?"

"Oh, Charlotte, your auntie's off to marry a stranger," Esther said.

"Not a stranger," Sara corrected. "A kind man who will …" Who will what? Not beat her? "We're going to Kansas City," she finally continued, over-enlivening the words.

"Oh, I love Kansas City," Charlotte said. Esther shook her head at the words. "What's Kansas City?" Charlotte added after a pause.

138

Esther nodded. "You've never been, dear," she said.

"Is it far?" Charlotte asked.

"Yes, it's far," Esther said.

"But I'll write you all the time," Sara said. "And I'll send you presents. There are a lot of presents in Kansas City."

"Can you go now?" Charlotte asked, eliciting a laugh from Esther and Sara.

Esther rose and got the girls cups of buttermilk and sat them at the table. Sara explained that they would be leaving on the afternoon train and that she had come to gather her things. "I still don't like it one bit," Esther said and shook her head. Sara explained that, actually, she had no things to gather, as they were all at Father's, and he had forbade her to enter the house, and besides there was not enough time. She could not go to the house and gather everything and make it to the train. Esther immediately offered to go to the house and to gather what things she could on Sara's behalf—"You're going to need everything you can get," she said. Once they found a place in Kansas City, Esther would send them on. In the meantime, Esther offered her an extra dress of her own, though it wouldn't fit exactly but it was loose enough cut that she would be able to wear it, as well as the necessary toiletries and a few other items. She put them into a carpetbag.

Esther stopped a moment, lost in thought, and then hurried to her bedroom and came back with a book. "I put this aside for you—what was it?—years ago now," she said. "About the time Mother passed. I was saving it for a wedding present, but …" Neither Esther nor Sara said anything for a moment. "So your husband won't have to go elsewhere for his cooking," Esther added with a sideways glance. It was a cookbook called *The Compleat Housewife* by a British gentlewoman named Eliza

Smith.

"Well, then, it is a wedding present," Sara said lightly.

"Yes, I suppose it is," Esther said.

And then it was time. Sara gripped the bag firmly with her right hand. "Well, Esther, I must be off if I am to make it in time," Sara said. "Thank you for the kind presents. I will not forget and I'll write. Please say goodbye to Gerald for me. And please explain to Maisie and to Ed. I will miss you all terribly." Esther gave her a long hug and the girls put their arms around her skirt and had to be pried from her and set back into their chairs. As Sara turned to go, Esther pressed something into her hand. It was a sum of money. Sara protested, but Esther replied, "It's little enough. Having never gone without, you do not yet know how desperately you will need it." Sara thanked her, and with that she was out the door.

Chapter 12

s Sara walked away there by the river, James was left with such of feeling of well-being. All his pain was gone and physically he felt almost normal. And there was his future bright and shiny before him. He and this lovely creature were going to be wed. He couldn't yet truly believe it. This one fact had so changed his outlook on what lay in his future that he brimmed with optimism.

So how to solve this problem of money? He began walking to the depot and cogitating. He did not have it. He was owed some from Ricci, but he would never see a cent of that. The absolute only thing he could think of was to ask Mrs. Smit for a loan, and so he turned and made his way to the boarding house, keeping his eyes open for any sign of Ricci and his crew. A long shot at best, as Mrs. Smit came in contact with many characters, and surely she had been hardened to the likes of him. But she was a woman whose soul was by nature charitable, and he must hope against hope that that would prevail. Mrs. Smit thought James incapacitated and in his room, but perhaps if he explained the situation, she would relent. Would the romance of an impending marriage triumph over cynicism? It sounded implausible, even to him, but what other choice did he have?

He found Mrs. Smit in the dining room overlooking the placement of the dinner service by the girl who came in to help. When Mrs. Smit saw him, she looked him up and down. "You mustn't be out of bed, the doctor said," she said. "Back you go, at once."

"That's a kind woman to say so," James said. "I appreciate your generous concern on my behalf." Mrs. Smit seemed gratified to hear it. James continued, "Only there is a matter to which I must attend that cannot be put off."

"What could possibly be more important than your good health?" Mrs. Smit said. "You don't realize the shape you were in when we put you to bed. You're lucky a rib didn't puncture your lung, and you there with air seeping from your chest, breathing your last." She looked at him again. "Back to bed with you, and I'll not hear anything about it."

"But, dear Missus Smit," James said, "you'll have to relent once you've heard my reason. I am to be wed."

Mrs. Smit looked at him, her face a mask of disbelief. "You say, wed? When did this come about?"

He couldn't very well answer that it had come about within the last hour, so he replied, "Just very recently, in fact. You are the first to know." Mrs. Smit seemed to be both gratified and skeptical at the same time. How to soften her up further? "You have the most gracious home here," he said, "and I've felt very welcomed." She nodded. He searched around for something more to say, but could come up with nothing, so he said, "But, you see, I find myself short. As you know, I am recently from prison, and I have not yet had the wherewithal to amass any savings, my small pension upon release having been immediately given over to you for your kind ministrations." He tried to gauge what affect this was having on her, and while she did not pull away in dismissal, she did not respond to his compliments. He plunged ahead. "What I ask of you, kind lady, is a small loan, little more than I handed to you upon my arrival, just until we can arrive at Kansas City and I can procure a position there."

Mrs. Smit crossed her arms. "Kansas City, you say? And you're to be wed—today?—you say? Forgive my skepticism, good sir, but did your mother also recently pass away?"

He could not believe that she could know that, and he said, "Yes, in fact—" and then he caught the twist of her head and how her body language spoke of disbelief.

"My good man," she said, "in the time that I've known you, you've been an honest man, and I try to take them as they come. I believe in charitable works as much as the next woman. You seem to be kind and forthright, especially for a man so lately imprisoned. However, your tale is a tall one, and me no spring chicken, you'll forgive me my disbelief."

He considered his options. She would not buy the truth, but she was a businesswoman, perhaps she would be persuaded by something else. He had to try something, as there was nothing else to do but this. He began again. "Let's say that what I said was untrue, that in fact I was not to be wed, but what I need is the loan with which to start a new business, to make my way fresh in the world, and you could consider the money paid back twice over once I've seen a profit. Would that make a difference?"

Mrs. Smit smiled, and James thought that his argument might have won her over, until she shook head and clicked her tongue. "Now, Mister Youngblood, here I was thinking you were an honest man. But now I know by your words that your character is of a much more rascally order, and therefore if I were considering it before, I would not stake my life upon it now. Besides, I happen to know that you are in the employ of one Mister Ricci, and that if you wanted the money, you could simply ask it of him."

Alas, all was lost. That was the end of it. Ricci, once again, had spoiled any chances he had. Why was it ever thus? Furthermore, the gambit had not worked and had in fact ricocheted awfully. There was no way now she would trust him. There was nothing for him here. All he could do was try to salvage what little was left of his reputation. He straightened his back and looked her in the eye and said, "Well, you won't believe it, but the first story is the true one, and I regret you didn't believe me. I'll be on my way, but remember me as an honest man, not the scoundrel you perceive. If you want to know the scoundrel, it's that no-account Ricci, as he's the one that did me thus." He turned and left her standing there and made his way out through kitchen door.

He had to find a way to buy some tickets. Could he offer to do work for the railroad to pay their way, as stowaways on ships often did? That did not sound plausible. The only thing that was left to him was to take the money, really the only way he was going to get it. That's how people like Colonel Moore did it. They didn't get by on their honest good work. They found ways to steal things, people's money and time, in order to take more than their fair share. He stopped in his tracks. He thought of all those rooms back in the boarding house, the one on the ground floor of the old gentleman whose cane was tipped with ivory and who had the sweets for the widowed Mrs. Smit. He was a man of means, and his room was on the ground floor and James knew from observation the man

144

generally took a walk this time of day. He could simply slide open a window or sneak in the side entrance. He could rifle the room and take just enough to pay their way. He would leave the room as it was, so the old man would not even know.

What was he thinking? He had never deliberately thieved money in his life, and he would not start now. He and his mother had in dire straits stolen a bit of food or clothing for warmth, but he had never stooped to common thievery, notwithstanding the issue of the horse. There was just nothing, absolutely no reserves upon which he could draw. He had nothing to sell or pawn. The buffalo nickel in his shoe would not begin to cover their passage. In that frame of mind, a pall of gloom laid over him, he found a wall to lean against, a place in the shade of the lowering sun, and he waited for Sara to return.

The platform was empty as Sara approached. She stepped up onto the boards and walked to the middle of the platform, her boots thumping. There was no one. She glanced back over her shoulder and then walked to the door of the station and opened it and put her head in, but there was no one in the waiting area. The stationmaster behind the window looked up and nodded to her. She went in and asked him about the gentleman who had just been in to purchase two tickets to Kansas City. He searched his memory, head shaking, and then replied that no one had purchased tickets to Kansas City in at least a week. This set Sara back on her heels. He had not purchased tickets? How could that be? She went out the door and back onto the platform. Still, no one was there. Had he changed his mind? Had he left her standing there, to be humiliated? She would have to return begging to her sister's, begging for a simple roof over her head and begging for Esther to intervene with Father and begging, begging, begging for the rest of her life. She let her carpetbag fall from her hand and onto the decking beside her. How could James have done that? His body language, his words, everything had spoken of honesty and forthright character and that he actually had meant the words he had said. How could it be, now, that he had gone? She picked up her carpetbag and walked farther down the boards, her the bag bumping her knees, the feeling of desperation growing within her.

But, as she approached the steps on the other side, there he was. He stepped from around the end of the building and in front of her. She saw him and took an involuntary breath. It wasn't all a dream. Here he was, here he truly was. She stepped to him, so relieved she felt the impulse to throw her arms around him, to hold him tightly to her, but she hesitated. She did not know him well enough for that and she did not know what his reaction would be. She looked into his face. He had unwrapped the bandage from his brow and the skin underneath was bruised and stitched. His expression was not at all what she had expected. She wanted all the signs of a joyful reunion, yet his face was distant, crestfallen—whatever it was, it was bad news. Once again panic rose within her.

"What? What is it?" she asked, putting out her hand though not touching him.

"I do not know how to tell you this, Sara," he said.

What was it? Sara felt everything crumbling around her.

"I have no money," he said, eyes on his feet.

What was this? No money? Was that all it was? A laugh of relief bubbled up inside Sara, but what came from her lips sounded like a scoff. At the sound, James quickly glanced at her face, startled, searching, but then what he found there seemed to reassure him somewhat, as his widened eyes relaxed a bit. She then dropped her carpetbag and threw her arms around him and hugged him tightly. "I've got money," she said, the relief of danger passed growing within her. "I have some money. It's not much, but I think it'll get us to Kansas City." She stepped back.

"You do?" he said and breathed deeply. "And you'll not mind us using it for our trip?"

"Of course not," Sara said. "Of course not. I am so happy it's of some use." She dug into her carpetbag and brought forth the money and handed it to him. He smiled broadly at her, relief flooding his face.

"I will pay you back," he said, "once we reach there and I get a good job. I will reimburse you."

"Don't be silly," she said. "We will be married by then. It all goes into a common pot, does it not? For our future?"

"Yes, but I feel I'm off on the wrong foot. Here it is, the beginning of our great adventure together, and I've not but myself to offer, and that's a poor thing at best."

"Not a poor thing," Sara said and leaned in and gave him a kiss on the cheek. "Not a poor thing at all. The exact right thing, the thing I most want in the world." Then she felt a blush rising and his face turned red too, but it was not awkward.

"Well, I will purchase the tickets then," James said. "Then we'll be off on our great adventure." His body, slumped the moment before, now straightened and enlivened.

"Please do, kind sir," she said, "and I'll be waiting right here for you."

He nodded and turned and went into the building. Sara bounced on her toes and smiled to herself. It really was true.

She walked over to a bench along the wall and sat, her back straight, turning it over in her mind.

"Sara?" The voice came from the edge of the boardwalk, and at first it registered as Father's, only the tone was all wrong. It was questioning, rather than commanding. It made her jump in her seat and then stand up quickly. But then when she looked down the sheltered boardwalk, it was the tall broad form of her brother Ed. Of course it was. Ed's voice was much like their father's in depth and timbre. She turned and walked to him, both so happy to see him and relieved that it wasn't in fact her father. Now she would be able to say goodbye to the one who gave her unequivocal support, someone who cared for her dearly. It was so kind of him to come. But then, when she looked at his face, she saw the set of the jaw, the narrowing of the eyes, the way his head thrust forward, and she knew that he was angry. Ed did not often get mad, but when he did, it was an awe-inspiring thing. His body in natural build and then from his physical exertions was large and powerful. She had seen him lift the corner of a loaded wagon and drive a spike into the ground with the swing of the mallet. Now he stopped and stood and glowered at her and then looked over her head and scanned the platform.

"Where is this man?" he said.

"Ed. Oh my goodness, am I glad to see you," she said. She put her arms around him, but he did not respond.

"The man who dares to …" He did not finish the thought.

Ed was angry at James? For what? For stealing his sister? He wasn't stealing Sara—Sara was going willingly. He was saving her.

"Look at me," Sara said. Ed continued to look past her, his jaw clenching. "Look at my face," Sara said more loudly. "Do

148

you not see what Father has done?"

Ed glanced at her face and then his expression opened up in surprise as he registered the bruise along her cheek. "What?" he said. He took her chin in his thumb and forefinger and turned her head, and she let him. He looked for a long moment, his face flattening and then sagging. "Father did this?"

"Yes, he did," Sara said, "and from what Esther said it's not the first time. I was too young, but surely you're old enough to remember Virginia and Mother? That's what she said. She said Father used to do it to her too."

Ed's look held for a minute as if he were searching his memory and then he looked down and nodded. "It is true," he said. "I do remember something." His shoulders slumped. Then he said, "But Esther said nothing of this"—he nodded toward her face—"to me."

"She didn't?"

"Well, in truth, I gave her no chance." He shrugged. "When I heard that, well, when she said … I didn't wait around."

"That a man was besmirching my womanhood?" Sara let the smile cross her face. She did not want to make fun of him, but she wanted to get across how silly the notion was. "I came willingly. We are to be married, you see. Did Esther not say that?"

"She might have," Ed said. "But how can you go with a man you hardly know? You can stay. I'll keep you safe. I'll protect you from Father." Earnestness crossed his face. "Stay," he added, simply.

"But I can't, don't you see? He ordered me out of the house. Before that, he ordered me to marry Chester." She let her distaste for the man come through in her pronunciation of his name.

Ed straightened. "He wants you to marry Chester?" They had talked many times about Mr. O'Hanlin, and they had agreed that he was awkward and unsavory. There was something off about him, and Sara now knew the ramifications of that character flaw.

"And that's not the worst part," Sara said. "Chester threatened my person. He implied that he would raise his hand to me once we married if I did not do as he said."

Ed's jaw once again clenched. He looked upwards and askance, his eyes narrowed, thinking. "That little piss-ant," he said. "Oh, sorry," he added, apologizing for the profanity.

"No, I agree," Sara said. "But don't you see? That's why I have to take my chances now. It's my only one. Oh, I know you mean well, but you cannot protect me, no matter how you try. A brother's love does not override the will of a husband."

Ed shook his head and put out his hands, palms up, fingers and thumbs spread wide in frustration and helplessness. He finally said, "I thought I could at least save *you*. I have long since gone under, but I thought, at least …" He continued to shake his head and let his hands drop.

Sara put her arms around his body once more and squeezed him. "I know you did, Brother. I know." It went deep, this feeling, and in that moment she wished with all her might that she could let him save her, that for once in recent memory he would be awarded a victory. But it was not to be.

Sara heard the door to the station open and close and then Ed stiffen. She stepped back, turned, and took Ed's arm and pulled him over to where James stood, watching them.

As James came out the station door, he saw Sara with her arms around a big man and he was stabbed with jealousy. Was she not to be his wife? How dare she, in full view of the public, show such affection toward another man? When she turned and pulled the man over, the familiarity between them—the way Sara tugged at the man's sleeve and the way the man let himself be led—showed James that they had long been intimate. It reminded James of how little he knew about Sara and that there were whole swathes of her life he knew nothing about. For all he knew, she may have been betrothed or, even, known men in the past, and the thought further stoked the embers of jealousy. But then James realized how big the man was and he saw the aggression in the man's stance and felt afraid.

"James," Sara said. "James, meet my brother Ed." Brother! He was her brother. The relief flooded James. "His dear friendship means the world to me. Ed, meet James, the man I'm going to wed." It was okay. It was the love of a brother, and Sara obviously was close to him. He must make friends with this man, or there would be trouble. No wonder the man was angry. James offered his hand, and the man looked at him through narrowed eyes, but then he glanced at Sara and then took it, and they shook. James made sure to press firmly, to pump his hand vigorously, and look the man in the eye. The best approach was to be forthright, to show himself a man of honor and good intentions.

"I am so happy to meet a member of Sara's family," James said, "especially one so obviously dear to her heart."

The man did not say anything, just let his hand drop. He kept looking at James, his face blank as stone.

"Ed," Sara said. "Ed! There's nothing you can do. Please, for my sake." She pushed his shoulder with her palm.

Ed glanced at her and then looked back at James. Then he looked down and shook his head. Ignoring James, he addressed

151

himself to Sara: "I don't know this man, Sara. I don't know if he picks pockets in the town square or saves children from burning buildings. I just don't know. How can I send you off with him not having a means to protect you nor to even know if you need protection? You're my kith and kin."

It was a very reasonable response. How could James lay his fears to rest? Well, in actuality, he couldn't, not in such a short period of time, but he could meet the challenge head on. James took a deep breath and said, "I honor your fears, Mister Moore. I know it is small comfort, but all I can say in reassurance is that I mean to do my best by Miss Moore. I have no proof in my defense, but know that I am an honorable man, and I mean to marry her and provide her with the best possible life I am able. It will not be the life she had here in Anamosa—that is true—but it will be the best life I can offer." James kept his eyes on the man's face as he made this speech, and then he waited.

This brother, Ed, kept looking at him, his head tilted to the side. "I hear your words, but words are small comfort during the darkest nights. If I were to hear of anything happening to Sara, I would be beside myself. Do you understand what I am saying? I would go to the ends of the earth to make things right." Ed let the words hang in the air.

This man was threatening him, but James did not blame him. He cared for Sara, and this was all he had to fight his ineffectuality. James did not take it personally. "I do understand," James said. "And nothing will happen to Sara. While my love is not a brother's love, it is nonetheless a husband's love, though fresh as it is, and I would not harm her for the world. And I would also go to the ends of the earth to protect her. All I have is my word, but my word will have to do." He kept his face nondefensive and open as he said this.

Sara smiled broadly at James and tucked her hand under his arm.

Ed continued to eye him, but then he pulled in a breath and let it out. He nodded slightly. "I do not like it, but it seems I have nothing to say on the matter." He turned to Sara. "I cannot believe you are to be married. It takes some getting used to, Little Sister." It was as close as he came to an apology. He wrapped his arms around Sara and held her for a long time. Then he turned to James and held out his hand and again shook it firmly. "You'll write," he said to Sara. "If there's anything I can assist with, let me know."

"We will," Sara said.

Ed turned to leave, but then turned back. "What is your name?" he asked James.

"James Youngblood," James replied.

"Well, Mister Youngblood," Ed said. He turned and left, glancing again over his shoulder at Sara as he went.

Chapter 13

ara and James sat on the bench next to the wall and waited for the train to arrive. They talked about small things and let their bodies relax into one another. They were both very aware that their shoulders rested together and that his knee bent over against hers. Neither pulled away. It was exhilarating.

It would be a three-day journey to Kansas City, and they planned to spend an additional day in Cedar Rapids to find a preacher to marry them. Their tickets were for coach, and what with the rail price wars they were able to get a good price. If they'd been traveling through the night, Pullman sleepers would have been the most comfortable, but they were spending two nights in Cedar Rapids, so they could save the steeper fare. Then they would continue on to Council Bluffs, stay the night there, and then the following day travel south to Kansas City. Their plan to marry in Cedar Rapids was a relief to Sara—she trusted James, but niggling in the back of her mind were all the stories of women whose reputations were ruined by a promise of marriage that never materialized. He did not try to put her off by saying that they would be married in Kansas City. He seemed as eager as she. For that, Sara was grateful.

People arrived onto the platform to await the train—an

older lady with a beribboned girl, a man dressed formally in a white cravat and tails who had once attended one of Sara's Father's dinner parties, and then two other men in work shirts and vests. They could hear the train before it came into view, hooting and then bell clanging as it entered the settlement. It chugged into the station and came to a screechy halt, enveloping them in coal smoke and heat, and then sat there creaking and chuffing.

James went to relieve himself before the journey, and he handed Sara her ticket and said, "Reserve us some good seats." Sara was eager to see the opulence of the train, as she had never ridden one. She quickly stepped onto the car closest to her, hoisting her carpetbag and pulling herself into the darkness by the handrail. The first thing to hit her was the overweening smell of unwashed bodies, sweat, urine, cabbage, animal feces, and dirty feet, with an undertone of something medicinal. This cannot be right, she thought. There was the rising gabble of people talking in languages Sara could not understand. It took a minute for her eyes to adjust to the dark interior, lit only by a few oil lamps, so that she could just make out what looked like a mass of people. Gaunt faces and round faces turned her way, and upon them she sensed boredom and fatigue and desperation and hunger. She put her hand up to the wall to steady herself and felt closely spaced wooden slats worn smooth from the caress of many hands. She glanced about and saw that every surface was covered with these slats—the bowed ceiling, the walls, the benches, the board-frame berths. Wooden slats held together with cordage served as shades on the small and widely spaced windows. It was as if she had entered a cattle car.

The area was crammed with people wrapped in clothing in

155

unfamiliar styles. Blankets and cloth bags seemed to be everywhere, falling from benches and piled in the aisle and under seats and berths and in the overhead slatted compartments. Where there were no people or cloth bundles, there were crates and trunks and wicker baskets. Sara had heard the term "impedimenta" applied to travel luggage, and now she knew why: there was no room to move about, to walk the aisles, even to stand. One woman held two chickens in a crate on her lap, and Sara swore she heard the low-level grunt of a pig.

Who were these people? Immigrants, most likely. These people were on the move, looking for a prosperity they did not currently possess. Just as she and James were, really. These people were very poor—one could tell from the state of their clothing and their cleanliness and their being crammed into this animal crate of a train car. Then a thought brought a lurch in the pit of Sara's stomach—Sara had no money either. God in heaven. She had just given what money she had to James, so technically she probably had less money than these folks. She was better dressed, she was traveling coach, and she came from money, but in reality she was poorer than these people. The more Sara thought about this, the more dire her circumstances became. She looked again at the passengers, and they looked to be wretched creatures. Could she be reduced to that? It was all too horrible to imagine. Sara flipped around and pushed out the door and stood on the platform, gulping air.

James leaned out of the door of a car farther down. "Over here," he said loudly, his voice carrying over the sounds of the train.

She quickly walked to James's train car and climbed the stairs.

"What kept you?" he asked.

"A wrong turn, is all," she said.

They entered the coach car. After the previous experience, it felt airy and light, with windows all along the sides and a high arching roof with architectural details designed to please the eye. There were people in almost all the seats, and there was baggage, but it did not litter the aisles. Twelve rows of high-back padded benches lined either side of the aisle, each bench seating two people. Stoves at either end of the car would provide heat, and there were ceiling lamp fixtures. In comparison to what she had just stepped from, it seemed the height of luxury. There was a calm, a sense of space and propriety, which gave her back her illusion of self-sufficiency.

The last available seats were rows apart from each other, and Sara and James made their way to them. They squeezed each other's hands before they parted in the aisle, but a kindly man in a bowler who was in the window seat next to Sara noted the exchange and offered to switch seats with James so that they could sit together. It was a simple kindness that touched Sara deeply. She thanked him once and again as he rose and scooted past her, doing a double-take on her face as he did. "Don't mention it, ma'am," he replied, moving down the aisle and backing aside to let James past. *Ma'am*? She had just been called ma'am for the first time in her life, and she wasn't sure how she felt about it. On one hand, she was soon to be a married woman, and so ma'am was appropriate, but did she appear so old as to merit the title?

As James approached, Sara held her palms up, offering him the window seat, but he smiled and shook his head, so she scooted over and he sat next to her. "Hello, stranger," Sara whispered. The train soon jerked and bumped into motion.

Brakes squealed, and the engine puffed and chugged. As they gathered speed, the level of noise mounted. The windows rattled, the wheels hummed, and all manner of metal on metal screeched and groaned and knocked, with people shouting to be heard over the din. Sara and James could not talk without shouting, so they settled in without a word. The window a few seats ahead on their side was open, and the air felt cool and refreshing, dispersing the odors of people in transit. Houses soon gave way to fields and open grasslands, with an occasional farmstead. Sara was content to relax back into her seat as it swayed and rocked. She was on her way, they were on their way. It was a while later that James turned as to speak to her, but he seemed loathe to shout, so after a few attempts, he gave up and with an obvious shrug gave up, though he did fidget a bit.

It felt good finally to be in motion. Sara turned to the window and watched the countryside roll by. It was new to her, as she'd never ridden in a train and she rarely made it far from Anamosa. The train hurled along at an incredible speed, faster than Sara had imagined possible, winding its way along a valley before climbing an incline and topping onto plains. Then it dipped again into a valley and repeated, and it felt as dizzying as a circus merry-go-round, up-the-hill, down-the-hill, dip-across-the-valley. Sara liked the way the fields circumscribed the green crops and how the long vegetation at their edges waved in the fierce wind and in the distance the clouds puffed up like over-risen bread. The lowering sun made the clouds glow, and rain streaked slantwise from their bruised bottoms.

Night fell, and the lamps were lit but gave only a dim light. The breeze in the window took on a raw edge. Why did these

158

people insist on keeping the window open? Sara stood and leaned forward and loudly but politely asked the woman two seats ahead to close the window, but she was met with stony silence. Then someone lit the coal stove behind her, and she realized why the window was open. The stove glowed red, emitting coal fumes, and she became hot, and then the cool breeze of the window felt good on her face and cleared the smoke. She wished that it would somehow balance out, but it did not, with her body too hot and her head and feet freezing. She wrapped her coat more closely around her and wished she had a blanket.

James's attention had turned inward. His fingers fidgeted and rolled into fists in his lap. It concerned Sara, as she could not tell what he was thinking. She had no idea what he was thinking, and it was too loud for them to hold a private conversation. But then, after traveling along in the fading light for some time, the train pulled onto a siding and slowly halted, screeching and groaning. Another train soon shuttled past, a blur and a roar through the window glass, causing the car to rock slightly. As they sat, the temperature evened out, and Sara warmed—it was nice—and the noise was much less. James glanced toward the people sitting in nearby seats, turned to Sara, leaned in, and said in a low voice, "Sara, there's something I must confess to. It is only right that you know before we marry."

The realization of his meaning sent a shock through Sara. What could he possibly tell her now, now that she had left home in his company with the full intent of marrying him. If it were so important, why had he waited? Holding herself stiffly, unsmilingly, she attended him.

"This is a difficult thing to impart, and I apologize for the belated nature of it." He was quiet for a second, his eyes on the hands in his lap, and then continued, "The reason for my residence in Anamosa was the penitentiary." She looked into his face, but he refused to raise his eyes to hers.

"Do you mean that you worked there? Were you a guard?"

"No, that is not what I mean. I was an inmate of that institution." His eyes remained on his hands.

Sara sucked in her breath. She knew about the prison, of course. Her mother and Mrs. Weiss had once paid twenty-five cents apiece for they and Lily and Sara to tour the facility. What had stayed with Sara were the looks on the men's faces as the women walked past. Some were stricken as if in remembrance of their own dear wives and children, some were indifferent, while some few looked wolfish and debased, and Sara had inwardly shook with fear as to what they would have done had there not been guards all around. Sara's breath seeped out as she peered at James's face. What could he have done to be placed, not in jail, but in a penitentiary? The possibilities ran through her mind, all of them unsavory.

"Wh-why?" she ventured.

James raised his eyes and searched her face. He continued, "I stole a horse. I got three years. I ain't proud of it."

"Why?" she repeated. It was as much a questioning of his mendacity as it was of his actions. Why did he steal horses, sure, but also why had he lied by omission up until this point? Yes, it was indeed a lie that he would offer himself as a good upstanding citizen when in reality he was a convict. It shot a bolt of self-righteous anger through her. If she had been standing back on the train platform, she would have turned tail and left him there, to go back to face whatever may come with her father. How dare he? Anger bubbled and churned. Not waiting for an answer, she said, "You lied!" She lowered her voice to a whisper, "You let me believe ..." She looked away from him and out the window, but the darkness beyond and the dim light within made it a mirror that gave back a misshapen image of her face, with his half-face behind. They were both grotesques, and it was all a shambles. "You led me to believe that you were ..." she said but let her voice trail off. An honest person, she added silently.

"Hey, Sara. Look at me." She kept her face to the window and her hands clenched. "Sara, for heaven's sake," he said. "I'm not proud of what I've done. It was a mistake. It was hard times, after Mam's last husband died. I was only seventeen, and no one would hire me, with us moving around all the time and not knowing anyone. Mam did what she could. We were hardly making it." He was quiet for a moment. "I was once so hungry then I ate boiled shoe leather, I swear. Finally, an uncle, the brother of Mam's last husband, offered to take me on, only he did not pay me. I worked in his employ for six months. I would not have stayed that long, but Mam kept saying, 'Just a little longer, he's got to pay us.' But he didn't, and I was so enraged that I took what we were owed. It was foolish." James's voice was pleading at first and then but ended in bitterness and anger.

Was it true, what he was saying? Had he once been so hungry he ate shoe leather? An image came to mind of the people in the immigrant car. She could imagine them so famished that they were forced to do that. The anger drained from her and she felt an ache rise within her for the boy she imagined he had been. The image in her mind of a convict and the image of James just did not go together. She shook her head. She would try to hold to the one that she believed, not this newly introduced counterfeit.

He took her hand in his and held it tightly. "If I had informed you of that fact, you wouldn't have … you would not be here now. Is that not so?"

It was true, though she hoped her face did not indicate one way or another.

"I'm telling you now," James said, "I am still the person whom you agreed to marry. I swear to you that I am honorable and I will make a good husband." He seemed to find encouragement in what he found in her face.

What could she do? Her only other option was to ride next to James all the way to the next station, purchase a return ticket—would he give her the money, then?—ride all the way back to Anamosa, and then face her father and submit, now and forever. She looked again at the glass and at the ghoulish half-images leering at her and thought, we are both phantasms, and this is the way of it.

"You'll marry me?" he said from behind her.

Without looking at him, she nodded.

"You will?" he said again.

"Yes," she whispered, keeping her face turned away.

Just then, the train lurched into motion. Sound rose—the rushing wind, the scrape and clack of wheels, the scream of the engine, the rising voices. Outside, it was inky black, and in the distance, lightning stabbed the sky. A raindrop streaked the window, and then another, accompanied by a loud tap tap on the roof, but then it stopped, a brief spate. They gained speed and topped a rise, to descend sharply down and then up again and then curve. Outside the window, a new light shown up from directly below. It was the wheels giving sprays of sparks as they rubbed against the iron rails, sparks that lit the window bottoms with an orange-white light. The rolling motion of the car and the push and pull of ascending and descending the hills, the streaks of lightning, the flashes of sparks, the din of noise, and the blank of darkness—it all seemed to blend into one assault on Sara's senses. She was suspended in this nowhere place where she heard too much and not enough, where air blasted her face yet she could not breathe, where it was dark and it was light, where it was cold and it was hot. The train moved on into the night, inexorably.

Chapter 14

I t was the dark of night when they disembarked at the Cedar Rapids train station. Lit with few lamps, the depot was a large and echoey space that held high ceilings and wooden pew-like benches, with the smell of cleaning unguents and dust. Rain thrummed on the roof. As it was so late, the depot was deserted except for a bored security guard and number of passengers who were spending the night in the station. There was a tiny man lying on a bench, his arms crossed over his chest and his bowler over his face. There was a family—a grandfather, a mother, two teenage boys, and a young girl—who came prepared with pallets that they rolled out on the floor.

James carried in Sara's carpetbag and put it down on the floor near a likely looking bench, one that was long enough so that both of them could lay down and with adequate curvature for some comfort. It would not be ideal to sleep upon, but it was better than the cold tile floor. They did not have the extra funds to expend for a room, and so he assumed that they would join the others who dosed in the station. He sat down and patted the seat beside him, inviting Sara to join him.

She remained standing. "What are you doing?" she said, irritation in her voice. She had not said two words since his admission and had avoided all contact, visual or otherwise. It had worried him, but then again, she was still here, so he hoped a night's sleep would temper her mood.

"I thought ..." he said. Was she so unaware of their financial situation—and how could she be?—that she would insist upon a hotel? They would barely make it as is, what with trying to find a place in Kansas City and food for a week while they got settled.

She glanced around the room, a bereft look on her face, the irritation of the moment before gone. She looked at him full in the face and said, "James, I do not think, well, I do not think I could stand spending a night in such a place. I do not think ..." Her voice trailed off. There was such a note of defeat, of desperation, contained in her words, that James thought she might break into tears, but she did not. She continued, "A bed, someplace private to lie down, that is all I ask." As she said this, her eyes pleaded with his.

He looked at her for a moment, weighing the amount of money, her money, in his pocket—he would have to be the financially responsible one, he could see that now. It was apparent that she had never known poverty, and so he must protect her from that knowledge as much as possible while also hoarding what little money they did have. But the look on her face was so pitiful and lost, all thought of sternness fled and he immediately gave in. It was her money after all. "Of course," he said. He would sleep on the floor.

Leaving Sara on the bench, James located and spoke with the bored security guard. He asked if the man could point them toward lodgings, ones that would admit guests this late in the evening.

"You and the missus?" the guard asked, looking over

James's face, his eyes lingering on James's brow where it was bruised.

"Yes," James said without hesitation but with perhaps too much emphasis. To cover, he said, "But perhaps one of less exclusive ones, if you know what I mean." By that, he meant that it was less expensive.

"Ah, I see," said the guard with a wink.

"No!" said James, realizing that the guard had misinterpreted his words. "What I meant was, we do not have much extra to pay for such lodgings."

"Oh," said the guard, visibly disappointed. After giving it some thought, he said that there was a boarding house not far from the depot that they might try. "Tell her I sent you her way. She *appreciates* the referrals," he said with another wink and then gave James the directions.

He went back to Sara and extended his hand, which she took, and he helped her to her feet. He gathered up her carpetbag, and they walked out into the night. The rain slowly soaked through their collars and cuffs as they made their way down the street. As directed, James turned a corner and about halfway down the block mounted the steps to a darkened two-story house with a lamp lit in the window. "Here's where we will stay," he told Sara. They stamped the mud off their boots as best they could, and then James knocked on the door, which was opened by a short frowning landlady holding a candle. She was a mound of a woman who stood reared back to counterbalance the tremendous bulk of her that hung in front, yet her dressing gown was lined with lace and a dainty lace nightcap rested upon her hair. After introductions, she listened to their request for lodging, nodded, and waddling side to side and breathing hard, candle in hand, she led them down the hallway to the back of the house and opened the door to a room not much bigger than a pantry that may have once been a shed addition. Windowless, it held a narrow bed and a narrow bureau with a basin and pitcher, above which rested a jagged sliver of mirror held to the wall with bended nails.

"This'll have to do," she said and turned and left, taking the candle with her.

And so it was in pitch dark that they prepared for bed. He thought about offering to stand in the hall while she changed into her night clothes, but how would that look? A husband leaving the room for his wife to change? It might raise someone's suspicions. Besides, it was so dark they could not see a thing and so her modesty would not be compromised. But, in deference to any misgivings she might have, James turned his back and said over his shoulder, "Sara, I'll just stand here with my back turned while you prepare for bed." There was silence for a moment, and then the frantic rustling of clothing as she changed and slid into bed. He decided not to undress and to use his coat for a blanket. Perhaps he could use hers for a pillow? He asked her, adding that he would sleep on the floor, and she said yes, relief apparent in her voice. And so they lay side by side in the dark, her on the bed and him on the floor.

"Good night, Sara," he whispered.

"Sleep well," she whispered back, and then they were silent.

James lay for a long time listening to her breathing. He did not like the distance he felt between them. They had been so close for that brief period of time, up until he had told her of his incarceration, and now he regretted the telling of it. He had thought it only right that she know. Perhaps he had been wrong. Perhaps it would have been better if he had kept his secret, and in all likelihood, she would never have found out. He did not think she was quite yet asleep, as her breathing was too rapid, but hearing it made him intensely aware of her presence there in the dark. It was not long before their combined breath warmed the room and gave the air moisture and a slightly animalistic scent.

She was lying there not two feet from him, a warm and soft female body. The thought prompted his breath to deepen. The only thing separating his body from hers was air and a few thing strips of cloth. That was all. Yet, those few feet of space combined with the cold distance he felt from her might as well be another continent, and the thought made him feel intensely alone again, despite her presence. He wanted to feel close to her, connected, and this want turned into a yearning. He listened to her breathing again. She was just there, right there, and all he had to do was to reach out his hand and he would touch her. He turned over onto his side so that he faced her direction, and in response the pace of her breathing quickened. Perhaps she was lying there, like him, wanting him to reach out to her, wanting to feel that connection, but like him afraid to extend herself.

His manhood responded. It had been a long time, a very long time. He had not lain with a woman since before he had been incarcerated, when a hired girl had come into his room in the middle of the night and kissed him in his sleep, her breath smelling rank with the rotting of her teeth. They had not said a word, just grasp at each other under the covers, and she had ridden him from above. The memory caused his body to respond even more, and his need of Sara, of touching her body, grew. After some hesitation, he reached out his hand to touch her, unsure in the dark of where to extend it. He finally decided to reach up high, so as not to accidentally bump a private part of her person that only a husband would have leave to touch. He made light contact with what felt like skin, but then she jumped violently and pushed away and bumped against the wall opposite.

"Oh, Sara," he said immediately. "I did not mean …"

She was breathing rapidly, as if she had run a distance. After a moment, she said, "Was there something you wanted?"

How could he encompass all he had been feeling in words? His impulse had been emotional as much as physical. He said, "I merely wanted to make sure you were comfortable." He hoped the disappointment did not show in his voice.

"I am," she said, and after a minute lay back down.

"Well, then, good night," he said.

"Good night, Mister Youngblood," she said, but then added, "I mean, James."

He finally fell asleep—Sara could tell from the lengthening and deepening of his breathing. She lay there tensely, her mind working. He had touched her—he had actually touched her. Her forehead still felt warm where his fingers had met her skin. What was he expecting? Had he thought to have his way with her, like so many men she had heard of, before they had entered into the bonds of matrimony? It seemed to fit with this new image of him, of someone who had been convicted of a crime. The penitentiary was full of such men who knew no bounds of decency and propriety. Men who could very well look like James—*just* like James, in fact. Perhaps he was indeed one of these men. He simply wanted to use her for what he could get—the gift of her femininity, her money, whatever he could take. Perhaps it had more to do with how tired she was and how vulnerable she felt, but she was too tired to check herself, and her mind sunk its teeth into the idea and bore down upon it like a bulldog.

What could she do? The one thing she knew, the one thing she felt most deeply, was that she needed to escape. She needed space and time to think. James had her money in his pocket, as well as their train tickets, and there was no way to get any of it from him without him knowing it. She must simply go. What seemed like hours had passed by the time she arrived at this decision, but as there was no window she had no idea how close to morning it was. So, after listening to his breath for a time to ensure that he was indeed asleep, Sara slowly and carefully pushed the covers off, slid down to the bottom of the bed, retrieved her clothes and her carpetbag, and let herself quickly and quietly out the door. He was using her coat, and so she would have to go without, but she felt lucky to get out of the room without waking him. In the hall after listening for any movement of insomniacs, she quietly and efficiently changed into her dress and put on her shoes, stowed her nightdress, and felt her way as best she could back the way they had come, trying to remember their movements of the night before. There was just a hint of light in the windows to assist her. She once tripped over a pair of shoes, and she walked into a coat stand, but she was finally able to make it to the front door. She turned the lock, turned the doorknob, let herself out, and pulled the door closed behind her. It had stopped raining. She immediately felt an enormous sense of relief, of freedom from entanglements.

She was able to find her way back to the train station without a wrong turn. They were not scheduled to leave until the day following this one, in order to give themselves time to marry, and so perhaps she had enough breathing room to wait until the sun rose and the stationmaster came and then she could work out a deal with him, or at least have him send a telegram to Esther. As the first rays of the sun peeked over the horizon, she stepped up onto the empty platform. With a sigh, she made her way to the bench along the wall, set down her carpetbag, and sat and leaned back. She took a deep breath—the air smelled pleasantly fresh from the rain the night before. She had not noticed, but the birds were singing raucously in the trees, and the slant morning sun beat down upon her and warmed her there on the bench. She wondered what time it was. Surely it would not be long until the stationmaster came. She must keep her eye out. She let her head fall back against the wall. It was very comfortable here. It made her realize how very tired she was, simply exhausted, and how tense she had been. She took a deep breath. It was indeed nice here. She allowed her eyes to close.

And then through closed lids she became aware of the sound of feet walking on boards and of people talking. Everything had shifted, and from the pressure on her shoulder and the side of her head she knew that she had lain down on the bench, her head resting upon her carpetbag. But what was this over her? She cracked her eyelids and realized it was her coat. Oh. It was her coat—she must have gotten cold and so she must have pulled it up to cover herself. But then it came to her: her coat was back at the boarding house with James. Oh my God! She opened her eyes and pushed herself up and there was James, sitting beside her on the bench looking out across the tracks. There were people on the platform, sitting or toting luggage or walking and talking, and the bell to the door tinkled

171

faintly as someone went into the station. It must be midmorning, as the sun was partway up in the sky. James sensed her movement because he turned his head, and his eyes were red-rimmed as if he had been crying. He looked into her face with such incredible sadness, his mind behind his eyes far away. He did not say anything, simply looked at her.

"Oh," she said, sitting up and straightening her clothes. "Oh, James." She glanced down the platform to see who might have noted her sleeping, but no one seemed to be looking. She looked back at James. He was so sorrowful there on the bench, so much like a boy who had been separated from his mother, that pity arose within her. It came to her that he must have woken to find her gone, the missing carpetbag evidence of her willful abandonment. They had made these plans together, to build a life, but she had shown herself to be untrustworthy. She herself, not him. What right had she to judge him so? She did not blame him for what he had done to be sent to the penitentiary—the actions stood on moral grounds, if not ethical ones—and her censure of him was uncalled for. And the thought of him placing her coat over her and sitting there patiently touched her deeply.

"Oh, what you must think of me," she said and hoped that he could see the repentance on her face.

"I don't," he said simply, and when she looked at him questioningly, he continued, "You must be feeling very alone. You are with a man you do not well know, and you have just lost everything that you have ever held dear, and you are faced with a future of uncertainty, without access to money nor friends." It was true, and his empathy caused tears to well up within her, tears she tried to blink back. He dug into his pocket and brought forth a bundle of money and a coin purse. He squoze the purse and shook out all the coins on top of the bills in his other palm, and then he thrust it all into her lap. Then he said, "I do not pretend to know the reason you left in the middle of the night. You do not have to tell me, if you so desire. Here is all the money we have left. It is yours. It would be enough for a return trip to Anamosa. You are free to go, if you will it." Sara glanced down at the money and then back to his face, which searched hers.

But then, in a rush, he pushed up off the bench and moved in front of her and knelt down, one knee on the boards and another bent in front of him, and held out his hands. He did not grasp hers but simply waited until she placed hers in his, and then he held them tightly. He said, "I do not know poetry with which to woo you, but all I can say is this: I would be honored—no, not honored. I want with all my heart for you to be my wife. I cannot say it any other way. The thought of the future with you brings me such joy, while the thought of the future without you is bleak and dark." He glanced off down the platform and thought for a minute before continuing. "I was sitting here thinking about my mother, and about you, and about how, despite my best efforts, I am unable to provide enough, enough ..." He shook his head. "I am not enough," he finally said. He looked intently into her face. "I can promise you this: I will do my very best by you, work harder than anyone, longer, to keep you, to honor you, if you will only agree to marry me." He took a shuddering breath and fell silent and waited.

By that time, tears were rolling down Sara's cheeks. She had been all wrong about him. Her first impression had been the true one—he was a kind and gentle man with only the best of intentions, and it was so wicked of her to succumb to the dark thoughts of the night before. Prison or no, he was an honorable man, and she would be a fool to trade him for all the supposed comforts in Anamosa—which was, after all, a life now lost to her. "Yes," she whispered. "Oh, James, I am so sorry. Yes, I will marry you."

The look of relief upon his face made it apparent how sure he had been that he had lost her. "Oh really, really, Sara? Oh." He held her hand to his cheek and glanced up at her and gave her such a bedazzling smile as she had never seen.

"Oh, do get up, James," she said with a returned smile and pulled on his hands.

He squeezed her hand before he released it and then rose. "Are you hungry?" he asked, sighing deeply. "While you slept I bought some food. It should still be warm."

When he asked it, she realized that she was indeed very hungry, and he sat back down on the bench and on his other side opened a package that contained fried egg sandwiches with butter and crisp bacon and lettuce. They sat there eating, glancing at each other and smiling over their mouthfuls. It was all right. They were once again in accord, and they both felt such relief.

Chapter 15

ate that afternoon, as Sara and James made their way to the house of a preacher, one whom the stationmaster had recommended, Sara considered the possibility: they were actually going to be married! Married. This man is going to be my husband, she thought. Up until that moment, it had been an abstract thing, a thing desirable but not particular.

An old folk rhyme came to mind: something old, something new, something borrowed, something blue. Suddenly, this silly ditty seemed of the utmost consequence. It was something tangible and concrete, something controllable, something that might bring them luck, and right now they needed all the luck they could get. Something old. Tucked into her pocket was her mother's watch, which she always carried. That would do. Something new. Well, she had nothing new except James, but that did not seem to fit the spirit of the thing. Something borrowed—perhaps she could borrow James's handkerchief. Something blue. The embroidered edging on her dress was a dark navy. Two of the four. This did not bode well, not well at all. She was a second-rate bride before the vows had even been spoken. It should not have disappointed her so, but it did.

They walked a short ways to a modest house with white

clapboards. The door was opened by a diminutive old woman whose stooped shoulders put her chin nearly upon her ample chest. She looked up at them under her eyebrows and smiled. Her white-haired husband stood behind and towered over her. He had a pot belly that was just the right size, suggesting comfort and health. James and Sara introduced themselves and explained why they were there, as the old couple listened attentively but eyed the bruises on both their faces.

The old woman said, "This is Reverend Potter, and I'm his wife, Missus Potter." She nodded and smiled, and the man nodded in agreement.

James said, acknowledging their curiosity, "We met with an unfortunate accident," raising his hand and indicating his face.

The old couple seemed satisfied with this. "Come in, come in, dearies," the old woman said, and both stepped back to let them enter. "Welcome."

Sara and James hung their coats and hats on pegs along the wall and set down the carpetbag, and old couple led them down a hall that smelled of wood smoke and of old people and of a shut space—mustiness and body odor and camphor. They entered a room containing a couch and a settee and an inordinate number of chairs grouped around the large fireplace's stone hearth. A small friendly fire sputtered in the grate, though the day was warm outside. The old woman grasped Sara's hand with both of hers, which were blue-veined, gnarled, and chilly. She squeezed it and then let go and waved for them to be seated on the settee, which they did.

"Can I offer you refreshment?" the old woman said.

James looked at Sara, who shook her head slightly, and then he said, "Oh, no, we would not want to put you out."

"Well, my dearies, seeing as you're here at the spur of a moment, it's no further bother," the woman said. She did not say it to be accusatory but rather just as an observation, and she stood smiling at them. James shrugged. The woman left and was gone for a few minutes, and the preacher stood smiling pleasantly at them, not saying a word. Sara and James sat and smiled back. Soon, the old woman returned with a tray of mismatched cups and saucers, a ceramic pot of coffee, and little bowls of cream and sugar. She set them on a side table.

"I am incredibly sorry to descend upon you like this," James said quickly after she entered. "We would not bother you if it weren't for our haste. You see, we're scheduled to leave first thing tomorrow, and, you see, we're …" His voice wandered to a stop.

"Young people," the old woman said, shaking her head, "so impetuous. Well, I guess we're living in impetuous times." She glanced at her husband, who nodded in agreement. She continued, "Let's see. Do you have witnesses?"

"No. No, we don't," James said. "We thought …"

"I know, I know. You did not think of it." The woman upended the cups on the tray. "It twill be all right. I can witness, dearie." She shook head and clasp her hands to her belly. "Many a wedding I have witnessed." She stood quiet for a minute remembering, a small smile on her face, and then looked back at them. "But, the Reverend Potter, he cannot be a witness. Can you, dear?" She smiled at her husband and then at them. "As he's going to marry you. You'll need another." Sara and James glanced at each other and then back to the old couple. The preacher nodded at his wife. "Yes, dearie, I know," she said to him. She turned to them. "Don't you worry. We'll fix you up. My sister is upstairs. She will not mind." Mrs.

Potter bustled up the stairs.

Something borrowed! Sara thought. She smiled broadly. Maybe it would in fact turn out all right. Maybe this was meant to be. If only she had something new, it would be a sign, an indication that it was meant to be. But she didn't, so she told herself, do not be so silly. It's just a superstition, it does not matter in the least.

The preacher poured three cups of coffee, handing each of them a cup. He poured a bit of cream into his cup and then indicated that they should help themselves to the cups of cream and sugar. Then he sat and smiled at them and sipped his coffee. Sara spooned in sugar and poured a bit of cream and then stirred. It was warm in her hand, and the creamy coffee smelled as if the angels themselves had brought it to earth. She took a gulp and her belly filled with sweet rich warmth. She closed her eyes and sighed. The coffee's vitality soon followed, and it too imparted a sense of well-being.

Sara glanced at James. He took his coffee black, which seemed so appropriate, so like him, strong, undiluted, earnest, undemanding. Forthright, even, his withholding of the truth notwithstanding. She put her hand on his arm and let it rest there for a moment before withdrawing it.

After a bit, Mrs. Potter bustled back downstairs trailed by a tall angular woman with a face like a bulldog—wide-set eyes, head thrust forward, lips pulled down in disapproval. The woman trailed Mrs. Potter down the stairs and then stood with her hand on the newel post. "Well, shall we get on with it, then?" Mrs. Potter said and nodded to her husband. He stood, put down his cup, and went to the fireplace and indicated that they should stand in front of him. They set their cups down and joined him. Mrs. Potter stood next to Sara and the grim sister stood next to James. In the whole time they had been within the house, the preacher had not spoken a word, and Sara was curious as to how he would perform the ceremony. But then, of course, he did begin speaking, his hands clasped in front of him, and his voice, deep and broad, was like a force of nature. It began low and rolling, thunder in the distance. It rumbled softly but then rose. It reached a mild crescendo, a peak in emotion, then released, murmured, as if echoing across a landscape. Then it gathered speed and momentum and began building again, and then peaked again, higher this time, louder. His lyrical words told of earthly vessels and sacred vows, of the love of God and its place within the sanctity of marriage. Then the preacher was silent for a moment, as if in prayer, and then he read their vows. They each promised to be true and faithful to one other until they shuffled off this mortal coil. He ended by saying, "Within the eyes of our Lord, you both have agreed to be joined in holy matrimony, and by the power vested in me as a divine servant of our Lord, I pronounce you Mister and Missus James Youngblood." It had come to pass. Sara was a married woman, and this man, this handsome capable man who looked at her with such intensity, whose presence made the very blood in her veins run faster, he was hers and she his. They were now intimate friends forever, simply by the uttering of these words.

Sara smiled broadly at James, who smiled back but then froze as if he remembered something. He held up his had to stop the proceedings and fished into his coat pocket with his other and brought something out. It was a pale blue ribbon attached to a heart-shaped jewel, a large fire opal that glowed red and blue and green under its milky sheen, which in turn was surrounded by two rows of diamonds. He held it out displayed in his palm to show Sara. Sara could not believe what she was seeing. It was quite an exquisite jewel.

"It's only made of paste," James whispered.

Sara was speechless. It was such a beautiful thing—that did not matter. She shook her head in response, and then nodded and nodded again.

"Well, it was my mother's," he continued, "so it means so very much to me, as I hope it will to you."

He held it up, she turned, and he tied it loosely about her neck. Sara fingered it—it had a reassuring weight and roughness. Not only that, she realized, but it was something new. Something new! Maybe not new in the strictest sense of the word, but it was new to her. Something old, something new, something borrowed, something blue. The rhyme, silly or not, had been fulfilled. It was in fact meant to be. The feeling of assurance spread through Sara, and despite everything she'd been through, she was now convinced that it was the best of all things, that God shined His favor upon them.

"Oh, my dears, my dears," Mrs. Potter sniffed. "Marriage is indeed the most beautiful thing in the world. You will be so happy, I just know it." She clasped Sara's hand and stretched her head up and Sara, anticipating her desire, leaned down so the woman could kiss her cheek, as Reverend Potter shook James's hand. The preacher extended his hand to Sara, so she stepped forward and shook it, and Mrs. Potter stepped around behind her to hug James. All the while, the sister stood stiffly by.

The Reverend Potter led them back to the small side table, where they signed a certificate of marriage. It was a form in curlicue script on a heavy creamy paper, decorated around the edges with cabbage roses and cherubs and bunting. James

180

signed, and then Sara. As she finished, she admired James's firm, regular, rounded script. Hers looked shaky by comparison. In turn, Mrs. Potter and her sister both signed, and then Reverend Potter. Her duties completed, the sister then gave them a curt nod, turned, and went back upstairs. Mrs. Potter insisted they sit and have more coffee, and to celebrate she retrieved from the other room little round cookies with nuts that were rolled in powdered sugar. The cookies melted in Sara's mouth and the powdered sugar went up her nose, making her cough and laugh. James laughed with her and took her hand. Soon, with thanks and a small tip extended to the Potters, they made their way back into the day as a wedded couple, marriage certificate carefully folded and put in an envelope and stowed in Sara's carpetbag.

The air was hot and steamy and the sun touched the horizon and cast a yellow light as James and Sara left the preacher's house and made their way, this time to a two-story hotel recommended by the stationmaster. James put his arm around Sara's shoulders, and she put hers about his waist, and they did not think about propriety. They did not speak but moved in tandem feeling each other's presences. This hotel was run by an old man with watery blue eyes and sleeves rolled up to his elbows. When the man spoke, his lips shaped the vowels into ooooos and his tongue clipped the consonants, his native vernacular having an uneasy relationship with English. He had the cook make them cucumber sandwiches, radishes, and sweet tea, which they took sitting in wicker chairs on the porch in hopes of catching a breeze off the Cedar River. They could see the mounding trees along its banks. They could smell the river too—muddy wetness and reeds with a faint undertone of rotting sewage. The few puffs of breeze brought the smell of the lilac bushes from the side yard.

They finished eating, and their dishes were cleared. Sara felt sticky with sweat and gritty with dust, but she was relaxed and not as tired as she thought she might be after the lack of sleep the previous night. The chair was comfortable, and her belly was full. She had been thinking that they could be any married couple, traveling the world, sitting on a porch, eating sandwiches and drinking tea. There was comfort in that, that people every day got married and took trips and ate sandwiches on porches. These people survived day to day, despite the spears and arrows life threw at them, and got through their lives.

"I wish we could go for a swim," Sara said.

James smiled but said, "Unfortunately, that's a skill I have never mastered."

"Oh. You can't swim? You are truly missing out. Though I haven't swum in years. Must be, well, eight or ten, anyway." As best as she could recall, the last time was when she and Lily and Ed and Cornell had gone on a picnic to the river, and the boys jumped in fully clothed. After a careful survey of the surrounding countryside, she and Lily had stripped to their petticoats and undershirts and had walked carefully up to their waists to cool off. But the thought reminded Sara that Lily was gone, which sobered her.

James was sunk down in his chair, his head resting on the top of the rolled wicker backrest, elbows propped on the armrests, hands resting on his belly, one ankle on top of the other knee. With a sigh, he sat forward and pushed himself to standing and dusted off his pants. He walked around the table and held out his hand. Sara smiled up at him and put her hand in his and let him pull her to standing. "Shall we retire early?"

he said. "You go on up to the room. I'll be there in a minute." It was considerate of him to allow her time to herself to perform her ablutions in private. It spoke again of his kindness and consideration.

Standing there beside him, she was reminded of how broad he was. He was not much taller than she, but her hand got lost in his, and his shoulders quite outstripped hers. He was a strong man. And a handsome man. Sara's stomach tightened at the thought. This was it. They were free to lie together. She was nervous about it, but she trusted him, so she was willing to follow his lead.

She stood and quickly took his hand in both of hers, leaned in and kissed him firmly on the lips, for which he looked at first started and then pleased. She then smiled at him and went upstairs. The room was spacious, with a large bed, a bureau and mirror, a wardrobe, a desk and a chair, and a rocking chair by the south-facing bay windows. There were matching brocade curtains and bedspread and soft towels and washcloths and rose-scented soaps and a matching eggshell porcelain pitcher and basin.

A long time passed before he came into the room, and she was able to stow her things, dress in her nightgown, give her hair 100 strokes, and wash up. As she waited, she thought about the first time she had seen him. How he seemed different from the men around him. The way she had wanted to touch him as they walked. His rough hands, how they'd held Miss Bailey's reins and clutched together in front of him in nervousness and their deft flip of the Barlow knife. She wondered what he looked like without his shirt, but then the thought embarrassed her. She wondered if he would require her to bare her skin. She didn't think she would be able to—it was all too much. But still, the naughty jolt was not unpleasant, not unpleasant at all. She sat in the chair to wait but then immediately rose and stood with her back to the window.

A knock on the door, and then James's voice called hello. He didn't enter until she replied, "It's perfectly all right—come in." His hat was tucked under his arm and a bucket of water hung from his hand. His face and his ears glowed pink where he had scrubbed them. "I thought we could, well, use some water. It's not swimming, but it will be revitalizing."

"But I've already washed," she said, tilting her head.

He shook his head slowly back and forth and smiled and held up his finger, indicating that that was not exactly what he meant. She nodded and smiled and sat down on the edge of the bed. He set the bucket on the floor and then began to undress. He took off his coat and hung it in the wardrobe, topped with his hat. He loosened his neckerchief and unbuttoned and pulled off his shirt and stowed them away, so he was in his braces and undershirt. He pulled his braces off his shoulders so that they hung around his hips and untucked his undershirt and then sat down on the bed next to her and began removing his boots. As James bent and moved, his muscles rippled. She could see them through his undershirt and in the legs of his pants. There was not a scrap of fat upon him and his body looked all of a statue in its classic form—carved, curved, smooth, and firm. Sara had never regarded a body in quite this way—it seemed perfection, exactly what a body was supposed to be, a worldly instrument. As he bent over his knees, she tentatively reached out and touched the muscle on his shoulder. He stopped moving for a moment but did not look her way and then continued to take off his socks. She traced the muscle as it came away from the tip of the bone and swelled and then reattached to another bone. He finished taking off his socks and then sat still, all of his attention turned to her, his head tilted a bit and his body twisted slightly.

With more assuredness, she pressed her fingertips against his back and shoulder blade, tracing the bone under the muscle. She pressed down along the edge of the shoulder blade and down his spine to the small of his back and felt the muscles woven flat, tight, and firm into his backbone. His muscles were strong and elastic. They held vitality, potential, possibility. They could be so gentle, but they could be undeniable too. She had watched him heft crates half his size, muscles quivering. He could've been a man like her father who chose to use his strength for violence, but he was not that man. Those were muscles that touched her so gently, that cradled her small hand. These muscles, this power, this body could be anywhere, could do anything, but he had chosen to be here with her. Something about that possibility, that that body held such power yet it served her, made her feel liquid inside. She leaned in and put her cheek on his shoulder.

The touch had been like a child's, tentative and soft, James thought. He sat up straight and put his arm around her shoulders and held her tightly. She was at once as long as he was but much more slight and delicate, with small bones in her wrists and fingers and small clavicles above the neckline of her nightdress. He felt the urge to stroke her, to pet her like an animal, but he was not sure she was ready for that—she had shown such modesty—so he said in a low voice, "If you would allow me, I'll brush your hair." Her hair was well-brushed, but of course they both knew that that was not the reason for his suggestion. He watched her as she stood to retrieve her hairbrush from the bureau. She passed in front of the window, and her form was backlit under her nightgown. He could see the slight curve of the small of her back where it met the round swell of her buttocks. He could see the cloth billowing around her breasts but he could also see their outline through the cloth. He stood and pulled the desk chair over to the bed and faced it away.

When she returned, he leaned forward and patted the seat and took the hairbrush that she handed him. She sat and with her hands pulled her waist-length hair out from between her shoulders and the chair back and let it fall behind the backrest. He began brushing. He started at the bottom and worked his way up as his mother had taught him to do so that the snarls, if there were any, would untangle more easily. She had already brushed it, though, so it went quickly and then he gave it long sweeping-but-gentle strokes and watched the way the straight dark strands gathered from her head down to fan and brush against themselves and the chair back, slipping and sliding. He leaned in and inhaled deeply. It smelled of her, like sun-warmed mud, earthy but verdant.

Sara tilted her head back and closed her eyes and sensed the soft rhythmic pull of the brush, the crackle of her hair, the hard wooden seat against her buttocks, and the slats of the backrest against her back. Even that insistent pressure melted with the strokes of the brush, and soon she couldn't tell where her body began and the world ended. Stroke, pause, stroke, pause. She felt near sleep, but then he rose behind her and stood by her shoulder and brushed the top of her head. The bristles scraped softly against her scalp and sent a chill down her spine. The heat of his body radiated into her shoulder, and she wanted to touch him. Not just touch him but pull him close. She opened her eyes and reached out, but he gently tapped her

186

hand. "Sshh," he whispered, "close your eyes," and lightly ran his palm over them, his calluses rough against her skin. She felt the warmth of his hand and her nerves tingled on her forehead and cheek where his palm has brushed her skin. She closed her eyes obediently and heard his steps on the boards as he moved across the room and then the tink of the tin bucket and the slosh of water as he poured it into the porcelain basin.

James moved back across the room and set the basin of water on the floor. He picked up a washcloth and dipped it in the cool water and felt its sun-dried stiffness soften. He lifted it and wrung it into the basin, the water sluicing through his fingers, but then a rivulet ran down each arm and off his elbows. He spread the rag onto his right hand, tipped her head forward and pushed her hair aside with his left, and washed the back of her neck. Her vertebrae pressed her skin outward and the water ran down the back of her nightgown and her shoulder muscles were delicate arches under her skin. He dipped the rag in the cool water again, moved the gown off her shoulder, and rubbed the soaked cloth over it, letting the water run down and wet her nightgown. He tilted her head back and let her hair fall down the back of the chair and rubbed the wet rag across her clavicles and she felt the cool drip and slide of the water down between her breasts and down her sides and then his lips were on hers and it was exactly what they both wanted and she put out her hands and felt his muscles pressing and tensing and she felt his arms rigid under her as he picked her up and put her on the bed and he felt her body, soft, give underneath him and curve to fit his own and the heat of her body against his and how wet it was making him wet through his undershirt and they kissed deeply their noses bumping as they turned their heads and his tongue in her mouth and hers ticking back at his

187

and the pressure between them and the heat of their bodies and the nerves tingling and wanting to be inside and the pressing pushing, not knowing where she ended and she began and the feeling rising deep within of wanting of wanting something so badly wanting until it comes in like water sluicing down their bodies, sluicing down through them and out, and then ebbing, ebbing, the warm darkness, falling, falling around them.

Part 2

Chapter 1

ara found Kansas City simply overwhelming. She had never before beheld so many factories, houses, trains, wagons, people, and horses crushed together in one place. She felt deafened by the trains and carriages and the roar of the crowd with their rumbling mass of luggage. Her nose was assaulted by the stench of the city—industrial smoke and the waste of animals and unwashed bodies and garbage and underneath the wet and rotten smell of the river—she closed her nose and breathed through her mouth to allay its effects. It all made her feel small and insignificant and very much the bumpkin that she was. She and James had entered Kansas City by train from the north, hovering over the impassive gray surface of the Missouri River on a trestle bridge and then skirting between its east bank and the tall bluffs before dropping down into the industrial heart, which rested in a bowl created by the Missouri River to the north, the Kansas or Kaw River to the west, and the tall bluffs to the south and east. The confluence of the two rivers lay at the northwest corner of that thriving metropolis, termed the West Bottoms, that sprawled across the Kansas-Missouri state line.

Sara clutched at James's arm as they pushed their way through the crowded Union Depot. She glanced at the noisy hoards and whispered in James's ear, "All these people. Will there be any jobs left for you?"

James set down Sara's carpetbag and glanced sideways at the crowds. Sara had sensed his mood darken as they entered the city, but now, after a moment's hesitation, he smiled and said, "As surely as there is ugly on an ape, piety on a preacher, temperance on a school marm, bravado on a boy."

Sara smiled broadly but stayed her course: "Really, James, you have been resident in a city before. Cities invariably have lots of positions available, do they not?" She could not shake the feeling of deep trepidation that had overtaken her.

In reply, James simply raised his eyebrows.

The crowds seemed to press around her, so she raised her eyes to the ceiling. Light streamed in slantwise through the tall Romanesque windows, and there was an oculus high up on the wall toward the vaulted roof peak with its circle of projected light centered on the tile floor. There was the music of a string quartet, barely evident above the roar of the crowd. Sara glanced at James. His head was cocked to the music, and he said in an animated voice, "I do not know, dear Sara," he said, "but let us dance as Rome burns." He extended his hand to her, which prompted her to smile and to take it. The quartet had just begun the familiar melodic strains of "Greensleeves" at a buoyant pace, and he took her firmly by the waist and hand and swung her round and round with such gaiety she laughed out loud. His ease and grace made her dance more elegantly than she believed she was capable of. They were quite a sight— statuesque, spinning and twirling, and witnesses could easily overlook his ill-fitting black corduroy suit for the mesmeric beauty of her swirling gray wool traveling dress edged in blue embroidery, her slender but womanly figure, her black hair pinned up under her small but stylish hat. They had never before partnered for a dance, and Sara was surprised at his command of the form. He would later explain that his mother had called upon him to lead from an early age, saying, "To dance is to woo. It is a vital proficiency, and as a man of the world you must know how." Much too soon, with its haunting final notes, the music ended and the dance was done.

Together they walked to a bench. Sara sat down and patted the seat next to her for him to sit, but he shook his head. "I must be off to look for our lodgings, the sooner the better," he said and put down the carpetbag at her feet. "You will be all right here, will you not?" She nodded, trying to keep the panic from registering on her face. He is abandoning me, she thought, though she knew it to be patently false. "I shan't be long, no more than a few hours," he added. He smiled at her and then turned and his form was quickly swallowed by the crowd. Sara gathered the carpetbag up in her lap, both because she feared it would be stolen and also as a means of protection for her person, a barrier, small though it was, against this unknown fast-paced world. She leaned back against the high wooden backrest of the bench and scrunched down, making herself small.

She watched the crowds for a while, but then time spooled out, she relaxed, and eventually she became bored. Her mind wandered to the curiosities of their journey. The train from Council Bluffs to Kansas City had been near capacity, and Sara had had to take a seat across the aisle from James next to a small woman elegantly dressed in blue and green velvet, with a plush hat sprouting peacock feathers. The woman smelled of a perfume that was at first flowery but upon further deliberation turned musky. Under her hat, the woman's auburn hair was carefully rolled and twisted and pinned with a single long ringlet dropped onto each shoulder to her rounded bosom. Her complexion was pale, upon which Sara though she caught the sheen of powder—Sara dismissed the thought, however, as it would be quite an unseemly thing to do. The woman sat with one leg tucked up under her skirt and a book in hand, which she ignored as she looked with empty eyes out the window. The woman's outward appearance was compelling, and Sara found herself repeatedly glancing over at her. The woman did not notice, or at least pretended not to, until suddenly she leaned in toward Sara, curling her body fluidly, and said confidentially, as if they had known each other before and were simply continuing a conversation, "It's Kansas City, then?" The woman's voice was high and animated, as if she were trying to draw Sara in with that single phrase.

This sudden intimacy flustered Sara, especially from such an exquisite creature, and she wished she had kept her eyes to herself, at least until she had had a chance to observe the woman a bit longer. "Yes," she said, "yes, we are." After some searching, she added, "So, are you and your husband traveling to Kansas City as well?"

With a burst of breath and a raised eyebrow, the woman said, "No. But I do reside in Kansas City."

"Oh! I am sorry. I did not mean to presume," Sara said. "My husband and I are transferring our residence to that fair city. That's why I ..." She did not finish the thought. She realized, then, that that was the first time she had used the phrase "my husband," and it swelled her with pride. She glanced over at him, where he sat looking vacantly down the aisle. She wondered what he was thinking. Then she glanced back at the woman, who looked pointedly across the aisle at James and then back to her.

"A fine specimen of manhood," the woman said. "And you should know that I have made the acquaintance of a few men in my time to whom I may compare. He looks, shall we say, sturdy?" She nodded firmly and tucked in her chin, and Sara nodded in agreement. "And handsome?" Yes, indeed, he was. "And in love. He looks positively smitten, does he not?" Sara glanced at him, and at present he had a bored look on his face, not at all expressive of such emotion. Sara wrinkled her forehead in distress. She suspected the woman of making fun of her and so wished her to stop, but on the woman went on: "But perhaps a bit down on his luck? Living off love, perhaps?" The woman tilted her head as she spoke, first one way and then another, her eyes crinkling at the corners.

Sara turned her face away from the woman and crossed her arms. How dare she venture suppositions about things of which she had no idea? What right had she to play upon Sara's good will? Sara resolved to have nothing more to do with her. Beauty does not excuse bad manners. But then the voice came in her ear, much lower and more resonant, "Aaaaaaaw. Looka here. We are such a fragile flower." Sara continued to ignore her. The woman continued, "Such a pretty face to have such a nasty scowl affixed upon it. Here. Let me make it up to you. Let me extend my hand"—she held out her gloved hand—"in the spirit of friendship and mutual benefit." Sara hesitated for a moment and then took the woman's hand and shook it. The woman pulled a purse from beside her and opened it and retrieved a calling card, which she handed to Sara. She said, "If there's anything you need, anything at all, do let me know."

The card on heavy paper was elegantly embossed with the name "Miss Danielle Rose, Laundress" and an address in Kansas City "by the City Market." Sara glanced at the woman. A laundress? Sara had no idea what to think about that. She certainly didn't appear as one would expect for a laundress. The woman smiled once more at her and picked the novel up from her lap and began to read. Sara glanced from the woman to the card and so as not to appear rude tucked it in her carpetbag.

In a short while, the woman put down her book and indicated that she needed to get out of her seat, so Sara obediently stepped into the aisle. The woman retrieved a crutch adorned with satin and painted extravagantly that had been tucked between herself and the wall. She pushed herself to standing and maneuvered her way out from between the seats, and it quickly became apparent that she had only one leg, with the opposing prop supplied by the crutch. Despite the impediment the woman was nimble on her feet, and with a nod she made her way down the aisle. Sara and James looked at each other and raised their eyebrows, and then Sara returned to her seat. The woman did not return for quite a long time.

As the train swayed and rocked, Sara had thought about what life might be like for them in Kansas City, and it suddenly came to her mind that she would have to cook for James. What with everything that had happened, she hadn't dwelt upon it before. What did one do to prepare food? There was boiling water involved, and one stuck things into the oven and then removed them, but that was the extent of her knowledge on the subject.

Then Sara thought of the cookbook Esther had given her, *The Compleat Housewife*, and with a glance at James, who sat with his head back against the seat rest and his eyes closed, she bent down and retrieved it from the carpetbag. She rubbed her hands over the smooth leather binding and fingered the guilt letters and the ridges over the binding string on the spine. It was an old and well-used book. She sniffed the pages, hoping to catch a whiff of dinners gone by, but it simply smelled slightly musty. She flipped to the title page. There was a detailed frontispiece of women in a huge kitchen, with light streaming in the tall narrow windows at the left. Shelves against the back wall held serving platters and pitchers, and from the ceiling hung a rabbit, a bird, and some vegetables that Sara was not sure she could identify. A women bent over the cooking fire in the hearth, and two elegantly dressed women chatted while standing before a table in the middle of the room. If only she were a woman of such station, she could let others worry about cooking—or, more correctly, she had recently been woman of such means and now she was not. The thought caught her unawares. This was true evidence that she had fallen in station and that her future was by no means assured, a truly disturbing thought. She focused again on the book. The full title read: *The Compleat Housewife: or, Accomplish'd Gentlewoman's Companion, Being a Collection of upwards of Six Hundred of the most approved Receipts in Cookery, Pastry, Confectionary, Preserving, Pickles, Cakes, Creams, Jellies, Made Wines, Cordials. With Copper Plates Curiously Engraven for the regular Disposition or Placing the various Dishes and Courses. AND ALSO Bills of Fare for every Month in the Year*.

She turned to the section with receipts. From the titles, most of them were for fancy dishes, not for beginning cooks at all. Carp Blovon and tench stewed with pitch-cocked eels and a calf's head boned and stewed with a ragoo of mushrooms and cocks-combs a la crème. These receipts called for fish and beef and chicken and other ingredients, and where and with what would she procure such items? Her task was now simply to keep her husband fed and happy, and she had no idea how that was to be accomplished.

Chapter 2

ames had never been this far west. The land felt much more open and spacious, with broad views of the long hills extending to the horizon. However, James was not impressed with what he had seen of Kansas City. It was just another city on another river—it stank of stock yards just like Chicago, it stank of industry just like Detroit, it stank of humanity just like New York City, and under it all the river's sewage left its trace. Nothing good can come of this, he thought. Why am I bringing my new bride to such a place? But they had chosen their path and they had not the funds to go any farther. One day in the not too distant future, they would buy a team of horses and go West. In the meantime they would be lucky to get through the next week or two. He must count upon the prospect of quick employment. He was aware, even if Sara was not, that that was the only way they would make it.

As a consequence of this dark mood, he pushed his outward appearance to the heights of giddiness. He had smiled broadly at Sara and stepped lively, and when he helped Sara down the steps and off the train, he picked her up by her waist and swung her round. She had the pale wide-eyed look of a child overwhelmed by a new experience, but she played along.

"Isn't it exhilarating?" he said. "Have you not been to a city before?"

She shook her head and ogled the surroundings.

"Oh, you'll soon be used to it," he said. "You'll be stepping onto moving street cars and cussing the horse cabs before you know it."

She gave a genuine smile at the thought.

After their dance, he left Sara sitting in the train station with a strained expression on her face. When he asked a man at the station who was sweeping the floor where there might be cheap but decent accommodations, the man shook his head. He said it all was a bit tough at present, as word had gotten out about the job opportunities in this city, and what he called those bastards from across the waters had sent word back to their whole bastard clan to come on over. "Ya can't see the prosperity what for the jigaboos and bogs and dagos and bohunks," he said. The man seemed disposed to continue his tirade, so James thanked him and turned to leave. The man nodded, but then added, "One thing ya might try. Boyer's Saloon. They's often work and things to be had out of there." The man told James where to find the place, and James thanked him again.

James had encountered such men before who blamed all the world's ills on the negroes or the Irishmen or the Prussians or what not. James himself had no strong feelings on the subject, as over the course of his life he had encountered good and bad in all brands of men, and a white man was just as apt to hold a knife to your throat and steal your money as any other man. And also it had been an ancient black man who had taught him all he knew about horses, and so he was disposed to think favorable of the negro race at least. He hoped this man's attitudes were not indicative of the city's. It could only foretell hard times, and he sorely wished to avoid hard times.

Boyer's Saloon was a little more than a mile from the station on the Missouri side of the state line. It would later be explained to him that Kansas had enacted prohibition, so that those in the city who wanted to imbibe simply crossed over to the Missouri side of the north/south line that split the bottoms in half. James made his way out into the close and stifling air along the boardwalk and through the crowds around the train depot and then turned off the busy thoroughfare onto a relatively quiet street lined with mercantiles and tinsmiths and booteries and dining establishments. He found the saloon easily enough from the man's directions and by the large sign with an aces-and-eights full house painted the upper right corner. He stepped up on the boardwalk and went in, the door resisting his hand as he pushed through. It took a minute for James's eyes to adjust to the darkness inside. The place smelled of the spittoons and beer and cigar smoke. The barroom was long and narrow, with the bar to the right and a row of small tables to the left. The bar ended toward the back to make room for billiards and more tables. Single men and men in groups of twos and threes sat at the bar and the tables, and men crowded around a card table in the back. Behind the bar, the bartender was a broad pale man with a waxed and curled mustache who was talking intently to a very large negro man in a brown suit. The negro man had his bowler in his hands and hunched forward and listened intently to what the bartender was saying. He had the darkest skin James had ever seen, and James was surprised to think that a bar would allow negros on its premises, but it soon became apparent that the man was not drinking but merely speaking with the bartender.

James approached the nearest end of the bar and sat down

on an empty stool. After a bit, the bartender broke off his conversation and came down the bar and rested both of his hands on the rail behind, his shoulders hunched forward. He did not speak, however, and just looked intently at James with his tan-colored eyes. James didn't want to drink and couldn't afford it to boot—and in fact had he had not but a sip or two his whole life as a reaction to the drinking of his stepfathers— but he knew that this man wouldn't tell him anything if he did not at least order something. "I'll have a whiskey," James said, glancing at the man's face. The man's stance bespoke aggression, and James knew better than to boldly meet his eyes. Still saying nothing, the bartender turned and pulled a glass and a bottle from the back bar, set the glass in front of James, and poured the drink. He named the price in a surprisingly high voice.

James paid and sipped his drink. The whiskey was rank and vaporous and he realized in order to get it down he would have to drink it all at once or not at all, so trying not to make his reaction apparent, he tipped the glass into his mouth and swallowed and then glanced out the front windows to avoid letting his face be seen. The thin liquid ran down his gullet burning the whole way and rested there uncomfortably. It did not take but a moment for its effects to be felt, and James was unprepared for his senses to fuzz and the slight dizziness to set in. The bartender had not moved from in front of him, just gathered in his coins and stood there. James hoped this was a sign of willingness on the bartender's part, but it did not look promising. So, taking advantage of the man's presence, he said, "Know of any lodgings around here?" Did his voice seem different from the effects of the alcohol? He hoped it was undetectable.

"Nope," the bartender said and turned his back on James and put the money in the cash box.

Why had the man at the station suggested this doggery? Certainly, there must be something. He didn't want to anger the bartender, but he was in sore need, so he said, "Know of anyone else who might be of help?" The bartender turned around and removed the empty glass from in front of James and then looked pointedly at the door and then back to James— it's time for you to leave, he was forcefully suggesting. There was no use arguing. This man would be of no assistance, and it would not avail to prod him further. James would return to the station and ask another individual. Surely there were lodgings in a city as large as this—he just had to ask the right person. So James took the man at his word and left the saloon, the door once again scraping the frame. The alcohol disoriented him, and his limbs were lazy and late in response, as if they were on too long on a tether—he was astonished that it had taken him so fast and so far. Perhaps it was his empty stomach. And his physical control was not the only thing it blunted. It also dulled the fine edge of nervous angst that inhabited him, and this was a feeling that he liked. His usually keen sense of the world and its dangers melted a bit into a soft smooth glide—not a bad thing, not a bad thing at all.

He had not made it far down the boardwalk when he heard steps thump behind him. Just as he was quickly turning, a deeply resonant voice said, "Sir? You looking for a place?" There was the large coloured man in the bowler hat. When the man stood next to him, James realized how enormous he was. His shoulders were rounded with muscle under his expensive but worn suit, and his neck was wider than his jaws. His black eyes were shaped like almonds, his lips and nose were pronounced, and his face was long and narrow, with a strong and prominent chin. He wore a white shirt with a white string tie, which set off his complexion even more. His face wore a pleasant expression, something James was thankful for, as that much power in a man was a scary proposition, but his face also held an eager quality, as if he were striving—like James, a man trying to make his way in the world.

"Yes, indeed, my wife and I seek long-term lodging," James said.

"I got a place," the man said, "and it will not cost you much."

James's hopes leapt at the words. James needed a place that was cheap—and he hoped decent, though that was a secondary consideration at present. He needed it expeditiously, and here was an opportunity not easily passed up. Could he trust this man? He looked him over again and considered. He was a black man, and that in and of itself did not sway his decision one way or another, but was he the type of man to be trusted with he and Sara's future? His association with Boyer's, given James's impression of that establishment, did not bode well, but the open expression on the man's face and James's gut feeling weighed in his favor. James's gut told him that this was essentially a good man but also a motivated man, a man doing what he had to to get ahead.

"What would be the cost?" James asked.

The man named a price, and James figured it was indeed low for a city price, though it was exorbitant by small town standards and more than James had on him at present. That was a problem. How could he get this man to take him at his word that he was good for it, provided he was able to find employ—everything rested upon that. If that didn't happen, they were good and sunk.

The man added, his eyes on the ground, a question in his voice, "But you'll not mind amalgamation, as my mama lives in that same building." But immediately he looked up and straight into James's eyes and said, "I want you to know so as there will be no trouble. Trouble with my mama is trouble with me. Sir." He said it not angrily, but firmly, squarely, to let James know that that point was nonnegotiable.

James understood his point exactly. He was providing for and protecting his family, just as James was. What could James say to convey that understanding? "I hold no grudges on account of who a person is, only what he does," he ventured slowly, watching the man's face. The man considered for a moment, and then nodded.

The man held out his hand. "I'm called Moses, Moses Thaxton." James took it and shook. The man's hand was enormous and warm and moist, and his grip was firm. James squeezed a little harder to even out the crunch of bones in his hand.

"James Youngblood," James said.

After they dropped their hands, Mr. Thaxton stood waiting, and James knew that this was the moment that he should pay, so he got out his wallet and began counting out his money. He did indeed come up short, with the man standing there watching him. The expression on the man's face closed down, and he looked at James through narrowed eyes. Maybe James would not be able to obtain this lodging after all. Mr. Thaxton had been honest and forthright with him—perhaps his best approach was to do likewise, though it had not often worked in the past. "I am sorry," James said. "I did not mean to misrepresent myself before. You asked if my wife and I needed lodgings, and I answered in truth. Newly arrived in this fair city and newly married, we are in fact sorely in need lodgings. But as you witnessed I do not in fact have the amount you named, and so all I can offer is that I am good to my word. I will in fact meet your price, but I need to find employ first."

The man tilted his head as he looked at James, arms crossed across his chest, and considered.

"I do beseech you," James said, "as I too have a loved one of the female persuasion that I hope to provide for."

At those words, the big man sighed. "I will indeed take you at your word, but I do not have the time nor the resources for you to be wrong. See that you aren't. Sir."

James nodded and handed over all the cash he had and then turned out his pockets and gave him the coins that were there. Mr. Thaxton watched him and then received the money but then stood there with it in his palm. Then he shook his head slightly and plucked a bill and a couple coins from the pile and without a word handed it back to James. Then he retrieved his own wallet and tucked the money inside, adding, "I am indeed sorry to inform you that jobs are scarce, for black or white. That is to say, there are a lot of them, but they all taken. You're only hope is if you got folks in town with connections. That so?"

James shook his head.

"Well, then, good luck to you," the man said. He gave James directions and handed him a key and turned back toward Boyer's.

Chapter 3

ara sat in the train station. She knew that James would be gone still awhile. She wished for a novel or knitting or someone to talk to to distract her, but she had none of those things, so she simply watched the crowds of people. The afternoon wound on toward evening, the light from the oculus elongating and then pinching out. Then she noticed a newspaper abandoned under a bench so she rose and retrieved it and settled back into her spot and began to read. A long story on the front page caught her eye. It was about a young woman of good parentage who showed promise as a singer but ended her life in childbirth among strangers. Her first husband had been abusive and a drunk, and then she was seduced and abandoned by a man of means. Sara had to stop reading before the story ended. It was all too close to Sara's own circumstances for her comfort—a woman away from the support of her family, left to the vicissitudes of men. It prompted imaginings beyond what had come to mind before. What if James didn't get a good job, or any job? Their connection felt very tenuous, despite his constancy—what if he decided to abandon her? How did she know that he wouldn't? What was she to do then, without a penny to her name? Then the thought occurred to her: It was now possible, in addition to

the above circumstances, that she was quick with child.

Sara glanced around at the great hall and at all the people, unknown to her and uncaring of her situation, and felt once again utterly lost. But then, through the crowd, she saw a figure coming toward her, smiling broadly and brandishing a skewer of roasted meat and a paper package. It was James. Once again, she felt him her knight in shining armor, come to her in her hour of need. She rose with her carpetbag and went to meet him. He greeted her warmly and with the good news: He had found lodgings that they could afford. The smell of the food reached her and she felt ravenous. They turned and sat again on the bench. At first, James refused any food, but Sara insisted, as she suspected he also had not eaten. The roasted meat was spiced in a way she had never tasted before, but it was delicious, and within the paper parcel was a baked potato, which James gingerly pulled into halves, as it was hot, and they ate as if it were an apple.

After they had eaten, they exited the Union Depot onto the wide bustling boardwalk lined by horses and carriages and cable cars. They made their way down Union Avenue, which teemed with people and animals and moving carriages and wagons, and made their way across the city. Five- and six-story buildings towered above them, and they passed groceries, bootmakers, druggists, eating houses, clotheries, tobacconists, ice companies, and much more. They walked over train tracks and under elevated rails for cable cars. Every once in a while, a cable car rattled past at alarming speeds, but neither Sara nor James mentioned taking one. Gradually, the low of cattle and the squeal of pigs rose from a dull roar to a hundred thousand individual voices, mournfully calling, and the smell of smoke, manure, and carcasses grew stronger, but then it faded a bit as they walked on past the district of the packing houses with their ubiquitous train tracks. Sara got so turned around, she could not have found her way back to the station if she had tried. Soon the uncanny off-angle buildings thinned out, and the surroundings became shabbier and dirtier and the odors shifted to those of excrement and garbage, which lay in the open gutters and along the road, and rainbow-hued water pooled here and there. The road narrowed more and more until it was nothing more than a dirt alley, and the buildings were tiny one- and two-story shacks. Sara would later be told that this part of the city was called "the Patch" and housed workers for the packing plants and stock yards of all races and nationalities—coloureds, Irishmen, Germans, Poles, Swedes, Italians, Croatians, Russian Jews, and many others, the strongest commonality among them being that they had little money.

Light faded from the sky, and the sunset glowed red along the horizon of bluffs to the west. Just when Sara believed the surroundings could not be more hellish, James led her up to a dilapidated two-story building, the ground floor of which was an overall factory with a sign that said Johnson's Dry Goods Ltd. Just past it, James turned down the alley. He went to the back of a building and through a door and climbed a dark and creaky flight of stairs. "Here we are," he said and fished a key from his pocket and opened the door. Sara stepped into the room and stumbled on the threshold. She caught herself but in the process stepped on the hem of her skirt and felt it tear. The window above the bed let in a dim light and faced the red brick wall of the building opposite. She could just make out the apartment, which was one large room with a bed on one side and a table and chair against the opposite wall. There was a stove for heat and cooking with an empty coal bucket placed next to it. Shelves held odds and ends of cooking utensils, cutlery, and dinnerware.

James stood waiting for her reaction and twirled his hat in his hands.

It was all Sara could do to keep from bursting into tears. She bit her tongue and choked out, "It's ... It's not too bad." She looked around, her forehead crinkling. Oh my God, she thought, my God in heaven. What have I done, what have I done? James seemed to be expecting more, so she managed to add, "Maybe I can sew a curtain?" James still did not seem satisfied, but she could give him nothing further, and they were silent. They had not a candle between them, so without a word they retired for the night. They changed, and as there was only one room, Sara did not expect James to remove himself but it was one more compromise in a long list of compromises, and once they climbed into bed, Sara turned her back on James and began to cry silently.

A while after, the darkness was pierced by a loud sustained hooting, which shot Sara through with panic and she sat up in bed. James put his arm out and pulled her to him to comfort her. "The factory whistle," he whispered. "You'll soon get used to it." She did not want to get used to it, none of it, not one single thing, so she pulled away and turned her back once more and continued to cry. James let her be.

Chapter 4

ara awoke realizing that she had just heard the piercing factory whistle once more. It had entered her dream of a flood of people coming toward her, chasing her, and she could not get away. In her dream, the people had stopped and turned at the sound and stood motionless, and she had wondered what it meant. As she woke, the early morning air was warm about her face and she could smell hot coffee. She rolled onto her back and took a deep breath and stretched, but then remembered everything from the day before, which prompted her body to clench. She pushed herself back against the wall to a sitting position and opened her eyes. James was seated at the table, his back to her as he read the newspaper, a tin cup of coffee at his elbow. Next to James on the table was a golden loaf of bread. She glanced around at the apartment. It was clean and swept and well ordered, at least. Had James done that quietly this morning, or had it been that way last night? There were sticks of wood from broken furniture in the coal bucket, and the coffee pot sat on the stove, steam curling from its spout. Over it all, the gentle light of from the window cast a glow.

Sara tried to remember her impressions the night before, how it had seemed the worst of all possible places, a descent into Dante's hellhole, never to return. But this morning's impression was altogether different. It felt warm and welcoming, more so from the thought of how James must have crept from bed before dawn and gone out in search of provisions, perhaps making multiple trips, and came back and made coffee. It filled her with such tenderness. She had been wholly uncharitable last night—after all, he was in the identical position, and he had taken it stoically. It did not cast her character in a favorable light to throw a tantrum about something he had no control over any more than she, and she felt ashamed of her bad behavior.

She flipped off the covers and went over to James and put her arms about him as he sat hunched there. He turned to her with such a hopeful expression on his face, his eyes curled wide and his jaw slack, it broke her heart. "Oh, James," she said, "I am so sorry. My actions were unforgivable." He shook his head and pushed his chair back from the table and drew her into his lap. She sat there curled against his chest, unused to feeling small and comforted but wanting it, craving it. It was exactly what she needed, and she hugged him tightly for a time and then pulled back and looked into his face. His countenance was once more one of happiness.

"Coffee?" he offered. "You can share my cup, as it appears the last person to inhabit this"—he hesitated—"*dwelling* lived solitarily." She reached for it and took a sip, carefully testing the metal rim so as not to burn her lips or tongue. "Shall we break bread?" he continued. "I think we can shift this"—he indicated the table—"to the bed so that we each would have seating. Though the one on the bed will have to be careful not to bump his chin." He smiled as he said it. They rose and shifted the table in such a way that a chair sat on one side and the bed was cattycorner to it. He insisted on taking the bed and they sat tearing off large hunks of bread and sharing a cup of coffee. They discussed the day's events. He would go out immediately to find work, while she would get their lodgings in order and provision it. He handed her their last silver dollar in order to pay for it and their key to the apartment so that she could lock it while she was away. Sara was nervous at the prospect. She was old hat at buying provisions, but first she would have to find her way to a market or a grocer. She would have to have the things delivered or tote them back, once again finding her way, not getting lost, and then she would have to figure out how to transform these humble materials into something edible. She was not at all sure she was up to the task. He would stop back by at noon to check to see how she was doing and for some lunch and then would go back out for the afternoon. They were soon finished with breakfast, and she gave him a kiss on the cheek as he left.

So much to do. Sara quickly dressed and pinned up her hair and put on her hat and coat and descended the steps and out into the morning. The sun shone brightly and there was a bit of a breeze, which somewhat brightened the surroundings and ameliorated the stench, respectively. Just behind the building, there was a small weedy back yard with a clothes line and a fire pit and a pump. Sara went through the alley and back onto the filthy street, but there were paths through the garbage, and maybe it wasn't quite as horrendous as it had been in her mind. She tried to decide whether to turn right or left. Right, she finally decided, back the way they had come, as she thought she had remembered a grocery along the way. The street they were on, a glorified dirt path, gave way to a busy street down which people strode purposefully and carriages creaked and jangled, pulled by horses with their heads down. Sara joined the traffic and walked a while but could not seem to locate a grocery. This area was much more industrial, with bootmakers and blacksmiths and the like. Sara went down the street and turned left and then left again. She thought that one more left would bring her back to the beginning and she could start again, but then it didn't and then she was hopelessly lost. It set a panic through her and she realized she did not even know her own address with which to ask someone directions, and so she consulted no one but instead simply wandered up one street and down the next, searching for something familiar. This she did for what seemed like hours, until finally she sat down on the edge of a boardwalk and stared forlornly at the street.

As James left that morning, he held no illusions about his prospects for work. His hopes lay in chancing into some manual labor for the first bit and then possibly plying his considerable skill with horses to find a better position. Perhaps he could muck out stalls in order to draw attention to his preferred manner of employment, so the first thing he did was to locate a livery and inquire within. The man, portly but kind enough, said that he had enough men working for him and he was not looking to hire. When James pressed him, he said that even the lowliest positions were taken, but perhaps there might be something at a blacksmith's down the road. James went to the blacksmith's, who was a small and wiry man with a large dark-skinned man working beside him. The blacksmith was polite but curt and told him there was nothing, unless he had references. James did not. He could not very well tell the man he had been in prison for the last two and a half years. And so it went. Everywhere James tried he was turned away. Near

214

noon, after hours of trudging, he made his way back to the apartment and went up the stairs. When he tried the door, however, it was locked. He rattled it and said Sara's name through the door, but there was nothing. Nothing? Two possibilities immediately popped to mind: Either she had not yet returned from her errands or she had decided that she could not live this life and had fled back to Iowa. Her rapid departure was not without precedent. But there was a market just down the way that he had seen that morning, and so she should have returned. She should be here. He pounded on the door and shouted her name, which brought the creak of the door opening down the hall. Wasn't his landlord's mother living in the building too? Wouldn't she have a key? He turned and said, "Wait!" as the door slipped shut. He walked down to it and knocked softly. After a moment, it cracked open, but only a crack.

"Yes?" came a voice down low, as if from a child, though it was husky and definitely not a child's.

"Would you be Thaxton's mother?" he asked.

"I be," the voice came.

"You would not happen to have a key to our apartment down the hall, would you?" he said. "We are the new renters, and I don't have my key."

"Where's the missus?" came the voice. "She went out, locking the door behind her."

"She did? Of course she did. But she has not yet returned and I want to enter to see if she left me a note." It sounded ludicrous even to him, because why would she leave him a note if he did not have a key with which to open the door to enter and read the note? "Did she have a carpetbag with her?" he added.

"I don't know you," came the voice, and the door was shut firmly in his face. He walked back down the hall and tapped again to no avail on his own door and so he sat down against it and considered. There were other possibilities. There had been something in the previous day's *Kansas City Star*, an article about a young woman spirited away by a disreputable man under the pretenses of employment. His intent, however, had been much more sinister, but his plan had been foiled by the woman's father. What if Sara had simply gone out and some man had approached her with misrepresentations and promises? Was she such an innocent as to believe him? James knew the dangers of a city, but Sara did not. Was she such a naïf coming from a small village that she would fall for such a scheme? He did not know. But there was nothing he could do about it at present. If she were gone overnight, he could go to the police station to report her missing, but in the meantime there was nothing. It would do no good to wander the streets as there was only a one in a million chance that their paths would cross. Still, if she were not back by evening, he would do just that.

James thought about his innocent Sara. She had trusted him, and hadn't he been a stranger?—though that was different because he was indeed trustworthy and of honorable intent. But she couldn't know what people were capable of, growing up the way she had in Anamosa, in a privileged and protected situation, with family money to remove her from all forms of harm. People had the capacity for evil. They often looked out after their own interests and desires and no one else's, and, not only that, all those painful feelings roiled inside them and prompted brutal acts. Persons living cheek to jowl such as those in a city were the worst because city life bred a certain carelessness with the lives of others, a survival instinct, and they did not risk or even put forth effort for strangers, nor even acquaintances. Perhaps it was different for those who lived well and graciously in the mansions on the Quality Hill above the city, but that was not the life James knew.

He stood and went back out to the streets. Perhaps he would stop for a drink with the coin in his shoe.

Sara did not know how she did it but finally after walking and resting and walking for hours, she came across something familiar, a leather shop that had a sign in the shape of a lady's fine boot. It was there she had turned onto the main street from the street in front of their apartment. She was so relieved she had a fleeting impulse to go inside and thank the owner for placing his store there. She turned down the street and made her way to her building and down the alley, up the stairs, opened her door with the key, closed and locked it, and then flopped onto the bed. She swore that she had never before been this thankful to be home. Home. What a word for such a place, yet she couldn't have been more grateful. She pulled the boots from her aching feet and lay for a minute and felt them pulse with fatigue. The light in the apartment had changed from the morning—with the sun full overhead, the light was flatter. She could hear the sounds of a horse and wagon along the street and the barking of a dog, and somewhere a door slammed and someone yelled. The bed seemed softer than it had the previous night. She thought about the impressions of the day, and when she shut her eyes her eyelids showed the blurred motions of people and horses and carriages, the same scene repeating over and over.

And then she was waking up. She had fallen asleep there in

the bed. She jumped up, her head still groggy from sleep. How long? At least an hour or two, as the light was different in the window—it was late afternoon and soon James would be home and here she was asleep and hadn't done the main thing for which she had been tasked for the day, simply preparing dinner. She indeed was a failure of a wife at her very first test. What was she to do? There was not a scrap of food in the house, them having eaten the bread that morning, but she couldn't go back out there into the city to procure some. She had not the vitality nor the know-how. She could not wait until he returned home, bone weary and perhaps cranky, to ask his help—his patience surely would only go so far.

Perhaps a neighbor might assist her? Shaking her head to clear lingering sleep, she went out the door and down the hall to the only other door on their floor and tapped lightly upon it. From within, she heard someone call, "A minute," and so she waited. The door was flung open and there stood a tiny old negro woman. A negro woman, in Sara's building! The woman's white hair was pulled tightly into a bun on the top of her head, and her skin was a wrinkled but rich brown. Her face held the classic features of the race. A broad nose with broad nostrils, yet it curiously came to a small rounded point, with a pronounced groove down to the upper lip. Her lower lip was broad and naturally lined underneath, and her small eyes were set far apart. Her face was long and narrow, coming down to a square jaw. She stooped slightly forward and walked with a cane. She wore a fashionable but old black dress and a maroon wool shawl. The woman's expression changed from smiling expectation to narrow-eyed wariness in an instant. She pulled the door partly closed and said in a low voice, "Yes?" Sara was not whom this woman had been expecting, and this woman was not whom Sara had expected. It all so shocked Sara that, had Sara's need not been so great, she would have turned tail back down the corridor and never returned. To Sara, all coloureds were servants, and she would no more ask for assistance, rather than command obedience, than she would plan a trip to the moon. It was an assumption she had not challenged—until now.

It all crashed in upon her—the long trip filled with uncertainty, a radical change of circumstances, the arduous but ultimately unfruitful day of walking, and then sleep cut short. Though she did not cry standing there in front of this stranger, it surged within her and she wanted to give up utterly and completely. She said, simply, "I am in need of assistance," in a voice that did convey her true necessity. She had never felt pushed to such limits. "I don't know what to do," she added, her voice trailing off.

The old woman appraised her for a long moment, longer than was comfortable. Finally, the woman said, "Well, what you standing there for then, child? Come in. Auntie shall fix you up." Her voice held no discernable regional accent. She stepped backwards and held the door wide for Sara to enter. Sara had not cried before, but the kindness affected her so greatly that tears started to seep from the corners of her eyes, which she tried to contain. The woman gave her the dignity of ignoring her sniffling as she led Sara into the kitchen and sat her in a chair and then moved about pouring water from a kettle into a teapot, scooping in the tea leaves, and then putting a matched set of cups and saucers, creamery and sugar bowl onto the table, along with spoons and a package of paper-wrapped pecan cookies that she called tassies. The china set was decorated with blue line drawings of a fine lady and gentleman out of doors on a walk, and the man had a cape and fine hat with a long gray ostrich feather, and the woman held a parasol over her shoulder.

Her preparations gave Sara time to recover and to survey her surroundings. This apartment was of two rooms instead of one, with a window toward the east with a view of the grand houses upon Quality Hill. The rooms were fitted out, though sparsely, with quality furnishings that showed age but retained some of their former glory. It all shook Sara's preconceptions and left her on a new but uncertain plane. This woman was none of the things she expected. Once preparations were complete, the woman poured Sara's tea, inquiring whether she would take cream or sugar and placing two cookies upon her saucer.

"Now then," the woman said, "what seems to be the trouble?"

Sara didn't mean to be so forthcoming, but something in the comfort of the tea and the woman's attentive countenance prompted her story to pour out. She told Auntie about her father's cruelty and about her trip and her doubts about her future. Auntie nodded and made affirmational noises and then poured her more tea. After Sara had finished, Auntie said, "You do in fact have the look of a new bride about you. I could tell that right off. Don't you worry. These things have a way of working themselves out."

"But James will soon be home, and I have not yet cooked his supper, nor do I have a thing with which to prepare it nor the skill with which to do it." It was such a shameful thing to admit, but she had already confided so much and it got to the crux of the present dilemma.

"Ah, I see," said Auntie. "Well, don't you fret. Auntie will get you fixed up."

"I don't have the coin to pay you," Sara said. "I mean, I do have a dollar but not anything of a smaller coinage."

"Don't even think upon it," Auntie replied. "I wouldn't take a penny." She rose and gathered ingredients upon the counter: potatoes and milk and a salt cellar and a couple of biscuits. She wrapped these in a towel and handed it to Sara. "There you are," she said.

Sara was so grateful for the ingredients she thanked Auntie profusely. Such generosity. Silence followed, though, as Sara stood there not moving—she had not the slightest idea what to do with these ingredients. How did one cook potatoes? And the milk? Was that to be drunk alongside the potatoes? Thank the Lord the biscuits were already baked—she didn't know what she would have done had she had to attempt biscuits. She felt sorely tempted to return to her apartment and begin to try things on her own, but these were her only ingredients and she truly was unsure even of how to boil water, so she stayed put and looked at Auntie, embarrassed. Auntie looked back at her, polite but unsure.

"I'm so sorry, Auntie, but what am I to do with these?" Sara finally added.

Auntie's eyebrows raised, and then she laughed loudly. "Heavens, girl, have you not made tater soup before? And such a fine strapping girl you are, but nothing but a new born chick. Well, we will soon fix you up. Let me show you." Auntie retrieved an apron from a drawer and also one for Sara. Faster than Sara thought possible, Auntie showed her how to stoke the stove, peel, chop, and boil the potatoes, first in water for a time and then in milk.

The whole time she kept a running commentary: "Don't

you just let that stove go at night. Make sure to put that fire to bed, or it will be a chore getting it started from scratch in the morn. As big a log as you can fit, so it burns the night through, and bank it with the ashes. Here, let me show you. You peel those taters. It's the lazy housewife who does not peel. Those peels go into making salt-rising bread, or to feed the hogs, or to help the garden along. You are not to waste a thing. Everything on God's green earth has its use, several times over. Don't forget that. Chop those but leave them a bit big. They'll stay together better, especially if you have to let it set on the stove for a while awaiting your man. The milk's not to boil too hard. It will curdle. Just let it simmer a bit. The more it simmers down, the better. Stingy with the salt. You can always add, but you cannot remove. The biscuits will indeed be a good complement. Here. Dampen this cloth a bit—not too much now—wrap it round the biscuits and place them back of the stove, in the warming ovens. I think your stove has the warmers? That will heat them up a bit." On and on.

Sara listened closely and stored it all for later. It was overwhelming, but in attending Auntie closely a bit of her confidence rubbed off, as Sara saw how easy it appeared. Perhaps she could do this. Once it was done, and Sara held a pot of potato soup with a dishcloth to keep from burning her hands, the biscuits piled on the lid, she thanked Auntie again and again. "I am so very very grateful. So very grateful. I do not know how I will repay you." Auntie shrugged off her thanks and held the door for her to go back to her own apartment. "I'll soon have your pot and things back to you," Sara said.

It was near dark when James returned. The soup had simmered nicely, the biscuits were warm and moist, and Sara had set the table with the mismatched dinnerware. James seemed in a hurry as he stepped in the room, but then his shoulders slumped forward. She went to him and kissed him on the cheek, and he put his arms around her and squeezed her tightly.

"Where were you?" he asked.

"Oh. At lunch?" She had forgotten all about it. "I must admit to having lost my way." She promised to tell him the whole story. "Oh! Your lunch. You did not eat. Did you make out?"

He said he had. "My innocent abroad," he added, smiling. Then he sat, and she helped him remove his boots. "Well, I am not yet hired," he said lightly, but his weariness was evident.

"It was just one day," she said. "Tomorrow will bring better luck. For both of us."

He took a deep breath and nodded and said, "What is that delicious smell?"

"Potato soup," she said, pride in her voice, "and biscuits. My first." She did not yet let on that she had had assistance from down the hall. "Let me get you some."

She served the soup and they ate as the room went completely dark. She told him about her day, trying to make it sound like an adventure. She left out the desperation and the doubt. She embellished her account of the people she had seen and places she had gone. She finished by admitting that she had not managed to procure supplies. James was on his second helping, which lifted his mood, and he said wryly, "Anamosa born and bred, are you not? Tomorrow you come with me in the morning and I'll show you where to go." Sara was relieved at his reaction. She ventured, "And may I ask— this may sound foolish on my part—but what is our address?"

James laughed loud and long and then told her. How then, he asked, had she managed supper? She explained about Auntie and the help she had received.

"I am afraid I will try your patience even further, James, as I master the art of cookery," she said.

"Well, you've done marvelously for your first go," James said and then explained that Auntie was the mother of the man who owned the building. A black man owned the building? Things were surely different in Kansas City than they were in Anamosa. The world was a many splendored thing, full of marvels, and her judgment of it was wrong on so many accounts. Well, she would just have to take it as it came.

In darkness, Sara poured water in the bowls and the pan, so that they would soak and would be more easily scrubbed in the morning. She and James got ready for bed, the darkness alleviating any shyness she held, and once they were in bed they made love, and as this was their second time she knew what to expect, and it was good.

Chapter 5

he next morning, which was sunlit and fine, James led Sara the opposite direction, and she was amazed how close the market was and, beyond that, the grocer. She had simply turned the wrong direction. As they were in public, James took his leave with a short bow, and she touched his arm and wished him luck. To herself, she said a small and fervent prayer to seek God's favor on their behalf.

The open-air market ranged in front of a row of shops, under their awnings and in tents and booths on the opposing side. Some sellers had nothing more than baskets on the ground, with no protection from the sun, which would be severe later in the day. In addition to the usual city smells, there were the odors of fresh fish and brewing coffee and roasting meat and frying vegetables from the stalls. Vendors called out, "Fresh catfish!" and "Best meat in town!" and "Get your fresh vegetables, healthful for your wee ones!" and "Pierogies, pierogies!" Sara walked through, keeping well back from the stalls so that a purveyor would not approach her nor bully her. There were vegetables galore. She recognized carrots and potatoes and tomatoes, but there were many others that she could not identify—leafy greens in many shades and green and red and purple bulbous vegetables with glossy peels. There were fruits and berries in many cheerful shades, purple and red and yellow flowers poking from containers of water, meat from animals she could and could not identify, fresh baked bread that smelled heavenly, honey, eggs, milk, jams and jellies, and barrels of flour. There were dry goods—colorful cloth and rugs and newspapers and tin pots and pans and brushes and brooms. A sea of men, women, and children teamed the market, walking between the stalls, bartering with those who were selling things, talking, and pulling wheeled carts or toting baskets, and a few dogs chased between the stalls.

What should she do? Sara had no idea what to buy and she had no confidence in her ability to discern prices and to haggle with sellers. This was unfamiliar territory and she wasn't sure she was prepared to conquer it. Besides, it was staples that she needed, of that she was certain. Green vegetables would go bad after a short period, and she needed flour and sugar and the like, so she continued on to the grocer's. Here, at least, she would be on familiar ground. Well, maybe not so familiar—she looked around with wide eyes upon entering the store. It was much bigger than her father's, taking up two connecting row buildings with doors cut between. There were teams of bustling clerks and counters on every wall. The store sold things she had never before beheld, such as ready-made mourning clothes and specialty kitchenware and foodstuffs in little cans from far away labeled in languages she could not read. The bulk barrels held the normal things such as flour and sugar and oats but also grains that Sara did not recognize. She wasn't sure what she needed—she hadn't had time to look in her receipt book—and so she did the best she could. Staples were what she needed, so she thought back to what she ordered every week for her father's cook Mini and bought small amounts of bread, flour,

Indian meal, sugar, molasses, coffee, eggs, butter, potatoes, dried beans, rice, lard, a little bacon, saleratus, salt, milk, some dried peas, and one can of peaches. She was careful to add the costs in her head as she went, assiduously having things weighed and keeping track, so that she wouldn't go over the dollar—she wasn't the daughter of a grocer for nothing—and the clerk handed her back two Indian-head pennies.

Sara was proud of this accomplishment. On her own, she had finally done something right and done it well. Maybe she could in fact live this life and manage to keep her husband reasonably comfortable. She squared her shoulders and nodded her head. She took an armload of groceries and then asked the clerk to have the rest delivered, as the store sign had advertised this service. She gave her address with instructions to go around back, and then she walked home without once getting lost. It was a day of firsts, and a day she would always remember with pride. Shortly after she arrived home, a small red-headed boy knocked on her door and brought in her groceries, and she tipped him a penny, to which he smiled broadly. "If you ever need help again, ma'am, ask for Charlie. That's my name," he said. She promised she would. She reflected, after he left, that the number of people she knew in this city had just doubled, and at this rate she would have met a whole raft of people before the week was out. She liked that feeling.

Her belly growled, as she had had nothing for breakfast but coffee. She put the groceries away on the shelves and admired how full they were. Then she thought she would eat something, so she pulled off a hunk of bread and slathered it with butter and sat at the table and ate it. The bread was crusty on the outside and chewy in the interior, and the butterfat melted on her tongue—there's nought better seasoning than the appetite, as her mother used to say. With all the missed meals so far, Sara's frock had begun to hang a bit loose on her frame, but she didn't mind, as she had always thought of herself as big, whether from her unnatural height or from the curves of her female body. As she finished her quick meal, she mused on the lessening of the stench of the city. Had it really diminished? Or was she simply getting used to it? Whichever, it had not reduced the simple pleasure of bread and butter.

James stopped back by for lunch. He ate a sandwich of butter and molasses, washed down with water. In the future, he said, he would like to take lunch with him in the morning, as it was a burden to make his way all the way back to the apartment. This would be especially true if he found work. She said she would devise something for him in the future. When she asked how it was going, he merely shrugged. "See you this evening," he said as he left.

Now came the question: What was she going to make for supper? Best to consider it early, in case she had to take a second crack at it. Wiping her hands on a rag, she retrieved the cookbook from her bag and opened it on the table. She knew that many of the receipts were for dishes she did not have the ingredients for. Certainly, if she had had the money, she could have run out to the market in no time at all, but her funds were spent. She took a couple of deep breaths and thought a minute. Certainly there were receipts in the book that she could cut back or alter to suit the ingredients that she did have on hand. Flipping pages, she found a receipt for a duck soup with dumplings. She didn't have duck, but she did have the flour, egg, and salt necessary for dumplings. What could she cook the dumplings in? She remembered the potato soup from the day before. Milk. She would cook them in milk and add a little butter. No. Fried bacon would give it good flavor. She could serve it with bread and butter and coffee. Perfect. Problem solved.

Sara carefully laid the book to one side and stoked the stove as Auntie had shown her. She put milk on to heat and put bacon in the skillet to fry. In the bowl, she mixed the egg dumplings. She didn't know what consistency the dough should be, so she hoped she'd gotten the measurements about right, as she didn't have any measuring utensils. She added a little extra flour, just in case. When the bacon was done, though it was uncooked in some areas and blackened in others, she pulled it out onto a plate and poured the fat into a small jar. It would make good flavoring and cooking lard, provided it did not go rancid. She watched the milk to make sure that it did not boil, remembering Auntie's admonition. When it was hot, she crumbled the bacon back into it and dropped spoonfuls of dough into the simmering liquid. She sliced a couple of thick pieces of bread and buttered them, put coffee grounds in the hot water, and set the table. She felt so proud. Once the dumplings were firm, she pulled it off to the cooler side of the stove and sat down in a chair. She wished James would get home soon, as she was hungry.

The afternoon wiled away, and then James walked through the door and Sara jumped up and helped him off with his jacket. "Supper's all ready," she said, nodding. "It's all ready." As he took off his boots and washed his hands, she ladled out the soup. To her bewilderment, the soup was a lot thicker than it had been earlier. It wasn't like the potato soup. This soup had reached a nice gravy. That is good, she thought, as it will fill the belly and stick to the ribs. She was quite dismayed, though, when she tipped the pan sideways while serving and a black pancake peeled from the bottom of the pan. The soup was burned. She quickly righted the pan and ladled his portion off the top. She hoped that the burned taste hadn't permeated the rest. She was careful that he didn't get any of the bottom portion and kept that for herself. Hers tasted burned, though flavorful otherwise, but there was no doubt. James didn't say anything about his portion, so she hoped that it was not too horrible.

After they went to bed, Sara lay awake thinking. How could she possibly learn to cook when she had no direction and she was scraping by trying to adapt things from that fancy cookbook? How would she remember everything she had done? She could ask Auntie's help, but Sara was sure she would need a lot of assistance, and Auntie couldn't be pestered day and night. So, out of necessity, Sara hatched a plan. When she had a bit of money, she would buy a commonplace book and a pencil. There, she would record all the directions for the receipts of everything she cooked. That way she could keep track of alterations and inventions and decide what to change the next time. If the receipt worked, she would have it, but if it didn't, she could alter the receipt until it did work. She would also make a list of hints—#1. Flour dumplings will thicken milk. Having an approach made Sara feel infinitely better, and she soon dropped off to sleep.

The next day when Sara told Auntie about the dumplings, Auntie chuckled. "Now you know. Flour's what you use to thicken things. That's how you make gravy. You make a roux. You know, a roux. Melt some fat—bacon or butter or what have you—and put in an equal amount of flour and let that bubble and fry until it browns. Then you add your milk or your stock and you'll have a nice gravy. You can add onions too, and cooked sausage or other savory leftover. What you made we call rivul soup. Haven't heard of folks putting bacon in it, though, though I bet it was *fine*. Rivul soup is a washday dinner because it's fast and easy."

Auntie had made some tea, and they sat sipping it and eating Auntie's delicious gingerbread with hard sauce and talking about cooking. "What is this tea, Auntie?" Sara asked. It tasted strange, like tar smelled, and Sara had had to ask for extra sugar.

"It's called lapsang," Auntie said. "I keep it for special occasions, such as visitors." Auntie nodded to Sara and offered her more gingerbread. "They smoke it to cure it. Something about it I always liked. Reminds a body that life is not at all times smooth and easy. It's got some darkness in there too, prodding the tasters. Such things make the best times better and the middling times less middling."

The more time Sara spent with Auntie, the more she grew to genuinely admire the woman, who in some small way reminded her of her mother. It was imminently comforting to have the specter of such a memory in such an unsuspecting place. In Sara's mind, Auntie quickly transmuted from an old slave woman—though Sara did not know whether she had actually participated in that institution and now she doubted it—into a kind maternal friend. As they drank their tea, Auntie talked and talked. She gave Sara suggestions for cooking eggs and potatoes and bacon and flour and Indian meal. She suggested Sara pick up some raisins. That way she could make Indian pudding with raisins and soda bread and cookies and rice with raisins. "Adds a bit of sweetness to life, which is important, too," she said. Auntie promised to show Sara how to construct biscuits and corn dodgers. She mentioned the best times to go to market to get the best prices. Early in the morn was sometimes good because sellers were eager for their first sale, and some were superstitious about that, but it was by far the most desirable to go at the end of the day when sellers were anticipating having to pack up all their leftover goods and haul them back to their places of lodging. You could often haggle a good price then, though you risked them being sold out of what you needed. Sara asked Auntie about haggling, and Auntie said you had to have iron in your eye and larceny in your heart, not a time to be womanish. Start low, she said, and the seller will always start high, and that way you meet in the middle at a reasonable sum.

Then Auntie stopped talking and cocked her head, her eyes focused in the middle distance. "Yep," she said, "it is that time," she said and rose. The sound of footsteps, not slop-footed tromping but rather a quiet creaking of the boards, came to Sara's ear, and Sara rose too. Auntie went into the other room and in response to a soft rapping opened the door. Sara wasn't quite sure what to do, so she stood there with her hands clasped in front of her. With the quietness of the tread, Sara expected to see a woman, but it was a man, a large coloured man with dark blue-black skin. He carried packages in his arms, which he set on kitchen table. "My son brings me groceries," Auntie explained to Sara. The kitchen seemed tiny all of a sudden, the man's enormous bulk filling the space. Sara folded her arms across herself and took a step back. She had never been in such close proximity to a black man, much less such a large specimen. If Auntie hadn't been there, she would have been alarmed. Not only his size and his coloring and the unified slope and curve of his face was unsettling, but also

232

there was something about the way he moved, his muscles and joints a little more coordinated than the average man's. He seemed a huge watch-works, everything connected and even a little more dazzling than the inventor had envisioned.

He wore a bowler hat that he slipped off and laid next to the packages on the table. Under the hat, his hair was shorn close to his head. He wore a brown suit, but under the suit his shirt was white, his vest was white, and he wore a white string tie knotted into a large drooping bow. He took off his coat and hung it on the back of a chair. Sara glanced at Auntie, whose face had opened up like a sunbeam, and she scolded the man affectionately, "You just take those and hang them where they go." The man shrugged, picked up his hat and coat, went in the other room, hung them, and then came back in and put both hands on his mother's shoulders and then reached down to hug her. He towered over his mother, but when he hugged her, he delicately shortened and curled around her in one smooth motion. Auntie's crinkled face opened up into a broad toothy smile as she fairly clucked, "Why, Moses. Thank you, son."

"The least I could do for a beautiful lady," he said, his voice deeply resonant. He took his mother's hand in both of his and then looked expectantly at Sara.

"Moses," Auntie said, "This is Sara Youngblood, my neighbor. Sara, Moses Thaxton, my son."

"I met your husband," Moses said. They shook hands, and Moses's palm radiated heat around Sara's cold fingers.

"Moses is a businessman," Auntie said, "and he has just begun an apprenticeship to become a lawyer."

"What is it that you're in business for?" Sara asked.

"Oh," Moses said, glancing up in the air, "a little of this, a little of that. A sort of jack of all trades."

Auntie invited them to sit and poured tea into a large blue speckled enamelware mug she pulled from the cupboard and cut an enormous piece of gingerbread, put it on a plate, topped it with sauce, and set it on the table for him. She then began unloading groceries and dry goods from the packages and putting them on shelves. Moses went into the other room and came back carrying the unwieldy rocker, deftly threading it through the door, which he sat next to the table. When he sat on its low seat, his head was level with Sara's.

"Moses," Auntie said as she filled her flour canister, her voice taking on a serious tone, "I've been meaning to tell you. You hear about the lynching?" Auntie's voice in that simple statement was loaded with the weight of past conversations and admonitions. Sara had heard nothing of any such doings, though of course she had not been in town long. Would she have heard of it even if she had?

Sara glanced at Moses. She expected his face to be serious, but he grinned instead. "That southern boy from over Crawford County way?" Moses said, his voice low and velvety. "Folks say they never knew a man to straighten a rope with more unstudied grace and earnest zeal."

Auntie turned around and put her hands on her hips. Her face contained the seriousness of the moment before.

Moses continued, "Seemed to throw the whole vim and concentrated energy of a lifetime into it. Calculated to win the respect of all."

"Moses," Auntie said in a level voice. "Don't you be challenging to God. It is not a laughing matter." She turned back to stocking the shelves.

"You always say, do your best," Moses added and then he winked at Sara. Sara did not know quite what to think about

234

that.

"So, Moses," Auntie said, her voice changing as if she were redirecting the attention of a two-year-old, "how'd your trip go? How was Saint Louis?"

Moses grinned even wider around his bite of cake. "Full of excitement," he said after he swallowed. "Railroad travelers are always so sociable." This was in direct opposition to Sara's recent experience.

"Excitement how?" Auntie said, mock suspicion in her voice. Auntie poured Moses and Sara more tea and then took a seat as Moses spoke. Then she settled in her seat, her face pleasantly set as if she knew what was coming.

Moses said, "So, I never got so well acquainted with my fellow passengers as I did on this trip. On the return, going about thirty miles per hour, another train telescoped us." He brought his hands together, one hand sliding over the other.

"Anybody hurt?" Sara asked with concern. Auntie shook her head and shushed her: It was nice that Sara was distressed but the question had no bearing.

Moses continued, "We were all thrown into each other's society, immediate social contact, so to speak." His face flattened into seriousness. "I went over and sat in the lap of a traditionally built southern woman from Baton Rouge." His voice smoothed once more. "Quite a lot of woman, overflowing with concern for my welfare." Auntie snorted but didn't say anything. "A girl from Chicago went over nine seats to sit on the plug hat of a preacher from D.C. She did it with such timid enthusiasm it shoved his hat clean down over his shoulders." This brought a chuckle from Auntie, as Moses pulled down his shoulders, elongated his neck, and pushed up the crown of his head. Sara found herself chuckling too. "This shy young man with an emaciated oilcloth valise left his seat, went over, and sat down in the dinner basket of a bridal couple who were wrestling with a picnic. Now, under normal circumstances, would he have risen with such impetuosity and sat down in the cranberry jelly of total strangers? I tell you." This last image so tickled Sara that she laughed till her sides hurt. "Yep, completely laid aside our cool reserve. Made ourselves entirely at home." He smiled smooth and wide, his eyes crinkled with humor.

After they had stopped laughing, conversation turned to more mundane things, with Moses and Auntie discussing the groceries Moses had brought and what to bring next time. They both tried to include her in the conversation, but Sara didn't say much and simply looked back and forth between Auntie's face and Moses's, which both held the inward-outward look of two people who only see one other. When Sara returned to her apartment, she felt vicariously suffused with that glow.

The rest of the week rushed by. When James found work and gave her money for the household, Sara bought a blank book and a pail for James's lunches. She settled into the routine of rising early to prepare James's breakfast and to pack his lunch. If she could, she assembled as much of it as she could the night before. Then, as soon as he left in the morning, she would haul water, take a sponge bath, and clean the apartment until it was spotless. She would cogitate on food and plan meals and go to the market, if necessary. Sometimes she would have tea with Auntie, and she tried to bring an offering if she could. Her own attempts at cookies and cakes flopped, so she was not always able to, so she would bring milk or something else. After, she would return and have a light lunch, bread and butter or leftovers and a little coffee. Then she would start supper. James would come home after dark. Some nights he could barely keep his eyes open. They went to bed right after supper, and days went by where he seemed not to have the energy to approach her in the dark.

One morning, Sara tore pages out of the back of her commonplace book to write letters back to Iowa. She wrote to Esther and Maisie and Ed. She did not write to her father, as she was sure the letter would immediately be thrust into the fire. To Esther she wrote about her wedding and the trip, her first impressions of marriage, her adventures in cooking, and what Kansas City was like, and she asked after Father's continuing health and if Maisie and Ed were managing. To Maisie she described the train trip and what it was like in Kansas City. She also mentioned Auntie and Moses. She tried to make it sound like the stories she used to tell Maisie at bedtime. Sara felt a stab of guilt as she finished the letter, as she had abandoned her, though she could not have done differently. For Maisie's sake but also to reassure herself, she ended the letter with an invitation for Maisie, when she was older, to come and visit Kansas City or possibly even reside with them. Probably just a dream, especially now, but it might give Maisie something to look forward to. To Ed, Maisie wrote about how well they were doing and James's adventures, somewhat elaborated, in employment. She took every opportunity to assure him of James's felicitousness toward her.

As the days past, Kansas City's temperatures soared, and it became humid and sweltering. It certainly was hot in Anamosa during the summer, but not at all like this. The metal roof above Sara's head concentrated the heat and the smell. Sara didn't know whether she would be able to stand it, as it was only early June, but she could and she did. She opened the window in spite of the smell in hopes of a breeze, and she made herself a fan. She splashed her face, neck, and arms with water whenever she felt she could not take it. She learned to cool things by wrapping them in wet rags, the evaporation having some effect, but wishing the whole time they could afford a cold box and to have ice delivered. She would add that to her list. At night she put foodstuffs on the little shelf out the window to take advantage of the night air, and to make small amounts of things so that there were few leftovers. She tried to do most of her cooking in the early morning or late evening, and she searched for more uncooked fresh dishes so that she wouldn't have to start the stove.

Sara also turned her attention to the laundry. James had purchased extra underthings and a nightshirt for himself, when they could afford it, but in all they did not own much clothing. Still, what they had needed laundered and there were the sheets and kitchen rags. She laughed when she opened *The Compleat Housewife* to the section on laundry. It began with the sentence, "Before starting to wash, it is essential to have a large light airy laundry with at least seven tubs." She didn't have seven tubs, but it was indeed light and airy, though it carried a stench, as she did laundry out back. She had to borrow the tub from Auntie. In the back yard of the building there was the pump where she retrieved her water and a fire pit. Once again, she asked Auntie how to do it, and so Auntie sat in the shade and gave directions. Sara soon found out why laundry was the task most universally hated. Wrestling large, hot, wet pieces of cloth to scrub them and wring them and hang them was almost too much for her at first. By the end of the day she had sweated circles around her armpits and down her front, and her hands were red and raw from the hot water and soap. She was so tired she couldn't even think. There was indeed rivul soup for supper.

The first letter to come for her was from Esther, with a letter from Maisie written by Esther tucked within it. Esther said that they were managing. Maisie had gotten over her cold and had become very upset when told of Sara's departure. Ed was getting by. "You know Ed," Esther said. "He doesn't say much." Father had taken it the hardest of all, Esther said, and the household was running as smoothly as could be expected without Sara, and Father was relying on Minnie for many things. Esther came over to help when she could. When Sara read this, she felt a stab of self-righteousness. Serves him right, she thought. Though Father had not confided in Esther, he had said nothing as she had went over to pack a trunk for Sara and sent it on.

Then Sara turned to Maisie's letter. It said:

Dear Sara,

I hope you are all settled in Kansas City. Esther told me that you married some man, and as she is writing she says your surname is now Youngblood. Did you not want to be a Moore anymore? (She insists I ask this question. ~ Esther) I would love to visit you there, only Father said that on no account can I go.

Why did you go to Kansas City? You left and I did not know what to think though Esther said for me not to worry as I would understand better

*when I was older, but I understand things just
fine. I've finished my sampler. You should see it
because it is beautiful. Please write me long letters
about your travels and come back soon.*

Your loving sister,

Maisie Moore

Esther's and Maisie's letters prompted such a complex variety of emotions that, despite the many tasks she had on hand, she took to her bed for an afternoon. She lay there, her mind chewing their words over and over, and after much ruminations she thought, I do believe I'm being silly. What is done is done. I cannot undo it, any more than I could have done differently at the time. I must move on. And with that, she decided to suspend her feelings of guilt over Maisie and leaving Anamosa, no matter their merit, and she would focus on the present and the future. She rose from bed and began to prepare supper.

A few days later, Sara's trunk arrived packed with so many good things that gratitude to Esther swelled in her breast and she vowed to send Esther a long letter and a small present, if she could find something with her meager funds. Possibly she could make something, a needlepoint perhaps, though her assessment of the value such things had somewhat lessened since coming to the city. The trunk was full of not only dresses and clothing and shoes but also cookingware and towels and blankets and a sewing kit and so many other useful household items that Sara would not have thought to include. It was as if it were Christmas, and Sara had received the best present of her life, all the more moving for it utility, timeliness, and unexpectedness.

Chapter 6

ames got up early every day to find work, with limited success. He stood in line at the packing factories and at the stock yards and anywhere men congregated for day work. He politely asked others if they knew of opportunities. He walked from one end of the West Bottoms to the other and up the bluffs into the city above to follow leads. Occasionally, a man would hire him to help haul something or move cattle or shovel manure or carpenter a shed or unload rail cars or shovel ditches. But these jobs paid the lowest wages and took a heap of going after. He tried and tried but could not procure full-time work to save his own life, no matter how much effort he put into it.

One morning, James went out as usual. It was overcast and raining lightly. A stocky man with scarred knuckles who had previously employed him once again used him to help haul furniture. James didn't like the man nor his team of horses, but work was work. The near side horse was a fine docile sorrel gelding of mixed breeding with foundered hooves, while the off side was a bony blue roan gelding with the look of a short Thoroughbred that had a blind cancer eye on its outside. The animal stank as if were already in the knacker's cart, and its skin was nubby from whipping. The animal was skittish and mean, and it had tried to bite James the first time he had walked past. James felt for the animal, as it was sunk in its own private hell, but he could do nothing for it and kept clear.

The man drove to an office building of turreted gothic architecture in the upper city, and then grunting and sweating in its shadow he and James lugged oilcloth-wrapped furniture from an office out onto the cart. Once they had finished, James walked around the cart to the offside to seat himself in the passenger's place, and at that moment out of the corner of his eye James saw a small child darted out from an alley and run headlong past the team of horses, coming up just behind the spiteful blue roan. James knew in an instant what was about happen. The horse sensed the motion in the corner of its eye and flattened its ears against its skull and hunched its back, blindly aiming a hoof at the hurtling figure. James sprang from where his foot rested on the step and swept the child to the side. His mind did not process his actions—he just acted. He rolled as he passed the horse so that his body was between the child and the animal, scooping the child up and feeling its light weight in his arms, but then there was a blow to his leg and he had a split second to think, that is going to hurt, and then it did. The hoof had not missed. The horse hunched again to aim another kick, and so James leapt sideways out of harm's way with the child in his arms and they came to rest upon their sides. It was no more than a second before the child struggled and ripped free and continued running down the walk without so much as a glance back. It was a boy in knee breeches, and James didn't even see his face. You are welcome, James thought, shaking his head.

James pushed himself to standing and assessed his injuries. The leg bore James's weight, so he did not believe it was broken. If the kick had been square, his bone could have shorn in two, as the old horse had quite a bit of muscle. It did hurt like the dickens, and when James pulled back his pants leg there was blooming bruise and a scrape that oozed sluggishly. As the pain pulsed with the rush of his blood, James took deep breaths to fight light-headedness. The owner of the cart came around and twisted the animal's ear to calm its restiveness and keep it from bolting, while the near-side horse stood calmly, ears flicking back and forth. Once the roan had calmed, the man came over to check his state. James said that he was fine, but then when they reached their destination and began to unload, the pain in his leg was too great, and James had to excuse himself and hobble home. He not only lost the rest of that day but also two more days' wages due to incapacity, which he and Sara could ill-afford.

The first day he spent with his leg up, and in spite of the financial woes it was heavenly not to be trudging through the streets but rather sitting at home and spending time with Sara. It was a mini holiday, though they went nowhere and did nothing but talk. It brought them closer. As soon as he was able, he was up and out despite the pain. He had to rest his leg every so often, which hampered his job that day of sweeping out train cars.

That evening, as James limped home along the crowded boardwalk, someone tapped him upon the shoulder. He turned, and standing there was Moses Thaxton with a woman on his arm. James's first thought was how beautiful the lady was. She wore a loose-fitting silk evening gown with a high waist and a pale peach-colored bodice that showed her honey-toned skin and a full blue skirt printed with peach-colored roses. The tops of her full breasts rose and fell above her neckline as she breathed. Her face held large lips like Moses's, but her nose was not broad, and James could not tell her particular mix of parentage. Her cheekbones and chin curved and jutted agreeably as she tilted her head, and her dark eyes were large and wide-set. James's second thought was alarm. Though the woman looked respectable enough, something in the liquid way she moved and the way she eyed James made him feel small, as if he were a rodent within range of a bird of prey. He immediately felt sorry for Thaxton, as the man seemed proud of this creature who hung from his arm.

"Thaxton," James said.

"You getting along all right?" Moses said.

"Fair to middling."

The woman nudged Moses with her elbow. "Do introduce me to your fine friend," she said, her voice low.

"Oh," Thaxton said. "Youngblood, James, wasn't it?" He turned to the woman. "This man and his wife are renting out above the factory," he explained to her. He turned back to James. "This is Olivia Beauchamp, soon to be Thaxton, my fiancé." She kept ahold of Thaxton's arm with her left hand but then stepped forward and held out her right hand, limp-wristed, palm down. James did not know whether to shake it, kiss it, or bow. With a glance at Thaxton, James tucked his hands behind his back and bent slightly at the waist, saying, "It is nice to meet you, Miss Beauchamp." He straightened, but she continued to hold up her hand, smiling, and the only thing for James to do was to take it, which he did awkwardly. "A pleasure to make your acquaintance, I am sure," she said in a low voice. When he tried to quickly pull his fingers away, she held them tightly for a split second before releasing them, and a small one-sided smile came to her lips.

James took a step back and said, "Congratulations. Congratulations to you both."

"We are much obliged to your well-wishing," Thaxton said. "Well, we must be on our way, then."

"Yes, of course," James said. He watched them as they continued down the boardwalk. He shook his head. Thaxton might be a big man, but James had some doubt as to whether he was man enough to manage that situation.

Days went by, and the search for higher-wage jobs or permanent employ continued, without much luck. James would find himself in a ragged semicircle of men in stained clothing all huddled into groups according to ethnic background, waiting for the foreman and his men to come out and choose a crew. They shuffled irritably. Here would be a group of coloured men, there a group of Nordic men, here a group speaking guttural German, and then three Irishmen would walk by, laughing and talking in a rough brogue, but they would only glance at the end of the line, shrugging their shoulders. An hour would pass. Some men would get angry and leave, some would walk up and meekly join one group or another, and others just stood, hollow-eyed, waiting. James got picked, or he did not.

One afternoon, instead of stopping, James too passed the restive crowd and kept walking until he reached a mortared stone wall skirting the mighty Missouri River. He scaled it, swung his feet over the top, and then sat hunched forward, his elbows resting on his knees. To the northwest, he could see where the Missouri came into view up by Goose Island where there lived a negro congregation and then down to the mouth of the Kaw River coming up from the south where it fed into the Missouri and then closer where it looped through the city and

246

then back to the east and north. The river water was oily brown from mud and humanity's waste and the filth of the city's factories, the dull rush of the water scraping its banks and rippling and swirling in grimy pools. It was a huge mass, sometimes surging, sometimes sluggishly pulling back, but nonetheless mindlessly moving forward, channeled by the massive banks.

James sat glumly as the sun turned orange and pink and then red and then faded to a pale yellow in the haze from the factories. As the light was dimming, the wall underneath him began to quiver and vibrate and rumble. At first he thought it could be an earthquake, as he'd never experienced one, but then the ground under his eyes began to seethe in discrete spots, and he quickly realized it was nothing more than rats as they emerged from holes under the wall. There were a few and then a lot and then what seemed like hundreds, streaming from under the wall. They escaped their burrows and then stopped and sat in groups, waiting for something. Soon steam erupted from a pipe that jutted from the wall below him, and blood, viscera, feces, and other unmentionable things shot out of the pipe and into the outfall channel. The rats squealed and fought each other, diving into the mass, retrieving chunks with their mouths and swimming to bare ground, pelts slick with blood, to devour them.

It was more than James could take. He pushed himself up, jumped down from the wall, and went home. There, Sara had a supper of fried potatoes, wilted greens, and only slightly dense biscuits waiting for him. Under the odor of dinner, the apartment smelled freshly cleaned, and it was orderly and bathed in the warm light of an oil lamp. Sara's hair was freshly done up, and she greeted him eagerly when he came through the door. During dinner, she told the story of Charlie, the grocery delivery boy. Though an orphan on the streets, the grocers employed him on deliveries, and though he worked only for tips, the clerks often gave him part of their lunches. She finished the tale by saying, "I'm continually amazed at all the little bits of good in the world." James did not respond. After Sara had done up the dishes and they had blown out the lamp, James gathered Sara in his arms and held her as closely as he could. He wrapped his legs around hers and pressed his face into the curve of her shoulder. He tried to pull her into him, to inculcate some of that goodness that she seemed to possess without even realizing it.

And then they made love, and Sara was surprised at the fierceness in his movements and the force of him. He began softly, considerate as ever, but then quickly his motions became jerky, forceful, falling just short of causing her pain. He seemed overdone, and within him Sara glimpsed this other unnamed and unnamable creature, its dark and shaggy head, for a brief second, rearing above James's and its sinewy arms and hands grasping at her. She heard its ragged sound deep in his chest—something immense yet inchoate. It was more than mere passion, and Sara was afraid for a moment. The very thing that prompted her physical attraction to him—his power and its possibilities—could it run out of his control? But then it was over and he lay beside her, her head on his shoulder, his arm cradling her, and it was as if the thing had never happened.

The next day, James went out once again on the never-ending search for a permanent position. By midafternoon, he could not take it anymore, and he felt an almost undeniable urge to buy a ticket on the first train out of town. It would be so easy. He turned and walked toward Union Depot. He had enough money in his pocket to buy the ticket and to last a couple of days—days in which he could be in the farthest territories and beyond claiming. He would be free once again. Sara, after all, had enough cash that she simply could go back to Anamosa where, in fact, she would be happier in the long run. He could not provide for her. It was that simple. The hopelessness of it settled in his stomach, and he stopped and stood paralyzed. He was trapped, trapped once again in that life he had led before, with someone to depend upon him and yet no one would offer him the lifeline of employment.

He began to walk again but then again stopped. No. He would not. He was a new man, and he had made a vow to stand by Sara no matter what. He would not run out on her. He sat down on the edge of the boardwalk and rested his head in his palms, elbows on his knees. The feeling of desperation brewed within him until he could not stand it any longer, so he pushed himself to standing. Across the street was a saloon, and so he walked to it and ordered whiskey straight up, and thus that wretched feeling within him was drowned.

Chapter 7

hen James woke the following morning, he felt tremendous guilt about his actions and vowed to make amends. The window showed it to be a sunny day. "I'm not going to work today," he told Sara as they lay in bed. "I'm taking you out."

Sara couldn't believe her ears. They had both been shoulder to the yoke ever since they came to the city—she had not had a day off, and James's only days off had been with his injury. James kissed her on the cheek and got out of bed. They ate a quick breakfast and changed from their night clothes. Sara pulled her best dress from the trunk—a black tailored jacket with buttons all the way down the front and a large round coattail that covered her hips and bustle and an overskirt of quilted blue silk held wide by a hoop skirt. She pinned on her best hat with its slightly crumpled ostrich feathers. Last she wound her mother's watch and then hung it around her neck on a ribbon.

When James opened the door, he bowed deeply. "At your service," he said. "Are you wearing your walking shoes? Cause we're going to cover some ground."

"My skirts will act as sails, my love, and I'll float wherever we go," Sara said.

First they walked over to the confluence of the Kaw and Missouri rivers. They stuck to the side streets to avoid the crowds. The sun on their backs warmed their shoulders, and something about the morning light made everything look fresh and new and seemed to dispel the horrid odor. Along the way, birds sang and a magpie followed them for a bit, fluttering from post to wall to ground, its black and white feathers whirring and blurring in the sun. Sara and James climbed onto the wall by the shore and sat watching a huge steamship with its puffing smokestack and its churning paddle wheel methodically making its way past them and up the Missouri. After a bit, it disappeared around the point. Sara wondered how much time it took for such a conveyance to make its way from the outlet of the Mississippi up into the Missouri and then past Kansas City and as far as it could go across the continent. It must take months, she mused. She thought about the amount of time they had been in Kansas City, the way the season had turned to summer, and then it came to her. "What day is it?" she said, and then without waiting for an answer, she exclaimed, "It's my birthday!"

James's face opened in surprise and then composed. "I knew it all along," he said, though there was no way he could have.

"You did not. You are a liar," she said.

"You'll never know." They smiled at each other and linked hands.

They climbed down, walked for a while, and then clambered up onto the walkway next to the elevated cable car tracks and looked over the vast cattle yards rectangling into the distance. Some trick of the atmosphere muted the bellowing and lowing of the herds. In the pens, a sea of bony backs

251

rustled and bumped. Every once in a while one would breech and place its hooves on the beast in front of it. Sara wondered if it gave the cow relief, but she supposed it was an illusion. They couldn't have seen past the dirty boards to anything green beyond.

Sara and James made their way back through the city and decided to make the effort to conquer the steep bluffs. The hill was lined with stepped Queen Anne style row houses with bay windows that were interspersed with Romanesque standalone houses with cupolas and yards. It would be so wonderful to live in a house like these, Sara thought. She could hardly contain herself and talked a steady stream. James followed along, not nearly as excited but genial enough. They made it to the top of the steep hill, out of breathe and thighs aching, and then they stopped to view the West Bottoms. From this height, they could see all of it, with its smokestacks and factories and train tracks circumscribed by the rivers, the people like ants below. As they stood, a wonderful smell came to them, and they followed it and bought potato pierogis from a streetside vendor and then found a place to sit on a low wall. The steaming fried dumplings were hot and dripping with butter, and Sara and James came away with greasy hands. The world went about its business, and for a moment Sara felt outside and above it all, untouched. The air was cleaner up here and the future brighter.

A cable car pulled up to a nearby stop. It was midafternoon, so the car was mostly empty. James nodded to Sara, eyebrows raised, and they got on and paid the driver. "No. Sit up here," James said as he pulled her into the seats at the very front. "I've got something to show you." The trained lurched to a start and then chugged as it threaded its way along the narrow alley between tall buildings.

"You ready?" James asked.

"Ready for what?"

"Ready?" he asked again and put his hands over her eyes.

"What—" She struggled to pull free but then she felt the train jerk and screech and then the front dropped steeply into space. It dove over a cliff, and Sara was thrown forward, almost out of her seat, though James held her tightly. She felt suspended from a rope over a canyon, dropping into the abyss. The car screeched and groaned and creaked, speeding up as it went. The hair stood up on Sara's arms and neck. She yanked James's fingers from her eyes. There was the West Bottoms laying out below them, and rushing up to meet them was Union Depot.

"The Ninth Street Incline," James said.

Sara was sure that the brakes would fail, and she tried desperately not to think of the stories she had read of streetcar accidents on the hills of San Francisco. Soon, though, they were safely at the bottom, and the track leveled out and the train slowed. Sara fell back against the seat and breathed as if she had been taking exercise. Her legs shook as they dismounted the train, and once they were out she smoothed her dress and adjusted her hat. James laughed at her. "You're like a cat licking her fur—so dignified after tripping on her own tail." She jabbed him in the ribs but then laughed too. They walked from the train station down the boardwalk.

"One last thing," James said and turned down a side street. He opened the door to a shop with a sign that read, "Geo. Paulson, Portraits and Photoengravings." Bells on the door tinkled as they entered. The shop was only a small room with a couple of chairs, a high counter, and a curtained doorway at the back. "We never got a wedding portrait," James said.

"Oh, really?" Sara said. "Oh, James, that would be so lovely."

Just then a small thin clean-shaven man hurried into the room through the curtained doorway and bowed.

"Mister Paulson, we'd like our portrait taken," James said.

"Yes, Mister, Madame," the man said in a nasally voice. "Right this way." He took them back through the curtain into a shadowed back room that seemed larger than was possible. In the dim light along each wall were sets for portraits, and at the very back, short stairs led to a landing with a doorway draped with a curtain. Close to them was the set of an elegant dining room and farther was a couch with a large painting behind it, and farther still was a chair in front of fireplace and also a tromp l'oeil of a garden scene, yet another of mountains and a lake. Sara really liked the elegant dining room at the front, but James shook his head and whispered, "Too proper." He pointed to the mountain scene on the right at the back of the room, and she raised her eyebrows. She was not a bracing outdoor milkmaid. She pointed to the fireplace on the left and he shook his head. He shrugged and pointed to the garden scene on the left. She whispered, "My thumb is about as green as this floor." They made their way through all the sets and reached the back of the room without choosing one.

They turned to Mr. Paulson, who shook his head. "Mister, Madame," he said and gestured to the wall. "Humm. A blank wall, perhaps? To set off your outfits. And a staircase, perhaps? Showing your bright future ascending?" He arranged them against the wall. He had them stand squarely facing him, their hands clasped in front. He took James's hat and set it on the floor out of the way. He adjusted her chin and his stance. He adjusted the curtain at the back so it was slightly open. Then he brought the camera over and hunched underneath the machine's draping cloth. He moved the camera to the left and then back to the right.

Sara noted that the braided carpet underneath them was ragged on the edges. This image was for posterity, their wedding photo after all. Certainly they had started with little to their names, but she was sure that she would not want to be reminded of that fact forever. "Umm, Mister Paulson," Sara said. "I think the carpet, umm, maybe without it?"

"Oh no," Mr. Paulson said, coming out from under the drape. "A blank floor will reflect the light and you will look like islands. You need the darkness to ground you."

"But it needs mending," she said.

"I know the perfect solution," Mr. Paulson said. "A chair will cover it." He bustled over and grabbed the chair in front of the fireplace. He drug it over to the rug.

"I don't think ..." Sara started to say and then saw James's expression, which looked to be losing patience. Then she said, "No, no, that'll do fine, I think."

He rearranged them. He sat James in the chair, and James immediately crossed his legs.

"Your hands, mister, are hanging at your sides. Maybe fold them in your lap."

James slouched in the chair, and then started twiddling his thumbs irritably.

"You, Madame, on his left, maybe like this?" He pretended to put one elbow on James's shoulder.

Sara moved to that position but her hoops pressed against the chair.

"No, no," Mr. Paulson shook his head. "Madame, you look like a bell being rung. You do not want to look like a bell being rung." He came over and pulled her backwards. "Now, elbow on the Mister's shoulder."

She tried to but it wouldn't reach unless she bent forward.

"No, no, no," Mr. Paulson said. "Mister, please, up straight." He pulled James's shoulders back so that he looked like an awkward bird. "Now, Madame," he said and pushed her this way and that until her skirt hung almost straight and her elbow was on James's shoulder. He put her other arm behind her back and pulled her shoulders back. "Up straight, Madame," He said. Then he went to the camera, put his head under the drape, and adjusted it.

He stuck his head out from under the drape. "Now, both of you, imagine something nice. And hold still." He took the photo, the illumination blinding both of them. Mr. Paulson said, "It will be a number of days. Come back next week." Their portrait done, they came blinking out into the daylight.

"I think Mister Paulson prefers stuffed people," James said with a grin.

Sara snorted. "Much easier to arrange, one would think."

Still laughing, James said, "Oh, look!" He pointed to the green awning across the street. "Ice cream. I bet they have strawberry."

"And chocolate," Sara added.

They went into the shop and ordered their ice cream and sat near the window and watched people walk by. It was lovely. They were tired from their adventures, and it felt good to sit and let the world go by and partake of a such wonderful delicacy, cool and luscious on the tongue. They soon finished. The ice cream had chilled them, which was refreshing at first, but then Sara was cold, and so it felt good to walk out into the warm day again.

Chapter 8

s Sara and James made their way home, they saw a young girl in a white pinafore walking along dangling two red puppies with big floppy ears from her arms and talking to a man on the street. The man listened to what the girl said but then shook his head and walked off. As Sara and James came by, the girl turned to them and said, "Would you like a puppy? They don't cost nothing. My papa says he's going to throw them in the river if I don't find someone to take them on." At closer view, the puppies were indeed small but older than Sara had first believed. They were just beginning to lengthen into grown dogs.

As the full day of liberation left Sara with such a good feeling, she did not want to let this pass—it seemed like a good omen—so she said spontaneously, "Of course, we would love to have such fine specimen of a dog. That's so kind of you to try to save them." Relief crossed the girl's face, who said, "Would you take two, then?" Sara considered it but then glanced at James's face, which was contained but set. James did not want one dog, much less two. "Oh!" Sara said. "James, would a dog be all right?" James did not respond, so she said, "It could be my birthday present. Please? Just one." He stood for a minute and then relented with a small shake of his head.

Sara turned to the girl. "I'm sorry, but we can only take one of them off your hands." The girl handed over the larger of the two, a female, and Sara took its wriggling mass into her arms. Its skin felt too big for its body, which was warm and solid and alive, and Sara was immediately overcome with a maternal kind of love. "I think I'll name you Opal," she said. She turned to James and said, "Opal was my mother's name." He nodded, smilingly resigned to the new acquisition. Sara hummed the whole rest of the way home, holding close the alternately limp and wriggling warm body.

Opal filled their little apartment with enthusiastic motion. When first set down, she immediately put her nose to the floor and seemed led by it on a meandering path all through the space. It was as if the nose had a mind of its own and the dog's body merely followed on a tether. Opal nosed under the bed and behind the stove and put her paws up on the shelves and tried to sniff the dry goods. She made her way over to the bed and tried to leap onto it but made it only halfway before flopping onto her side on the floor. She stood back up and shook herself, undaunted, and continued to sniff about. After a time, even James seemed charmed by her earnest zeal as she nosed his ankles. As they were not particularly hungry, Sara made a light supper of cucumbers and tomatoes, in which Opal showed interest, and Sara had to push her away. As Sara peeled and sliced, she realized she had no idea what she would feed the dog. She had seen advertised Spratt's Patented Meat Fibrine Dog Cakes, but they could hardly afford to feed themselves, much less buy expensive specialty items for a canine. It would have to be leftovers from the table, then, though she had previously done her best to apportion things so that there were very little that was left over and nothing went bad, even if she had to stomach a dish that hadn't turned out very well.

When Sara threw the cucumber peels into the garbage bucket, the dog knocked it over with her attempts to get at them, and so James rose to take it out immediately. "Hungry little monger, aren't you?" Sara said. "What shall we feed you?" She glanced at James's face as he let himself out the door. He raised his eyebrows and nodded his head in such a way as to convey to Sara that that was precisely what he had been thinking all along. But then he shrugged and shut the door against Opal, who tried to follow him. Deprived of her target, she went to the corner next to Sara's side of the bed and walked in circles around and around before settling on the bare floor. When James returned, he and Sara sat down to their supper. Opal came over and would not leave them alone, insistently staring up at them with soulful eyes and pawing at their legs. "I'll impart better manners," Sara assured James as they tied a cord around her neck and to the head bedpost, where Opal pulled against it for a time, whining, and then once again settled down. After supper, Sara untied her and gave her a scrap of hard bread crust and leftover boiled potatoes on a layer of newspaper, which the dog wolfed down without hesitation and then lapped from the dish of water that Sara had put down. As they got ready for bed, she took the dog out to do its business, and Opal obediently squatted in the yard and peed.

After they were in bed, the dog once again circled and lay down on Sara's side. Sara snuggled into James's chest, who put his arms around her. She said, "Thank you so much for the present, for your generosity, despite any misgivings you might have."

"Anything for my queen for the day," came his answer.

In the middle of the night, they were shocked awake by a

mournful howl. At first, Sara had no idea what was happening. It was like a wolf baying at the moon, only it was loud and right next to them, within the apartment itself. They both sat up in bed. Then Sara heard the click-click-click of dog claws and once again, more softly this time, came the distinct drawn-out full-throated baying.

"What in the world?" Sara said.

"Well, that just proves she's a hound of some sort," James said.

"A what?"

"A hound dog. A hunting dog like a coon hound or a bloodhound."

"Ah, she's lonely," Sara said.

"Or she needs to go out," James said and rolled over with his back to her to go to sleep.

Sara snorted and got up and tied the cord around the dog's neck and took her out. Opal obediently squatted and peed and pooped. James was again asleep when Sara returned and snuggled into bed next to him.

Thus began Sara's new passion for everything dog. She struck up conversations with people on the street who were accompanied by dogs, and when they had an extra penny she tracked down the cat's meat man and haggled vigorously for the least disgusting contents of his wheel barrow, which James assured her was the decayed flesh of horses who dropped dead in the streets. She introduced Opal to Auntie, who just shook her head and said, "You be wanting a child." Sara tracked down a receipt for hard tack from an old man who swept front stoops for coins—some said he'd campaigned beside Napoleon as a drummer boy. The original directions were nothing more than a dough of flour, water, and salt rolled out, cut into rectangles, pierced with a fork, and then baked into a hard cracker, but Sara added stock or bacon fat or mashed vegetables or even animal blood, if she could get any. Opal loved the biscuits and would stare at the shelf where they were stored.

James scowled and growled at first but soon he too would pat the dog on ears when he came home, and he sometimes volunteered to take her out for her morning or evening constitutional. He attempted to teach her to fetch a stick, which she ignored, but he took it in stride and instead taught her to search out things that he or Sara had touched. "Find it!" he would say as he released her from the cord around her neck, and then once she got the hang of it she would locate the object without fail. When James returned from these communal treks, he would whistle as he washed up for supper.

After a few weeks, Sara remembered to stop back by the portrait studio and pick up the photo. Her impression of the image was that they both looked startled and lost, which was not at all her fond memory of the day.

Chapter 9

ne gray and drizzly day, James was out looking for work. The boardwalk made water-dulled thumps as he walked, rain dripped off his hat and down the neck of his jacket, and thick mud coated his boots. The awnings of the stores did little to keep him dry, as the wind blew the moisture in sideways, but he stopped and leaned against a wall anyway.

Bam! A loud noise startled James. At first he thought it was a screen door whapping shut, but then Bam, Bam!—the sound was unmistakable. Gun shots. They came from next door, that doggery, Boyer's Saloon. The door scraped open and a man in a policeman's uniform stumbled out through the opening, across the boardwalk, and then fell off into a large puddle. There was no outward evidence of wounds—no blood yet showing—but his movements were proof enough. He landed on his knees and managed to push his feet under himself, but that foot slipped and he fell forward onto his belly. Then, something worse than the frantic discoordination—the brown pool of muddy water around the man's shoulders swirled bright red. The man struggled feebly to raise himself from the puddle, quickly becoming weaker and weaker, until it was all he could do to keep his face above the water, though his limbs shook with the effort. He struggled a bit more and then succumbed. His face sank below its surface.

James's first impulse was to go and help the man, but then he didn't. This was a policeman, and so the circumstances of his shooting were sure to be convoluted, and it was Boyer's from which this man ejected, where unsavory characters were sure to abound. James was an ex-convict, and involving himself in this manner would inevitably cause much complication in his life and possibly even endanger Sara. This he told himself as he stood and watched the policemen quiver with the effort to keep his head above the water.

Across the street, a man jumped from the boardwalk and hurried over to the policeman. The man was large and wore a brown suit and a bowler hat. James caught a glimpse of his countenance—it was Moses Thaxton. Moses quickly knelt and pulled the man's face from the water and then grabbed his shoulders, pulled him from the puddle, and rolled him over. The man no longer struggled to breathe nor moved at all, though Moses put his face down next to the man's mouth evidently to check, but by the looks of him, he was past that. James should have been the one to do what Moses had done. Shame made him cringe, but still he hung back.

Then it all unfolded very quickly. At the first sound of the gunshot, people in the busy street had stopped. When the policeman fell into the muck, they had stared and glanced around, looking for perpetrators, perhaps, or looking to their neighbors to see whom would step forward. No one else did, only Moses. People saw the policeman's uniform and talked excitedly to each other, and then more people gathered, and soon there was a crowd whose faces twisted with concern and then quickly turned to anger as they saw Moses. Then one man from across the street stepped forward, pointed his finger, and looked back at the crowd behind him. "It's the nigger!" he said. "He's the one that done it!" Moses, who had been concentrating on the man, glanced up and then saw the crowd. A look of terror crossed his face, his eyes saucers, his jaw slack. He pushed himself back onto his knees and held his hands up, fingers spread in front his body. Keeping his hands there, he moved his foot under himself and pushed to standing and then held up his hands as if someone had a gun trained on him. He slowly looked around at the crowd, who at first hushed and then at once began murmuring and shouting.

Someone said "Get him!" but just then three policeman came running up. One of them blew a whistle, and when the crowd realized it was the law, they hung back. The crowd's faces showed guilt, anger, and feigned innocence. "Now, listen here," a policeman shouted. "You all go about your business. Nothing to concern you here." Moses said a few words to the policeman and then gestured to Boyer's and another of the policeman went inside, gun drawn. The one continued to talk intently with Moses for a minute, then he and the third policeman led him away. Relieved of its target, the crowd seethed. They talked loudly and tagged along after Moses and the two policeman. James followed well behind as they made their way down the street and then on to a jail. They took Moses inside and shut the door behind them. The people stood outside and milled. Time passed. Some found seats, but by late afternoon, the crowd had swelled to fill the street outside the jail. A couple of boys climbed up on the fence opposite. James found a place a little ways down an alley where he could see the crowd in front of the jail. Eventually, a group of thirteen men assembled, shouldering the courage of the crowd. One of them walked into the jail. After a while, he came back out, shaking his head. "They won't give him to us," he said loudly to the crowd, and a murmur rose. Then the sheriff himself stepped out and began orating. He explained that this negro man that was being held was not a suspect at this time, that he had not even witnessed the crime and had simply been acting out of goodness for his fellow man. The police were just holding him for questioning. To this last statement the crowd murmured angrily.

The sheriff went back in, and then a little while later he came back out with five deputies and a man in their midst with his face covered by a handkerchief and his hat pulled low. This man wasn't Moses, James could tell, as he wore overalls and his frame was not nearly as large. A white man, as it turned out. James had the quick thought: What man was so foolish and so brave as to put himself in the shoes of someone who was the focus of such rage, simply to save a fellow human being? It was a thought that further shamed James. The crowd was fooled but for a moment. They surged forward and pressed against the deputies. Then someone shouted, "That's not him!" and the crowd realized that they'd been fooled. They surged past and into the jail. There was shouting and disturbance, and then they came back out dragging Moses. By this time he wasn't wearing his bowler or jacket, and his shirt hung cockeyed upon him. His face was bloody and mashed, his expression matching the blank darkness of the sky. The crowd surrounded him and swallowed him whole, though even beaten down he towered over them. The sheriff and policemen drew their guns, but it was no use. Unless they were prepared to fire into the crowd, there was nothing they could do, no matter how they tried to press their way through. What could James do?

265

Nothing.

He followed the crowd. The late afternoon light was fading, and the moon rose and glowed like a fired pine knot. When the crowd got to the Bluff Bridge, one man produced a rope and another stood on the railing and tossed it over the supports above. They spent some time tying a knot in the end, handing it back and forth and discussing between themselves the proper way to tie a noose, but then they had it tied and they put a rope around Moses's neck and forced him to climb the railing. At first Moses refused, but the men beat him until he attempted it. The rain made the rail slippery, and it took a couple of tries for him to accomplish the task. James hoped the rope would snap his neck so that it would be over expeditiously and Moses would not suffer unnecessarily, but the affair did not get that far. Someone fired a shot into Moses's chest, which propelled him up and back and off the bridge. Some in the crowd cheered. After a time, they pulled the body up and propped it against the railing. Someone fetched a photographer and others fetched lamps, and they all took turns holding an umbrella over the photographer and posing in the rain next to the body.

James had seen enough. As he left, he saw a large group of policeman standing off to one side. They had been there the whole time, doing nothing just as he had. The world was a horrible place and the good character of men was simply an illusion. And so James found a saloon and got stinking drunk.

Chapter 10

arly the next morning, James told Sara what had happened. He said Moses Thaxton had been lynched and shot, though Moses had not done the deed he had been suspected of. When Sara pressed him for details he shook his head. "You do not want to know," he said. He had gotten in late the night before, after Sara had gone to sleep listening to Opal's soft snores, and this morning he had woken with a headache that kept him in bed.

"Do you think Auntie knows?" Sara said. "I had better check on her." She went down the hall but hesitated outside Auntie's door. What was she going to do? How does one cushion the blow of a dead loved one? She did not know, but she knocked on the door anyway.

Auntie opened the door, and when she saw Sara she smiled. "Well, do come in, girl," she said. "I was just making some cornbread. Moses and his wife are coming to supper." She led Sara into the kitchen. "Did I tell you about his wife? It was all so sudden—he got married just the other day, you see," and then she whispered, "a baby well on the way, you know." Her voice was steeped with excited pride. "A grandmammy at last. He married a right classy lady from Saint Louis. Her father is a doctor, they tell me." Sara followed Auntie into the kitchen.

She wanted to stop Auntie from saying all these things because it hurt to hear them.

"Auntie, please," she said. "I have some bad news. Won't you sit down?"

"Sit down? Girl, I'm in the middle of making cornbread. You'll just have to wait till I pop it in the oven." However, Auntie must have sensed something because her voice trailed off and she slowly dropped into a chair. "What's the matter? What is it?"

"I truly don't know how to tell you." She hesitated and then said, "Have you heard from Moses today?"

"Moses? Why, no. As I said, he is calling this evening."

"But Auntie, he won't be, calling that is. I don't know how to tell you. Moses is dead. James, my husband, he saw it happen, last night."

"Dead. What? Dead? No. You're talking foolish. You see, he just stopped by yesterday morning, and he and his wife will be here for supper," Auntie replied, her eyes misbelieving.

"No, Auntie." Sara said. "I am so sorry. James was downtown. A policeman was shot. Moses didn't do it, but it didn't matter. The crowd"—of white people, she couldn't say it— "didn't believe it though. But James saw the whole thing and Moses didn't do it. But the crowd, they killed him. Oh, I'm so sorry."

Auntie's face scrunched with concern. "You must be mistaken, because, as I said …" Her voice trailed off and she thought for a minute and then looked back at Sara's face. Sara tried to convey her concern, her veracity, her empathy, all in glance. "He was a fine man," she said. "In no way deserving of such a terrible fate. I can't begin to …" Auntie continued to take it in, eyes on Sara's face but unseeing, and then she bowed her head and stared at her hands in her lap. She put her head to one side and let out a quiet wail, "Eeeeeeeeeee!" It started high and then fell to a lower register. Her body began to rock and sway. Then came her voice, high again, "Eeeeeeeee!" and wavered there. Her face was scrunched in pain. "Eeeeeeee!" Auntie's voice rose, louder and louder, until it filled the room to the rafters and then sputtered to a stop. It continued on, as Auntie's world was overcome with grief. It was as if Auntie had been preparing herself for this moment for a long time, as if she had feared it and now that it had happened she was ready to believe it. She abandoned herself to it.

Sara sat with Auntie for a long time. She didn't know what to do to comfort the old woman, so she got up and made tea. She put the water on to boil and searched through the cupboards. She found a small paper package labeled "lapsang" and poured in the loose leaves. Dark undertones for dark times, she thought. She put in spoonfuls of sugar. Auntie, though, did not touch her cup and simply sat there rocking and crooning.

"Is there anything I can do, Auntie?" Sara asked after a while. "Anyone I can send for?"

Auntie shook her head and choked as she said, "They'll be coming for me soon enough." Sara stayed with her for a while longer and then returned to her own apartment, assuring Auntie that she was just down the hall if she needed anything. James had left the morning's *Kansas City Times* on the table. Holding Opal in her lap, who for once lay tranquilly, Sara searched the front page to see if there was a mention. There was. It recapped what James had said, though they seemed to think Moses was the perpetrator. Lower on the page, though, was another story that reported that the negro people had rioted because the wrong man had been lynched.

269

She put Opal on the floor and felt a self-righteous anger grow within her. She could not help but think about her brief meeting with Moses and how he seemed the noble negro, the original Uncle Tom who through Christian faith cared for the people around him. Moses had given lodging to a white couple in desperate need, and then it was a mob of whites who did him in. Sara then determined that she would attend Moses's funeral. She was not one of those offensive individuals who did not believe in the humanity of the black race. Maybe once upon a time she had not much considered the idea, but now she knew from personal experience that negros and whites were cut from the same sacred cloth. She would attend the funeral out of respect for Auntie and all the help she had given her and also to represent those of her race with more generous sympathies. So, later that day, when she heard steps on the stairs, people coming and going past her door, she poked her head out. She saw a well-dressed black woman tapping on Auntie's door. "Excuse me," Sara called, "but when and where will Mister Thaxton's funeral be held?" The woman raised here eyebrows but after a second's hesitation imparted the information. Sara thanked her.

The day of the funeral, James left for work, and once again Sara put on her best black dress. Opal was excited, anticipating being taken out, but the dog would have to be left behind in the apartment. Sara hoped that she would be back in time so that Opal would not mess on the floor. She had not told James of her plans. She not sure exactly why. Perhaps it was because she was not sure how James felt about negroes. He seemed cordial when she mentioned Auntie, neither censorial nor particularly interested. Sara certainly knew how her father would have felt about it, and perhaps it was that guilt that made Sara keep her own council. Perhaps too she was afraid that James would forbid her to go, and she very much wanted to present herself as token of goodness. And, perhaps, deep down, she had a more personal reason to go, one that she would not admit to anyone, least of all herself, which was this: the one time she had met Moses, he had been such a compelling figure of a man. How could a person of such strength and vitality no longer exist in this world? She wanted to witness for herself.

Thunderheads with swollen blue-black bottoms were gathering when Sara came out into the daylight. It would storm soon, but for now the sun still shone warmly. The funeral was being held in a church all the way over by Goose Island—the policeman on the street had hesitated and wrinkled his forehead when she had asked about the address—so Sara took a cable car, even though they could not really afford it. Sara fretted that she hadn't brought an umbrella and that Opal would not be able to hold her water until Sara got home. She wondered where in the city James was working that day. After a circuitous route, across the Kansas River, up the bluff, and around through the residences, the cable car finally came to her stop. As she stepped down, the cable car operator said loudly, "Ma'am? Are you sure this is where you want to go, ma'am?"

"Yes, of course," she said. Did he think her such a ninny as to not know her own purpose?

He shook his head and said nothing. As the cable car rumbled off, Sara straightened her skirt and took in her surroundings. It was an area of residential structures, modest but better than the small dilapidated dwellings in the Patch where she lived. By comparison, they looked quite stately, and they even had yards, though only a few were fenced. An ancient coloured man sat leaning forward with his hands propped on a cane across the way on a house stoop. He stared at her unwaveringly. How rude, Sara thought. Even as she turned the direction she supposed was the church, his eyes followed her. She walked to the end of the block and then turned and crossed the street to find the address, and there was the church, a white clapboard structure—the only thing distinguishing it from a narrow house were the double doors on the front and the small steeple with a bell on the roof peak. There was also a sign hanging from a wrought iron support upon which was written Brown's Chapel Free Will Baptist Church. A coloured man and a woman stood on the walkway. When they spied her, they stopped and stared, the woman politely, the man with a stony look on his face. Sara smiled politely at them, but they didn't respond and, if anything, withdrew. Maybe this had not been such a good idea after all. Sara continued past them and made her way up the steps. The first drops of rain spattered against the shake shingles as she let herself into the foyer as quietly as she could. The doors to the main chapel in front of her were open, and through them Sara could see rows of people seated in the benches, some dressed in black, some in white, and many of the women in elaborate hats.

The preacher, a tall man with a vaguely French-looking mustache and goatee, was on the pulpit, his voice booming, rising and falling with emotion. In front of him was the large casket that was draped in a black fringed cloth. "When Job was in the depths of despair," he said, "was he afraid?"

"Yes!" said members of the congregation, their voices holding conviction and shuddering with feeling.

"Did he not say Lord?" the preacher said.

"Lord, Lord!" the congregation said.

272

"Did he not say Lord?"

"He said Lord!"

"He said Lord, why hast thou done this to me?"

"Amen!"

"Behold, the fear of the Lord is wisdom, and to depart from evil is understanding!"

"Amen!"

"Salvation comes from the Lord!"

Sara stood mesmerized by the scene. She had never seen so much energy in a church, so much movement. Emotion crackled in the air. People shouted and stomped their feet and waved their fans. The rhythm of the words washing over her, Sara took a step forward. "I would not go in there, if I was you," came a voice at her left elbow. Sara started and glanced down. Sitting on a bench was a young negro woman with a suckling baby in her arms. The woman was small but amply built. Sara's eyes fixed on the side of her round breast and the baby's vigorous sucking motions but then Sara caught herself and tore her eyes away, embarrassed.

"What?" Sara said.

"I said, I would not go in there, if I was you."

"What do you mean? I'm a friend of the family's, of Auntie's." Sara felt foolish—What was Auntie's real name? She had no idea.

The woman pulled the baby from her breast. As the woman held the baby with one hand and rearranged her clothes, the baby smacked its lips contentedly. "I'm just saying, I would not go in there just now, you being a white woman."

"I came to pay my respects," Sara said, straightening her shoulders.

"Whether or no you respect a black man, you had not better

273

go in there."

Ignoring the woman, Sara stepped into the chapel, which held the fusty odors of a crowd closely packed. She stopped and stood at the back, just as the preacher continued, "Jonah was angry. Lord, he said, I'm angry enough to die! Take away my life, for it is better for me to die than to live!" Sara was pushed roughly from behind, causing her to stumbled sideways. The woman with the baby pushed past her and walked noisily down the aisle. As the woman passed by, people turned their heads and looked. She continued until she reached the front pew, where she knelt and whispered to someone seated there. The people glanced from the woman to the back of the church where Sara stood. One by one their eyes turned and fixed on Sara.

The preacher stopped speaking. There was nary a light-skinned face in the crowd. All eyes focused on her, intent, narrowed. For a long moment, there was silence, and no one moved. Then, someone did stand up, a tall thin woman on the right. Those around her joined her, and others, and soon everyone in the room was on their feet in a wave and a rush. There was the thump of people bumping the pews and the rustle of clothing, followed by a loud bang as someone dropped something, causing Sara to jump, but then it was quiet again. Sara looked from face to face. She had rarely seen such raw emotion. Fear shot through her. All that emotion was focused solely upon her. What were they capable of? Had they truly been rioting? She could now believe it. And, really, what had she expected? To them, she was a white woman, representative of the white race, and one that had the temerity to impose herself on their private grief. But that is not what I intended, she cried silently. I meant for the best.

A large woman stepped forward and grabbed Sara's arm and held it, and Sara tried to pull away, but another smaller woman stepped forward held her other side with a fierce grip. "What is God's name do you think you are doing?" the first woman hissed. "You defile our church just as you defile our men." She pulled her roughly backwards so that Sara lost her footing. The noise of the crowd rose and undulated, an angry murmuring, though Sara could not make out the words. The women did not wait for her to regain her footing and instead dragged her along as she scrambled backwards trying to get her feet under her and ripping the back of her skirts. People with enraged faces crowded in after them, and Sara feared that in a moment they would take up her feet and then rip her limb from limb. With so many eyes, there would be no witnesses, yet so many witnesses, just as it had been with Moses.

But then Auntie, leaning upon the arm of a young woman, appeared before her. Auntie's face was changed since the last time she had seen her. It had been dragged earthward under the weight of its grief. "Shshshshshshshshsh," Auntie said loudly to the two women and to the crowd, raising her free hand and patting at the air. "Shshshshshshshshsh." It visibly affected the crowd. They no longer stood forward on the balls of their toes, and they glanced from Auntie to Sara and back. Seeming suddenly very tall, Auntie looked down at where Sara hung from the women's arms. "Sara," Auntie said, "You go along." There was iron in that voice. She nodded to the two women, who simultaneously let Sara drop to the floor. "You go on." Auntie's voice came softer.

Sara got her feet underneath her and straightened her skirts and her shoulders and took one last look at Auntie. Then she turned and pushed out of the church and into the pelting rain.

Fear and relief were upon her, and she ran unheedingly, her feet splashing through puddles. Her dress became soaked through with the rain, clumps of mud hung from the hem, and her shoes became heavy with the weight of it. She ran on until, breathless, she could not manage, and then she slowed and walked quickly toward home. Now she knew. She had been so naïve. It didn't matter that she and Auntie were friends and neighbors. That tender bond of mutual affection was simply irrelevant. The historical weight of it would get in the way, today, tomorrow, perhaps always. And she began crying— whether for herself or for Auntie or for Moses, she did not know.

Chapter 11

hough James felt guilty about the time away and the money spent, he began stopping by a saloon earlier and earlier, especially if he did not find employment for that day. It was either that or do something more drastic, he reasoned. Just a bit of respite, he thought. He tried this establishment and that, but then he happened upon the Climax Saloon, which was not far from the apartment. It was tiny, just a few stools and a table or two. The first time James frequented the establishment, the proprietor, who resembled a large egg on very tall stilts, enthusiastically chomped his cigar and patted his ample belly as he regaled two men who stood at the bar. James slumped onto a stool and took off his hat and laid it on the bar. The bartender interrupted his telling to make his way down to serve James, who did not make eye contact as he ordered whiskey, neat.

A smile in his voice, the bartender said, "I'm Jim. People call me Big Jim. Haven't seen you in this fine establishment before. New in town?"

"No," James said, gulped his whiskey, and set the glass on the bar, indicating that it should be refilled.

The bartender poured another drink and said, "That's on me." He chuckled, "I was just telling old Joe and Karl here about the shooting and hanging. Shot and hung all at once. Guess they wanted the job done right."

The taller of the two patrons moved down the bar. He was thin, with a broad weatherworn face and squinting eyes that formed a peak at his central brow and a full drooping mustache. He wore no tie nor collar on his white shirt and his pants showed wear at the knees. "*Joseph*," he said to the bartender. "I ain't Joe. *James*," he said, speaking to the bartender. His voice held a bit of an accent, some vowels rounded, some cut short. He grinned and winked at James. The other patron followed down the bar. He was a smaller, broader version of the other patron, though he was clean-shaven and wore round spectacles.

The bartender said good naturedly, "My father hear you say that, he would likely as not beat the daylights out of you, soon as look at you." He turned to James. "What'll we call you?"

"Name's James," James said.

"Jim it is, then," Joseph said. "There'll be two of you." Then he laughed deep in his belly, which rose to his chest, his whole body moving with it. It was a contagious laugh, even against one's will, and James felt it catch hold of him and lift his mood.

"We'll take another smile," Joseph said, pushing his glass forward and then nodding also at James's.

The bartender poured them all refills and then one for himself and toasted with it. "To Joe and James and Jim and … What'll we call you, Karl?" he asked the other man.

"Karl," Karl said, in a surprisingly deep voice.

Joseph and Jim hooted with laughter. James found himself smiling.

"To Karl," Joseph said and drank. The bartender drained

his glass and then nodded to them as he went to wait on a table.

"It is a pleasure to meet you, James. So, what brings you to the finest establishment in all of KC?" Joseph said. "What do you do?"

"Not much. And that is a problem," James said.

"Job hunting, eh?" Joseph said. "Looks like it's hunting you." He glanced at Karl, who nodded.

James nodded in agreement.

"It's a wicked and wondrous world," Joseph said.

James began to regularly frequent the Climax Saloon, so named for a race horse and Big Jim's betting luck. James often met up with Joseph and Karl. If he was the first to arrive, they would join him at his table, and if he came in after they, they waved him over without hesitation. Joseph and Karl were brothers by the last name of Soijka from the area of southern Silesia on the European continent. Their father claimed lineage to good King Wenceslaus the Second, they said, and their mother's family had moved up from the Hungarian empire. Joseph and Karl were two of fourteen children. When Joseph was not much out of his boyhood, he had been caught in a raid and conscripted into the Austrian Army, only to escape one night back to his native village. His family had quickly consulted and decided their salvation lay in sending Joseph to the west in hopes that he could find passage to America, and at the last possible minute they also consented that Karl should accompany Joseph, giving their sons their last florin. Eventually, the whole Soijka family, those who had not died in the cholera epidemic of 1867, had immigrated and settled in eastern Missouri.

One night at the Climax, James, Joseph, Karl, and another man sat around a table and drinking and playing cards. They'd

279

just dealt a hand when a group of people entered the bar. Joseph let out a long low whistle. "What a fine piece of cat meat. Sure enough sell yourself down the river." The fourth man at their table, who was a married man like James, took one look, shook his head, laid down his cards, and stood up. "I am off to the pisser," he said. James, who was seated with his back to the door, turned to look. First in the group was a short round pale man in tails and a top hat. Despite the man's broad girth—he had narrow shoulders, a ballooning belly, and scrawny legs—the suit fit him well, though the cummerbund was forced into submission below his belly. His shoulders were thrown back, and his head stood high on a bulging neck. As he made his way to the bar, he smiled and looked from man to man, taking them in, sizing them up, and if any man held his eye, he slowed for a moment and fixed them with a stare before moving on.

Just behind him was a most beautiful honey-toned woman, who was a full head taller than the man and dressed in an elaborate ball gown of a rich purple satin overlaid with a fine black lace in a floral pattern. It was cut almost indecently low on the shoulders, with only bells for sleeves, and the high waist did not disguise the fact that the woman was far along with child. Around the woman's neck and nestling between her large breasts was an elaborate necklace, diamonds upon diamonds dropping down in long loops that flashed in the gaslight. Like the man, she too held her head high and her shoulders thrown back. As she followed the man, she laughed, a high tinkling that elongated and then descended to a low husky whisper. The woman removed her black lace wrap and draped it over her arm, allowing every man in the bar to take in the long sweep of her neck and the delicate curve of her shoulders and the heaving swell of her breast. The couple was followed by two very tall, very broad men whose aggressive natures were writ large on their well-dressed bodies.

Reacting quickly, Big Jim had a drink poured and placed on a cork coaster before the round man even stepped up and put his foot on the railing. Big Jim bowed twice with his head as the man approached. "Pendergast!" the short man said. "It is once again nice to see such a fine figure of a man." He patted his belly with one hand as he removed his top hat with the other, which he set upon the bar. "I was touring around and I said to myself, what better place to showcase our fine city than the intimate milieu of this fine establishment. Let me formally introduce you to an associate of mine." He stepped back and held up his hand to allow the woman to step forward. "Mister Pendergast, I would like to introduce you to Missus Thaxton." His face became serious. "Unfortunately, she has recently found herself a widow, and I was attempting to raise her spirits."

"A pleasure to make your acquaintance, I am sure," the woman said and held out her hand, which Big Jim took and bowed his head and kissed firmly but politely.

"Very commendable of you, sir," Big Jim said to the man. "And what may I get the lady?"

"She will have a brandy for her nerves, I think," he said, eyeing her in such a way as not to ask her approval but instead to show that he had the right to observe her in this way.

James knew who the woman was, of course. Unlike Moses, however, James did not pity this man. He seemed to have everything in hand, and it might be the beautiful lady who had to watch herself.

The man and Big Jim continued to chat, while the widowed

Mrs. Thaxton hooked one elbow on the bar, the rest of her frame relaxing into an angular curve. Over her shoulder, she looked from man to man until her eyes rested upon James's face. They stopped there, and a smile came to her lips. James met her gaze and didn't look away. She calmly looked into his eyes and then cast her eyes down over his shoulders and torso, which were twisted to look at her, to the floor and then slowly back up to his eyes and held. It was then that James let his drop. She laughed again, a high tinkling that fell down, down, to a soft low whisper, and then she turned to her gentleman friend and ignored the room.

Another week, another day, James, Joseph, and Karl sat drinking and taking turns playing at the cards, Karl quietly winning per usual, but in such a way that neither of the other men much minded.

Joseph looked at Karl for a long minute and then said, "What you say, Karl? Let him in on it?"

Without looking up from his hand, Karl shrugged and tipped his head as if to say sure, why not?

Joseph turned to James. "You seem yet to be struggling with your employment prospects."

James nodded and shrugged. It was true.

With a final glance at Karl, Joseph said, "We got a job that we do regular like. It's not in any way pleasant, but it pays well. You are able to handle yourself. You interested?"

"Yes," James said, trying to keep the depths of his gratitude and desperation from his voice.

"But before you say yes," Joseph continued, "it ain't exactly what you call legal." He raised his eyebrows.

Just what James needed, to be thrown once again into prison for shady dealings. The way his luck was running, he would quickly be caught and incarcerated. He sighed. However, the thought of steady employ and working with these two amiable men quickly overwhelmed any objections. James couldn't remember the last time he'd felt this good about other men.

Joseph sensed James's hesitation. "It ain't illegal for us," he said. "It's illegal for them, our employers." James nodded, listening. "Well, technically, I suppose it's below the board for us too, but it is not us the law would go after. They want the big boys. You see, there is parts of a cow that most people would not eat, if they were to know what they were eating, see? And there is parts of a cow that nobody would eat, excepting if it's put in a nice pickling brine or stuffed into a sausage." Joseph's tone was very reasonable. Karl nodded and smiled in agreement. "It's illegal for the packing factories to do it, but they do, and they pay us pretty well to take care of it for them. Huh, Karl." Karl nodded again.

"Is it regular work?" Perhaps if it were illegal, the pay at least would be decent on account of the danger of being caught.

"Need you ask? How many cows you think go through those packing factories in a day?" Joseph said. "We do, however, wait until the sun sinks low before we perform our duties." He smiled. "So, what do you think? Agreed?"

Without hesitation, James agreed.

And so it was the next day that James met the Soijka brothers in a narrow alley behind the Armour Packing Company as the sun sank below the horizon, Joseph toting a coal oil lamp. James had explained to Sara that his job situation had taken a turn for the better—if everything panned out, they would have regular money coming in—but that his hours has shifted to the evenings. She had said nothing in response, though she looked at him sideways with her forehead scrunched. "It will be much better," he assured her, and he had hoped that it was true. At the packing plant, Joseph brought out a key and opened a recessed door, carefully locking it behind them, and they made their way through almost-deserted stairs, hallways, and rooms, some with the wet fresh smell of meat, some that stank of ripe blood and viscera and feces. Their breath wisping white in the chill, they walked through a low-ceilinged cavern of a room that was scored into alleys by long wooden trenches. Along the ceiling tracing the trenches were gantries with chains and hooks for hoisting carcasses. James's boots alternately sloshed and slapped and peeled from the pools of murky liquid, which were being pushed into holes in the floor by the few straggling men. Others wielded hoses and brushes and washed the benches and floor. Joseph nodded to one of the men and said, "Evening, Jurgis." The man raised a hand and nodded.

The three men left the huge room and once again wound their way down through a maze of corridors, down a series of stairs, and into the windowless bowels of the factory machine, Joseph stopping briefly to light the lamp. They reached their destination—a long and narrow windowless room with a tall counter under a gantry. As Joseph held the lamp aloft in the gloom, Karl pushed something upwards on the wall—*kachunk*. In response, a dim glow sparked in the center of the room. It was a single bulbous light. It took James a moment to realize that these were the lamps that were driven by electricity. There had been rumors of them coming into the Additional Penitentiary before his leaving, but he had not yet seen them. He had heard that, back East, they were as common as horse carts, every city employing them in their central areas. James walked over to the bulb and reached up and tapped it. It was surprisingly warm, even in that short period of illumination.

"I wouldn't do that if I were you," Joseph said. "They're a bit temperamental. Break it, and they charge us an arm and a leg and we still have to do our work by the coal oil."

James nodded and took a step back. For all the hoopla, it did not impress him much. You could get more light from a candle, he thought. Joseph blew out the lamp.

"And it ain't enough light to keep you from slicing off a thumb," Karl said, handing James a huge cleaver with a long handle like an axe. "Modern miracle or no."

Joseph snorted in agreement and said, "It won't keep away what you can't observe, neither. Best to keep from cutting yourself at all, if you can help it. There's nasties that can't be seen."

Then he walked over and unlatched and opened a tall door with a small channel above it set high in the wall. He unwound a chain from a set of hooks and pulled on it, causing it to rattle along its traces. Karl joined him in the tugging, and soon cattle carcasses hung by the back hocks issued from the door. Of course, James had butchered before, working among rural farms as he had. A cow carcass generally showed ruddy striations where the muscles were covered by a sheen of viscera and showed white where the bone and tendons emerged from the muscle. The muscle was firm and taut and sprang back to the touch, cool and dry, smelling like wet grass in a shady spot, with symmetrical graceful curves and a layer of white fat frosting the rib cage. These that jerked along on the chain looked nothing like that. Some showed yellow and green striations in their muscle, some were lopsided or missing limbs or parts, some had deep gashes along their sides that were coated with a thick black crust, some were overly small and some overly large, and some looked suspiciously normal. A wave of odor washed over James. The stench of sickly putrid meat, like the contents of the cats meat man's wheelbarrow. James sucked his breath through his mouth in short bursts to avoid its subjugation.

"Downers," Joseph said and nodded. "Beauts, aren't they? I do believe you might be buying the family's meat from now on," he added, chuckling.

Karl picked up his carcass blade and moved next to the line and began work. Joseph showed James his job, which was to pull the chain to move the carcasses, with Karl's help if necessary, and then to use the huge cleaver to chop off the most disgusting parts and flip them into a waste tub. He pointed out a low rack with a handsaw and hack knife and other tools to help with the work. Next, Karl walked along the right-hand side and made a series of cuts to break up the carcass, and Joseph made a similar series of cuts on the left-hand side. They halved and quartered the animals and then chopped them down further into large cuts of meat. They dumped them into one of two wheelbarrows—one for the indistinguishable that was taken to blend in with the other meats, and another for the disgusting that was taken to sausage production. Some cuts brought about a lively discussion of the merits and demerits of that particular specimen and the barrow to which it belonged. The waste went to the bone meal works. It was all about maximizing output, about volume, Joseph said. All but the moo, Karl added.

They soon developed a rhythm, though at first it was all James could do to keep up with the brothers. He chopped as quickly as he could, but Karl seemed to be right on his heels all the time. No sooner would he walk down the line with a chunk and a scrrrrrrape and a whap, then he would set down his cleaver, careful not to cut himself nor to hit the blade anywhere, which would dull it and expose it to further filth, and then grab the chain to move the next series of carcasses through the door, the empty hooks disappearing through the wall opposite. After much effort, he began to get the hang of it. Soon he was able to glance over and watch as Joseph and Karl worked. Their timing was perfect and they kept up a lively banter as they went. The carcasses swung wide as Karl batted them one way and Joseph batted them back. Karl swung his cleaver and whistled and grunted and yelled, "Yours, Joseph," and "Watch her, she's a'swinging." Joseph followed in perfect time with "Right back atcha." On it went, Karl on one side, Joseph on the other, and James imagined he heard a waltz in the background, with a chop, step, swing … chop, step, swing. And they included him in the banter. They grinned as they ejaculated, "Did you piss on that one, James?" and "You're holding up the works, Game Leg," and "My nagymama could move faster." He grinned and bent to his task.

And so it was James joined them every evening and was reasonably paid for it. Over time, with James scarcely noticing, that hard and painful place in his chest, that empty hole he'd tried to fill with whiskey, eased. James no longer felt the urge to board a train to nowhere, nor to run away. Am I content? he wondered. It had been so long, and he wondered if he had ever been. Certainly Sara induced in him a feeling of broader purpose, but in a different way, similar to the way in which going West inspired him. It was in a grand way, in an untouchable way, in a deep way. Not this, though. Being with Joseph and Karl contented James in an everyday basic way, in a relaxed no-strings-attached way.

However, though the pain went away, the rotgut remained. Shots of whiskey, gallons of whiskey, streams, rivers, torrents of whiskey. It no longer served as medicine—it served as oil on hinges and wax on floors and glue between boards. It was part and parcel of the daily round of men who worked hard. Three or four times a week, James walked a Virginia fence rail through the streets, crawled up the stairs, and let himself into their apartment drunk as a skunk. He might only manage to take off one shoe before falling into bed and into the sleep of the dead.

Of course, Sara was by no means oblivious. James smelled of whiskey and cigar smoke and often was slow with headaches when he arose in the late morning. She quickly surmised that he imbibed. She wasn't shocked nor particularly upset at the fact. He worked hard, and so he deserved to relax, and good money was coming in. Sara's father often had had a brandy after supper. Sara knew that temperance was the most desirable, but she understood James's need to partake. Plus, James was in a better mood these days, what little she saw of him. He would hum as he mended a button on his coat or cleaned his boots or would affectionately kiss her cheek or lay his palm upon her shoulder. At first, she had feared that it was perhaps something closer to his heart that kept him out late at night, but she did not detect any of the signs. He did not smell of perfume and he was as affectionate as ever, excepting when he was tired. It had also crossed her mind that his work might be somewhat of a more clandestine nature, that out of desperation he had allied himself with associates of decidedly less than upstanding natures. They patently needed the funds—

she understood that now—but then again what good would that be if he were to be arrested and jailed once more? She could understand the mistake he had made in the past, but she did not want to entertain the notion that it might be an element in his character, that he was base by nature.

But then one early Sunday morning shortly after dawn Sara awoke at Opal's restless pacing, wanting to go out, and James was not there beside her. She quickly searched her mind: he had said nothing. Quickly, her concern mounted. Something must have happened to him. Immediately, newspaper reports inundated her mind. Men killed in work accidents, in shootings, in lynchings, by runaway horses, in boating accidents, in tram accidents, in bar fights, run over by wagons, freak accidents in the street, killed by wild dogs. These thoughts worried at her mental fabric as she lay there, covers pulled tightly to her chest.

But then she heard booted feet on the stairs, a commotion, something being dragged. Step, scrape, step, clomp. Opal stopped in the middle of the room and let out a low woof and then another. There came a tap, tap, tap, light but deliberate on the door. Opal started barking and ran back under the bed and barked from that relative safety. Sara stiffened. What was she to do? It couldn't be James, as they had made a second key. It was way too early for visitors. It could only be bad news. Whomever they were, they must not see her like this. She was in no presentable condition, and anyone with a lick of manners would not tap on someone's door at this hour. That caused a jolt of fear to go through her—she had heard of scams in the neighborhood in which someone knocked and as soon as the door was opened the robbers burst in upon the unsuspecting. Maybe the mere presence of a dog would deter such criminals?

Again came the rap, rap, rap, louder this time, and Opal barked again in response. She pushed the covers off, told Opal to shoosh, and hurried to the door and opened it a crack but kept herself behind it on account of having no robe handy. There stood two men whom Sara did not know, and they had a third man between them hanging from their shoulders. She immediately recognized James as that third man, and she said under breath, "Oh my God, he is deceased." She opened the door wide and stepped out from behind it.

"No! No, no," said the taller of the two men. "He's drunker than ten Indians, that's all. Took but a picayune too much, he did."

He was simply drunk? This prompted anger to surge within Sara. If she had to make herself eat near-spoilt boiled cabbage for the sake of economy, if she had to forgo even basic necessities such as a new pair of undergarments or butter for the table, he could at least be home to sleep so that he could do his job so that they had enough money to survive. She stepped back and jerked her head sideways, indicating that they should bring him in, which they did. Sara shut the door behind the men and turned and followed.

They put James on the chair, and the taller one who had spoken before turned to her. "Where are my manners?" he said, extending his right hand. "I apologize. I am Joseph Soijka, and this here's my brother Karl." He gestured to the other man, who was trying to prop James on the chair. The other man pushed James, completely limp, against the backrest and then stepped back, his left arm across his chest and his right hand cupping his chin. As James ever so slowly toppled sideways from the chair, the man caught him and righted him. Once again the man tried to prop James, and again James slowly toppled, the other way this time. Opal ventured out from under the bed and was soon nosing, tail wagging, under the men's feet. The taller of the two men reached down and patted her head. Some guard dog, Sara thought.

With a shake of his head, the shorter man gathered James up and drug him to the bed, and the tall man went to help him. They place him there, tugged off his coat and boots, and pulled the covers over him. He emitted a loud snorting snore and in response his mouth opened but he slept on. Sara, so recently ejected from the warm bed, wanted to object to his placement, but that was, after all, the most logical place for him, and she was now up for the day anyway. This made her again aware of her semi-dressed state, and she quickly found her robe and put it on. When the men had finished putting James to bed, the shorter man said something in a low voice to the taller of the two, who glanced at Sara and nodded.

"We are infinitely sorry for the inconvenience," the taller one said. "It was entirely our fault, for which we beg your forgiveness." He glanced at the shorter man, who nodded vigorously in agreement. "He had wanted to return home earlier in the evening, but we kept him away, insisting upon his company for our, well, let's just say, our personal entertainment, which was of course wholly selfish on our part. To make up for this, Karl here would like to fix you breakfast, just as he used to for our dear departed mother." The tall man pulled out the chair and gestured to indicate that she should sit. She did, pulling Opal up into her lap, partly for the comfort, partly to keep her from bothering the men. "I'll just pop out and get some extra coal for the stove, as I see you're low. Let me assure you: You are in good hands with Karl here," the tall man, Joseph Soijka, said. The other, Karl Soijka, smiled and nodded.

Just then, another loud snore emitted from the bed.

Joseph Soijka left with the coal bucket, shutting the door firmly behind, and the brother Karl moved about the room with the deliberate step of a draft horse. He did not seem to move fast, but things were quickly done. A few times during the procedure, Sara had put forth a statement about the weather or some other general topic, as she felt uncomfortable sitting while this stranger made her breakfast, but Karl Soijka had simply nodded pleasantly. He soon placed a plate of biscuits and gravy and a cup of hot coffee in front of Sara and bowed slightly and smiled. As she ate, he took the dog out with her gestured permission, returned, and then stood back against the wall, his hands behind his back. Soon, his brother Joseph knocked on the door to be let in, which Karl did. Joseph brought not only coal but also a parcel of groceries, including what appeared to be fresh strawberries, which he placed haphazardly on the shelves, insisting that she eat while he do so. She tried to insist that they eat too, but they smiled indulgently and ignored her. Opal lay on the floor and looked up at her and her plate with soulful eyes. Joseph let out a steady stream of talk, and his words were interspersed with "Eh, Karl?" and "Karl thinks" such and such. When Joseph had completed putting away groceries, he pushed James's legs over and sat on the bed and continued talking.

Once Sara had finished, the men insisted upon gathering up the dishes and scrubbing them. "Yes it is," Joseph said to Karl as they finished, "time to go. Do not worry about James. He will be fine, though I might imagine he will wish he were dead." And at those words, for a split second, anger flared and Sara wished he were in fact dead, that some unfortunate

292

accident had befallen him, but horrified at herself she immediately retracted it and severely chastened herself. They ducked out the door, and it came to Sara that these were likable men, even though she did not want to like them.

Chapter 12

he first thing James became aware of was his temples and how they reverberated with a thousand hoof beats. His head also seemed swathed in cotton, and he immediately wished he were again asleep. Then he was aware of his stomach's prickly roiling. Had he thrown up? Was he going to? He swallowed at the bile in the back of his throat, rolled over, and put his arm over his head and dozed. He awoke again with a start and realized that he was indeed going to throw up, so he sat up, looked around, realized that he was home—how in the hell did I get here? he thought—and then leaned over and threw up onto the floor. He had not eaten since the afternoon of the day before—it had been the day before, hadn't it?—and now the sun in the window indicated it was afternoon. What came from his mouth was bitter green-yellow stomach bile. Though there was not much volume, he continued to dry heave, his body contracting and convulsing, and he had to brace himself from falling headfirst from the bed. It went on for what seemed a long time, and when it eased, his stomach was sore from the contractions, the interior of his throat rubbed raw. He sat back up and glanced around for something to wipe his mouth but, finding nothing, grabbed his shirt by its tails and pulled it over his head and then wiped his

mouth with it. As he wadded in a ball and tossed it onto the floor near the mess, intending to use it to clean it up, he caught a glimpse of Sara sitting across the table from him, a cup in her hands, her gaze leveled at him. Her face was stony, and when she saw him looking at her, she did not look away nor smile. He glanced from her to the mess on the floor and back.

He pushed back the covers and stood to try to clean up the mess, but then a wave of dizziness came over him and he fell backwards onto the bed. From underneath the bed came the scrabble of claws, as Opal scurried out and over to Sara. Sitting on the bed, he bent over his knees and picked up his shirt and swiped with the liquid, and then slowly and carefully, using the bedstead for a prop, he hoisted himself to standing. She watched him without saying a word as he crossed the room, let himself out of the apartment, gingerly went down the stairs and out the back door, and under the pump washed out the shirt and threw it over the clothesline. Opal followed him, wagging her tail and getting under foot. He pulled himself back up the stairs and at the door realized he did not have his key, and so shaking his head he tapped lightly upon it.

After what seemed like an inordinate amount of time, the door opened in front of him. Opal ran through the opening, and by the time he came through Sara had reseated herself on the chair and was placing her hands firmly around the cup. Across from her on the table was a plate that held biscuits, with gravy in a pool beside them. When his mind registered the food, his body reacted in two directly opposing manners. His stomach first growled with hunger but then nausea gripped him again and he had to swallow hard. Some food in my belly would be good, he thought. He walked over to the table and, without speaking, using his hands, asked if the plate was for him. She did not answer, simply lifted her shoulders. He pulled from underneath the table the three-legged stool they had purchased for a second chair and sat and began eating, slowly at first, testing his stomach with each bite, and then more quickly as he became sure it would stay down. Through it all Sara sat there brooding.

His anger began to rise. What right had she to be so suddenly self-righteous? He put food on the table, did he not? He provided for her and treated her kindly and did his best by her. He did not beat her. He did not force himself upon her. He tried to make her happy. The anger bubbled higher. It combined with the pains of the hangover and the tired wretched feeling he had inside and the doubt that perhaps she had every right to be angry. It soon felt near to overtaking him, and it was all he could do keep from standing up and upending the table and breaking things. He grabbed his coat and shoes and stalked across the room, almost tripping over the dog, and let himself out, not allowing himself the pleasure of slamming the door but instead closing it carefully and quietly. He sat on the back steps and put on his boots and then began walking. He did not watch where he was going, simply strode on, the same thoughts churning his mind. Unfortunately, it was his day off, and so he had no work to go to that night. He walked and walked until the thoughts slowed down. It was dark by then, and he returned to the apartment and let himself back in. She lay reading a pamphlet in bed by the coal oil lamp, Opal lying next to her, and when he came in she looked up. Her eyes were puffy and red as if she had been crying, and her face opened up to him, receptive, but still she did not say anything. He refused to speak as well, and he looked at her, set, neither unreceptive nor accusatory. He undressed and washed his face and hands and

296

prepared for bed. She put the dog down and moved over to make room when he got into bed, and he climbed in and put his back to her and pulled up the covers. As he lay there, he could hear her breathing behind him. She was facing him, wanting him to turn over, he could tell, but he didn't and after a time, she too turned her back to him, and in that way they went to sleep. The next day, she was up when he woke. She made his breakfast and fixed his lunch pail, and he got ready and went out to work, and neither of them spoke a word.

Sara once again felt as if she were back under the aegis of her father. His protection and guidance came at a high cost, she now realized, and he had demanded that she anticipate his needs without much direction. This situation brought with it an intolerable pressure, a pressure that had returned now with James, made worse by the fact that she believed that she was in the right. Unsettled, she went about her day. She fed the dog. She cleaned the apartment and planned supper. Looking at her receipt book brought Auntie to mind, and since she had not seen Auntie since the funeral, she resolved to knock upon her door, if only to check how she was fairing. After a quick excursion to the shops for the few items on her list, she did just that. She went down the hall and tapped on Auntie's door. Auntie cracked it, and when she saw that it was Sara she slowly opened the door. "Do come in," Auntie said. Auntie looked the same, only thinner, and upon closer inspection there was a blank look about her eyes and a set to her jaw that had not been there before. She was kindly enough, but Sara got the impression that her mind was not in the present moment. "Sara," Auntie said. "Just the person I've been meaning to, ah, inquire of. So good of you to anticipate my need."

"Of course, Auntie," Sara said, trying to think how to tread this particular social terrain. "Our teas and chats have been terribly missed." Sara truly meant it. Auntie led Sara into her kitchen as usual and indicated that she should sit and went about making tea in her usual way, although she did not fully open the cupboard doors as she did so, just slipping in her hand and quickly shutting them. The tea tasted weak, with an odd flavor, and Auntie did not offer milk nor any nibbles on the side. Their chatting about the weather and other things seemed strained at first, but then they fell into the old pattern and it came much more easily. Auntie still had a somewhat distracted demeanor, but she readily engaged in conversation. After a relatively short time, not wanting to overstay her welcome, Sara showed indications that she would soon leave. "Well, I must be thinking of supper," she said, but in response Auntie hoisted herself from the chair and went into the other room. She soon returned with sheets of paper and sat down, placing the papers on the table between them and smoothing them out. "I will tell you," Auntie said, "I have been somewhat concerned as to what will happen to this building."

"Is there a problem?" Sara asked. A quick dread settled in Sara's stomach, but then Auntie held the papers out. Sara took them but gave the old woman a questioning look. Auntie shrugged and looked down at her hands. Sara glanced at the papers and saw that they were legal documents of some kind, with Moses's signature in broad firm strokes at the bottom. Sara looked back to Auntie and said, "These are legal papers?"

Auntie did not meet her eyes. "These old eyes, not much for ciphering. Even in my youth, I had bit of difficulty with it," she said.

Why would Auntie be ashamed of poor eyesight? Her

eyesight was not so poor that she couldn't make her way around the kitchen. "We must purchase you a hand lens so that you can ..." Sara let her voice trail off as she tried to remember whether she had ever seen Auntie consult a receipt. She had not. Also, the one time Sara had brought over her receipt book to get Auntie's advice, Auntie had waved it away, saying, "I don't need no book to tell me how to roast vegetables." There weren't any books in the apartment, nor any newspapers. Sara had not once interrupted Auntie in the midst of a novel or writing a letter. And then it came to Sara: Auntie could not read. Sara glanced at Auntie to see if she realized that Sara now knew. Auntie held her face tight around the cheekbones and the eyes, and Sara saw that she was embarrassed, and had Auntie's skin tone been lighter a deep blush would have been apparent, Sara was sure. Attempting to smooth things over, Sara pulled her chair forward in a businesslike manner and cleared her throat. "Absolutely, Auntie," she said. "God just isn't fair with His gifts sometimes, is He?" She focused her attention on the papers and read through them.

The papers were handwritten in a well-formed script. It was Moses's will, which said that his wife Olivia would receive a property Sara knew nothing about and that their building would be left to one Margaret Soule, along with the sum of ten dollars. Sara looked up at Auntie. "Would your name be Margaret Soule?" As she asked, she fervently hoped so.

Auntie nodded her head and smiled. "Yes, it is."

"Did Moses say anything to you when he left these papers for you? Did he say what it was?"

"Only that I would be provided for, that I had nothing to worry about. He said he wanted to leave them here for safekeeping." Auntie hesitated for a moment and then continued, "But in truth I got the impression that he did not want a certain person to stumble upon them. What do they say?" She nodded to the papers.

"They say that he left you, Margaret Soule, this building and ten dollars. It's his will."

"Oh," Auntie said. "And it says he left it for me?"

"Yes, it does."

Auntie sighed deeply. "That is such a relief. You don't know … Well, the young Missus Thaxton"—her voice took on a wry tone as she said the name—"did stop by a week ago and she said, well, she didn't say, but she hinted that she would be needing me to move out, as she had plans for this building."

"Well, you can tell her that you have the legal documents that prove she can do nothing of the kind." It felt good to be able to come to Auntie's defense, to play an active role in comforting her.

"It is a relief as well that he thought to leave me a little something, though I do not suppose I shall see a cent of it."

"Why is that, Auntie?"

Auntie did not seem inclined to answer but instead rose to make another pot of tea. This time, she left her cupboard door standing open, within which the shelves were nearly empty, but then she seemed to remember herself and quickly close them with a glance Sara's way. Sara quickly averted her eyes. Auntie's cupboard was bare.

"Say," Sara said, trying at nonchalance, "you know, I have really got to run, as I have to go by the market by way of the shops before supper. I was thinking: I will pick up a few things for you while I am out, shall I? It would not be any bother at all."

A look of relief came onto Auntie's face, but then she

quickly closed it off. "That is very kind of you, girl, but, well …"

"Your, let us say, immobility hampers you a bit, so allow me to fetch things for you. It really is no trouble."

Auntie said nothing for a minute and just looked at Sara. There seemed to be struggle going within her.

"What is it, Auntie?"

Auntie shook her head and as she did Sara realized that her eyes shone with moisture. Sara wanted to rise and comfort her, yet she did not have the confidence that it would be accepted so she stayed in her chair but leaned forward, her hand outstretched.

"Oh, Missus Youngblood," Auntie said. "I could not ask it of you, you being a young wife and just trying to make it."

Auntie did not have the money to pay her back—that was what concerned her, Sara thought. "You'll not worry a thing about it," Sara said as breezily as she could manage. "My husband has recently came upon solid employment and our future appears assured. Let me help you. It surely is no bother." In truth, she had saved but little, but what little she had she was determined to use to aid this kind woman. At those words, Auntie took a shaky breath, and then Sara did rise and help her to her seat. It took a minute for Auntie to regain her composure, dabbing at her eyes with a handkerchief retrieved from the pocket of her skirt. Sara poured the last of the tea into her cup, laid a hand on her shoulder and then took her leave. She immediately went out and purchased as many staples as she could afford—flour, eggs, cheese, potatoes, dried beans, rice, and the like. She even purchased a small package of raisins, remembering Auntie's admonition about the sweetness in life—surely, she needed some now. Sara spent all the money she had squirreled away in tin can behind the shelf—Auntie needed it more than she. She returned home with the delivery boy Charlie at her heels. She apologized that she could not tip him but instead gave him a cookie from a batch she had recently attempted, which he quickly ate while patting Opal on the head. He eyed the plate once more, even though the cookies were not very good, so she gave him three more. He left with it, and then she took the bounty down the hall to Auntie's rooms. When Auntie let her in, she laid them on the table. Auntie had been able to produce a few coins, that were mismatched and looked very old—heirlooms, perhaps?—but Sara refused. "It is the least I can do," she said.

Auntie thanked her. "My Lord, girl," she said, "I do not know what I am to do with all this goodness."

"You are the font of much more goodness than I," Sara replied and then returned to her apartment to prepare James's supper.

Chapter 13

t was pitch black when Sara was shocked awake by a pounding on the door and the startled barking of the dog. As she tried to shake the sleep from her mind, she realized that she had been hearing knocking and barking for a time but that the sounds had translated into her dreams. She sat up, shook her head, pushed off the covers, and rose. "I'm a'coming," she said loudly, with a glance into the darkness where by the noise Opal once again crouched under the bed. She made the time to locate her robe and put it on and fumbled to light a candle, which she carried to the door with her. The pounding came again, this time with a voice yelling something through the door. She cracked it open and there stood the two brothers once again, James slung between them, only this time they had ahold of him by his knees and armpits.

"Oh my God," Sara said, this time her voice carrying rather more disgust than anything else. So James had not let but days pass before a repeat performance. The anger rose in her and she gritted her teeth.

"No!" the taller brother, Joseph, who held James's shoulders, said. "Tis not the same. Your James is injured, possibly with mortal consequences. A gantry collapsed upon his head. Look, see." He lifted James up as if to say, here.

The anger was strong in Sara, as she had been woken from a sound sleep, so the words took a minute to register. "He … What?" She looked more closely and saw a cloth wrapped around his head. "Oh my God," she said again, this time with the intonation altered to match the horror as it dawned upon her. Oh my God, James has been killed! She stepped to the side and waved them in. "Please, please," she said. They brought him in and deposited him on the bed while she lit the coal oil lamp. She set this on the end of the table near the bed. "Is he breathing?" she asked. "Has he said anything?"

"No," Joseph said. "I mean yes, he is breathing, but, no, he has not yet said anything. He has not come to since the damn heavy bit of metal struck his noggin."

"Let me see," she said. Karl scooped under James's armpits and held him in a sitting position while Joseph located the end of the cloth and unwrapped James's head. The cloth was clean at first but then seeped blood became visible, and then Joseph had to pull off the last bit where the blood had coagulated and glued the fabric to the wound, which was on the crown of James's head, hair clumped and matted around it. Sara held the lamp as close as she dared to peer at it. It was hard to see through the hair—the blood had stopped flowing, as far as she could tell, but that was about all she could see. For a head wound, there seemed a lot of blood, she thought. She could not see if the skull had been punctured, nor could she see anything that she imagined to be brain matter. She lowered her ear next to his face to sense his breaths, which came measured and even, unlabored. A good sign. "We've got to wash it," she said, gesturing to the wound, "to stave off any infection. And a doctor, we must have one."

"I'll go," Joseph said and turned and left. Sara was glad for a moment that it was Karl who stayed, as his quiet steadfastness had a calming effect upon her, while Joseph talked rather too much, at least for a moment like this.

"Hold him," she said and went to the stove and dipped her finger in the water that was always kept in the pan at the back. It was lukewarm and would do. As she did so, Karl hefted James onto the table, Opal trailing behind. "Easier this way," Karl said. It was, though it reminded her a little too much of preparing Lily's body for burial. She placed the lamp on the chair behind her and the basin under his head, which Karl held, and she poured water over the wound, while the pain she imagined made her wince with empathy. The water ran red into the basin. She could not get a good look at the wound with the hair in the way, so she retrieved her sewing scissors and as gently as she could sheared away a patch of hair from the area. When she washed it again and held up the lamp, she was able to see a long gash in the scalp and what she thought was a slight indentation in his skull, which made her shudder.

She had heard stories of men kicked in the head by horses or otherwise injured and how they were never the same after. One man had remained a vegetable until he eventually died, while another's personality was so altered that he had to be placed in an institution for the criminally insane due to his nighttime incursions into women's bedrooms. Up until that moment, she had not thought of the consequences of this wound—she had not realized the extent of it, and now that she saw the indentation it dawned upon her that he might in fact be irrevocably altered or even die, or she could be left with his mortal body, his mind long gone. She would have to tend to that body and if enough time passed find a means to support herself as well. A knock came on the door, and she went and

305

let in Joseph and the doctor, a small man with a neatly trimmed mustache and beard and round spectacles. With the help of Karl, Sara holding the lamp, the doctor examined James, nodding his head and humming under his breath.

When the doctor was done with his examination, he told them that, although it may not look so, James had been incredibly lucky. "A gantry of the size and weight described by Mister Soijka could have caused such blunt trauma as to kill him instantly. This was a much more glancing blow, and as such did not crack open the skull, merely dented it a bit, and the tissues underneath appear intact." He paused and then went on. "We will not know the true extent of the damage, however, until he awakens. But I must warn you that there is a chance that he will not awaken. The brain is a mysterious instrument, and it can be severely injured with no outward signs. As you attend him, monitor his breathing—if it changes drastically, if it becomes much slower or more labored or faster, it may be a sign of either his immediate recovery or his inevitable demise." His words chilled Sara to her core—the wound could go much deeper than the outward signs. "I will suture the scalp, but other than that, you simply need to keep the wound clean, him comfortable, and hope for the best. The sooner he awakens, the better his chances will be." Then he swabbed the wound with a sweet-smelling liquid and brought out a curved needle and thread from a small kit and sewed up the wound. Through it all, James showed no signs that he felt any pain, nor sensed anything at all. The doctor then packed up his equipment and wrote out his bill, which he left on that table. "You may call on me if there are any changes."

Once the doctor was gone, they moved James to the bed, removing his shoes and his coat. Then, with sober looks on their faces, the Soijka brothers left, saying, "If you need anything, do not hesitate to let us know. Send someone." They gave her an address. "We will stop by to check on him, and on you, in a day or two." The window had just begun to lighten with the rays of morning sun.

Left alone with James's inert form, Sara collected herself. First, she must see to James, see that he was as warm and comfortable as possible—that was the best thing. It would aid in his recovery. She tied the cord around Opal's neck and took her for a quick morning constitutional, thinking it would also keep her calm. If she were to get too restless, Sara resolved to tie her in the yard so as not to disturb James. When they returned, Sara removed an extra blanket from her chest and spread it over him. She could not think of what else to do, so she sat on the edge of the bed. She looked into his face, which appeared calm and restful, as if he were simply sleeping. She put her hand on his forehead, which was neither hot nor cold. This was her love, her passionate intimate companion. She swallowed hard. The planes and curves of his features seemed altered, as if he were already half-gone from this world, and she felt the tears rising within her. She took his hand into both of hers and held it to her chest and closed her eyes. She began to pray. "Please, God," she whispered, "do not take this man from me. He is the partner to my soul, my heart's desire. I will do anything, whatever you need me to, just leave him for me." Tears spilled from her eyes and ran freely down her cheeks. She sat for a long time, pressing his hand, pushing with all her interior might toward God and toward James, willing him to heal, to recover, to open his eyes.

She stayed that way for a long while, and when she was done she took a deep breath and opened her eyes. She remembered the doctor's admonition about monitoring his breathing, and so she bent down and listened. It was the same as before. She would be assiduous in its monitoring, she decided. She rose and washed her face and dressed, determined to keep the structure of her days. So, on that first day, she checked his breathing every quarter hour, and there was no change. She cleaned the apartment, made food for herself and for Opal and for James, should he open his eyes. She gave him a warm sponge bath when he micturated and defecated in the bed. She then placed an oilcloth underneath him, so he would not stain the mattress. She also moved his arms and legs a bit, gently, to get the blood moving. That night, not wanting to disturb him, she made a pallet on the floor, and Opal joined her to sleep. The next day, she kept to the schedule, and still, there was no change. The extra food she had made the day before, she ate herself. Again, she moved his arms and legs. Opal sometimes would crawl up into the bed beside him and lay, an inscrutable but sympathetic expression on the dog's face. Sara hoped he could feel her warm body next to him and that it comforted him. On the third day, sometimes an hour would pass before she would think to check his breathing. Once, she tried tickling his cheek to see if there was a response, but there wasn't, and another time, she even resorted to pinching him fiercely on the arm, which she immediately regretted, but the fact that he did not respond further darkened her mood. Opal seemed to sense it, and slunk around her heals, as if both fearing her mood and also wanting to console her. Once on the fourth day she thought she had seen a twitch, a movement in his hands, but then she had to admit it was purely her imagination. She began to worry, however, at his not being able to take in any liquids. His face took on a slack sallow cast,

308

and his lips began to chap. How long could one last without water? She was not sure. Surely a week at the outside. How many days had it been? Should she try to force water into him? Would he swallow, or would she drown him?

Sara ate sparingly and fed Opal the minimum she felt necessary, but still, in four days, her stock of groceries was depleted. She had not had much in reserve, between not wanting it to go bad and not having much money to spend on large orders. She had also spent her reserve funds on Auntie, though even as the hunger gnawed in her belly she did not regret it. When she searched James's clothes, she found that he had but two pennies in his pockets, a measly sum. Soon she was forced to concoct bread and water pancakes, which tasted better than she had thought, drizzled with the last of the heated bacon grease. Opal seemed to think them the highest delicacy. On the fifth day, she ran out of everything.

She sat at the table, her head in her hands. Whom could she call upon to give her employment? She knew no one well enough, excepting Auntie, and Auntie was in no position to give her a job, not to mention the racial complications. Whom did she know in Kansas City? She was acquainted with the grocery clerks and some of the people in the market and with Charlie, the delivery boy, but she knew no one intimately. Laundry—wait, did she not know someone who was a laundress? That beautiful and peculiar woman on the train. She had had money. She was well off. She could pay Sara for her labor. Sara searched for her card, and there it was, still tucked in the pocket of the carpetbag. Upon the card, it stated that the woman, Miss Danielle Rose, was a laundress. That was right— the woman was not married. Well, maybe Sara could do laundry for her. She was not above that, not now. She must go see her.

Sara worried about leaving James alone, but surely she would only be gone an hour or two. It mustn't be far, as it was near the market. He would be all right, with the faithful Opal here to keep him company. If she were to be gone longer, she would have had Auntie look in on him—surely, Auntie could and would do that—but as it was, she would only be gone an hour or two.

She left the apartment and began walking. Much to her exasperation, it took her a good hour of wandering, first a couple of blocks one way and then a couple of blocks the other, to find the address, which materialized as a small hotel in the middle of the block. As Sara stepped through the door, a bell tinkled. The entryway opened into a long dark hallway straight ahead and a set of stairs on the right. There were mirrors on the upper half of the wall and squares of wood paneling on the lower half, and red velvet draperies with gold tassel trim lined the doorway to the hall. The floor was tiled in small white and red tiles, with the word "Rose" worked into the floor by the entry. Miss Rose must indeed be a wealthy woman to afford such lavish surroundings.

No one seemed to be around, however. Undecided, Sara looked first down the hall and then stepped over and looked up the stairs. On the landing, a little girl peeked around the end of the newel post. The reflected light from the doorway lit the girl's uncontrolled cascade of red hair. "Hello," Sara said, trying not to scare the girl. The little girl ducked behind the banister, and Sara heard her feet thump on the carpeted stairs as she retreated. Ah well, perhaps she will retrieve someone, Sara thought, and sure enough, soon down the stairs came Miss Rose herself, agile upon her crutch. Miss Rose was more beautiful than Sara remembered, even in her satin dressing gown. "Good morning," the woman said. "I am sorry to have kept you waiting. I am Miss Rose. You are?" Sara introduced herself and explained that they had met on a train a month or two before. "Ah," Miss Rose said, "yes. I remember. You were newly wedded. Well, we don't usually receive visitors this early in the morning, but here you are. Won't you follow me?" Was it early? It did not feel early to Sara. Miss Rose ushered Sara into a parlor, a large room that was close and unaired and smelled of perfume and cigars. It contained a number of small velvet and brocade couches with claw-foot legs and plush chairs in groups, heavy maroon draperies, a number mirrors with gold frames, and a red Persian rug. An upright piano stood on one wall and a large fireplace on another. Miss Rose gestured to a couple of chairs. Once they were seated, Miss Rose laid her crutch into what appeared a ready-made stand and said, "So what may I do for you?"

"You offered on the train," Sara said, "that if I ever needed anything …" Sara's voice trailed off. Was it proper to come out and ask for a job? Well, that was what she was looking for, so perhaps directness was the best approach. "I'm looking for a job. My husband, you see, has recently been the victim of an accident." She found herself choking over the words, so she stopped speaking and left it there.

"I see," Miss Rose said. To Sara's shock, she removed a cigarette from a silver box and lit it with an ornate silver lighter. Women did not smoke. They just didn't. Miss Rose inhaled deeply and after a hesitation said, "Well, then, what can you do?"

"I can play that piano," Sara said, gesturing to the instrument.

"That's lovely, dear, but I already have a piano player, and a fine one at that." Miss Rose waited.

"I can sew. I can cook a little." Could she claim that? "I can clean. I can do laundry. I am a hard worker." Sara tried to keep the desperation from of her voice.

After a moment of thought, Miss Rose smiled, showing her teeth and crinkling her eyes. "I am sorry, my dear. Where are my manners?" She rang a bell on the side table and soon a thin woman entered carrying a pot of coffee and assorted delicacies on a silver tray. There were fruits and breads and chocolates and cigars, even a small box that turned out to be snuff. The pot, the sugarer, the creamer, and the spoons were all made of heavy silver. The serving woman poured each of them each a cup and, unasked, doused both with cream and sugar. She looked tired, as if she had just awoken, and her motions were mechanical. The woman's eyes were half-lidded, half-seeing. The brown hair piled upon her head was disordered, the top button on the back of her collar was undone, and she smelled heavily of perfume and something else, something sweet and smoky, something Sara had never smelled before. Task completed, the woman wandered from the room, after which Miss Rose held out her hand to indicate Sara's cup and, taking up her own, sipped her coffee and said, "Tell me about where you are from, Love." Unsure of what Miss Rose wanted, Sara told her about overseeing her father's house in Iowa, how she was responsible for coordinating and managing so much of it. Miss Rose asked a polite question here and there, prompting her to continue, her manner of listening making it easy for Sara to talk. Finally, Miss Rose fixed Sara in a steady gaze and said, "Well, Love, we do have positions available, but not for a cook or a housekeeper. How much do you require the money?"

Should she admit the extent of her need? Well, it was a fact. "We do need it," she hedged. "We do."

Miss Rose tilted her head coyly and said, "The position might involve things that are distasteful to you. What would you think of that?"

Distasteful? What could possibly be more distasteful than starving to death, your husband lying in a bed, slowly dying? "I'm a hard and willing worker," she said.

"I am sure you are, Love, a hard worker, and a determined wife, but I question your willingness. You do seem to be a good conversationalist. You are a practiced hostess. I could even see a glimpse of the coquette about you." She considered for a minute, and then she said, gravel in her voice, "See, what I would require of you is to entertain some gentlemen friends of mine." Sara searched her mind. What did she mean? "You know what I am saying, my dear. You are not a halfwit," Miss Rose continued. "You know, to keep them company during the night." Her eyebrow was half-raised. Realization dawned upon Sara's. A prostitute! A girl of the frail but fair order. Sara's face became hot. She could not believe her own naiveté. Without a word, she pushed herself to standing. She caught a glimpse of a smirk on Miss Rose's face as she pushed out of the room and across the tile out the front door, the sound of the bell loud in her ears. She ran down the street, blindly, glancing behind her as if she were being followed. She ran until she could not breathe, and then she turned into an empty alley to escape the crowds on the boardwalk and collapsed on some steps.

Sara's internal voice streamed incessantly. What could that woman possibly be thinking? Did Sara look like the type of woman who would do such a thing? Never, not in a million years, would Sara ever stoop to such lows. She was a respectable married woman. She would starve first. Still, the thought came to mind that she had gone to the woman in desperation and asked for the job. Other women must have done the same thing, only they had accepted the terms. Why? What was the difference between them and Sara, exactly? A vast amount, Sara insisted to herself.

As she sat, the thoughts roiling in her mind, the sun rose to its peak and shone down through the narrow gap upon her on the alley steps and then fell, dropping her in shadow again. Still she did not move. The world continued to reveal itself as not at all what she imagined—a surprise, sometimes nasty, around every corner. Before, she had been sure that there was right and wrong, that people had their places in the world, positions that did not alter, that character was fixed. But now she wasn't so sure. Maybe, like she and James, like Moses, some people jumped in with both feet but then found themselves caught, and the only way they saw to save themselves was by less-than-savory means. Or they did not save themselves.

After a while, Sara calmed, and her mind cleared. She relaxed her tense shoulders and stretched her legs. She felt the warm breeze blow down the alley. Somewhere she could smell sausages frying. She took a deep breath. Her stomach rumbled—she was hungry, indeed.

The door behind her banged open. A round-bodied red-headed red-faced woman with sweat pouring off her grabbed Sara by the arm and jerked her to standing, and in her surprised state Sara let her. The woman let out a stream of words. "Lollygagging on the stoop? Why didn't you come to the front? You are late, late, late, late. One thing Molly don't stand for, it is tardiness. Get your arse in here. Come on now. Quit

314

your dawdling. There's an apron. Put it on now. Let's go." She pulled Sara into a short hall that was stacked with kitchen supplies—barrels and sacks and parcels and large pots and pans stacked to the ceiling on the shelving on either side of them—and Sara could hear the commotion of the kitchen beyond, with its most heavenly of smells. There was the mouth-watering odor of meat cooking and the moistness of stew bubbling and the rich scent of cake baking. Sara took a deep breath, feeling fortified by the mere odors.

"You are the cook's helper they sent over, are you not?" the red-faced woman said.

Under normal circumstances, Sara would have immediately protested her mistake and cleared up the trouble but in her present state of despair said nothing. She quickly reasoned that God had answered her fervent prayers and sent her a small boon. In response to the woman's question, she simply nodded vaguely, superstitious as not to bear false testimony. The woman said, "By the way, I go by Nellie." The woman wiped her hand on her apron and held it out. Sara took her hand and shook it firmly. Nellie took Sara to see the owner and head cook, Molly, who was a fleshy woman with tiny eyes buried in the mounds of her cheeks and black hair pulled tightly back into a bun at the base of her neck. She moved with ponderous ease, a large boat chugging through the tide, and she belted out orders as she flipped meat and stirred pots. Everyone jumped at her command. At Nellie's introduction, she eyed Sara for a minute, nodded her head, and turned back to her work. Sara vowed to keep out of her way. Nellie set Sara to chopping vegetables, and all the while she worked she worried that the real cook's helper would appear. She did not allow it to slow her efficiency, however. She needed this job.

315

After Sara finished chopping vegetables, Nellie sent her out front to clean tables and sweep. The dinner crowd was thinning, and Sara had to weave in and out of people moving toward the door and standing in line to pay. She'd just loaded a tray of dishes when in came an old woman hobbling on a cane who wore a white dress aflutter with ruffles and lace. Her skin was a warm brown, but she was so thin her chin stood out in a sharp V, and her hands were gnarled, almost indistinguishable from the cane. The woman held the arm of a middle-aged man whose head bowed toward her. The man had the same dark hair and brown skin, but his face held a vacant look, and his clothes seemed not quite to fit, not so much in the cut but in the way he inhabited them. If Sara were to judge, she would say that they were of Spanish extraction. They made their way to the register and spoke to Nellie. Across the room, Sara could not hear what they said, but as Nellie attended them she glanced at Sara and then turned and went into the kitchen. Molly pushed through the doors into the dining room and wiped her hands on an towel, followed by Nellie, who went back to the register. Sara edged closer.

"The position is filled," Molly said loudly. Sara was now caught and would be summarily thrown out on her ear! She quickly turned her back but kept her attention on the proceedings.

The old woman leaned forward and said something softly to Molly.

Molly said, in her loud voice, "Madame, I do not care what you were informed. The position has been filled." This time Molly glanced her way, and Sara wanted to sink into the floor.

Agitated, the old woman pounded her cane on the floor. "Are you not good to your word?" she said. The man standing

316

to one side tilted his head sideways, eyes focused on the wall.

"I gave no word," Molly returned.

"The person gave word," the old woman insisted.

"I cannot help that," Molly said and turned back toward the kitchen.

The woman dropped her cane with a clatter and slowly let herself down to her knees, the man beside her supporting her. When she was down, she waved him away. She said, loudly, "Please, good woman, give my son a job."

Sara immediately felt horrible about it all, no matter her need, so she stepped toward them. Molly, meanwhile, had turned back to them, and when Sara approached, Molly looked straight at her and said, "Sara. Kitchen." Sara hesitated, Molly's gaze fixed upon her the whole time, and then she capitulated and turned to the kitchen. She hear Molly say, as she went through the door, "Dishwasher," and then she named a measly wage. "Nellie, you take care of it." She then followed Sara into the kitchen and ignored her for the rest of the day.

Later in the day, a tall thin sloping drunk, unshaven and unwashed—Molly's husband, so Nellie informed Sara—slunk in and was served a bowl of beans and cornbread to eat. He was not charged, and he slunk back out. Nellie told Sara that Molly had given strict orders that he was to have whatever he wanted to eat but by no means was anyone to give him any money, not even their own money. But, Nellie said, with the resourcefulness of a dope fiend the man found infinite new ways to separate Molly from her cash. Once he had set up a scheme whereby he convinced some regular patrons that he could receive their money for their meals and they did not have to come to the counter. Another time, he took a delivery at the back door and then quickly hawked the wares in the market. He

317

was not to be trusted, Nellie said.

For the rest of the day, Nellie gave Sara directions, and during lulls, Sara worried about James alone in the apartment. Would he be all right? But she made sure to focus on her work and finish her tasks before Nellie came to find her. She kneaded dough and washed pots alongside the new dishwasher—she quickly learned that there was something not quite right about him. Mr. Montanez was his name. He was an industrious enough worker, but he did not talk but to say "Yes, ma'am" and "No, ma'am," and his movements were awkward, as if he were a little tetched or slow in the head.

Around seven in the evening, Nellie pulled her aside. "Guess that's enough for one day. You'll do, by golly." She cupped her hand next to her mouth and whispered. "I'm glad it's you and not that spic, me working so closely by." Sara kept her reactions off her face. Harmless Mr. Montanez, what she knew of him, did not seem to warrant such vehemence, but Nellie was entitled to her opinions, Sara supposed. Nellie let her out the back alley door, saying, "Here's your day's pay." She handed her some coins. "You look like you are needing it. Your wages is good for the job, but you run the risk of Molly's temper. That's why people leave—Molly can be a bear. Don't take her too seriously, though. Your hours are from nine in the morning to seven in the evening, so you'll work through dinner and supper." Nellie smiled, "And you get to eat your supper. And, if there's something left over, you can take some home." Nellie handed her a can of soup and then disappeared back through the alley door. Gratitude flooded through her. Money in her pocket, hot soup in her hands, Sara made her way home, tired but happy. She'd never before been paid for her labors, and it felt good.

Chapter 14

ames is alone in the darkness just before a dawning. It is cold and he cannot see anything for the blackness, and loneliness pulls at him like gravity. It is the singularity of himself in this nonplace that makes him feel the worst—he is utterly and irrevocably isolated. Then he senses movement at the corner of his eye. It is utter darkness, so he does not know how he sees the movement but he does, and he is aware that it is spreading, little patches of it breaking out across his field of vision. Perhaps it is a sound, a rustling, or perhaps it is that he feels himself watched by eyes that are not human. One of the patches scuttles from one place to another place, and then another scuttles, and he feels himself surrounding by the chitinous clickings of legs. His fear rises, but he knows he must move forward, and so he continues his slow way—is he walking?—toward a destination. He does not question the destination but he knows that if he reaches it, things will change, his existence on this plane will be altered. He wants this change to take place, though he also knows it could be a change for the worse as easily as for the better. It does not matter. His time here is weighted with such frigid isolation, such kinetic darkness, he wants it more than he's wanted anything in his life, it seems.

But then he is aware of a smell. It is pungent and acrid, a smell that he had sensed before, and he feels he is in a cesspool, and it rises above his ankles, his knees. The anticipation of it, the cold creeping up his extremities, makes him gasp for air, and he is aware that he is slowly drowning. It makes no sense that his ankles are covered with liquid shit and he is drowning in water over his head, but logic does not hold in this nonplace. Despite the smell and the water over his face, he is thirsty, so thirsty it's as if he were in a desert, a place so parched he would give anything for moisture on his lips. He would kneel in this filth and put his face into it just to have the feeling of moisture upon his tongue. But then a barely discernible crack of light shows upon the horizon. Is this the alteration he's been hoping for, the one that will change everything? He cannot know, but there it is brightening, orange and gold and white, expanding in front of him. Is it a sunrise? It does not seem to be, as it is not localize enough. Rather, it is continuous along a crack, which is widening by the second, getting brighter, and now he is aware of a sound, a whining low and undulating. It stops and starts and stops again. The desperation grows as the light dawns. Will he be able to make it? Will he reach the light? He struggles—against what he does not know, but it is heavy and it holds him and he cannot strive, he will not make it, and he fears the light will recede. He pushes with all his might. He isn't pushing exactly, but it is him willing himself forward, up and out, pushing himself away from those night threats toward, toward?

And then James became aware. At first it was the strong odor that came to him, the smell of dog piss and shit. He knew the smell, with its character different than that of horse shit. Next, he was aware of a horrible pounding within himself

320

somewhere, and he felt split in two with the pain. He pulled himself inward. He wanted to return back to wherever he'd come, to that blackness that did not have pain. He felt himself sink backward, but his being screamed *No!* despite the pain. He knew that if he let himself slip back that he would never again escape and he would be trapped in the darkness. So he embraced the pain, and the light brightened. His senses descended into his body. The throbbing pain localized in his head, and he wondered whether he had the king of all hangovers. He tried to remember, to collect his thoughts despite the distraction of the throbbing. He found that he simply could not remember anything. What was the last thing he remembered? Leaving the apartment to go to work—he was not sure which day. Sara had not felt particularly well, a little tired it seemed, and that late morning—his early morning—he had taken Opal out for a walk while Sara napped.

Click click came the sound of the dog's toenails on the floor. He opened his eyes to a blinding light and tried to push up to sitting with his arms. His body was stiff and weak and sluggish to respond. When he lifted his head, the pounding came on with renewed force and prompted nausea to rise within him. His head collapsed back onto the bed and he lay there, breathing hard. He opened his eyes again, this time without trying to move. He was home in bed—he could tell by the familiar view of the ceiling. From the floor, Opal let out a low whine and continued to pace, click, click, click. Then he was aware of how thirsty he was. It gave his mouth a metallic taste, and when he moved his tongue his mouth was papery and sticky. He tried to work up some saliva to clear it, without luck. Carefully, gently, he turned his head to survey the room. The change in position caused such pain to start that he closed his eyes again and remained that way for some time. As he lay there, he heard Opal walk to the bed and put her paws upon it and whine, and then she kicked herself up on the bed and nosed at his arm. He could feel the wet coolness of it. She circled once and then lay beside him, and he felt her warmth, which was a comfort. He was not alone anymore. And then it really came to him—he was not alone anymore. Unaccountably, a sob rose within him, which he did not try to quell but rather let it come out of his mouth. He was in the world he knew, and he was not alone.

But where was Sara? He tried to speak but only managed a groan. He opened his eyes once again and carefully surveyed the room. She was nowhere in the apartment, though he did spy a pile of dog pop surrounded by a yellow puddle upon the floor. How could she have gone and left him in this condition? And what exactly was it that he had? Again he tried to remember, without luck. He felt he had to do something. With all his strength, he pushed with his arms, trying to raise himself, but he only managed to lift his head a bit, and then he lay there panting at the effort. He was in fact alone, except for Opal, and helpless as a newborn babe. He needed a drink of water, he needed to move as his body was stiff and sore, and he suspected he was hungry too, though it had not yet shown itself. He lay in bed helplessly, staring at the ceiling. Frustration quickly mounted to a wildfire of anger, quick and overwhelming. The anger consumed him, but he could not much move and so he helplessly lay there, stewing, until it was spent, and he slept.

Then there was the movement of Opal jumping down off the bed and the sound of the door opening and James opened his eyes in time to see Sara come through the door, a large tin can in her hands. She set the can down on the table and greeted Opal and then James heard her say, "Ew. Bad dog!" and she took the rope down from its hook and wrapped it around the dog's neck and then added, "Though it's my own fault." He tried to move, to indicate to her his need, but he could not, and she went back out with the dog. A while later, she returned, let the dog off the cord, and cleaned up the mess. She sighed deeply as she sat down on a chair to take off her boots. With all his might, everything he could muster, he tried to call her name. It came out as a sort of a groan, and at the sound Sara sat up quickly. "James?" she said. She looked at him and saw his open eyes and jumped up, one shoe on and one shoe off, and stumped over to him and sat down and took his cheeks gently in her palms and turned his face toward her. "Oh my God, oh my God, James!" she said. She looked into his eyes, searching—for what he did not know, but her eyes were wide and bright. She put her head down on his chest and said, "You're back. Thank the Lord, you are back." She scooped her arms under his sides and held him rather too tightly and hugged him. "I was about to give up hope," she said. "Can you speak? How do you feel?"

"Water," he tried to say but did not manage to make himself intelligible.

"Are you in pain?" she asked, craning her neck to look at the top of his head. He did not know why.

"Uh huh," he managed, and this time communication was established.

"Well, I wouldn't wonder," she said. "You've had quite a crack on the noggin." She smiled broadly. "Oh, James, I was so afraid. But now, you're back." She hugged herself with both arms but then looked down at him and said, "You must be as thirsty as a camel. Here, let me get you some water." She rose and got a glass of water and, carefully propping his head forward, tipped some into his mouth. Oh, it was the sweetest thing James had ever tasted. It was the elixir of life, and he wanted to gulp in pools. But then she pulled the cup away. "Nnnnnnnnnn," he said, but she shook her head. "We must go slowly. You have not drunk a drop for five days. Six, actually, since the accident occurred the day before." The accident? He was in an accident? Again he tried to remember, and again there was nothing. However, the throbbing in his head was testament enough.

Again she raised the glass and let him drink. He swallowed quickly but then due to his supine position choked, just managing to clear his airway. "Easy, there," she said. Again, she let him drink, just a sip at a time, and then said, "Enough." But he was burning with thirst! He must have it. He protested as vigorously as he could: "Nnnnnnnnn!" But she was adamant. "You will throw up," she said. "Let's give it a minute." But in a minute, he was asleep, and he slept. It seemed no time at all, though, and he was shaken awake and given more water, which he was grateful for. Again he slept. The next time he was awakened, she gave him a warm broth, a nectar of ambrosia. The salt was the saltiest he had ever tasted, and the meatiness was the most luscious he had ever sampled, though it was nothing but liquid. She also did something with the lower part of his body, lifting it and wrapping something around his hips, and he felt the cold air on the bare skin of his legs and groin. Again he slept. Thus a pattern was established. All night long, she would wake him and give him water or broth, which he took gratefully. He was never aware of her lying beside him, and he briefly wondered if she slept, before he was unconscious again.

Then she was shaking him, and when he opened his eyes, there was another face next to hers—a brown wrinkled face. Sara said, "This is Auntie, from next door? She will look after you today. I must go to work." To work? Sara worked? He had just a minute to think, that is not right, a wife should not be forced out to work, before he was fed more broth and once again he fell asleep. The next times he was awakened, it was to the stranger's face, to her husky voice urging him to drink, and to her cold but firm hands helping him raise his head. At one point, he awakened to pain so bad tears streaked involuntarily down his cheeks, and the brown face then put something into his mouth, a strange tasting liquid that burned slightly and said, "Swallow, child." He had, and then he had slept. And then there was Sara again. This time, she spooned a thin gruel of oatmeal laced with milk and butter. Ah, the taste of butterfat sent a chill of pleasure down his spine. He slurped hungrily and even managed to say the word, "More," which she obliged him.

Slowly, over time, he was able to remain awake for longer periods, and whenever his pain got too bad, Sara would give him a spoonful of the fiery liquid. As he recovered, Sara was able to tell him what had happened. Again, he could remember nothing. When he was able to lift his arm, he felt the top of his head. His hair had been cut in an area on the crown and the short bristles poked his hand. There were bumps of tissue on his scalp and what he found out to be the poking of threads where the wound had been sutured. It was tender. Probing it as much as he dared, he discovered an indentation, which sent a chill through him. It had been bad, this accident. After some days had passed, Sara gave him a spoon of fiery liquid and then, using her sewing scissors, removed the sutures. He passed out from the pain, despite the liquid.

However, slowly but surely, he improved. He was able to sit up, and then to read, and then to stand, and then to walk. He approached each new task with trepidation, in fear that the trauma would have stolen it from him, but it had not. These skills were merely rusty from their not being used. The only persistent symptoms were a numbness in the pinkie and ring finger of his left hand and the persistent headache that eased somewhat over time but did not dissipate completely. The lack of activity, however, and the thoughts of his inabilities kept returning and often sent him into a foul mood, but sometimes at the thought of what might have happened he would be joyous, thankful for his mere existence.

The Soijka brothers called from time to time, often with gifts of bread or a newspaper or, once, a bouquet of hastily plucked flowers for Sara. He did remember them, his job, and their bouts of drinking. At some point, they made reference to a night he had been out till after the dawn and Sara had met them at the door and what trouble he had been in. He did not remember it, and he protested, as it seemed so out of character as to be unbelievable. They laughed and said, "You got yourself out of that one all right, though it nearly killed you." Sara went out every day except Sundays to work, and old Mrs. Soule—he found out quickly that her surname was not Thaxton—would stop by a few times a day. He was relieved when he could rise and use the chamber pot on his own, without her assistance, as it embarrassed them both. Though he felt awful that Sara was forced out to work, her cooking improved immensely, and those dishes she brought home from her job were absolutely divine compared to past fare. He began to put on weight, due to his inactivity, and for the first time in his life, he developed just a bit of fat upon his belly. He looked forward to the day that he could return to work, as he missed the physicality of it and the way it structured his days, and his mood lifted somewhat as he became more convinced that that day would actually come.

Sara was overjoyed at James's steady recovery. Each new task he was able to perform put her over the moon. As it progressed, she realized how over those dark days she had begun to accept his trance state and so his recovery seemed miraculous in all respects. She was patient and optimistic at all turns, even when she was tired from her days at work. She felt she owed him that. The only way he was to completely recover is if he kept his fortitude, if he kept pressing on, and the only way he would do that is if she prepared the ground in all manner possible.

Sara's employment at Molly's was for weekdays and Saturdays, with Sundays off. Her morning routine began early as she helped James clear his bladder and bowels and prepared food for him for the day. If she had time, she helped him to stand and walk a bit. She rushed off to Molly's between 8:15 and 8:30 to make sure she had plenty of time to walk the distance. She worked all day, only resting to grab something to eat, and when the workday was through, she trudged home carrying an odd bit of stew or pie or bread for supper. Their apartment suffered. It was all she could do.

Though it was hard, Sara liked her job. She learned how to cook. At first, she had been assigned the hardest and most time-consuming tasks. She chopped endless piles of vegetables and swept and mopped miles of floor. While she was doing these tasks, she watched what the others were doing and if she finished her task early she would offer to help them with theirs. She watched how things were made and noted the receipts in her book at home. Molly's tongue became less sharp, and she began assigning Sara tasks that still required a lot of time but also more skill. Sara made and rolled out pie dough and mixed and kneaded bread. She browned meat for stew and simmered bones for soup. Sara soon found that she had a knack for cooking, despite her past inabilities. She had a mind for detail—she always remembered to check the roast in the oven and to pull the gravy off before it scorched. She didn't oversalt things, and she was patient enough to let things simmer slowly when they needed it. She had an eye for appearances, as well. When she made a pie, she always topped the crust with a half-moon to remind herself of her long lost mother. When she made biscuits, she was careful to cut them evenly, and she cut them into diamonds rather than squares, which had the added benefit of making them crispier. Whenever she could, she tried to make things elegant. Elegance was unusual in this eating house, but Sara remembered the suppers back home in Anamosa, and she tried to inculcate a little of that into this dreary little corner of the world.

It set her apart. Nellie rolled her eyes when Sara tried something new, but Molly didn't, and that was what was important. Nellie soon began to get on Sara's nerves. It was the little things. She talked too much with everyone, which left Sara with more work to do. It was not that Nellie was lazy, but instead that she was easily distracted. Nellie would set Sara up with something to do, intending to help her, and then she would go off to get something and then would not return for a half an hour later as she chatted with a customer. By that time, the job would be done. Nellie apologized, but that would not stop a repeat performance.

Nellie also could not make up her mind about anything. The soup was a prime example. Nellie was in charge of preparing the soup for the next day. "Shall I use the leftover roast to make vegetable soup? Or maybe dumplings? Dumplings sound good. I think dumplings," but then she would start cutting up vegetables. "Oh, I was making dumplings. Oh well. We will make vegetable soup." Then she second-guessed herself. "No, no. It's supposed to be cooler tomorrow so dumplings would have been better. Oh!" Then she would get flustered. It wasn't just the indecision. Sara found lots of little things that bothered her about Nellie—the way she patted her hair when certain men came in the restaurant, the way she held her body stiffly as if it were a bird that was about to fly, the way she talked nonstop. However, Sara felt guilty about being bothered, as none of the things that Nellie did were harmful, and she had a good soul.

One evening when Sara returned to the apartment, a letter sat on the table for her. It had been delivered earlier by the Express man, James said, and as it had been addressed to her, he had not opened it. She immediately recognized the tall loopy scrawls of her father's chirography. It was addressed to "Mrs. Sara Youngblood," as if he could not stand to write the Christian name of her husband, or he refused to know it. Sara told James who it was from and immediately felt an urge to throw the thing in the stove and burn it. Instead, she let it set on the table while she helped James to bathe and set the table for supper and they ate. The envelope, however, was always on her mind. After supper, though, as they sat there, drinking cups of tea, she finally summoned the courage. James did not comment

329

but merely eyed her as she ripped the flap. She read:

Daughter:

Esther tells me that you are established in Kansas City and that all is well but that your husband struggles to achieve a secure position. I write to tell you of my communications with my associate, Mr. Frances Xavier, of Xavier's Grocery and Dry Goods, Kansas City, in which I informed him of my intention to give your husband decent employment. Mr. Xavier has agreed to the arrangements. Should your husband turn out to be an adequate worker, he will be paid a living wage. These arrangements are made in memory of your mother, at Esther's request, and against the forces of reason.

Your father

Sara sat stunned. It was the best possible outcome. It was begrudged, but it offered a way out, a chance for them to possibly make more money, what with her having a job too, and then they could possibly get ahead. This could be their ticket to a better life. She glanced at James, and doubts immediately surfaced about her being able to persuade him to take a new job. He had a job, and it was evident his enjoyment of that situation, even though he had not been able to join the Soijkas for quite some time. How best to approach the matter?

330

"Well, then," James said, "what does it say?"

"He says," she began and then stopped. Frame it as it benefits him, she thought. "You have often complained of the exhaustion of working at the packing factory, no? And it is dangerous work, as evidenced by the severe trauma you received. Is that not true?"

He looked at her but said nothing, his eyes narrowed.

She hurried on. "He offers an opportunity for employment unlike you've been able to obtain as yet." His face clenched. Whoops—she realized the miswording of her plea immediately and began to backpedal. "What I mean to say is, he offers a job, here in the city with good pay and regular hours"—she supposed—"and less demands upon your physical person. He offers us a future that we would not otherwise be able to achieve." Her voice was pleading.

"Out of the goodness of his heart," James said, "your father, a man who beat you and bullied you, offers us work?" His eyebrows were raised.

"Yes," she said. "There are no encumbrances. My sister Esther convinced him. If there is anyone who could, it would be her. Please, do not resist this."

"And what of my previous commitment to Joseph and Karl?" Stone was in his voice.

Sara felt increasingly frantic. Now that she had seen the opportunity of this job, she did not want to let it go. It seemed to her, more and more, that if they let it escape, he would continue to drink and they would be pulled into the morass of poverty, and it became more and more imperative that he take the job.

"Please," she begged. "Please? At least talk to the man?"

Anger rose on his face, a quick flash. It happened so fast,

she did not think it possible. He rose, but in his weakened state, he could not do much more than pace the room, his presence bristling. She went up behind him and put a hand on his shoulder, which had diminished in strength and size over these past weeks. She said softly, "You do not need to agree to it. Simply talk to the man. See if it might suit our needs." When this got no response, she said, "You'll be in no condition to return to the other job for a number of weeks yet, while this job will be less physically demanding"—she hoped—"and hence I would once again be able to return home." She knew as she said it that it bothered him that she had to go out to work. In truth she enjoyed the job, but this was the tool that she hoped would accomplish the task of getting him to take the position. She hated herself for having to use it.

When he heard the words, his shoulders slumped. "Yes," he said almost inaudibly.

"What?" She could not hear him.

"I will talk to the man," he said, more loudly, "when my strength allows it." He went and lay in the bed, his back to her.

Chapter 15

avier's Grocery and Dry Goods was located near the Missouri River and its wet stench. Rain fell softly as James eyed the building from across the street. He had had to rest only a couple of times on his way there, but he planned to step on a streetcar on his return as the trip had drained him. Sara had supplied him with the money to do just that, and it made him feel like a boy again at his Mam's knee, begging for a penny. It prompted an undercurrent of simmering anger to rise and then fall, but to remain there, just below the surface. It was a festering stew that had bubbled within him ever since the accident.

People bustled in and out of the grocery at this early hour hauling baskets and paper-wrapped parcels. It did a good business, which was a propitious sign, but James liked the job he had. He would go in, talk to the man, and then have his excuse to turn the job down. That was all. A bell tinkled as James opened the door and then softly shut it behind him. It took a minute for his eyes to adjust to the interior gloom. The place smelled of overripe fruits and of the wood of freshly sprung packing crates. Two high counters and glass cases ran on either side the length of the long narrow room. Essentials such as flour, rice, soap, and meal were sold from the counter on the right, and nonessentials such as candy, patent medicines, and cookware lay on the shelves on the left. Every space was filled with stacks of dry goods or opened crates. The little space not taken up by goods was occupied by customers waiting in line or browsing. Light shown from a door at the back, through which James could see another room stacked with unopened barrels and crates. The scene was presided over by a quick small man, dark-skinned, who sat on a tall stool at the cash box. His hands seemed to have a life of their own as they smoothed the counter, made loops through the air, fingered each item as he tallied things up, and snapped and clapped. The man wore a red embroidered vest over a white shirt with ruffles, and his dark mustache was well waxed, through which came a steady stream of talk: "Missus Perkins, how are you today? Haven't seen you in a while. You know you cannot get along without Mrs. Partridge's chamomile soap. And Lucy, how does she stay away from those peppermint drops? Just corn meal and eggs today?"

The proprietor turned and yelled toward the back of the store, "Custer. Custer!" In response, a thin stooped figured stood framed in the light of the back door. The man's head and shoulders were bent so that he looked at the floor, and his black hair, shorn just below the ears, fell forward and covered his face. The sleeves of the man's coat stopped two inches above his thin wrists. The man's wool pants, baggy around his waist, were held up with a bit of packing cord as a belt. Standing there in the light, the man twitched his shoulders, as if the clothing did not set quite right. "Custer!" the proprietor bellowed, "get Missus Perkins here a half dozen eggs and a pound of Indian meal. And *ehshehwoh highahts.*" He turned and continued his steady stream of chatter as the man disappeared from the door. "You know how they are, Missus Perkins," he said conspiratorially. "Lazy as all get out. You have to get after them." The man soon emerged from the back. He set the eggs nestled in a small basket on the counter next to the man on the stool and then turned and scooped yellow meal from a barrel. He turned back and poured the meal onto a paper-lined scale on the counter, carefully adding weights. The man's eyes were focused on the scale, but James couldn't help but feel that they took in everything—him, the woman and tall girl leafing through dress patterns, the man looking at tobacco, the boys near the candy jars, the woman with the girl child piling things on the counter, and the man sitting on the stool behind the counter chattering. The flat eyes seemed active in their stillness. After measuring out the meal, deftly wrapping it into a paper bundle, tying it with a string, and placing it on the counter, he turned and disappeared out through the back entry.

James pretended to look at the tin kitchen implements hanging on the back wall as customers stood in line to pay. He hoped that the people would thin out, but they did not. He waited as long as he could, until the man at the counter started watching him. It seemed he could wait no longer, so he stood in line. When he made it to the head of the line, the man's hands stilled in front of him, and he cocked his head. "What can I do you for?" he asked, glancing down at James's empty hands.

"You received a letter. About having me work for … with you," James said, glancing behind himself at the man standing there.

"A letter? I don't recall a letter. You will have to wait. Go to the back." The proprietor gestured widely with his right hand and then turned to the man behind James. James had no

335

choice but to wait. He made his way to the back and propped himself on a barrel so that he could see along the counter where the man perched. It felt good to be seated. The thin dark man, whom was called Custer, appeared at the back door with a large crate in his hands. Custer set down the crate, pulled open the screen door and held it with his hip, deftly picked up the crate, threaded through the door, let the door close quickly but silently behind him, catching it with his foot just at the end, and then deposited the crate on the floor. Then he turned and made his way back out. James continued to watch him as he brought in another crate, set it on the floor, and then back out. James glanced at the proprietor, who continued to ignore him, and then he got up and held the door for Custer. Custer stopped for a second, his eyes still on the floor, and then made his way through the open door. When Custer made his way back out the door, James followed him. In the alley was a pile of crates. Custer picked one up, and so did James, choosing a small one, as he did not trust his strength. They developed a rhythm. Custer would come out of the door and hold it for James, who carried a crate, and then James would hold it for Custer. As a matter of necessity, James always chose the smaller crates, and by the end of the task he was sweating profusely and his legs shook with the effort, and he hoped the man would not think he was deliberately shirking his share. The back room was soon full, and the alley emptied. Neither said a word. The task complete, James perched back on the barrel, thankful to be seated, breathing heavily. Custer turned an empty crate on its end and sat. He pulled a knife from the sheath on his belt and began to trim his fingernails. Still, he did not look at James, but again James felt like he took in everything.

The man perched on the stool in front ignored James for

336

what felt a long while. Finally, the crowd thinned, and the man glanced back to the back entry. He seemed startled to find James still sitting there on the barrel. He looked away for a second and back and then said, "Hey, you. What you want?"

James stood and walked back up to the counter. "You received a letter from a Colonel Moore of Anamosa, Iowa. He said something about a job. A job with decent pay." James looked him in the eye, daring him to disagree. He hoped that the man would eject him from the building, and that would be that, end of story.

"Oh. That." The man's hands came to rest before him and he stopped talking for minute. James stood there. The man asked, "So what is it that you do?"

"I'm pretty good with horses," James said

The man's hand gesture took in the store. "Horses?"

"Yep."

"Not much need for that. Are you strong?"

Formerly, James had been strong, but now he was not. To avoid the question, he said, "I have kept books." When he had been in his early teens, he had worked briefly with the man and wife in their business selling eggs and produce, and the woman had taken an interest in his education and had taught him the fundamentals of bookkeeping.

"*I* keep the books," the man said, smoothing the counter in front of him. "*I* keep the books."

"Well, then, there is obviously nothing much you can do for me." James turned to walk out the door. He felt a weight lift from his shoulders.

"Wait!" The man jumped off his stool and came around the counter. He was a full head and a half shorter than James. "I seem to recall the letter now. Yes. The letter." He fingered his lapels and put his hands in vest pocket, pulled them out, and then put them in again.

"You don't seem to be in need of anyone. You've got ..." James gestured toward the back.

"No, no. No! I have something for you. I am sure we can work something out." He stroked his lapel.

The desperate tone in the man's voice told James that Sara's father, the Colonel, held some sway with this man and that he had put his demands rather more forcefully. James could only guess at this man's motives, as well as his father-in-law's. There was a history there, that was for sure. "Nah. I am not seeking a crate-hauling job." He turned and walked out the door.

The short man followed him. "No. Wait! I ... I have a clerk position. Yes. A clerk position. Yes. We can work something out." James ignored him and continued down the street, the man's voice getting smaller behind him: "No, wait!"

That was that. James felt satisfied, though very very tired. It was all he could do to make it home. He immediately took to bed and slept that night and well into the next morning. It was not until the next evening after supper that Sara asked him about job. They sat on the back stoop under the overhang, watching Opal nose about the back yard in the rain, the sky darkening behind the clouds. He felt badly having to tell her, but he was also defensive. What right did she have to order his life in such a way? It was a man's decision to work where he will, and she had no say in it.

"How did it go?" she asked.

"Go?" he said, determined to play dumb.

"Yesterday. At the grocery. Inquiring about the position."

He felt the anger rise again. She was nosey, she was

impertinent, she was simply overstepping her bounds. "Fine," he said.

"So you have the position?" Her eyes brightened.

"I did not say that." He would not give her an easy satisfaction.

"What?"

"I said, I did not say that I had the position."

"Well, do you?" Genuine perplexity crossed her face.

"No, I do not." He rose from where they were sitting on the back porch of the building and went inside. She followed him upstairs, Opal left behind, and into the apartment.

"Did he refuse you? Oh my. Wait until I telegraph my father. He will set it right."

"No," he said forcefully. "It is not like that. Telegraphing him will do no good."

"He flat refused you? He cannot!" Her voice rose in its self-righteousness. "He cannot. My father—"

He cut her off. "Your father will have nothing to do with this. I am not taking the position. Yes, I spoke with the man. Now, leave it be. I am not taking the position." The anger boiled within him.

"You what?" Her eyes were wide with incredulity. "You, you. You did not take it? He offered and you did not take it?" Her thoughts moved behind her eyes, and she shook her head. "How could you?" She turned away from him and walked out through the open door to their apartment and stood for a moment. Then she returned, her shoulders set. "You must take this job. You simply must."

"Are you fucking listening to me?" he said, as shocked as she at his own curses, at his strong reaction. But it bubbled and boiled and he felt the urge to strike out in anger, to break something, but instead he walked away from her and out the door and down the steps. Immediately she came pounding down the steps after him.

When they were once again on the back stoop, she said in a level and forceful voice, "You listen to me, James. If you do not take this job." She hesitated.

"You will what? What will you do?"

She made up her mind. "If you do not take this job, I will leave you. It does not matter if I return to Anamosa or simply move to another part of the city. I can support myself now. I do not need you. And you are well enough to damn yourself to hell."

He turned to look at her face, and in it, he saw that she was serious, that she would indeed leave him, that very night if necessary. She had the look of the converted, and all his fears were realized. He could lose everything. He was not even sure that he yet had the strength to keep himself in a job, even with the Soijka brothers' charitable natures. He had fought so hard to get her, to keep her, to support her, everything, only now to lose her—the thought broke something inside him, and he sagged upon his frame. That was it then. He had obstacles from without and within his household, and even those closest to him conspired against him.

"I will," he said softly.

She peered at his face, her anger still writ bold across her own. "You will what?"

"I will take the position," he said.

She pulled back, her shoulders relaxing into their normal position, and she tilted her head and thought for a moment. "All right," she said, and then with more emotion, "you will? Truly?"

340

He nodded. She rushed to him and put her arms around him. "Oh, James, you do not know what this means to me, to us. It will mean the difference for our future. It will be all right, you will see." He turned to walk back up the steps, and suddenly he felt the strength go out of him, and she supported him up the stairs and into the apartment.

The next day, James returned to Xavier's Grocery and Dry Goods. As if he had not moved, Xavier sat on his stool, his hands smoothing and patting the counter and the merchandise as he totaled purchases and took money. James heard his voice even before he entered the store. "Yes, Mister Jones. Those suspenders you ordered should be in next week. I see your wife's craving lemon drops again. A good sign. A good sign, eh?" Xavier glanced up as James carefully closed the door. "Ah. What have we here? Someone looking for a job, perhaps?" His voice was cheerful, but his lips did not form a smile. "Yes, sir, I will be with you as soon as I finish with Mister Jones here." James made his way to the back room and sat again on the barrel. Custer was nowhere to be seen. James sighed and prepared for a long wait, but Xavier surprised him. He finished up with the man at the counter and climbed off his stool and came into the back. "Was I right?" he asked. "You rethink my offer?"

"Yes, Mister Xavier, I did."

"It's a deal then, a deal." Xavier rubbed his hands and then clasped them together as if his fingers were cold. Then he held out his right hand. James took it in his own. The man's grip was slack, and as they shook, the man's gaze slanted sideways. "Colonel Moore did not mention your name?"

"It is Youngblood. James Youngblood."

"Aaaah. Mis-ter Youngman," Xavier puffed with

satisfaction. "Happy to have you. You can begin your illustrious career by opening these crates." He turned and made his way back to his stool and addressed the next customer. "Yes, yes. Miss Sorenson. You're bonnet is lovely today. That new cloth we got in last month, isn't it?" James turned to the crates. He sighed as he looked around for a bar with which to pry the crates open.

James's job at the grocery turned out to be that of delivery person and general help. The man who helped Xavier, an Indian James decided, rather than a Mexican, was gone for days at a time, but Xavier took it in stride, so it must have been arranged. When the man—James hesitated to call him Custer, if only in opposition to Xavier's snide tone—was gone, James took over his duties of retrieving and weighing, opening and stocking, dusting and sweeping. At first, it taxed James to his limits, but the regular exercise soon strengthened him physically, though he found that he brooded more than ever, and it was a challenge to keep his temper in check. Xavier never put James behind the counter, so he did not actually act as a clerk. He delivered and fetched things. Xavier did not seem to trust the other man with money, and he only grudgingly allowed James to handle money, and then only because he had to as a delivery person. Still, Xavier made him bring back the duplicate receipt and count out change in front of him, which Xavier would meticulously enter into his black accounts ledger. However, for all the menial jobs that Xavier had James do, he paid him reasonably well. James suspected that that was part of he and the Colonel's deal—Moore had specified that he be paid well, but he had not specified what jobs James should do.

At first, Xavier was polite, never quite saying please and

thank you, but a formal note was in his voice nonetheless. Slowly, though, the tone changed. He started parading him in front of customers and saying nasty things. "What do think of my errand boy, Missus Blake?" he would say. "He's past his prime, as an errand boy. Could be quicker. Why, just last week, he broke a dozen eggs." Xavier would smile smugly. Needless to say, James had not broken the eggs. Some of the customers looked at him with pity, some with skepticism, some heartily in on the joke. Xavier would say, "What do you think, Mister Perkins? I have the most expensive go-fer in the world." His lips would curl into what should have been a grin. He would slap the counter. "But, you know, my business partner insisted." Then he'd look right at James and say, "You'd think they were related," and then he'd smile for real. James took it in stride and bit back his tongue. What else could he do? But, he needed to watch the man. Xavier would try to get away with as much as he could, that much James knew.

James dreaded going to work. He never was late—why give that bastard an excuse to fire him?—but it was all he could do to drag himself out of bed every morning, pick at his breakfast, trudge to the store, and hold his tongue all day. His physical strength may have improved, but his mental and emotional strength was stretched mighty thin. On his way home, James rarely stopped by the Climax Saloon—it was too painful—but he did inform the Soijkas of his new position. They said they were sorry to see him go, but as they needed someone they hired another man. It felt as if a door had been slammed in James's face.

The only thing of interest at his work was the tall dark Indian man, the man Xavier called Custer. There was something about the man that fascinated James—a quiet thoughtfulness, a careful and deliberate manner, and even as the man waited on customers and did everything Xavier asked him, he did not appear beaten down. James thought he saw an intelligence, a shrewdness behind his eyes. When they worked side by side transferring barrels and crates and unpacking them or hauling out garbage, James thought he saw that the man's shoulders would relax just a little, but when Xavier came into the room, the man tightened and vibrated like a plucked wire.

One day, as he and Custer sat out back eating their lunches, James read the paper. The rain had abated somewhat, though it was still overcast, and they sat in the lee of the building. An article about the Kentucky Derby caught his eye. It reported that Kansas City's own Thoroughbred Brandywine, owned by one Thaddeus Blachley and jockeyed by Erskine Enders, had won that race, as well as two other derbies just this year. James always read about the races when he got a chance. Reading about it was second best to being there, feeling the thrill of it. He did not gamble, and for him it was all about the horses. James had worked with Thoroughbreds, though he'd only ridden a western saddle—not the English that jockeys rode.

He finished reading and folded the paper. Custer turned to him and said, "Some rain."

"Yeah," James said.

"By the way, my name is Ohnohnehwohneshk, but people call me Thomas Prairie Dog. I'm Tsististas, from the mountains out in the Territories." He gestured northwest, the direction that the Missouri River came into the city. He seemed about to continue, so James waited to see if he would say anything else. After a minute, he did continue. "The mountains are a long way away, so I haven't been there since I was a boy."

344

James nodded. "My name is James, James Youngblood." He put out his hand. "I'm from"—he gestured to the northeast—"the plains." Thomas considered it for a second, nodded, and then held out his own hand. Smiling, they shook.

Just then, Xavier came out to check on them. When he saw them, he scowled and walked back into the store. James shook his head. Thomas glanced at James and nodded his head toward Xavier's retreating back and said, "He taught me English, and he was also the one who taught me how to curse." Humor glinted in his eyes, but then he became serious. "My father knew. My father was a wise man."

What could his father have to do with Xavier? James did not prompt him. Instead, he waited.

Thomas continued: "Yep. My father became a Christian when his second wife converted. He was a spiritual and deep-thinking man."

James nodded.

"And when Mister Xavier came to our camp trading," Thomas continued, "my father paid him what he asked. Then my father asked him for a receipt."

James glanced over at Thomas. Thomas's face looked serious. He wondered if Xavier had stolen from Thomas's father.

"Xavier told him he did not need a receipt," Thomas said. "He told my father, 'I'm an honest trader.' My father, though, he shook his head. He told him, 'I have to be ready for judgment, when that day comes, just as you have to be ready for that day, and I do not want to have to go down to where you will be to collect that receipt.'" Thomas kept his eyes down on his hands as he finished.

James snorted and looked at Thomas, and Thomas glanced

over from the corner of his eye, and soon they were both smiling.

Chapter 16

ne Sunday, while Sara was in the apartment darning a sock and James was out, Sara heard feet on the stairs and then past her door and the heavy thud of something dropped down the hall by Auntie's door. Opal let out a low woof and raised her head. Not wanting to be nosy, Sara kept her door shut, but she was curious and put her ear to the crack. She thought she heard the voice of a woman followed by that of a man. Sometime later, the feet, quicker this time, retraced their steps across the landing and down the steps and it was quiet again. Carefully, Sara opened the door, but there was nothing to see and she had to catch Opal from running past her. Later that afternoon, Sara heard a high-pitched noise, long and drawn out. Sara would have thought that she had imagined it, but for Opal pricking her ears too and tilting her head. Sara heard the sound again that evening just for a moment. Soon, she begin to hear it at odd hours, though it never lasted long, never long enough to locate where it originated. The more she heard it, the more it sounded like the cries of a baby. Was she tetched? When she heard it late at night, lying next to James, she rolled over and touched his shoulder. "You hear that?" she whispered.

"Huh?" he said, lifting his head.

"Did you hear that?" she repeated.

"Huh? Uh-uh," he mumbled and went back to sleep.

The next Sunday, Sara sat down with a cup of strong coffee and her commonplace book to note down a receipt, when there was a tap on her door. James was sleeping. Opal barked, as usual. Sara rose quickly, so that a knock would not rouse James, and opened the door. It was Auntie, her face pinched with concern. She was in a heavy wrap and carried her hat and gloves, and she walked with the assistance of a stout polished stick with a carved knot at the top.

"Good morning, Neighbor," Auntie said. "Hope the day finds you well?"

"Indeed it does," Sara replied. She wanted to invite her in for a cup of coffee, but James was sleeping and Auntie was obviously on her way out. Against her better judgment, though, Sara said, "Would you like to come in for a cup of coffee?" She immediately regretted it and glanced back toward James.

"No, but thank you kindly," Auntie replied. "I am sorry but I must run. But before I do I have a favor to ask."

"Oh my gosh, of course, anything," Sara said, immediately curious about what Auntie might need.

Auntie glanced back toward her apartment. "I be running out, but, well, I have recently been charged with the keeping of my grandchild, Moses's baby boy, and I cannot tote him out with me, yet I must get some milk to feed him."

So that was what the noise had been. "Yes?" Sara said.

"I was wondering if you might poke your head in and check on him from time to time. He is a fairly easy one, not at all like Moses in that regard, but, well, you know." She shrugged and looked up into Sara's face. "I hope to be gone no more than a half hour, hour at most, and he is sleeping, but you never know."

"Say no more," Sara said, "of course, of course. It will be me returning the favor, as I am deeply in your debt." Then Sara remembered Auntie's limited mobility. "Wait. Why not let me retrieve the milk for you? I can be there and back as quick as a wink."

This caused Auntie's face to pinch further. "That is very kind of you, child, very kind. However, it is not just milk I'm after. I have some other business to which I must attend."

"Of course," Sara said, "of course."

"Well, here is the key. He is sleeping, but you might poke your head in soon, just in case."

"I definitely will," Sara said.

With that, Auntie turned and made her way to the steps.

A question came into Sara's mind, and so she yelled, "Wait, Auntie! What is the baby's name?"

Auntie called over her shoulder, "Moses. Well, Jeremiah Moses, but I call him Moses." She carefully but deftly began to descend the stairs, much more quickly than Sara imagined possible.

The response caused Sara to involuntarily bow her head before she turned back into her apartment and shut the door. Sara then wondered why Auntie was taking care of the boy. Where was the mother? Well, who knew about these things?

Sara returned to her coffee and commonplace book, only to be distracted by the thought of the baby. Should she check on him? Auntie had said he was sleeping, and Sara did not hear his cries—surely, if he awoke, would he not start crying? She was not sure. She tried to think back to when Maisie was a baby. From what she could remember, Maisie would often cry when she awoke, so Sara turned to her pencil and her coffee.

But it niggled at the back of her mind. The baby Moses, was he a crier? Was he a wiggler? Could he roll off the bed? Could he smother?

She jumped up, grabbed the key, and went down the hall. She let herself into Auntie's apartment. No baby in the sitting room, so Sara went into the kitchen, where next to Auntie's bed was a beautifully made cradle. It sat fairly tall in its frame, its sides were solid and unslatted, and its wood was a dark brown with simple but beautiful carving that was rounded and cupped from years of use. She moved quietly up next to it and peeked down over the edge. The baby Moses was wide awake. He had the slightly scrunched look of a young baby and his dark eyes were wide open and looking toward the ceiling. His brow was wrinkled between his wide-set eyebrows, as if he were thinking hard upon something. His skin was lighter than Auntie's but not much. He had round nostrils like little circles and a broad lower lip. Sara was surprised—except for the darker skin, baby Moses looked much the same as newborn Maisie. As Sara stood quietly next to the cradle, the baby's manner changed. The wrinkled lines on his forehead smoothed, his eyebrows shot up, and he smiled. One second his face looked like a walnut, and the next it opened like the sun. He smiled broadly for a second and then kicked his feet vigorously and waved his arms. His eyes did not focus on her, but his actions seemed to indicate that he knew she was in the room. She pulled up a chair and sat down next to the cradle and put her hand down to the baby. He clutched it in his fist and shook it up and down. That's where Auntie found them an hour later—Sara leaned over the crib, chin in hand, and Moses clutching her other hand in his fist.

It became Sara's habit every evening to pop in to see

Auntie and Moses, and she thought about them while she was at work. When she visited, she tried to bring something, usually milk but also soup or biscuits or the like. Auntie, she figured, had rising expenses, with Moses on cow's milk, rather than at the breast. It was not long before little Moses seemed to know her voice, and he would turn his face toward her when she spoke. The first time she held him, Auntie put her in the rocking chair and put a pillow under her arm and nestled the baby onto her lap. He was heavier than she had expected, and warmer, and it felt so good, so right, to hold him. It made Sara long for a baby of her own.

Work went well. Mollie trusted her more and more, even looking to her where she once looked to Nellie. She gave Sara the responsibility of overseeing the soup, something that made Nellie frown, but neither of them said anything to the other about it. Nellie did not seem to hold it against Sara, however.

Then, on yet another day of pelting rain, Sara was out front in the dining room mopping the floor in a corner when Molly's husband came in. It was just as the breakfast customers were clearing out, so there was confusion as there were two lines side by side, one to order food and another to pay. The lines bulged and crossed, as men chatted with each other and made their way toward the counter or the door. Mollie's husband evidently did not spy Sara. While streams of men milled around and Nellie's back was turned, he slipped by and put his hand in the cash box and then melted back in with the men who were leaving. He did it with such calculated ease that Sara was sure he had done it before.

Sara did not speak up, though, and she was not sure quite why. She didn't want Nellie to get into trouble, that was for sure, and she did not want to provoke Mollie, so she kept silent. It was probably something that had been going on for ages. It could even have been one of those things that were agreed upon but never spoken of, one of those things between husband and wife that are best left alone. None of her business. But then late in the day Molly's husband came back. Sara was in the kitchen up to her elbows in wet sticky dough and Molly was preparing a roast, the pepper in the air making them both sneeze, while Nellie had just left the kitchen for the store room. The kitchen door banged the wall as Molly's husband pushed clumsily through it. He pulled himself up tall in an exaggerated manner and stood there swaying and blinking.

Molly glanced at him and then her jaw tightened. "You're drunk as a dog," Molly said, squinting her eyes.

"Naaaaaaaaaaa," he said, his head wobbling on his neck in an attempt to shake it back and forth. "Well. Maybe … jess' … one." In slow motion, with utter concentration, he shook his finger at her to emphasize his point.

"You no-good son-of-a-bitch! Where did you get the money? Let me ask you that. Where did you get it?" The flesh on Molly's arm swung and swayed as she gestured with her hand.

"Money? I … Let me jess' say, I deserve that money. Uh huh. Deserve it," he said, this time trying to shake his head up and down. The effort unbalanced him, and he sat with a whump on the barrel of flour. He seemed to forget for a minute what they had been speaking about, but then he remembered. "You can't accuse me … Fair and square."

Molly reddened. "Accuse you? So you did take it." She paused, but then cocked her head and added, "Or did Nellie give it to you again?"

The muddle of gears of the man's mind turned. He grinned

and gave his head an exaggerated shake. "You can't blame me. Nellie's such a nice girl. She felt sorry for me. Her breast is not made of granite, like some I could mention." This amused him, and he began hooting with laughter. Sara sucked in her breath. He was insinuating that Nellie had given him the money, the no-account. She had seen it with her own eyes. He had stolen the money.

Molly began sputtering. "You no-good son-of-a-bitch—you take your sorry arse out of my kitchen! I'll deal with you later."

The husband, giggling and snorting, stumbled out into the dining area, and they heard the rattle of him hitting tables and the thump of the front door as he let himself out.

Molly's face was a mask of fury. "Nellie, get your arse in here!" She yelled. The magnitude of her anger made Sara feel small.

It took Nellie a moment to make it to the kitchen. There was dust in Nellie's hair and on her apron. "Yes?" Nellie said.

"You are fired!" Molly did not even try to explain.

But, Sara thought, Nellie did not do anything. It is not Nellie's fault. Sara had seen it with her own eyes. Sara stepped around the table and put out her hand as if to say, wait, I have something to add, but Molly turned that terrible gaze on her and raised her formidable eyebrows. Sara could see the look come in to Molly's eyes: If you say one word, you are gone too. At least this is what Sara would tell herself later, after she was promoted to Nellie's position with a raise. She would tell herself that the reason she did not say anything was because she would have lost her job too. Cowardice, pure cowardice on Sara's part that she did not speak up, and it was a thing that she would regret to the end of time, the day that she did not stand up for that innocent party.

Nellie's face turned white. "What? I ..." she sputtered.

"Get out now. I've had quite enough of you." Molly grabbed Nellie's arm and pulled her out the kitchen door. Sara followed quietly at a distance. Molly wrested open the cash register, pulled out some money, and thrust it into Nellie's hands. Then she shoved Nellie toward the door, in front of the gaping customers. By this time, great sobs escaped Nellie's chest and her eyes sparkled but she did not try to argue.

Chapter 17

ne Friday, as James and Thomas worked together in the back room constructing a shelving system, Thomas turned to James and said, "I've got something for you. I help a man with horses." After a moment, Thomas added, "We could use someone like you."

James nodded. "Sure."

"Not much money, though. At first, anyway."

James snorted. "Didn't think there was, beings as you are still working in this shithole," he said.

"It's because I love my job." Thomas shrugged and smiled with his eyes. "Tomorrow, Saturday. Meet me at 10 at the cable stop just down the way." James nodded, and they went back to work.

Saturday morning it was raining lightly as James walked to the stop where Thomas awaited him, and James was glad he wore a long duster coat. They took the cable car over the Kaw and up the bluffs and out into the city beyond. They passed stately homes and then modest homes and then rundown shacks. They rode on and on, out into the countryside, woodlands and fields on either side, to a tiny station, a small shack along the tracks, where they dismounted the car. So far from the city, and what with the rain, the air smelled fresh and pleasant. There to meet them was a stiff man in a formal coat and an oddly old-fashioned bicorne hat. He ushered them into a closed carriage pulled by a single horse and took them, rocking and bumping, farther into the country, and all the while the ubiquitous rain softly fell. James wondered at the luxury of the coach and coachman—Thomas must be valued by his employer if the man sent such a vehicle to retrieve him. The land they passed over was rolling and open, cut with fences into velvety green fields and paddocks and dotted with horses, cattle, and mostly depleted haystacks. There were small woodlots and winding streams swollen with rain that cut between the mounds of hills. Here and there were farmhouses and barns, which were invariably large and well-kept.

They topped a small rise, and out before them lay a wide and deep meandering valley with stately trees skirting a generous drainage. Down among an extensive copse of oaks, a large barn with long outbuildings was skirted by corrals and paddocks and a small horse track. The first thing that came to James's mind was how much it was all worth and that whoever owned it must be a rich man. As they approached, his impression was confirmed, as there was an imposing house among the oaks. The house seemed foremost designed to impress, with three floors skirted all around with porches. Baskets of flowers hung between every support pole, and well-mulched ornamental bushes and flowers decorated the edges and walkways. The carriage swept past the house, by the barn, and through the outbuildings beyond, and James caught a glimpse here and there of people performing their duties. It was a busy place.

The driver stopped next to a long outbuilding near the barn, and Thomas and James dismounted. Thomas led James into the dark interior of the long building. It smelled of hay and horse manure and saddle leather, and the interior gloom took a moment for the eyes to become accustomed. Men worked here and there, carrying buckets of grain and mucking out stalls. There was a large room, and then beyond were rows of large horse stalls on either side of a spacious center aisle. In the large room was a horse, a huge bay Thoroughbred, sixteen or seventeen hands with excellent proportions and powerful haunches, but its head was a somewhat big. The horse hung his cheek next to that of a short black and white paint horse, who occupied a stall and stuck its own head out over the gate. James glanced beyond the pair at the other horses' heads that loomed over the stall gates. Except for the paint, they were all Thoroughbreds, expensive ones. This was a horse farm for racing stock, no doubt about it.

Thomas lead James around the big horse, giving it a wide berth, and on the other side stood a man who was both small and extremely slender. He was recovering from an injury, as his left leg was well-wrapped and he was supported with a crutch under his armpit. However, his bearing was one of confidence despite the fact that his face held a youthful look, perhaps due to its thinness. His facial features showed him to be of negro blood—his skin was a dark brown and his nose cut a broad rounded wedge down the middle of his face. He was in the process of directing another man in the grooming of the large horse. "What the hell do you think you're doing, Paddy?" he barked. "One of those horse's hooves is worth more than you and your whole family put together. If you can't use proper technique, we'll get a groom with hands more capable than meat hooks." The man surveyed the groom for a minute but then turned and saw Thomas. His face transformed to a much

357

more pleasant expression as he did so.

"Thomas!" the man said.

"Babe," Thomas replied.

"Have you come to save me from ineptitude?"

"As a matter of fact," Thomas said and gestured toward James. "This is James Youngblood. He seems quite handy."

"We'll see about that."

Standing so close to the man, James realized how very tiny he truly was.

Thomas continued, "James, this is Erskine Enders."

Where had James come across that name before? It nudged the back of his mind. Oh well, it would come to him.

"And this is Brandywine," Enders said. "He's a pretty good horse, when he's not a leg breaker."

It couldn't be. James now remembered: This was the jockey and the horse he had read about in the newspaper, the jockey who had won the Kentucky Derby, the Tennessee Derby, and the Coney Island Derby on this horse, Brandywine, within the past year. That would make this the estate of Thaddeus Blachley, a man among men in the horse racing world. James suddenly felt very small, smaller than this small man. He was usually confident of his abilities with horses, but he suddenly questioned whether he would measure up to these standards.

"Well, shall we?" Thomas said. Enders nodded.

Thomas turned to James and gestured to the tack room, and so they entered its gloom. James looked at the racks. Instead of western saddles, they were all English. Of course, they were English—this was a horse racing stable. As much as James had been around horses, he had only ever ridden a western saddle, never English. Thomas handed James a bridle with a snaffle bit and then gestured to a saddle and a small blanket. Then he grabbed a set himself. The saddle and blanket were of no consequence at all, as light as a child's. When they stepped back into the aisle, the large bay Brandywine was being led away, a tall dun was led in, and the short black and white paint was let out of its stall. The man handed the halter rope of the paint to James. "That's Twister," Thomas said. "You'll ride him." Twister? Good name—let's hope he didn't live up to it. Just then, down at the end of the alley Brandywine let out a sustained high-pitched whinny as he was led around the end of the stalls. "Twister and Brandywine are buddies," Thomas explained.

Thomas then walked up to the dun, took the lead from the man, slipped the bridle over the horse's nose, and put the bit in its mouth. James did likewise. The familiar movements of working with a horse were soothing, and James leaned in slightly and inhaled the sweat scent of the animal. He patted the horse on the neck, letting it get used to him, and then lifted the bridled over its head, making sure that the bit did not slip under the horse's tongue. The horse took the bit readily into its mouth and chewed on it, the metal clinking against its teeth. James tried to watch Thomas out of the corner of his eye as Thomas strapped on the English saddle. It was most likely just the same as an Western one, but he wanted to be sure. He did not want to look the fool, especially to Enders, who stood across the way with his arms folded, watching. James rubbed the little horse's back to make sure that there were no stickers or clods of dirt that would cause irritation and then turned and retrieved the saddle and blanket. He placed the blanket right up next to the withers and then placed the feather-weight saddle with its stirrup draped over the top gently upon the blanket. He glanced over to see the horse's mood. It stood ears forward, eyelids drooping. Well, the horse was gentle—that was a relief.

There was some question as to how James would mount with such a high stirrup, but he pretended the horse was bareback and leapt into place. Enders looked on impassively. Once Thomas mounted with a leg up from a groom, Thomas turned his horse and walk through the open door, and James followed, feeling a precarious balance on the unfamiliar saddle. As they exited the barn out into the misting rain, behind them came a resounding thump and a loud prolonged whinny—a horse was protesting within. James and Twister trailed Thomas and the dun out onto the road. After a bit, James leaned forward in the saddle to get a better view of how Thomas was riding. Twister broke into a trot. James settled back as best he could and Twister slowed back to a walk. The signals to the horse, in English riding, were somewhat more subtle than he was used to. Instead of the heel to the ribs, as one did in western riding, it was the forward stance that urged the horse, but coming astride Thomas gave James a chance to view how Thomas was doing it. Following Thomas's example, he adjusted his single hand on the rein to both hands and tightened the tension a bit, plow rein-style. As James expected, Twister bowed his head, paying closer attention to James's movements. But from stem to stern, this way of riding felt all backwards, like trying to knot another man's tie. Thomas slowed the dun to allow him to catch up and then raised his eyebrows—you ready? he was asking. James shrugged. Ready or not.

The dun began to trot. James shifted forward. Obediently, Twister broke into a trot, and the two horses trotted side by side. It seemed natural to rise and fall with the movement of the horse, to post, as Thomas did. Moving at this speed, things felt more natural and in balance. He leaned farther forward and Twister broke into a long slow lope. At that point, it all seemed to click for James. In motion, this riding felt smoother and more free, less like he was anchored to the ground through the horse, more like he was being launched to fly. He started laughing and glanced back at Thomas. Thomas was smiling as he loped up beside him. "You *have* been on a horse before," Thomas yelled and urged his horse forward too. It felt wonderful—he was free in a way he hadn't been in a long time. There was the pell-mell motion and the beat of hooves like his heart pounding and pounding and the mist-filled air on his body pushing his hat back and streaming into his lungs and wind-induced tears mixed with rain in rivulets across his temples and into his ears and his body breaking free.

His little horse kept up with the dun. They were in a dead run when they topped a rise and the ground dropped sharply in front of them. They reined in and stopped, the horses stamping and blowing. Below them the wide expanse of the Missouri River, high in its banks, spread out in a long loop from east to west, its blank green surface deceptively calm. They rested a bit to give the horses time to recover, and then they turned their horses back, walking, letting the horses cool.

They were walking up the final rise before the descent to the barn when a huge dark animal burst over the rise. It looked so big and moved so fast that for a split second James thought it was a bear, though of course the gait was all wrong for that animal. "Brandywine," Thomas said loudly, almost a curse. In no time, the bay Thoroughbred was on them, showing no signs of swerving. Instinctively, James signaled to Twister to put some space between himself and Thomas so that the bay could thread between them. Obediently, Twister sidestepped left. At the same time, James whooped, "Hah! Stop!" The big bay slowed somewhat as it ripped between he and Thomas. If James had been on a bigger horse, the short stirrups would have saved him, but since Twister was half the animal's size, James's leg was wrenched by the force. "Damn," James said as his leg flopped back in place. Gingerly, he flexed it—it was fine, though it might be a bit sore in an hour. Twister snorted and stepped nervously but did not bolt. Thomas spun the big dun and chased the bay as it circled back around in front of James, broken halter rope trailing. The bay pulled up short in front of Twister and snorted and puffed. James urged Twister forward and grab the halter rope. Brandywine jerked his head back and almost ripped the rope from James's hand, but James held tight. James's weight shift had urged Twister into a trot, so now James pulled back on the reins slowing him to a walk. Brandywine trotted forward and lowered his head so that it was even with Twister's and blew into the other horse's nostrils. Then they walked, and the bay calmed somewhat.

"Like an abandoned lover," Thomas said when he circled up to the other side of James.

"It's a course that does not run smooth, for sure and for certain," James said.

Two riders met them on their way down the other side of the hill. They rode up to retrieve the big bay, but when the man tried to pull the halter rope and separate the two horses, Brandywine protested, so they rode nearby so that the big bay was near Twister. As they approached the long building with the stalls, James caught sight of a man with a white beard, shoulders squared and standing stiffly on the back porch of the big house. The man was hatless and dressed in a swallowtail coat. Would that be Blachley? James wondered. He didn't move as they walked up the road and into the long building.

Thus it became a pattern every Saturday that James accompanied Thomas out to Blachley's. He soon settled into the routine of the place, and it was not long before Enders's expression became less sour and he nodded occasionally. He even began to greet James by name. Then, one Saturday that Thomas was laid low with the grippe and James was there alone, Enders called him aside. Another man took the lead rope of the older Thoroughbred James had been riding so that James could follow Enders out of the barn into the sunlight, which for once had broken through the thick clouds.

"You'll do," Enders said.

James did not know how to respond, so he simply bowed his head.

"I'm in need of another man, one who can handle himself around these animals." Enders's voice was gruff.

James tried to keep from his face the thrill that shot through him.

"You'll not be handling the prime stock, you understand." James nodded—he would not expect that. "But we need someone with a feel for horses to keep after the other mounts, the ones past their prime, and so on."

James nodded vigorously. Oh, how he wanted to say yes. This was his dream job. He would be working with prime specimens of horseflesh all day, every day. He would be out from under the thumb of Xavier, a dream come true in many respects.

"Someone dedicated to their welfare," Enders said. "You'll need to move into the bunkhouse. I'm looking for a single man who can travel a lot. Someone who can get up at midnight and so tend to a sick horse. Someone who understands when they need patience and when they need a crop to the haunches. You strike me as that man."

James's shoulders dropped, and he bent his head. He was not single. He could not move into the bunkhouse and be available all the time. He looked into Enders's face for some hint that he would accept a wife after all. There was none. For a moment, he wished fervently that he was in fact single, that he would be free to come and go as he pleased, free to take this position, but he was not, so he said, "At present, I am not in a position to accept your generous offer." When Enders eyed him, eyebrows raised, asking him why, James said vaguely, "I currently have obligations that I cannot shirk."

"No chance of you giving them over?" Enders said.

"At present, I am unable to accept your generosity," James said and hung his head.

Enders looked at him a moment and then shook his head. "Suit yourself."

That evening, as James rode the cable car home, he grieved. Once again, he could not pursue his dream.

Chapter 18

ne day toward the end of a week, Sara felt tired all day as she worked at Molly's, but she forced herself into industriousness. James was not there when she made it home, so she laid out his supper and put herself to bed. She hardly awakened when he came home. The next day was the same—she was sleepy, and she wanted nothing more than to escape to a store room and put her head in her hands and close her eyes. The next day was Sunday, so she was able to sleep in. She also took a long nap in the afternoon. Perhaps I'm coming down with something, she thought, but she did not have the sniffles. Perhaps it was the summer complaint—something she ate or a stomach bug, as her stomach was a little upset. She had no diarrhea, however. The problem worsened, an uneasy scraping feeling in her belly, and she found she did not want to eat anything, though she forced herself at least to nibble on some bread. She began to avoid coffee, first of all because it might further upset her stomach but second because it seemed to have altered in taste. At first, she thought it was because the supplier of the coffee beans to Mollie's had been changed, but then she realized that the coffee that she made at home was the same, so it couldn't be that. The condition perplexed her, so in the evening she went

down the hall to Auntie to seek her advice and to see if she had any remedies. No sooner were the words out of Sara's mouth than Auntie smiled down at Moses, who sat in her lap determinedly shaking a very large spoon.

"I know what's the matter with you," Auntie said.

"Why are you smiling?" Sara said.

"Because I know what you don't seem to. You are a new bride, all right."

A new bride. What? Oh. Of course. Sara felt the color rise in her cheeks at her own obtuseness. She had been so focused on work that she had not taken the time to realize that she was with child. It had occurred to her in the past that she may soon become pregnant, but she had not connected it with her physical symptoms. Thoughts and feelings rapidly came and went. A surge of happiness first—I can have a little one just like the adorable Moses—but then concern—what about her job?

Then further concern—what would James think? He had accepted the dog readily enough, but his objection had been about another mouth to feed. How would he react to this news? Especially considering his present mood, which had been dark. His quick rises of temper had somewhat abated, to be replaced by a glowering silence. She did not think she was its cause— she hoped fervently she was not—but whether or no, it was there. She spent the rest of the evening cogitating how she might approach the telling of it to James. She did not know how she would do it, and the more time she spent thinking upon it, glancing over at his stony countenance, the more she felt afraid. He already felt trapped in this new job, and would not a baby further entangle him, weigh upon him all the more? Nonetheless, she resolved to tell him first thing in the morning.

And so she was up early to prepare him his favorite breakfast—bacon, eggs, toast, and fried potatoes. He arose when she did and went out and purchased a paper and sat reading it while she bustled around. She kept glancing at him, trying to gauge things.

James saw her sidelong glances, and it irritated him to no end, even as he knew the special breakfast was for his benefit. Why was she treading like a long-tailed cat in a room full of rocking chairs? Was he such a horrible monster that she felt she had to be so careful? The blood rose within him. He treated her well. He provided for her as a husband was bound to do. Anger rose higher within him. She had forced him, blackmailed him, pushed him until he had no choice. She meddled in his affairs, where she had no right to be. If he had only steered clear of her, taken her for the bad omen that she was, he would not at present be in this fix. He would be free to make his own choices.

"I made your favorite," she said as she set the plate beside him.

He gritted his teeth, said not a word, and continued to read the paper, afraid that if he began to speak he would not be able to contain his rage. She sat down beside him and began to eat her breakfast. Opal whined from where she lay next to the bed, chin on her paws. It set his teeth on edge to such a degree he began to eat faster. He had to get out of this apartment before he exploded.

Sara craned her head to see the front page and then said, pleasantly, "I see that this is one of the wettest springs on record."

James grunted and continued to shovel food into his mouth.

"James," Sara ventured, "there is something I have been

367

meaning to talk to you about."

What now? Had he not given until he bled? "*What*," he said forcefully. "What now?" He chewed his lips to bite back the other things he wanted to say.

"What?" she said. "What's the matter?" There was a note of bewilderment and unease in her words. She was quiet for a minute before she said, "Are you all right? Lately, you have—"

He cut her off, "Lately, I have what? What, Sara? Lately, I have not been the cheerful little toady that the rich spoiled she-bitch expects?"

Her eyes widened. "What?"

Once he began speaking he had a hard time stopping. "You cannot just let it rest, can you? You have to meddle. You have to prod. My God, Sara." He rose and pushed his dishes across the table violently, so that his utensils ended up on the floor and his half-eaten food spilled onto the table.

"No, I ..." Her eyes showed fear.

"I cannot take this," he said. "I am going out." He grabbed his hat and coat and left, the rage still roiling madly within him. When would it ever end? He stewed as he walked. He saw his future laid out before him, a series of causes and events, with little or no control on his part. His only escape was death, it seemed. He hung his head and trudged on.

It did not end once he was got to Xavier's. James did as Xavier ordered and went to work in the back room, but in no time, Xavier hollered from up front, "Hey, you, boy!" James gritted his teeth and walked to the doorway. He did not say anything, simply stood there. "In the upstairs storeroom," Xavier said. "A box of cinnamon. And make haste." Xavier did not even look James's direction, but instead focused on the customer in front of him, so James walked behind the counter to retrieve the keys. Out back, James unlocked the alley door to the stairs. He had only been trusted to retrieve things from this storeroom a few times. It was where Xavier kept the smaller more expensive items. On the other side of the second story, Xavier had his apartment, James knew, which Xavier also kept carefully locked. James looked up the stairwell. Even with the bottom door wide open, it was dark. He tried to locate which key might open the store room, but he could not remember, so he chose a likely candidate before he entered the darkness.

James reached the top of the steps and was met with a thin line of light cutting vertically across his face. It wasn't from the storeroom—Xavier's apartment door was open a crack. James walked over to it and grabbed the door handle to pull it closed. Why Xavier kept it locked, James had no idea. It was not as if anyone would steal anything, anyway, since the downstairs stairway door was always locked. Xavier was a skittish man, no two ways about it. James was about to pull the door closed when he thought, what would make a man so skittish? What could he possibly have in his room that would be worth that much? He hesitated. Normally, he would not have given it a second thought and would have simply yanked the door closed, but now he wondered. Why was he so nervous?

James pushed the door open. The room was disappointingly bare. There was a bed with a blanket of army issue dark wool, a chest of drawers, a steamer trunk, a chair, and a desk. It had a funk, as if it were never aired. There were no curtains on the windows, but they only let in a diffuse light through their dirty panes. The floor was not swept, and dust lay everywhere except upon the top of the desk. James turned to pull the door closed when something caught his eye: On the desk's surface were two ledgers open side by side. The ledger with the black

369

edges he presumed was the one he had seen Xavier working on downstairs. The other, edged in red leather, he had not seen. Comparing two ledgers. Why would one compare two ledgers? To see how your profits compare to last year, perhaps, as Xavier had boasted last month that Moore had congratulated him on the store's tidy profit. Why else? Another reason would be if you kept two ledgers at the same time, one that showed one thing and one that showed another. James's mind began working.

With a glance back down the stairs, James pushed through the door. He leaned over the chair and looked more closely at the contents of the ledgers. Xavier's script was spidery and cramped and leaned over backwards—it was hard to read at first—but by comparing the books he could make it out. The pages of both books were labeled with the same June date, and seemed to list exactly the same items. Holding his place, James flipped the covers closed. One was labeled "Ledger of Accounts, Xavier's, 1885." The other was labeled, "Frances Xavier, Personal Accounts, 1885." Flipping them back open, James compared the columns. In addition to columns of dates and items, the black ledger had three columns of numbers, while the red ledger had five. The numbers in both first columns were the same, but the numbers in the second were slightly different. The third columns in both held the running totals from the second columns. In the red volume, the fourth column held very small numbers, sometimes hundredths of a cent, and the fifth kept a running total of the fourth. Comparing the second columns, James figured out that the fourth column in the red ledger held the difference between the second columns in the two ledgers. The scoundrel. James would bet that Colonel Moore knew nothing of those small amounts, tiny

370

amounts that over time added up to tidy sums.

There came the frantic thump of feet on the stairs. With instinctive guilt, James stepped back just as Xavier burst in the door. He glanced at the ledgers and then at James. "*What the hell* are you doing in my room!" Xavier screamed, his face puffing red. "Get your arse out of here—now." Xavier flung his arm the direction he had come.

James stood still for a second and then, obeying a strong impulse, leaned over and picked up both ledgers. "I think I just made partner," James said.

"What? What? You stinking little pig!" Wild-eyed, Xavier launched himself at James. James twisted his body, protecting the ledgers and sidestepping. Xavier's rush was more frantic bluster than anything else, and because James ducked sideways, Xavier's momentum slammed him into the steamer trunk and sent him sprawling onto the floor. Xavier lay there gasping and holding his leg. After a minute, he rolled over and onto his knees. His eyes narrowed as he pushed himself to standing. He stood there thinking and then seemed to arrive at a decision. "Please, Mister Youngblood, please," Xavier said. "Please, Moore gets his. He's happy. I work hard. I pay you well. Where is the harm?" James backed next to the door and said nothing. Xavier glanced at the door and then at the ledgers in James's arms and said, licking his lips, "I deserve that money, I deserve it. When we were in the War, and I saved his arse, more than once. He does not appreciate that fact. He sent me packing like a nigger who'd done wrong, the bastard. He sent me out to the god-forsaken Territories and told me, 'Xavier, make something of yourself,' as if I had not already given him the ultimate gift."

"The esteemed colonel seems to have a pretty good head on

his shoulders," James said.

"I deserve it, damn it, I deserve it! I make more money in a month here than he does in a whole year in that little backwater he calls home." Xavier mumbled, "Gentility, my arse."

"Sit!" James said, pointing to the chair. James had been thinking frantically, trying to figure out the best course of action. Xavier continued to mumble as he sat, crouching in the chair. "Tell you what we are going to do," James said. "I will keep these." Xavier jumped to his feet, his eyes wide. James backed into the doorway. "Sit," James said again. Xavier remained standing. "Sit, or Moore will be happy to see these." Xavier narrowed his eyes and sat. "I just made partner," James said. Xavier sat still and did not say a word, and after a moment James said, "I'll take that as a congratulations. This is what we will do. You keep doing what you do best, buttering up the customers, ordering the inventory, happy little monkey that you are, and I will take over what you do not seem to do very well, which is to keep an honest book." James gestured to the desk. "Write it. Get out a pen." He waited as Xavier hesitated and then retrieved a pen, ink, and paper from the desk. James dictated, pausing after each phrase so Xavier could write it: "On this day, the tenth of June, in the year of our Lord, one thousand eight hundred and eighty-five, I, Francis Xavier, reward James Youngblood for his faithful service"—Here Xavier paused—"Write it," James said. Xavier did. James continued, "for his faithful service a partnership in Xavier Grocery and Dry Goods. Now sign it. We'll take care of the legalities later." James hoped it was enough to hold up legally. He had no idea, and the thought occurred to him that Colonel Moore might not be keen to the idea, but he would figure that out as they went.

"Over my dead body," Xavier growled.

"No," James said. "We will, or Colonel Moore will find out about these ledgers."

Xavier said nothing and looked at the desk. James stepped over to the desk, retrieved the paper, and stepped back into the door.

"Two more things," James said. "One. Thomas and I get raises."

"Who the hell is Thomas?" Xavier said.

"Whom you call Custer," James said and clenched his jaw, trying to hold his temper. "And that's the second thing. You call Thomas *Thomas*, unless he wants to be called something else, and you call me Youngblood, got it? No more, 'here, boy.'"

Xavier sat for a minute and said nothing, his eyes showing his mind skittering behind them. He did not say anything. With that, James backed out the door and gestured for Xavier to go down the stairs. The only thing meaner than a wild cat was a cornered wild cat—he would have to watch Xavier closely. Once Xavier was at the bottom of the stairs, James turned to the storeroom to get the cinnamon. He carefully locked the storeroom door behind him, pulled Xavier's door closed, and carried the cinnamon and the ledgers and paper downstairs.

When James came out into the main room, there were no customers. He walked up to the counter and laid the cinnamon in front of Xavier, who viewed him narrowly. "There you are. Did we not have a customer in need of this?"

"We seem suddenly to be short on customers," Xavier said as he moved out from behind the counter. James took a step back and then saw that Xavier held a pistol, a Colt repeater. "And me here thinking about how God giveth and God taketh away," Xavier said, feigning a smile. James did not know that he kept a pistol in the store. He should have guessed that. He should have anticipated, but he had no time to plan. What to do now? Xavier stretched out his arm and pointed the pistol at James's chest. "I killed lots of men in the war. What's one more?" he said. James took another step back, as far as he could go, so that he rested against the showcase on the opposite side of the room. "I will take those ledgers," Xavier said. James tried to think quickly. Could he rush the man? Could he duck behind a shelf? If he acted quickly, he might be able to surprise Xavier. But in the time it took for the thought to come to him, Xavier sensed it and calmly aimed the pistol at James's leg and fired. Bang! James jumped to the side, too late, but for whatever reason—whether Xavier meant to miss or he was simply unlucky—the lead did not pierce James's leg. At such close range, the sound caused James's ears to ring. James glanced at the door to see if the noise had attracted any onlookers. "Just stopping a thief," Xavier said, his tone reasonable. "And who they going to believe? An upstanding businessman and contributing member of society? Or an ex-convict, such as yourself?" James could not help the shock of Xavier's knowledge from registering on his face. "You did not think I knew, did you? Well, I did some digging of my own. Turns out, the upstanding colonel has a horse thief for a son-in-law. Something I am sure he will be happy to know. Hey, maybe I should shoot you to save the taxpayers the expense of a trial. They will probably give me a medal. Just like they did in the War."

What could James do? Once again, he was cornered with nowhere to turn. This was the end of the line. Hell, maybe he should let Xavier shoot him and get it all over with. Then he

374

would no longer be trapped in his life. It would be easier in the long run. But instead he hung his head and held out the ledgers. Xavier scuttled forward and retrieved them, along with the paper. "That's a good boy," Xavier said. "Now. You are fired." He nodded. "That felt good. Now get your arse out of here." He waved the gun toward the door.

There was nothing James could do. He went to the door, turned the lock, and let himself out, shutting the door behind him. He turned and began walking, not sure what he was going to do. He had not walked far when he saw policemen striding toward Xavier's, and so he accelerated his pace, putting as much distance between himself and the store as quickly as possible. His initial reaction to being fired was relief to be out from under Xavier and that horrible position. At least he and Xavier agreed upon that. He felt elation as he walked the streets a free man. He would not have to bite his tongue any more for a simple paycheck. He slowed. But now where would he go now? He wandered until he ended up at the Climax. He had not intended to go there, but there he was. He went inside. This early in the day, there were few customers, and Big Jim stood reading the paper.

"Ain't seen you in a while," Big Jim said as he served him a whiskey. "You look like you've recovered nicely from your unfortunate accident."

"Yeah," was all James said and found a table in the corner. He did not feel sociable, no matter how friendly the face. He sipped the whisky, and his elation soon drifted to brooding pathos. What was he going to do? It came down to this: Because he had a wife, he could not find a job, and because he could not find a job, he could not keep his wife. It was an untenable position, with him caught in the middle, a pressure that was as excruciating as it was inescapable. It seemed, suddenly, that the only way he was going to make anything of himself in this world was if he were unencumbered and unfettered by such conventional morality. The only thing standing in his way, now, was Sara. If she were not his wife, then he would be able to take the dream job at Blachley's. He would be free once more, free to do as he willed, free to achieve some success in this life.

Was he really considering what he thought he was? He went to the bar and ordered two shots of whiskey and downed them in quick gulps. He went and sat back down. All Sara had to do to save herself was to go back to Anamosa. One telegram, and she was set, what with the Colonel warming. She would be the better off for it, and he would too. But, even if she did not return, she had said herself that she did not need him, had she not? She had her job at the dining establishment. He was merely a prop in her life. With that, and the courage imparted by the whiskey, he made up his mind. He would not return to the apartment, and he would take the job at Blachley's, and that would be that. He now declared himself free from bondage. He rose, squared his shoulders, and left. With the few coins in his pockets, he took the cable car out into the countryside, ignoring his qualms of conscience. Because Enders was not expecting him, there was no car waiting, but he walked for a ways, rain dripping from his hat, until he was invited to set on the back of a freight wagon that was going his direction. He diverted his mind by fervently trying to recite what he remembered of "The Rime of the Ancient Mariner." It was late afternoon before he reached his destination. He located Enders and told him that he had decided to take the position. With a nod, Enders accepted, and that was that.

All the while, the rain pounded on.

Chapter 19

t rained and it rained. It rained in the mountains and on the plains all across the Midwest. It rained on snowdrifts in the Rockies that melted and fed the pools that fed the streams that fed the rivers. It rained on fields and farms. The water pelted off trees and buildings and gathered along roads and in ditches. Soon it was moving, shifting, following the call of gravity. It gathered things as it went, first soil and sand, then sticks and branches, then bushes and rocks and then whole trees. It pushed over wagons and pulled over bridges. The monster rolled in its bed and then riotously broke free, scraping its banks with boulders and buildings grasped in its watery paws, bawling out its rage and impotence. And still it rained. The river swelled, and swelled some more, first three feet, then ten. It burst the banks of the mighty Missouri and the banks of the Kaw. It came together in an enormous rush at the confluence of the two rivers and tried to claim the land back for the ocean.

When James left that morning, Sara did not know what to think. She sensed that his mood had gone beyond anything that had come before. She sat stunned for a long time, but then she rose, cleaned the breakfast plates, and took Opal out and tied her in the back yard, which was where the dog now usually spent her days, and was off to work herself. It was all Sara could do, really—keep to her routine, take comfort in the things upon which she had influence. It chewed at the back of her mind all day, and she kept making foolish mistakes, enough that Molly gave her a questioning look. She would have to do better, so she bent to her efforts.

And she had not even told him of the baby.

James did not return home that night. At first she thought possibly he had gone out drinking as he used to, but then he was not there in the morning when she awoke. She continued to worry about him. Perhaps he had met with another accident? The world was such a dangerous place, particularly for men. She worried all that day, and into the evening. Still, he did not return home. She was forced to consider other things. If he were not dead, what else could it be? Would he choose, finally, after everything they had been through, to abandon her? She could not believe it. He had rescued her, and he had put so much effort into their mutual survival. Why would he simply give that all up, over a silly argument? Men went on two-day drunks, did they not?

On the morning of the third day, Sara rose to the surface of her sleep and sighed. She had slept heavily. She pushed herself to sitting and for a fine moment everything felt right with the world. Her stomach, for once, was not upset. She took a deep breath. But then, she realized that James was still not beside her. He, once again, had not come home. Sara tensed, her mind going quickly over the topic, and then she pushed from her bed. This was not something she could ignore anymore, not something upon which she could simply hope for the best. He had truly disappeared, and there were only two real options for

379

what happened: either he was dead, or he had chosen not to return. Either was horrible to contemplate, but it also meant that she had to try to arrive at the truth, and she had to make plans for her own survival.

To accomplish the first goal, after work, she would go to his work and ask after him, she would contact the police, and she would go to see everyone that she knew he was acquainted with. She might even put up posters and adverts in the newspaper, if the other searches brought nothing. To accomplish the second goal, she immediately sat down with her commonplace book and did some figures. She arrived at a balance. If she were extremely careful and provided nothing unexpected happened, she could continue to live in the apartment on her own with her cook's helper salary. There were two major obstacles to this, though. One was that there were bound to be unexpected expenses, and when that occurred, she was sunk. Second, she was with child, and when the inevitable occurred, she would not be able to work for a while, and then she would be sunk, once again. But that was the future, and for now she simply had to get through this day, this week.

Thus, plan in place, she got ready for work. She was in a hurry, as she was running late, so she skipped breakfast, rushed into her clothes, and let herself out of the building, Opal on the lead behind her. As she came through the door, the rain pelted her and ran into her eyes. She wiped them and considered returning for her parasol, but she did not to, as she was running late already. She pulled at Opal's leash as she stepped down off the back stoop and—splash—into running water, a scant inch sluicing around her shoes. The rain did not collect in this part of the yard, only further on, and she glanced out around her and could not believe her eyes. Water ran everywhere, with few bare spots. It was a muddy red color, and floating in it were sticks and debris that could not have originated within the yard. She listened. There was the drop-drop of the rain and the drip from the eaves, then she heard the splash, splash, of someone running in the street out in front of the building. A voice yelled, "Get out of here, get out of here, don't take nothing, the river's coming, the river's coming!" Then splashing and the voice receded.

The river? Oh my God, the river. The confluence of the rivers, and all the rain. Had she not been paying attention? Had no one predicted this? Where were the people who were supposed to know about such things—was it not their job to warn people? Well, it did not matter. This was it, God had spoken. What did she need to do? Get to higher ground, up to the bluffs, expeditiously. She would have just enough time to grab a few things, she thought, but she would have to leave most of her belongings and hope that the building did not get swept away. She would take Opal, of course, and—Auntie and Moses! She had to help them. There was much to do. She quickly tied Opal to the back stoop, which would allow Opal to stay above the water, and she turned and dashed up the stairs and ran down the hall and pounded on Auntie's door. "Auntie, Auntie! Quick, hurry!" She kept pounding on the door. After time interminable, Auntie opened the door, shaking her head. Her hands covered with flour. "What is it, child, that won't wait a second for an old woman ..." Her voice stopped when she saw Sara's face. "Why, child, you are white as a ghost."

"Auntie! Get Moses, we got to go."

"What?" Auntie said, wiping her hands on the apron at her waist. "I just put Moses down for a nap."

"Well, get him up. There's a flood coming. We got to go."

Auntie looked at her blankly.

"Auntie, believe me when I say, the rivers are rising. They've reached the back porch. You've got to come immediately."

The realization dawned on Auntie's face, and she nodded vigorously, already turning toward the kitchen.

"I will return for you forthwith," Sara said over her shoulder and returned down the hall to her apartment. She fumbled to unlock the door and went in, intent on gathering things. First, she pulled the shelf away from the wall and grabbed her coffee can. She pulled out the money and put it in her purse. What could she carry things in? The carpetbag came first to her mind, but it was storing clothes and things and she did not think she had time to unpack and pack it and she would not want to carry that much anyway, so she found a large kitchen towel and spread it out on the table. She grabbed a loaf of bread and a hunk of cheese and put it on the towel. She had nothing to carry water in but a bucket, and such a conveyance would be nothing more than a nuisance. Indeed, it was ironic that she would need water. Next, she went to her trunk and flipped it open, and there lay all her treasures. All the material goods in this world that mattered to her. How would she choose? How could she take some and not all of it. Her mother's watch. The faux opal necklace James had given her. A Bible her father had given her. A handkerchief embroidered by little sister Maisie. Her commonplace book. *The Compleat Housewife*, given her by Esther. A carved chess piece her brother Ed had made when she was a child. Her fine clothes. Her sewing kit. All the extras and necessities essential to her life and her days. She quickly felt overwhelmed, but then she

382

shoved the feeling aside. There was no time for that.

She bent to retrieve her mother's watch, the opal necklace, and Maisie's handkerchief. The rest would have to sit tight until the floodwaters receded and she returned. Surely the building would stand. Nonetheless, she felt a sudden and terrible grief, as if she were abandoning her family and herself with it, but she swallowed hard. With one last look, she flipped the lid shut and put the things in her purse and wrapped up the food and tied the towel, and she was ready. She glanced around the room. There the portrait of her and James on their wedding day stared back at her from the shelf. She quickly grabbed it and put it too in her purse, and then it was time. She put on her coat and let herself out of the apartment, carefully locking the door behind her, and ran down the hall. She pushed through Auntie's door and was greeted with Moses's unhappy cries.

She said, "You ready, Auntie?"

Auntie was. She was dressed to go out, with Moses in her arms, a cloth bag over her shoulder, and the cane in her hand.

"We must be careful with this," Auntie said, lifting her bag, "as it has a glass bottle of milk for Moses." Indeed. Milk would be hard to come by, and Moses would need something to eat. "Faith in the Lord," Auntie said as they left the apartment.

"Here, let me take Moses," Sara said to Auntie, who handed her the baby. Auntie hobbled down the stairs as fast as she could, followed by Sara with Moses. At the bottom, Sara scooted around Auntie, opened the door, stepped through, and held it for Auntie, who came through.

Auntie took one look out over the watery yard and said, "Oh, my Lord in Heaven. Where's Moses when you need him?"

Yes, Sara thought, having a capable and caring man like

Moses here at the moment would be Godsend, and she tugged on Auntie's arm. But then she got it: the parting of the Red Sea. "Or maybe the ability to walk on water?" Sara said.

"Shhh," Auntie said, blushing a little at the blasphemy and shaking her head.

The water had risen, carrying with it a stench, having swept up all the garbage and sewage in the streets. They could hear it, too—a deep rumble, an ominous grinding that transmitted through the ground under their feet. But then Sara realized that the Opal was missing from the stoop. The rope was still tied, but the dog was nowhere to be found. "Opal," she called. "Opal?" Idiot dog. A fine time to run away. "Ooooh-paaaaalll!" she screamed, giving voice to her anguish. Nothing. What a time for the animal to run away. And there was nothing they could do about it. If they took time to search for her, she was sure that they too would be swept away. But it was Opal, her darling attentive, enthusiastic Opal. But there was no time. The water had continued to rise, and Sara reached for Auntie. "Now. We've got to go now," she said.

They both took a breath as they stepped out into the moving water, which was now up to Sara's ankle and wetting the hem of her skirt. Even at this depth, it pulled at her feet, a powerful force. They splashed down the alley and out into the street, which was chaos. First, Sara glanced up and down for Opal, but she was nowhere to be seen. In front of them, men, women, and children splashed by, running or striding fast, the women's skirts soaked up to their knees from the wicking of the water. Mothers with children holding fast to them and to the older siblings. Men carried things, household items, a bedroll, a gun. One man walked by with a dining room chair strapped to his back. Carts pulled by horses and tipping with goods sluiced through the water, and handcarts haphazardly piled with furniture were pushed by men, their families trailing behind. Sara and Auntie turned and joined everyone heading east to higher ground. Sara walked as quickly as she could, but she soon found she had to slow so that Auntie could keep up. She offered her arm, which Auntie took, gratefulness on her face.

They passed two men tilting back chairs against a wall on a high boardwalk. They were drinking and laughing and yelling at passersby: "What you running for, you chickens?"

"You had better hope you turn into ducks," Sara said under her breath.

Further on, a man dressed in preacher's robes had climbed atop a statue of some city father, and his voice, hoarse, with a foreign accent that Sara could not place, carried out over the water. "Heed the words of Zophar the Naamathite. The joy of the godless lasts but a moment. He will perish forever, like his own dung. The food in his mouth will turn sour in his stomach and will become the venom of serpents within him. God will make his stomach vomit them up. An unfanned fire will consume him, the earth will rise up against him, and a flood will carry off his house, the rushing waters of God's wrath."

His voice disappeared behind them as they hurried along the boardwalk until it dipped under still-rising water, where they had to splash down the street, their skirts now soaked to their knees and weighing upon them. Sara wished that she had thought to tuck hers up, but there had been no time and it was not proper. Even with Sara carrying Moses, who was heavy for his small size, Auntie began to slow, first a little and then more, her breath coming fast, the muscles of her limbs shaking with effort. As they made their way east, the ground underneath them began to climb. At first the water rushed in faster than the grade, but then the grade began to outpace it, and soon the water rose a bit slower. Sara gauged where they were. Perhaps they could catch a cable car. Would a cable car be running?

"Just to the cable car stop, Auntie," Sara said.

"You a fool, girl?" Auntie replied. "They do not let black folk onto the cable car."

Did they not? Of course they didn't. Sara hadn't thought to consider that. It raised her hackles, and she said, "They will this time, or I'll … I'll …" She was not sure what she would do. How could she get them to accept Auntie as a passenger? They rounded the corner to the next cable car stop, and there the car sat, empty and silent. It was not moving. There must not be any electricity. Of course there wasn't. It was all under water. Tiredness descended upon her, and Sara felt a sob rising in her throat. What were they to do? But, then, like an angel from heaven, a man walked up driving a team of six mules in harness and began hitching the team to the front of the car. People saw what he was doing and began giving him money in exchange for a ride.

Sara led Auntie up to the man and asked, "How much for a ride?"

The man looked them up and down and said, "For you, five dollars."

"Oh, good, I'll take two. Will the baby—"

The man cut her off. "For you, I said. We don't take no niggers."

The anger rose in Sara, and she sputtered, "Well, I …" trying to find something to say. She glanced at Auntie, who, though obviously very tired, was tugging at her sleeve, trying to get her to continue on. "No, wait," Sara whispered. This man was obviously taking advantage of those in need. If that were his motive, than surely he could be bought. Sara handed Moses to Auntie and dug into her purse and pulled out all her money. There was a goodly sum. She separated out half of it and walked up to the man. "Here," she said.

The man took it and counted it. "What do you take me for. An idiot?" He handed it back to her. "I know what would convince me, if'n there was time." He laid his hand upon her shoulder, but then with a grin, he turned back to others.

"No, wait, here is all of it," she said. "It's all I have." She dumped it all into his hands.

He looked at her, raising his eyebrows. "If you're going to waste my time honey, these people will get mighty cranky. They are my paying customers, after all." So without hesitation Sara brought out her mother's watch—she loathed to part with it, but the living were more important than the dead, and her kind mother would have wished it so. "Here. This too. Take it."

The man accepted it but looked at her and shook his head. "That old hag ain't worth it," he said, "but if'n you are going to pay, I will take it." He indicated that they could board.

Sara turned and helped Auntie onto the car. There was little room left, but to Sara's utter disbelief a white man in modest clothes spied their plight and rose to give Auntie a seat in a corner. He nodded in sympathy, and Sara thanked him profusely. She put Moses on Auntie's lap and stood right next to her, clutching the sideboard. They were given sharp and nasty glances by some of the other passengers, but no one said anything. When the car was full, and the man shooed people away. He handed some money to a tall boy that looked about sixteen or seventeen and told him to keep the others off the car, which the boy did with a thick bough the man handed him. The boy circled the car and swung it viciously at anyone who came near. By this time the water was up to the boy's calves, and the rumble was increasing. People were running by, and wood and debris floated past. The heavy rain and dark clouds made it look like night was coming, or perhaps a tornado, even though it was only ten in the morning. The man pulled the whip from his belt and cracked it over the mules. "G-wan," he yelled. "Giddyap, mule. Giddyap." At first nothing happened. The car was full and it seemed stuck to the tracks. But then it jerked free and began to creep forward. Slowly at first, it crept along, creaking and groaning, but soon there was a spray coming off the wheels and they were on their way up the incline to the bluffs. Sara breathed a sigh and put her hand on Auntie's arm, whose eyes were wide with fear. Just like Sara's own, she was sure.

Sara looked back toward the city. There, suddenly, whoosh, a huge flame burst over the middle of the West Bottoms. The brown and white-capped water sparkled red and gold with the reflection of the flames. Then high above them came a voice. "Haaalp," it screamed. "Haaalp!" Sara tried to find the source and finally located it in the upper stories of one of the tall brick buildings they had just passed. It was a woman leaning out a window and screaming, "Help me, someone! I need help. I am in dire straits!" The woman's voice held that quality, not simply of someone in hopes of rescue, but of someone in extreme terror, someone whose safety was threatened. Sara glanced at the faces of the people in the car around her. Some gazed toward the sound, a detached and complacent look on their faces. Others heard the woman and turned their faces away. None, however, moved to act. Would not someone go to help this woman? "Damn it," she said under her breath. If she were in such a situation, she hoped to God someone had compassion beyond themselves. And there was the matter of Nellie haunting her mind—she had not done a thing then and had regretted it ever since. It certainly was the duty of mankind to help those in need, was it not?

Sara glanced at Auntie. The car was headed higher up now and the track was clear ahead. Should she stay with Auntie to make sure she and Moses got to safety? They had made good progress, on much higher ground and closer to being out of the water. Or should she help the woman? Auntie looked at her and then glanced toward the building that held the woman. Auntie nodded slightly with a look of understanding on her face. In that split second, Sara made a decision. An uncommon certainty descended upon her—that Auntie and Moses would be fine and that this was a defining moment in her life and if she did not seize the initiative, her character, her life, would be irrevocably changed for the worse. She had to help this woman.

She bent over close to Auntie and said, "Don't let a soul prise you from this seat." She handed Auntie the towel with the food, kissed Moses roughly, and turned and pushed her way down the aisle, to the complaints of other passengers. Hoping it was not too deep, she then took a breath and stepped from the moving car into the dark swirling water. It splashed up around her but her feet quickly touched bottom. It was over her calves and pulled at her skirts and threatened to swipe her feet from underneath her. The woman screamed again from the window above, "Haalp!" Sarah moved toward the building, and the water deepened, first over her knees and then her thighs and to her waist. Sara would have to swim to make it to the building. There was nothing for it. She shed herself of her coat and wished that her skirts were not so long, but still she waded deeper and when it was deep enough she pushed off, trying to kick as her skirts swirled and twined around her legs. She tried to reach down and pull them out of the way, but when she did her head ducked under the water, so she put out her arms again and tried to swim again. It crossed her mind: What had she been thinking? She may forfeit her life for the vanity of believing she could help another. And then the current caught her and swung her around like a ballerina, and the undercurrent grasped her skirt and pulled her down, down, under the water. She kicked and kicked, trying to get her legs untangled, swinging and pushing wildly with her arms. Her head stayed under the horrible dark water.

Chapter 20

hat morning, when James walked up to the long building through the storm, Enders was frantically directing men in loading tack and equipment and Thomas was there too. When Enders saw James he gestured to a man holding two saddled horses, Brandywine and Twister. Enders said, "Thomas, it's up to you and him to get the mares from the back pasture. I don't need to tell you how important it is that this gets accomplished. And you'll have to use that hothead Brandywine—the other horses are occupied. Hurry, they report that the water's soon to reach the far end of the pasture." Thomas nodded and then mounted Brandywine. James quickly mounted too, and they were off at a trot through the opposite door of the long building, where the wind whipped James's hat off his head and blew it away. They leveled out into a lope and crossed the creek, which was swollen with water, but it was wide and fairly shallow. Still, Brandywine hopped on his front hooves before he plunged into it. Once across, they loped through an open gate. Brandywine kicked his heels and jerked his head at the pressure of the rein, wanting to open up and run. Twister calmly loped after him.

They sped through a pasture and then a grove of oak trees where the muddy path narrowed to a trail, and they ducked wind-whipped branches as they went. Thomas got the worst of it and had to crouch low over Brandywine's withers to avoid them. Even James on the shorter Twister was struck by flailing limbs. They soon popped out of the grove right next to a second gate. Thomas dismounted and flipped the latch from the post and unhooked it. He led Brandywine through the gate, James urging Twister after them. By this time they could hear a low rumble over the roar of the wind, something of huge magnitude, and James did not know what it was. Then came the faint sound of squealing horses. Thomas left the gate open and turned to mount Brandywine, but the horse heard the others and whinnied, cocking his ears in their direction and shaking his head. He high-stepped away as Thomas moved to mount and, since he was tethered by the rein, he sidestepped a circle around Thomas. Once the huge bay stepped so that he faced away from the mares, Thomas leapt onto his back and barely made his seat before the huge bay took off in the direction of the mares. Twister snorted and took off after them. There was no way the little horse could keep up, so they fell behind.

James and Twister crested a hill and were met with a truly awesome sight. The Missouri River in the distance, usually flat and green, was now red with silt and white with breakers, and its reach spread out way beyond its normal extent, past its forested banks. The light smell of the rain was overpowered by the heavy odor of wet earth, and the extending floodwaters roared and rumbled like some beast as the rocks and logs that it carried scraped against the ground, roiling and breaking and dipping as it crested rocks and bushes and trees and hills, leaping up and over, white-capped and angry, dragging things down with incredible force. Its forefront crept up this vale and that drainage at an incredible speed, dark and bulging with sticks and debris like a giant fast-moving amoeba, parting around obstacles and merging on the other side before overcoming them. On the hill below James were Brandywine and Thomas racing toward a band of fifty or so Thoroughbred mares, which pounded toward them, followed on their heels by the fast-moving water. The flood waters must have surrounded them and cut them off, as their coats were dark with water, and James could make out one mare straggling behind, stumbling horribly as it tried to keep up, a red splotch on its chest. They must have had to break through a fence to escape their pasture, or maybe she was injured by floating debris. In a second, the band engulfed Thomas and Brandywine and, as they swept past, Brandywine reared and turned back the way they had come toward James and Twister. James pulled up. He glimpsed Thomas standing upright in the stirrups as the bay twisted and plunged. When Thomas and the bay had almost turned, they floundered sideways, the horse losing its footing on the muddy embankment. The only thing that saved them was that they toppled into the mares, which propped Brandywine up long enough for him to gain his footing. James winced—God help Thomas, as part of him was undoubtedly pinched in the interstices. And then he and Twister were engulfed, the roar of hundreds of hooves, the flying mud, the drenching water, all pushing them backwards. Twister snorted and sidestepped, keeping clear as best he could. Smaller than most of the mares, Twister was almost bowled over by mare after mare, who ran blind with fear, but he and James survived after being buffeted this way and that. Twister was a surefoot, and James would take a surefoot over a racehorse any day.

Once the herd had passed them, Thomas and Brandywine

pounding behind, Twister pivoted and took out after them. They reached speeds they had not previously achieved, and Twister seemed to skim the landscape. James heard a huge crash and glanced to his left and saw the water thrusting up the valley, pulling down trees. James and Twister were able to catch up with the herd over the next hill as they bottlenecked near that last gate. James saw Brandywine rear again as Thomas fought to hold him back so he wouldn't pressure the herd against the pole and wire fence. Nonetheless, the herd pushed too hard and two mares tumbled through the fence. One immediately struggled to her feet and ran to catch the others, but as the other mare struggled to rise, she could not, her foreleg below the knee dangling and swaying sickeningly from of bit a skin. Normally, such a horse would be shot and put out of its misery, but there was nothing that could be done. "Damn!" James said. At last, the remaining mares made it through the gate. Brandywine jumped after them and into the flank of the herd as it pushed into the forest. James and Twister were close behind them. The trees hemmed in the herd, and they slowed. The branches whipped at them, and James caught flashes of the herd ahead. In the middle of the trees, there was a loud crack and the herd seemed to boil and erupt, some back toward him. James just caught sight of Brandywine leaping wide to the left and into some trees. In a second, James and Twister were on the spot, and there was the twisted and broken trunk of a new-fallen tree across the trail. Twister jumped it and slid in the mud on the other side, but he stayed on his feet. From ahead came a loud panicked whinny of a horse.

Twister and James broke out of the grove, and right away James saw something was wrong. Brandywine was in the middle of the mares, his head high and his muzzle twisted to his left like he was trying to see behind him, and Thomas was not on top. The saddle was still resting by the withers but canted to the left, held in place by the breast strap. Then the horses moved apart and James saw for a split second Thomas's body hanging down the left side of the dark bay, his foot caught in the stirrup. Only Brandywine's height kept Thomas's full body off the ground and dragging wide, where he would have quickly been trampled. Hopefully, the leather of the breast band would hold so the saddle stayed up. James slapped Twister on the rump and urged him on, and they pushed into the herd of mares, who seemed to tower above them. "Hah, hah," James shouted and slapped the mares with his hands, trying to part the herd. He had to get to Brandywine and Thomas before the horse made it all the way through the herd and broke out into the open. Otherwise, Twister may not be able not catch him, and Thomas would be the worse for it. "Hah, hah! Get outta the way, you bastards!" James screamed. Twister reared and put his front hooves on the mare in front of them. She scooted out of the way and made a gap that Twister shot through, and then they were behind Brandywine. They would have to get around him to the right so that James could avoid Thomas on the left and catch Brandywine's bridle. Again, James urged Twister ahead. Twister skirted the haunches of the big horse and ducked around a mare. Just then Twister and Brandywine broke free of the herd. "Go!" yelled James to Twister and shifted forward. For a second, Brandywine didn't seem to know he was clear, and that second was all Twister and James needed. They were up next to Brandywine's head. James reached with his left hand and grabbed the rein, which was still looped over the big horse's withers. When Brandywine felt the tension he jerked to the left, trying to pull away. It jerked James off balance in his saddle, and there was with no pommel or swells to hook into. James wasn't sure he could maintain his balance, nor the leather of the rein would hold.

There was only one thing to do. He held onto Brandywine's rein as hard as he could with his left hand. He dropped his own rein and leaned forward and hugged Twister's neck with his right, leaving his own rein to go where it would. Together, the horses and their riders shot through the second gate, thank goodness with enough room that Thomas did not knock against the gatepost. Once through the gate, James pulled his feet back in the stirrups so that he was on tiptoe, twisted, and leapt toward the big horse and wrapped his arms around its neck as he landed, holding on for all he was worth. He miscalculated, and instead of landing on the horse, he was only able to grab it around the neck. For a second, the world seemed to turn upside down as Brandywine reared and then swung wide to the left. Then a huge splash as they hit the water of the creek, spray dousing them all. James felt it on his legs and filling his boots and then up to his waist as it reached Brandywine's chest. James could not swim! But the support of the creek buoyed James just enough that he was able to grab a better hold. The bay plunged and then slowed. The water was pushing at them, but it took a moment for James to realize that they were being pushed the wrong way, upstream instead of down. The flood had reached past this point and was pushing them up the drainage.

Distantly, James heard shouts from the far side of the creek, but he had to get to Thomas. Thomas was underwater as Brandywine floundered. James grabbed the saddle with his left hand and put his right arm over the top of the withers. He used both arms to pull himself onto his belly on the saddle, causing Brandywine to sink farther and to snort and paddle frantically. Thomas floated on the other side, yanked by his left leg, face up but bobbing. Frantically, James grabbed Thomas's boot and the stirrup and yanked them apart. Luckily the water had released the pressure of the connection. James held onto Thomas's leg as James's body slipped over the butt of the horse and out of the way of its kicking legs. As soon as they were free, James quickly sank under the water, head and all— he could not swim!—but even so hand-over-hand pulled himself up Thomas's body. Panic gripped him. He could not breathe. How was he supposed to swim and hold Thomas at the same time? They would both drown. He did not know and was forced to let go of Thomas for a moment as he scrambled with all his limbs to get his own head above water. He kicked fiercely with his legs and scrambled with his arms, mimicking a horse. Just then he was bumped on the shoulder by something large and wildly swinging, and instinctively he reached out. It was a log of considerable size and he was able to grab it by an outpoking knot as it swirled around him, and when he was able to breathe he grasped the scruff of Thomas's neck with his other hand, but Thomas was sucked underneath the log and James had to struggle to pull him free. In the meantime, the force he applied spun the log along its long axis and dumped James back into the water. The log spun away, leaving James on his own to swim.

Once again he tried the one-armed horse paddle and was able this time to raise his head above water. He yanked at Thomas and pulled him over on his back so that his face was out of the water, while he frantically tried to paddle with his free hand. Luckily, Thomas seemed to float readily enough.

Between each stroke, James's head bobbed and he took in a mouthful of water, but he persisted, helped by the rushing waters that pushed him toward the bank. He pushed and struggled, trying to keep his head out of the water and trying to keep Thomas's as well. Then there was a splash as men threw him a rope, which he grasped and was pulled forward, dipping down under the water again, until men jumped into the water and grabbed him and Thomas and pulled them to shore.

They were deposited side by side. "You all right?" James's man said. James nodded as he coughed violently. James lay there for a full minute gasping for air. Once he had some semblance of breath, he rolled over and looked at Thomas. Blood flowed freely from a gash in Thomas's forehead, making grisly trails down his wet face, and he was pale, and James was not sure if he was breathing, but he soon began coughing. He continued to cough and cough, his face wincing in pain, his arm held up around his chest, until finally he opened his eyes and shook his head, gasping and gulping air.

James grabbed him by the material of his shirt. "You bastard," James said, "I thought I was going to have to breathe for you too."

Thomas shook his head again, which gave him another fit of coughing. When it subsided he touched his forehead and winced and then looked at his bloody hand. "I liked it better dead," Thomas croaked.

Chapter 21

nd then Sara's head broke the surface of the dark water once more. As it did, she heard words being shouted, but she could not make them out, as her ears were filled with water. She shook her head and thrust out her chin, trying to break free, trying to breathe, trying to clear her senses. Flailing her arms wildly in the direction of the sound, her right arm hit something. She grabbed it with both hands and it was long and narrow and wooden and she held it tightly. Next thing she knew, she was being hauled up out of the water. She tried to help, scrambling and pushing over the top of a large heaving thing in front of her, and as she struggled strong hands grabbed her under the armpits and pulled to help her. But the water would not easily relinquish her skirts, and it was all she and her unknown helper could do to pull her legs onto the boards. She lay there panting and trying to recover. She was lying on a well-built piece of boardwalk that floated as a raft, and a man—a boy, really—stood over her. He wore clothes that were too short for him, as if he had shot up in height recently. His sandy hair lay long upon his neck, and he had a pock-marked and pimpled face, a large pointed nose, and big ears.

"You all right, lady?" he asked.

"Yes," she said, her breath caught in her throat. "Thanks ever so much to you."

The boy turned and grabbed the pole he had fished her out with, and then stepped to the side and poled the raft to keep it from turning. The building—she had to get there to help the woman. "I need to go to that building," Sara said and pointed as it slipped away beside them.

"You crazy, lady?" he said. "The flood's going to take it down the river, along with everything else in this God-forsaken place."

"There's a woman in there, a woman in need of assistance." Sara scrambled, trying to push herself to her feet. She stood and swayed as the raft pitched, getting ready to jump in again.

"Stop," the boy said. "Just stop. I'll get you there. Does not matter whether you drown now or later." Skillfully, he poled the raft around the end of the building. "You are going to have to go in a window, as the doors are all under water." He pushed the raft up against the building in an eddy under an open window. "This is as good as it gets," he said.

She reached up and grabbed the window sill. The boy wedged his pole, trying to keep the raft next to the building. "Now," he yelled. "Now or never."

Adrenalin pumped through Sara's body, and she bent her knees and then jumped. She was just able to get her body over the sill, her elbows wedged within, but her skirts ran water and dragged her down. Damn skirts. What she would not give for a pair of those silly-looking bloomers. She struggled to pull herself in, but her body would not move. The weight of the skirts were almost too much for her, and it was only the wedge of her elbows that kept her there. She glanced down, and the raft and the boy were gone, pulled on by the current, and so she had to get herself through the window, either that or she went back in the water. She kicked as hard as she could against the building, stubbing her toe and heaving. She was able to work first her belly and then her hips onto the sill and brace her arms against the inside window frame. She pulled and wiggled and scraped and finally, thankfully, defying the weight of her wet clothing, she flopped through the window and onto the floor and lay there panting. She would have bruises and scrapes in numerous places, she could tell. She heard the woman's voice echo down the staircase: "Haalp!" "I'm coming," she said irritably but not loudly. "Hold your horses." With a sigh, she pushed herself up, tried to wring out a little water from her clothing, and then made her way out into the hall and then up the stairs. Which floor had it been? She decided that it was the next floor up. She had come in on the second floor, and the woman had been up above. She mounted the stairs and then searched from one end to the other, calling out, trying doors, but there was nothing but darkness punctuated by the shadowy forms of desks and chairs and cabinets. It smelled of dust, and once she heard the rustle of something moving, some small animal. Perhaps the woman was the fourth floor. She went up another flight of stairs and walked one way and then another, forgetting to call out, but then she heard a yell from behind her. She walked the other way and then jumped when the sound of the woman's call came from the door just at her elbow. She found the knob in the dim light, turned it, and went in.

This was a mid-sized office, with two desks facing each other across the room, some bookshelves, a small stove, and a couple of extra chairs. The woman clothed in a long white nightdress was on her knees on a bench and leaning out of the window. She turned when Sara heard the door open. "Thank

God," she said, a catch in her voice. "Oh, thank goodness!" She pushed herself off of the bench and struggled to stand, and when she did, she put her hands on her hips, with her elbows cocked out to the side. The way the woman canted backwards, as if to counterweight—this woman was with child and very close to her time. She was younger than Sara had expected, maybe mid to late teens. Her hair was dark and curly, and it lay in dry fuzz around her face before it submitted to a long braid down her back. Her eyebrows made dark dashes above her large dark eyes, contrasting with her pale skin. Her shoulders were slender, despite her extended belly. The woman began to walk toward Sara, but then she grasped her belly with both hands and doubled over in pain and sank to the floor. It was not simply close to her time—it was her time. No wonder the woman was frantically calling.

Had this woman ever given birth before? As young as she was, Sara thought not. "Do they come very often?" Sara asked, after the fit had passed.

"They come and go," the woman said in a soft low voice. "They are close but then they spread out."

"Well, I would think that they would have to be fairly regular to do the job, so we may have some time." Sara knew a little of what to do from Esther's birthing, though she did not have the resources she needed, such access to clean water and a bed. If nothing went wrong, they would probably be all right, but if anything were to happen, there was nothing that Sara would be able to do.

The woman looked up at her with wide eyes, and so Sara said, "Don't you worry. You will be fine. It's a natural thing and it will take care of itself, just you see." Relief came to the woman's face, and though Sara knew that it was not that easy—and she was sure the woman knew that too—for a moment they both felt better. "I am Missus Sara Youngblood," Sara said. She held out her hand. The woman took it. With her other hand under the woman's arm, she helped her to rise.

Once she was on her feet, the woman said, "I cannot tell you how pleased I am to meet you." They looked at each other and smiled at the incongruity of formal introductions. "I am Angelique Demichel," the woman said, "but you must call me Angelique."

"Certainly," Sara said, "and please call me Sara."

"Do you know about, um, birthing?" Angelique asked, the vulnerability in her face making her look even younger than what Sara supposed was her age.

"A little," Sara said. "I have attended a couple. But, you know what? Though you cannot tell, I am in the way too, just like you."

Angelique smiled in response. "It is the woman's burden to bear," she said. But then a fit came upon her, and she moaned and bent over. It was a short one and passed quickly. After it had passed, Sara helped her to one of the chairs to sit down. She then walked over to the stove and held her hands up to it. It was still warm. She cracked open the door, and there were coals glowing among the ashes. "We need to warm this room," Sara said. She went over and pushed down on the sash and closed the window. "I will work on getting this fire built up." Sara picked up the two remaining lumps of coal in the bucket by the stove and stuck them in the fire. She took the poker and stirred it and shut the door and latched it. "That'll hold us for just a bit," she said, clapping her hands to shake off the coal dust. She looked around for something to make the woman comfortable. Probably best if she lie on the floor. She helped

Angelique to lie down. The wooden chair behind the desk had a seat cushion tied to it, so Sara removed it and gave it to her. Then she spied another coat on the other side of a coat tree, so she unhooked it and brought it over. "Here, put this over you so you do not take a chill." The woman did as she was told. She lay on the cushion behind her and pulled the coat over top of her.

"Is this all right?" Angelique asked.

The woman needed reassurance. Of course she did. "Yes, that is perfect. You are doing fine." The woman nodded and pulled the coat up to her chin. Sara looked at herself. She was wet through and through. "What a sight I am," she said. "I hope you won't mind my immodesty—I need to rid myself of some of these wet things." She untied her overskirt and draped it over the back of a chair next to the stove. She untied two underskirts till she was down to just one and draped them over desks and on the coat tree as best she could so that they could dry. Just then there was a loud low noise coming from outside, and the building shook. Sara glanced at Angelique, whose sat up, body stiff with fright. Angelique said with a shaky voice, "The wind, I think. It's been doing it for a while."

"Let's hope so," Sara said. She was skeptical. Could it be the water against the foundation? She certainly hoped not. What else would be causing the building to shake so? Sara glanced around. What next? Well, she would have to see if she could round up some water and some food. "Is there any water?" Sara asked Angelique.

"I have no idea," Angelique said. "I have never been in this building before. I simply took refuge in it from the storm when the water first rose."

"Well, you make yourself comfortable," Sara said. "I'm

going foraging."

It was getting darker. A glance out the window showed the clouds glowering above and the pounding rain, and the water still swirled below them, much higher now. Well, nothing to be done there. They were truly trapped. God, let the building hold. She let herself out into the dark hallway and began searching every room on that floor and then on the one above. In one room, she was able to find some water in a metal pitcher and in another she found tea, a little sugar, and even a peppermint stick. She also found more coal. That ought to keep us for a bit, she thought. She also came across a yellow tabby cat sitting in an open window staring out over the water. "Hey kitty," she said. Its eyes followed her, more with disdain than concern, as she looked through the room. She left it alone. Coming back down the stairs she again heard the scurry of small animal feet. Normally, it would have bothered her, but under the present conditions, it was oddly reassuring. She did not attempt to go down the stairs to the floors below her—she was not sure where she would be met with water. When she came back to the room, Angelique was on her back with another fit. "Are you all right?" Sara asked when it was over. "I am," came the panting voice. Sara put the pitcher of water on the stove to heat, and soon it began to boil. Using a scarf from the coat tree, she removed it and put in the tea and let it steep. There was a cup in the sideboard in the room, so she poured it, put in the sugar, and took it over to Angelique, along with the peppermint stick. She kept nothing for herself. "Here you are," Sara said, and once Angelique took the mug, Sara went and sat in the chair. In the silence that followed, there was loud sipping of hot tea, the snap of the stove, and the rain tapping on the window. The room had warmed, and it felt almost pleasant.

Sara's hair and clothes had dried somewhat, and she was sleepy. She would lay down on the floor to nap, she thought, after a while and she did.

Throughout the rest of the day, Angelique's contractions came and went. They were irregular, sometimes far apart, sometimes closer. Sara wished they had something to eat, and so she went on another foraging run. She managed to find some more coal and an orange, and that was it, but she peeled the orange and gave it to Angelique, who insisted she have a portion as well. Sara also found more water in a bucket, which seemed clean. She was thankful for it because she had become thirsty, and it tasted sweet. The dark afternoon turned to evening and what little light there was faded. Still, rain pounded on the window, and the wind whipped at the dark water as it rushed by. The building shook every so often, and Sara still did not know what it was. To pass the time, she watched out the window for a bit, and although she could not see well for the rain, she could make out things floating by in the dark water, things that might be wooden walkways and logs and wagons but also carcasses and other things that were white and dark that Sara did not want to look too closely at. Something was burning behind their building, and as it got darker the faint glow bounced off buildings across the way and gave everything an orange cast. When Angelique drifted off, Sara too lay down on the bare floor and slept.

Later, she woke with a start. It was dark. The room was starting to chill, so she heaved herself up and walked over to stoke the fire. When the flames caught, it cast a glow over the room. When she glanced at Angelique, the woman's eyes were wide open. They shone brightly, and it took a minute for Sara to realize that she was quietly crying. Sara left the door to the stove open and went over to Angelique and crouched down beside her. She put her hand on the woman's arm. "Are you okay? What is the matter?"

Angelique shook her head and started sobbing.

"You will be fine," Sara said. "Women go through this all the time, and they are fine." She could not help, though, but to think of her dear friend Lily. She was kidding herself and Angelique when she said it, as they both knew it. Childbirth was a dangerous time.

"No, no," Angelique said, laying her head to the side. "You do not understand."

"Well, then tell me, tell me what I don't understand," she said

"I won't live through it," Angelique said. "I won't make it through the night. I know it."

"How do you know it? You are not a teller of fortunes. You cannot see into the future." Sara's voice came out a little too harshly, and so she tried to soften it by saying, "Of course, you will be fine."

"No. You don't understand. The women in my family ..." Angelique's voice choked to a stop. She put her head down into her arms, which rested on the floor, and her shoulders shook. But then a contraction grabbed her, and she took a big gulp of air and lay there breathing heavily and squirming, but it soon passed. Then she was quiet.

Not knowing quite what to do, Sara hesitated. Would this woman accept her embrace? Well, this is no time for propriety, so she lay down behind Angelique on the floor and put an arms around her and held her. The woman did not move away. "Shshshsh," Sara said, as if she were comforting a small child. She patted her shoulder.

407

After Angelique had quieted, Sara said, "Really, women do this all the time. They've been doing it for centuries. There is no reason—"

"Yes," Angelique said, cutting her off, "but not the women in my family. Not my mother. My mother died. I was her only, and she died because of me. It will be me this time—I have known it forever."

And yet she had allowed herself to become pregnant? Granted, a woman had little leeway in such things, but still, if Angelique had always believed that she would die in childbirth, why had she married? Why had she allowed herself into such a position?

"But you are not your mother," Sara said, keeping her voice firm. "You are you, and what happened to her does not foretell what happens to you. The future is a blank slate that only God knows. We don't know. In fact, it's pretty uppity of us to think that we know the future," Sara said, smiling, hoping Angelique could hear the joke. She had. She made a soft sound, and then they sat in silence for a while, listening to the sound of the rain and the wind. It seemed to be letting up a bit. Sara got up and shut the door to the stove and came over and sat back down in the dark.

"Is that not the truth," came Angelique's voice through the dark. "I did not know what I was going to do, here in the building all alone. And then you came." They sat in silence for a while. Then she said, "I think you should know, for honesty's sake: I am a fallen woman."

She was a prostitute? Sara pulled away from her. She felt revulsion rise within her, urging her to get up and leave the room. Like that woman at Miss Rose's and Miss Rose herself. This woman had thrown propriety to the wind too? Was she of such low moral character? Sara felt duped, as if the woman had trapped her with false promises, and this caused an anger to rise within her. She wanted nothing more to do with her, but what could she actually do now? She was trapped. The self-righteous anger boiled within her, but then another contraction caught Angelique and the sounds through the dark showed that it was a particularly strong one. Sara's anger softened. Were not all women subject to the same trials and tribulations at the hand of Mother Nature and of God? No matter what their situation or station in life, they all had to brave the perils of motherhood. It was the great equalizer, and queen and pauper alike were subject to it vicissitudes. Still, she held back.

Once the fit had passed, Angelique said, her breath short and panting, "Please, please, dear Sara—may I still call you Sara?—don't abandon me. Everyone has abandoned me. My mother before I even knew her. My father left me to his sister, who did not care for me. And then my Amedee. He said he would be true and faithful, and when I let him … do what he so desired, it was because I loved him so and I trusted that he would be true and faithful, and that he would marry me. You believe me, do you not? Please believe me."

So she was not a prostitute, then, but simply a woman who had been abandoned by a man, much like Sara. There was a clear distinction in Sara's mind between a promise of marriage and prostitution, and due to her own close call with that latter institution she would not have accepted the fact had it been so. But such was not the case. Angelique had been in a situation similar to Sara's—she had trusted a man. In Sara's case, the man had married her, but not so in Angelique's case. And now, had Sara really been abandoned by her man? She did not know, but it was possible. Any residual anger faded away, and she felt enormous sympathy for Angelique. "I do believe you, and I will not abandon you." She said it with conviction. Angelique had sensed her anger, but now she hoped that she sensed her forgiveness.

Another fit took Angelique, and Sara reached out and rubbed her back. And then, sooner than Sara thought possible, another contraction came. They began to come faster and harder, one after another. Outside the storm may have calmed, but inside it felt like a storm of its own. Soon Angelique's focus turned inward and her breathing came more ragged, and she did not speak. The contractions came faster and closer and longer until they seemed one long uninterrupted effort. Sara sat next to her and made encouraging sounds. It went on and on. Angelique was drenched in sweat and got weaker and weaker. The contractions seemed to grab her and rip her apart, but still the baby showed no signs of coming out. This can't go on much longer, Sara thought, and sat back. Her shoulders ached as if they were stabbed with knives, and a headache pounded right above her ears. She realized she was taking all Angelique's tension into her own body and fighting it, trying to support, to push, to hold it all. She could only imagine what Angelique was feeling.

"Much more of this," Angelique said, panting through clenched teeth, "and I'll have to jump out that window."

"What do you feel like?" Sara asked. "Do you feel like pushing?"

"What do you think I've been doing here, napping?" Angelique snapped. And then, more softly, she said, "I feel like I have to go to the outhouse, but I can't. I'm blocked. It won't come out. " Helplessness was in her voice.

What could Sara do to help? She wished she knew more,

410

she wished there was a midwife here, but then she shook her head. It could not be helped. Sara had to figure it out her own self. She had to arrive at a new strategy. She could do something, for something needed to be done.

Chapter 22

t was mid-afternoon before they got Thomas installed in the bunkhouse to rest and they rounded up the horses that they could find and got them to higher ground and they secured what things they could against the storm. The water was still rising, but the barn and outbuildings were all high enough that there was almost no chance that the water would reach them. James was physically exhausted, and so he went and got a meal—hearty ham and beans and cornbread—from the kitchen, which was kept open to feed all the men laboring against the disaster. He found an out-of-the-way corner in a chair on a leeside porch, set his food in his lap, and began to eat. The storm still raged, but the porch was deep enough that the rain stayed off him, and he wanted privacy badly enough he braved the residual lashings of the wind.

He could not take his mind off Sara. What was happening to her? The apartment and the dining establishment where she worked were downtown in the West Bottoms. There was no escape for her from this awesome disaster. If she had not had proper warning, she would be stuck down there. Worse, she would be swept away in the flood. He believed that it had the force not simply to wash things away but to knock things over, buildings even. She could swim, so she said, but that did not matter a hill of beans in water as forceful as this. You could not keep your head above water if a vicious undercurrent pulled you under and pinned you. Or a log came along and rolled overtop of you and knocked you on the head. There were numerous ways to meet your maker in a flood like this. The lightening. Falling debris. Riots and lawlessness. Tornados—had there been any?

And then the image came to his mind of the first time he had laid eyes upon Sara. The penumbra of light in which she had been bathed as she came walking from the end of the alley behind her father's store. How he had thought for a moment that she was his mother and how odd that had been. How he had instantaneously felt an attraction to her, which at first had been physical, but then had quickly transmorphosed into intrigue. He did not remember many of the particulars of their first conversation, but he did remember that for the first time in a long time—possibly ever—he had felt at peace. Something about her had given him a sense of himself that he had not possessed previously—a man on his own, without his mother, yet capable of joining in the common dream of mankind to make a life and future for themselves and those they loved. Something about her confidence, her focus on him, had so possessed him that he would have given anything to have her. And then, by some miracle, he did have her. How had that happened?

He thought the first time they had made love, how he had sensed her modesty and had not undressed her, though he had sorely wanted to see her naked body. The feel of her soft wet skin pressed against his and the distinct smell of her—her hair like warm grass, her body pleasantly of sweat, her womanly places musky and fecund. Just the remembrance prompted his

413

manhood to respond, even in his exhausted state. In that moment, he wanted her right there beside him, to have her firmly within his possession. Then came an image of her laughing. He did not remember exactly when it had been, but the sun had poured in from the side, and she had had her hat off. Amusement had taken command of her face and had possessed her, her eyes squinting and her cheeks pulled back, and he was moved at the memory of its sheer beauty. He had not seen her laugh in weeks, perhaps a month, since his accident surely. It was the weight of trying to make ends meet plus his accident that weighed her down. And, if he were honest with himself, he would admit that it was not just the accident that kept her from smiling. It was also himself, his demeanor. Something about the accident had awakened a rage within him that he had not known that he possessed.

Not only that, but it was his fault that she was now imperiled. He had been a coward and a fool and a sniveling worm, had he not? He had taken the easy out and abandoned her, and now when it was his supreme duty above all to protect and save her, he was not there. He had acted like an impulsive child. If she were harmed or—God forbid!—killed, it would be entirely his fault. He felt the guilt settle onto his shoulders and in the pit of his stomach. It had been his fault when his mother died, too—she had gotten sick because he had not been there to save her, and he had not been there to save her because he had stolen that horse, once again on an impulse and in a rage. He felt the vicelike grip of guilt tighten further, and he felt for a moment that he could not breath. He put his food aside on the floorboards and leaned over, propping his elbows on his knees and his head in his hands. The thought did come to him, though: he could not change the past but he could affect the

414

future, and as he sat there he made a vow that he would. He would immediately do his best to find her and save her if he could. He might already be too late. He pushed himself up and picked up his plate and took it to the kitchen and went to find Enders.

When he finally found the man a half hour later, Enders had just come away from talking to Blachley, he said, and there was a troubled look on his face. It had not gone well, apparently. Of course not—the storm damage alone was going to cost a pretty fortune to repair, not to mention the mares who had been killed or had to be put down. Had James had a choice, he would have waited for the storm clouds on Enders's face to dissipate, but there was no time—he had to leave now—and so he launched into his speech.

"Enders, I wanted to express how much this job is a Godsend, and how much I appreciate the chance you have given me." Enders narrowed his eyes at this. "I have done the best job for you that I was able, and I hope in some small way I was able to contribute to the operation. I hope after I have had my say that I can continue in your employ. Horses are … well." James did not have the words to express the complexity of his love for them, so he let it go. "But I was not entirely truthful with you. I do indeed have a wife, who is now in the city amidst the floods, and I must go and try to find her, if I can. I must go immediately."

The understanding of James's words crossed Enders face, and anger prompted his eyes to narrow and his jaw to clench. "You deceptive bastard," Enders said. "God help your wife. I have no further use for you. One thing I cannot abide is mendacity, not to mention disloyalty, and so I want you off the property immediately." So that was it. He had truly lost the position of his dreams. Enders stuck his fingers in his mouth and whistled, calling for a groom, but James did not let it get that far. "I am sorry you feel that way," he said quickly, adding, "Please give my regards to Thomas." He stood and walked out the door and out of the building and into the driving rain.

He started walking toward the city. The wind-driven rain lashed against him and the mud caked his boots and made his feet heavy and sloppy, and he fell down twice in the first mile, but he kept going. It was the least he deserved. He walked and, though he could not see the sun to tell the time, the light in the storm-darkened sky waned and soon it was night. Sometime during his trudging in the darkness, he reached the cable stop, but of course no cable cars were running—not this time of night and not in this storm—and so he continued on. It was deep in the night before he came into the city, and he was wet through and through, exhausted and stumbling in the dark. He began to meet wagons creaking their way through the dark coming the other way. They moved slowly and had no lanterns lit, as the rain would certainly put them out, and the teams of horses or oxen were led cautiously along by the person in front. People were also out walking in the dark, hurrying along, some carrying burdens, and he came across camps by the roadside, some with fires if there was a semi-sheltered spot in the lee of building or a tree that would allow such an endeavor. The buildings and the houses became more frequent, and some had windows lit. The rain let up somewhat, for which James was glad. He came upon a crowd in front of a lamplit newspaper office, and someone told him that a man was going to come out and tell them the state of affairs. He needed information, but he also wanted to get down to the bottoms. He decided to wait and was rewarded soon by a man who came out into the lamplight and orated the following.

"I will not lie to you. Conditions are grim. This flood is the largest since the Great Flood of Forty-four. It's up twenty feet and rising. There have been innumerable damage and loss of life and property. We will post a list of those who are missing here at the paper and will publish free of charge those names, as well as those who are confirmed to have shuffled off this mortal coil. We would appreciate you all keeping us informed of those who are missing and those who have been located, one way or another. And I call upon you, as God-fearing citizens, those of you with a home or of means, please extend a helping hand to those who are less fortunate. That is all." As he turned to go back into the building, another man stepped up beside him and talked to him for a second. Then the first man raised his voice again, saying, "In the spirit aforementioned, this gentleman would like to speak to you—"

The man, breaking in, said, "We've got a fire downtown, over the hill not a mile from here, and we need able hands to fight it. We have a wagon standing by."

James was so tired, and the thought of the relative luxury of a wagon ride moved him—if he had to fight fire for its reward, so be it. He stepped forward and volunteered, and soon he and number of other men were loaded in the back of a wagon. Despite their rough and squelching path, James's head bobbed to his chest, and he slept for a short time. When he awoke, the sky begun to lighten. By the time they reached their destination, it was light, though still dull and gray with clouds and rain. As they dismounted, water flowed in the streets covering over everything but the high spots. It had a sheen of grease and chemicals and reeked of sewage as it ran between the buildings and lapped at the boardwalks. Up ahead they could see a plume of smoke. Soon they were wading and then it came up to their knees. The current pulled at their ankles and the bottoms of their trousers. Still it got deeper.

"We will be in need of a boat before long," someone said.

"Just up here," the man in charge said and gestured. As they rounded the corner of a building, they could see flames in some of the bottom-floor windows on one side of a large apartment house that threatened to catch the buildings crowded around it. A few men with buckets threw water in the windows and formed a chain in through the door and out into the running water. Just as James and the men sloshed up, one of the second floor windows burst with a *chunk* and a *tinkle* of glass. Light gray smoke billowed out into the dark gray air. James and the other new arrivals formed a second line of men that curved through a bottom floor door and snaked up the stairs. Smoke obscured the view, but it was not too thick. There must be something, a hole in the wall or open windows, drawing it off, James thought. They put James to work in the second floor hallway. It was hot, which was welcome after the cold driving wind and water. Buckets sloshed as they were passed hand to hand as quickly as the men could manage, and most of the buckets were less than half full by the time they reached James. On the other side of the wall was the crackle and roar of the fire, the crash of something falling, the woof as something was engulfed in flame. At first the motions warmed and revived him, but then they became repetitive, and his mind blanked— turn, grasp the handle and the base, turn, hand it on, turn, grasp another, turn, hand it off, turn …

Time passed. James did not know whether they were making progress or not. Some men came in to relieve other men. James's back was getting tired and so when two men came up the stairs and one said to James, "You look like you need a break," James nodded and moved so the man could take his place. He did not want to interrupt the line passing buckets, and he also wondered about the flood, and so as he rounded the end of the line by the stairs, he ducked into a room on the side away from the fire. He looked out a window. The flood waters had topped the boardwalks, and there were a few boats with men rowing this way and that. He could see the bright reflection of the fire rippling on the waters, and men staring at the building he was in. As he stood there, he heard a *thump, thump, thump*. Again, a *thump, thump, thump*. Was it someone running up the stairs? There it was again. No, it could not be. It could only be the sound of a person calling for help, pounding on the floor above. He ran out into the hall. Heat engulfed him. There was chaos as men were passing buckets in the flickering glow of a couple of doorways. Smoke scratched his lungs, and James coughed.

On the far end of the hallway, flames licked a doorway. Someone yelled, "We have to get out of here, now!" Men responded, turning to scramble down the stairs. James grabbed a tall man as he passed and pulled him from the line and said, "There's someone upstairs," James said.

The man glanced at the line of men disappearing down the stairs and said, "You are crazy."

"No, I heard it. There is someone upstairs."

"If anyone is upstairs, they would have gotten out hours ago," the man insisted and turned to the stairs.

"No, no! There's someone up there, I tell you. I heard it. Someone's pounding on the floor." James shook the man's shoulder. If someone was indeed up there—and he was convinced there was—he would need help.

The man hesitated. He glanced down the stairs and then up the other stairs. "Well, if we are going to do it, we had better do it now."

James took the stairs two at a time, the tall man right behind him. The hallway was engulfed in smoke, and the end of it was a wall of flame. James coughed and pulled the tall man into a crouch. "Here. It was coming from here." He skirted the stair and pushed on a door. The door was locked, but then they both heard it: *thump, thump, thump*. Putting his ear to the crack below the door, he heard a croak, "Help! Help!" James straightened and looked at the man and nodded. "Someone in here." The tall man stood, backed away from the door, and then kicked it. It took two tries, but the door burst open. The tall man coughed and then went into a crouch again. They pushed into the room, which was bare except for a bed. In the bed lay an ancient man who had a cane that he was using to thump on the floor. When he saw them, tears streamed down his soot-blackened face. He held out his arms like a child and croaked, "Thank you. Oh, thank you." The tall man grabbed the old man under the armpits, and James grabbed his bony legs. He was light as a pillow, which was a good thing because they had to half crouch as they carried him out the door. A wall of heat met them. James thought he felt his hair singe.

They rounded the top of the stairs, the tall man going first holding the old man's shoulders. Halfway down the stairs, there was a groan, and the stairs beneath them sagged. "Damn," the tall man yelled. "Run!" They rounded the stairs on the next floor down and the walls began to crumble. They were halfway down the last set of stairs when James felt himself thrust up as the stairs buckled. He was heaved forward

420

over the heads of the old man and the tall man. He felt his head and shoulders smack into something hard, and then he blacked out.

Nothing.

And then, out of the darkness, James felt a wetness. His legs and his body were wet with cold water running over them and tugging at his clothes. There was smell of mud and waste and the sound of rushing water. How long had he been out? He did not know. He distinctly remembered flying through the air just before he hit. He moved his body, but as soon as he did, his arm shot with pain. He opened his eyes and saw that his sleeve was burned and his arm was red and bubbled with blisters. He winced. Where the water lapped felt cool, so he lowered it into the water. Relief—it stopped hurting, though James did not want to think about what infecting agents floated just there across the open wound. He flexed first one leg and then another. They seemed fine. His other arm seemed fine. He looked around him. The fire was out. The sky was open above him and water rushed by in front of him. He twisted his head and saw that the building had collapsed behind in a huge pile of jagged lumber that steamed and smoked. Around him in a perfect rectangle lay a door frame—that must have been what saved him. He twisted his head the other way, and sticking from the rubble was a leg. It was long and well-muscled and looked to be the leg of the tall man. He saw no sign of the old man. James turned away.

The pull of the water on his body became stronger. It soon covered his chest. He would have to swim for it. Though he had survived the swimming incident the day before, he was loathe to tempt fate yet again, but here he was, with no choice. Had he not vowed that he would risk his life to find Sara if he could? Now he would have to risk his life not only to find Sara but also to save his own. He tried to push himself up to sitting but then something held him back—his clothes were caught under large chunks of splintered wood debris, just behind him on his right side. He pulled but nothing gave. He shrugged his coat off his left shoulder and peeled his arm out of the sleeve, turning it inside out. He shrugged it off his right shoulder and then looked at his burned arm—this was going to hurt. As gently as he could, he lifted the coat and pulled his left arm back through what was left of the sleeve. "Aaaaaaaah," he breathed, as his raw nerves scraped against the cloth, shooting the pain of exposed nerve endings up his arm. "Shit, shit, shit!" he said. He felt his senses get fuzzy, like he was about to pass out. Can't, he thought, I cannot, or I truly will be done for. He lowered his arm back into the water and coolness returned. With his left hand he patted water on his forehead. After a second, he felt clearer.

The water soon covered his chest and continued to pull at his legs. He pushed forward to sit up, and this time it worked. His coat was the only thing caught. Under the water, he cautiously tapped the boards under his feet. They swayed and dipped as he did, threatening to collapse. Frantically he looked around for something to help him float. The boards around him were either too small or so intertwined that he did not think he could pull them free. But just then he spotted something large and round and dark bobbing just upstream. It lazily rolled in the current and a leg rotated into view. He saw that it was a bloated cow, risen to the surface by the decomposition gas building within it. That would have to do, as he had to have something or he would not make it. He crouched and then launched himself into the current. The cold water enveloped him and took his breath away as he unsuccessfully tried to keep his head above the water, but then he surfaced as the current swept him wide around a corner and into the body of the cow. He grabbed a leg and then pulled himself nearer for a better hold. The odor hit him—rotten stinking decaying flesh assaulted his nose and made him choke. He almost let go of the animal but then did not—it meant the difference between life and death, smell notwithstanding.

The water pushed him and his cow raft fairly rapidly down streets. They bounced off the walls of buildings and they swirled in eddies in the lee of buildings, and he felt things bump underneath him and up against him, things that he did not know and did not want to know. He prayed that nothing nearby was so large as to crush him or to pull him under the water. He tried to find placed to grab hold and pull himself out, but there were none. But then he swung around another corner and saw ahead of him a panorama of the wide Missouri gaping before him, the waters roiling and cresting and foaming like an ocean's rough seas and debris swiping into the air as it thrust through the waves. If he got in there, he knew that he would never make it. That would truly be the end of it. But, ahead to one side, James caught sight of a lone tree bending slightly in the current, a tall cottonwood, and the water was high enough that its leafy branches dipped and swayed in the water. That was his only chance. He pushed off from the cow as hard as he could and flailed in the water. Trying to keep the image of a horse paddle in his mind, he kicked and pushed with his arms, water splashing. He was lucky, here the water was flatter and had not reached the roiling peaks he could see out ahead, but the current picked up, threatening to shoot him past the leafy branches, so he kicked as hard as he could.

He was just able to grab at the greenery as he shot past, and his luck held—he feared for a split second that he would grasp nothing but leaves, but his palm wrapped around a good-sized branch. He hung on. Fighting the water that threatened to pull him under and to break off the limb, hand over hand, he pulled himself toward the trunk. Slowly, using all the last of his strength, he made it to the trunk and pulled himself up into a crotch of the tree, and unless he tucked up his legs, his feet were in the water. He tried to push himself up farther, but only succeeded in scratching his arms and almost losing his grip, so he sank back down to where he was. Soon he was perched uncomfortably with both of his arms around the trunk. He hoped the water did not rise any farther. The roaring wind and rain beat the swaying tree, and James shivered and looked out over the roaring water. It spread out all around him like a rolling ocean, with flotsam and jetsam cruising past. In the distance he could see the tops of buildings, and he saw flames rising in the bottoms. He looked up at the bluffs, and he could see dark spots where crowds of people stood and watched. The thought crossed his mind to shout and wave, but then it would not matter. They could not see him without a lens and they could not hear him over the roar of the water. Besides, he had not the strength.

But then he heard the strangest sound. It was low and then undulated higher, and he realized that it was the baying of a hound dog. He twisted to look behind him, upstream, and there, canted at an angle, was the roof of a building, the very peak jutting from the water. On the peak stood a wet red dog, baying. It could not be, but it was. Opal stood there straddling the peak, her head facing downstream. She lifted her muzzle once more, and the sound of her baying voice was time-delayed coming over the water. James searched beside her and what little he could see of the roof, but there was no one else. It was a relief, but then it was not. "Opal!" James screamed. "Ooooh-paaall!" The dog turned its head in his direction as the building swept past the tree, not too close, but the dog did not seem to see him, and then her head turned back downstream to what lay in her future. Just then the building rolled in the water, and James lost sight of the dog's form behind the tipping roof and then the walls that followed. That was the last he saw of her, though he frantically searched the waters nearby. At that, something broke within him, and he began to cry, though the sound of his loud convulsive sobs were drowned out in the roar and his tears mingled with the rain.

Chapter 23

omething had to be done. The baby was stuck. It only made sense, as Angelique was such a small person. Sara tried to think of all the ways one got something out of something else without damaging either. There had to be more force applied. Sara could not squeeze the poor girl—that would not help. Angelique would have to squeeze more herself, now before her strength waned. So, how could she help Angelique squeeze harder? She thought of the force of water outside, pushing against the building and wished that she could borrow just a smidgeon of it for the present cause. And then it came to Sara that the water flooded not simply because there was so much of it but also because it obeyed the laws of nature, it followed the call of gravity. That's what her sister Esther had done at both of her birthings. She had not taken it lying down—she had walked and squatted and used gravity to her advantage.

"Let's try something else," Sara told Angelique. She looked around the room. "Let's try this." She got up and pulled down some heavy ledgers and stacked them next to Angelique. Then she herself sat down upon them. "Here. Lean upon me. Crouch in front of me and put your hands upon my knees, and let gravity do some of the work. While you are pushing, it can be pulling." She helped Angelique pull herself so that her back pressed against Sara's body. Sara felt how thin and small she was, but how heavy too through the pressing of her hands. Angelique arrange her shift up onto her thighs so that her legs were bare and free to move.

Inspiration struck her again as another fit struck Angelique. "Angelique, listen. I want you think about your mother." Angelique groaned, though due to the pain or Sara's words, she did not know. "But I do not want you to be sad. The time for grief is over. I want you to let yourself be angry. This curse that all women bear stole her from you. Otherwise, you might have known her soft embrace and her sweet words. But no, you did not, and it was—not because of you, you are not to blame—but because of this. Let the anger take you. Use it to push this baby out of you."

Angelique groaned and strained. Then it eased just a bit and she took a breath and said, "And that hornswoggler who called himself a man."

"Yes!" Sara said. "Let the anger come to you. Use it!"

Upon the heels of the last fit, another took Angelique, and she let out a low moan and strained. "Now it's ... Now it's ..." she moaned. She clutched and pushed Sara so hard Sara winced as Angelique's fingers bit into her thighs. She put her arms around Angelique's shoulders to steady her back against her chest. Then Angelique screamed, "Uuuuhhhaaaaaaaaaaaaahhttt!" a long high-pitched screech that caught up short as Angelique went limp against Sara's chest and lay gasping for breath. Sara felt something fall upon her foot.

"Are you okay?" Sara whispered.

Angelique said nothing but nodded.

"Here, let me put you on the floor. You did it!" She lifted Angelique over onto the coat and crawled around in front of her. There between her knees was a tiny child, seemingly much too small for the size of Angelique's belly. She could just make out the shape of it and then realized that morning must be coming as there was light in the window. She was able to see that the baby was blue and green with a yellow coating and the umbilical cord with its bluish white sheen pulsed red with blood. It was a boy. He choked and coughed and then cried, weak and wavering at first but then more loudly.

Sara laughed with relief. "It's over. You did it, and you are alive."

Angelique smiled and nodded and tried to sit up. "Boy or girl?" she breathed.

"It's a boy."

"I think he came out backwards," Angelique said. "That's why it was so hard. My backwards little boy." She reached out her hand and touched his foot.

Sara put the baby on Angelique's chest, who pulled the coat overtop of him. The baby calmed. Sara glanced at Angelique's face. Angelique's mouth was open and her eyes were wide and she was shaking her head. "Something's wrong," Angelique said. "It's not over."

"Just the afterbirth," Sara said.

"No. That's not it. Something's wrong."

Sara pulled the boy to one side and put her hands on Angelique's belly. Another contraction hit, strong, and Angelique buckled. "Noooooooo!" she wailed.

Angelique's belly was too big, and the boy was too small. The contractions were still strong. What was it? Hadn't Esther's follow-up contractions waned?

Sara and Angelique's eyes met. Angelique said, "I think there's another one in there."

"No, really?" Sara said and immediately began to arrange things. She put the baby boy, still attached, to the side as well as she could, and she began to move to get behind Angelique, but Angelique breathed, "No time!" and pushed and between Angelique's legs bulged and then, with a grunting push from Angelique, the baby's head emerged. It looked upward, toward the ceiling, and for a second it seemed to have a questioning look on its scrunched face. Then out it came in a rush, Sara's hands there to catch it. It had almost none of the yellow coating, as if the rush of waters had washed it clean, and it didn't cry. Instead, it coughed a couple of times and it began breathing just fine. Angelique let herself carefully down onto the floor, breathing heavily, tears streaking her face. "It is a girl, I believe. A boy and a girl." Sara choked with wonder. A rush of emotion flooded through her and tears streamed down her face. Angelique's face held relief and joy and pain. Sara gathered the boy and put him on Angelique's chest and then gathered up the girl and put her there too.

"That's right, my little stoic one," Angelique said, "you will have a long life and many children. The curse is broken. And there will be plenty of time for tears later on." And then she laughed and Sara laughed and then they continued to cry. Sara lay down next to them and put her arm around them. She thought about the time to come and how, given some luck, she too would soon have a small miracle of her very own. They lay nestled in the warmth of their mother's body, waving their arms and trying to lift their heads, their eyes open wide with surprise.

Chapter 24

It was not until the next day that Sara, Angelique, and the two babies were rescued by boat. They had run out of water and had had no food besides the peppermint stick and an orange for the duration of their stay. The babies slept constantly, and when Angelique was not sleeping she fretted whether the lack of adequate sustenance would affect the babies, but it they seemed to be getting along fine, as far as Sara could tell. Their water did not run out until the morning of their rescue, when Sara was finally able to flag down a boat by waving a large scrap of white underskirt out the window. As they waited, they had discussed what they would do *when*—they did not say *if*—they were rescued. Sara did not know if her apartment would still be there. She explained to Angelique that she lived on the second floor. "Well, maybe it will be all right then," Angelique had said, but Sara could see the skepticism on her face. Angelique had lived in this city for all her life, and she had heard the stories of previous floods. "I do not believe my aunt's residence will still be there. And as much as I despise the woman, I hope she made it through as well."

"What will you do?" Sara asked.

"I will go to my father's home up among goats," she said.

"The goats?" Sara said.

"You know, the goats and the rabbits?" Angelique said. When Sara gave her a blank expression, she said, "They call those who live up on the bluffs the goats and us here in the bottoms the rabbits. My father lives in one of those ridiculously pompous homes up there." After a moment, Angelique said, "What will you do?"

Sara was silent for a moment, as she had no idea. She had not told Angelique about the missing James, as she was not sure what to do. She would have to see what remained of her life—her apartment and her job. She would once again try to find James, but with the chaos after the flood it would be even harder. If there was nothing left, if she there was no apartment, no job, and no James, not even a dog—a wave of grief at the mere thought overcame her—then she would have no choice but to telegraph her father, or Esther, rather. And she had a baby on the way. There was that. She would just have to see.

Angelique, sensing her hesitation, said, "You can come with me to my father's house. My father is not an ogre, though he is stiff as an old board. He knew of my condition, and though he did not approve, he will not turn me away. He simply did what he has always done with me, which was to shuttle me of Aunt Ginny's."

Relief flooded Sara. She would have a place at least for a short while, long enough to perform her searches. "I ... I would be greatly honored and greatly indebted to you," she said.

"No," Angelique said, "I owe you my life. It is I who am indebted to you." She smiled up from where she was nursing the little girl, whom she'd decided to call Chloe after her mother. The boy she had named Nicholas.

And so they were rescued and they went to the home of Angelique's father, which was indeed a mansion upon the hill.

Her father was tall and thin with a hook nose. He greeted them kindly enough but then disappeared, and Sara only saw him at suppers taken in the echoey dining room. They dressed in long formal gowns for dinner—Angelique lent her one—and spoke in polite addresses, much like it had been back in Anamosa. Rather than comforting Sara, it only served as a contrast to her current life and made her more miserable.

All of Sara's energy went into finding pieces of her former life, and after the flood had somewhat receded she made trips down into the disaster that was the West Bottoms. She found that the building of her apartment had been completely swept away in the flood, and Opal was gone. Dear Opal. She supposed she would never see her again. Such a sad and senseless thing, weighing heavily within the accumulation of events. Everything, all her possessions, were gone. The dining establishment had remained standing, but Molly had decided she had had enough—she was leaving her husband and returning back to California from whence she came. Molly had been almost apologetic when Sara was finally able to track her down. So Sara had no job. She searched as well as she could to try to find Auntie and Moses, but they had completely disappeared—whether they had survived or no, she had no idea. She told herself that of course they had survived and they simply had been absorbed back into the black community. Auntie certainly had enough friends—and relatives, Sara supposed, but she did not know—to give her aid in her time of need. She vowed to continue to inquire.

And then there was James. Sara could not locate the Soijka brothers to ask them. When she went to Xavier's, the place stood but was abandoned. She searched her mind for other people she could ask, but she could think of no one. The people

432

James had mentioned were nothing but names to her, and she had no way of knowing who they were or how to find them. She went to the police department and tried to report a missing persons, explaining that he had been missing before the flood. They simply gave her a skeptical look, as if to say, "Lady, your case is but one in a thousand missing persons, and he probably ran off with another woman." But they did take down her information and her present address in case they found something. She went to a newspaper office to consult their list of missing and dead, but they explained that since James had technically been missing before the flood, they could not add him to their list. They did add hers, though, to the list of survivors and where she could be contacted.

She stayed on at the Demichels, helping Angelique with the babies when she was not out searching. She became more and more desperate, finding a dead end at every turn. But then one evening at supper, Mr. Demichel, as he always did, began to relate the interesting items in the paper, and he mentioned the rescue of one James Youngblood from a tree in the middle of the floodwater.

"What?!" Sara said. "Who?"

"Er, um," Mr. Demichel said, "I believe his name was James Youngblood. Oh, that is your surname too." She still had not told them about James.

"That is my husband," she said with rather more surprise than she meant to convey.

Mr. Demichel and Angelique both gave her a questioning look, but she did not know what to answer. Instead, she said, standing up from the table, "Where is that paper? May I see it?"

"Well, that story was actually a few days ago," he said. "I

believe we have thrown it away."

Sara shook her head in frustration. "What did it say?"

"It was part of a story about miraculous rescues during the flood," Mr. Girard said. "It simply said that one James Youngblood was rescued from a tall cottonwood surrounded by floodwaters at the edge of the river. That was it."

So he was indeed alive! That gave her such solace, and she lay in bed that night simply overjoyed, but then as she lay there falling asleep, it came to her. That did not answer the question of what he had been doing. Once again sorrow came to her. Had he indeed left her? The next morning, the first thing she did was to go to the newspaper office and inquire about the story. It took them most of the morning to track down the reporter, and when they did, he said he had no idea where Mr. Youngblood was. He had been rescued and then melted into the thousands of other displaced persons. Yes, healthwise he had appeared fine. So she would have to continue her search.

That evening, she sat upon a chair in the sloping back garden of the mansion, which overlooked the West Bottoms. The rain had stopped, a fresh breeze blew softly, and the warm sun was a fiery ball sinking below the horizon. From this distance, the utter devastation was less apparent as the bottoms sunk into the shadow of the bluffs opposite. Sara lay against the high back of the chair and closed her eyes. Perhaps she would never know, she thought. Perhaps her previous life was nothing more than a dream, but for the child growing in her belly, and her future was simply to merge back into her old life, a fate she must accept. The thought did not grieve her as much as she thought it would, as a certain numbness had overtaken her, and she felt empty, washed clean by the flood. All that striving, all that devotion, come to nought. Perhaps the child wasn't even real. It was as if it were she who had been erased.

And then she heard the sound of someone moving behind her. The person walked around her chair and then stood in front of her. She opened her eyes, but the person was bathed in the golden red glow of the setting sun, a penumbra of light that left their features indistinct. "Sara?" came the voice, but instead of the high and soft voice of Angelique that she was expecting, it was deep and resonant and desperately familiar. It was her own dear sweet James.

The End

Acknowledgements

"I knew that there had been times in the past—
terrible times—when people had destroyed
others in haste, in fear, and had brought about
their own destruction." —Lois Lowry, *The
Giver*

Thanks go first and foremost to Ma Strong, my great
grandmother, and Frank Strong, my great grandfather, on
whom Sara and James are based. And there are many real
incidents upon which parts of this story are based—I thank all
those people who lived it.

I would like to thank my agent Rachel Stout and Dystel &
Goderich Literary Management for your kind thoughts and
input. I would also like to thank Roxanne Rhoads for her
invaluable efforts.

This was the first novel that I wrote—and rewrote and
rewrote over many years—and great many people have given
me feedback and encouragement along the way: Jessica, Nina,
Naomi, Kerry, Meg, April, Terry, Alison, Karyn, Bruce, Mark,
Caskey, Alyson, and Rachel. There was a wonderful man at a
very small conference when I was first starting out—I don't
remember his name—but he very kindly read the first couple of
chapters and gave me encouragement when I most sorely
needed it. For this, you will go to writers' heaven.

I would like to thank my family: my mom to whom I owe
my love for family stories, my dad for his kindness and his
forbears, my sister Nikki for her love of reading and happy
endings, my sister Jerri for her unwavering support and
enthusiasm, my sister Randi for her cheerful optimism, my

sister Tonee for her example, my brother Jim for his love of science fiction (and hence my love of science fiction), and my brother Rob for all things Western. My sprawling clan is the reason I am who I am.

And to my inlaws, I owe you my heart—particularly you, Jean, as you're the kindest and most wonderful person. I'm not only just related to you all—I love hanging out with you. Thank you!

Finally, to Steve, Elizabeth, and Eli: thank you for taking me for granted and allowing me to take you for granted. I love you more than you can know.

– Tamara Linse, Laramie, Wyoming, 2015

Reading Group Guide

Earth's Imagined Corners
Tamara Linse

In 1885 Iowa, Sara Moore is a dutiful daughter, but when her father tries to force her to marry his younger partner, she must choose between the partner—a man who treats her like property—and James Youngblood—a kind man she hardly knows who has a troubled past. When she confronts her father, he beats her and turns her out of the house, breaking all ties, so she decides to elope with James to Kansas City with hardly a penny to their names. In the tradition of Willa Cather's *O Pioneers!* and Zora Neale Hurston's *Their Eyes Were Watching God*, *Earth's Imagined Corners* is a novel that comprehends the great kindnesses and violences we do to each other.

The author Tamara Linse jokes that she was raised in the 1880s, and so it was natural for her to set a book there. She is the author of the short story collection *How to Be a Man* and the novel *Deep Down Things* and earned her master's in English from the University of Wyoming, where she taught writing. Her work appears in the *Georgetown Review*, *South Dakota Review*, and *Talking River*, among others, and she was a finalist for an *Arts & Letters* and *Glimmer Train* contests, as well as the Black Lawrence Press Hudson Prize for a book of short stories. She works as an editor for a foundation and a freelancer. Find her online at tamaralinse.com and her blog Writer, Cogitator, Recovering Ranch Girl at tamara-linse.blogspot.com.

Letter from the Author

Dear Reader,

What should I say about *Earth's Imagined Corners*? There's so much to tell.

This is the first book I wrote, and the first novel. I had been writing my whole life, but it wasn't until 1999 that I claimed "writer" and began writing lots of fiction. I almost immediately tried to write a novel—this novel.

Very quickly, I realized fiction is one long resistance against writing the first thing that comes to mind, against cliché, and that I knew nothing about writing fiction, not really. And so I continued to work on the novel but then I also wrote loads of short stories. Short stories are so demanding, little diamonds that demand perfection, and that taught me so much about writing. These stories became the collection *How to Be a Man*.

I wrote on and off for years and finally achieved a first draft. Then I got feedback from some very patient writing friends, though the manuscript had a long way to go. They were insightful but very kind, as true writing friends are. Then I tried to get an agent, with minimal interest. When I say minimal, I really do mean minimal. And so I put it away and wrote another novel, which is *Deep Down Things*. After 11 years, I got my lovely agent, and then we queried publishers with both the novels. In the process, I majorly rewrote them both—again, from scratch, just keeping the plot. *Earth's Imagined Corners* almost turned into two novels, but I really felt the parts needed to remain together. Then, after feedback from my agent, *Earth's Imagined Corners* was shaped into final form.

The story is based on the lives of my great grandparents, Frank and Ellen Strong. Ellen Noble grew up in Iowa, while Frank grew up in Illinois under the name "Frank Wood" and moved across the country with his mother, Elizabeth Zenana Robinson Maettison Wood Strong Howard Staats. She was born in Virginia, and family legend says she danced at Tom Thumb's wedding, married five times, and died in Red Willow County, Nebraska. She's an elusive figure, and I had a heck of a time tracking her down through geneology. I still know very little about her.

Legend also says that Frank worked for an uncle for a year and was not paid, and so that's why he stole two horses and was sentenced to the Additional Penitentiary in Anamosa. Family legend turned out to be true. This is from the records of the penitentiary.

A. Henry Zierjacks being sworn testified as follows, am 33 years of age, reside Franklin Twshp. Bremer Co., a farmer, have known Frank Wood 4 or 5 years. I worked for Harper R. Smith know that he Smith lost a horse about Jan. 12th, 1882 saw tracks going north from the stable, followed the tracks towards Henry Adams and found that Frank Wood had eaten supper at Adams that night and had left about 9 o'clock, the day after F. W. was arrested he told me in the Bremer Co. Jail at Waverly that he took the horses asked me to do what I could for him to get him off easy, he said he watched me the night he took the horse until I went to bed. I talked with him today he told me he took the horse.

441

John Carstensen sworn testified as follows, age 23 years, Residence Waverly, am Deputy Sheriff of Bremer Co., Ia. Know Frank Wood, first saw him about Jan. 14th, 1882 in custody of Sheriff of Floyd Co. in Chas. City I served a warrant on him and took him into my custody, he said it was all right commenced crying and said he had stolen the horses and had sold them to Waller Bros. Charles City. On my way to Chas. City saw Louis Harper who told me he saw a man with two gray horses he was riding one and leading the other which had a harness on. The description he gave me both of the man and the horses agreed with the description of the horses and Frank Wood when I found them at Chas. City. Met several other men on my way to Chas City who gave me descriptions of a man with two gray horses in his possession going in the direction of Chas. City each description agreed exactly with the horses and Frank Wood when I arrested him. When I brought the horses back Mr. Stotts claimed one and A. Henry Zierjacks claimed the other for Harper R. Smith. I never heard F. W. deny the stealing of the horses but have heard him on several occasions admit to the stealing and claimed it was poverty that drove him to.

Frank and Ellen met at the town pump while Frank was still incarcerated—not, as I have them, after he gets out. Ellen, of course, knew that he was in prison. They married, changed their name to Strong, and then moved to Kansas City, as Sara and James do. Here is Frank and Ellen's wedding portrait, upon which I base the scene in the photography studio.

Frank and Ellen Strong

The Strongs had a grocery store, and we still have the advertisement that ran in a KC newspaper on July 16, 1889.

Cast Your Eye on This!

WE DON'T WANT THE WORLD!
BUT WE WANT ALL THE TRADE

Our Price List Calls for:

12 lbs Granul'd Sugar,	$1.00.	2 lb. Can Pumpkins	.10
13 " Light Brown "	1.00.	Strawberries, 2 Cans.	25.
2 Pkgs Arbuckle's Coffee,	45.	Tea, per lb., from .90 to ,25.	
2 " Dillwith's "	45.	Fine Imperial Syrup	
3 lbs. Extra Moca "	1.00.	p'r Gal.	.50.
5 " " Rio "	1.00.	Cider Vinegar, " "	,20.
4 " " Gov. Java,	1.00	5 to 8 Bars Soap for	.25.
2 Cans Tomatoes,	.25	Best Tobacco. per pound.	.45.

27 Varieties of Candies.

Cig rettes. Cigars. Tobaccos. Lemons. Oranges, Pears.
Pineapples, Peaches, Bread and Cake.
BUTTER EGGS AND COUNTRY PRODUCE A SPECIALTY.

MEAT MARKET!

Is supplied with the BEST FRESH and SALT MEATS.

COAL, WOOD, HAY, FEED &c.

At WHOLESALE and RETAIL.
Goods delivered anywhere in or outside of the Consolidated Cities.

FRANK STRONG,
S. 5TH ST., ARMSTRONG, KAS.

Reproduction of advertisement for the Frank Strong
Grocery in a July 16, 1889 newspaper

444

Their daughters, including my Grandma Bessie, were born in Missouri and Kansas. They eventually move west across Nebraska supplying ties for the railroad, and they are in the vicinity of the Wounded Knee Massacre. At one point, Frank chased Ellen with an ax, and at another point Ellen went out to confront an angry mob of Frank's employees while Frank hid under the bed. Ellen cooked for the crews, and the story goes that she cooked breakfast one day, gave birth to my Grandmother Bessie, and then went back and cooked the evening meal. At least that's the story. This part of their lives is the subject of the second book in the series, *Numberless Infinities*.

Finally, they settled in northern Wyoming and started a hotel and livery in what was initially called Strong but is now Lovell. The Mormon community moved in and looked askance at what went on there. I don't know if it was a brothel, but I don't think so. The liquor was probably enough to be looked down on. The Strongs went in partners with other townsfolk to start a brick and tile factory, which eventually burned down, and there was much finger pointing. At one point, the whole town was moved two blocks south in one night. These events are the basis for the third part in the trilogy called *This Lowly Ground*. After the brick and tile kerfluffle, my family moved 25 miles north to the base of the Pryor Mountains. This is the ranch on which I and my six siblings grew up. Frank passed away in 1914, and Ellen, who was known to everyone as Ma Strong, lived until 1950.

I came across this entry in the book *Progressive Men of the State of Wyoming* (A.W. Bowen & Co., Chicago, Ill., 1903).

Strongly endowed by nature with clearness of vision, quickness of apprehension and alertness in action, so that the opportunity presented for advancement have neither escaped his knowledge or been neglected in use, Frank S. Strong has made steady progress in the race for supremacy among men and the acquisition of this world's good from time to time, when, at the age of twenty, he lifted the gage of battle in life's contest for himself, until now when, at but little over twice that age, he is comfortably provided with a competence, being well-established in his chosen line of business and secure in the respect and esteem of his fellow men. Mr. Strong's interesting and adventurous life began in the state of Illinois on February 8, 1861. His parents, John and Elizabeth (Robinson) Strong, were natives of New York and early settlers of Illinois. When he was ten years old they moved to Iowa, and there he completed his minority, lacking one year, and received a common school education. In 1881 he started out in life for himself, coming to Nebraska and locating in Red Willow county, where for a number of years he was actively engaged in farming. From there he went to Fort Scott, Kan., and was engaged in railroad work for a number of years, and then in Kansas City he opened a merchandising establishment. In 1889 he left the comforts and allurements of city life and went to the wild country of the Black Hills, casting in his lot with its rush of fortune seekers; but, instead of following the almost universal occupation of mining, he engaged in railroad work and found it profitable until 1892, when he came to Wyoming for the purpose of joining the great army of enterprising and hardy men who were engaged in the stock industry. For three years he prospected for a suitable location for his enterprise, working at various useful occupations, and in 1895 took up land on the border of which the town of Lovell has since grown up. He owns 720 acres adjoining the townsite, and in the town itself he owns and conducts a hotel, livery barn and saloon. He also owns 320 acres of land in Montana and has on it 150 fine cattle

446

and fifty well-bred horses in addition to the stock he owns in this state. He was united in marriage with Miss Ellen J. Noble, a native of Wisconsin, but reared in Iowa, at the time of marriage a resident of Denver, Colo., where the ceremony was performed on October 19, 1885. They have two children, their winsome daughters, Lulie E. and Bessie F. Mr. Strong is not only a prosperous and enterprising man who pushes his own business with vigor and success, but he is a broad-minded, far-seeing and public spirited citizen, whose interest in the welfare of his country and state, and in the town in which he lives, is manifested by continual activity in behalf of all means of advancement and improvement for them and the benefit of his people. He is well-esteemed as a leading and useful citizen, whose services are of high value and whose example is an inspiration to others in the line of every good work.

I wish I could have met Ma Strong. She was a strong and amazing and kind woman, and she was always adopting strays and helping people. We named my daughter Elizabeth after her—Elizabeth's middle name is "Strong."

The lives of my great grandparents aren't the only things that I fictionalized. I did a tremendous amount of research for this book. After all, it's much easier to research than to write the damn thing.

The American Memory Site of the National Archives is an amazing resource for researchers, and much of their material is online, and so I didn't have to travel to Washington D.C. to access it. Fortunately, there are birds-eye views of downtown Kansas City from 1879 and 1895, perfectly framing my time period. I could have gone so far as to tell you which streets Sara and James walked down.

And I also have the tremendous good fortune—for me, not for the residents of KC West Bottoms—of having a vast photographic evidence to draw from. That's because the Bottoms flood regularly, and people take lots of photos during these natural disasters.

There are many other things based on fact.

Work began on the "Additional Penitentiary" in Anamosa, Iowa, in 1873. In 1884, the name was changed to the "State Penitentiary." In 1885, it held 281 inmates. Electric lights were actually at the prison when James would have been there—they were first used in December of 1882 Fictional purposes—sorry. The inmates wore the broad horizontal black and white stripes and built their own prison, first in wood and then in stone.

The cookbook *The Compleat Housewife* by Eliza Smith is fact. First published in 1727 in London, the cookbook was republished almost verbatim in 1742 by the Virginia printer William Parks. It was the first cookbook published in the Colonies. The description of the book and its title page is real.

"The Patch" was a 4.5-acre area in the West Bottoms north of James Street and west of Ohio Avenue. It lay west of the Armour Packing Factory. If anything, I built it up a bit. The *Kansas City Journal* reported in 1910: "On this little spot of land fifty-nine houses have been built, of every kind of building material from pieces of driftwood to scraps of asphalt paving. The little shacks are built up against each other, and many front doors in the settlement look out on some neighbor's cow lot." Citizens of the Patch were evicted in April of 1910 and the land was sold for $200.

In 1900, *The 18th Annual Report of the U.S. Commissioner of Labor* reported the following prices in Chicago: a one pound loaf of bread $0.05, a quart of milk $0.06, a pound of flour $0.02, and a one-pound rib roast $0.13. Small, dark, two- to three-room apartments rented for $4-10 a month, while better housing could cost $100 per month. Men worked an average of 290 days a year and made $553.52, while women worked an average of 295 days a year and made $313.42. I extrapolated backwards to estimate wages and prices.

Inventions such as electricity were making their way across the continent. Electrical infrastructure began reaching Iowa, Missouri, and Kansas in 1882. Kansas City had mule-drawn cable cars in 1881, but by 1885, they were powered by electricity. If you remember, the Transcontinental Railroad was completed in just 1869.

In 1881, an African American man named Levi Harrington, 23, was lynched—hung and shot—from the Bluff Bridge for killing a policeman named Jones, a crime Harrington did not commit. It got little coverage in the papers because it happened the same day that Jesse James was shot in Saint Joseph. The lynching that Moses and Auntie refer to previously is that of Joseph Lawrence, a black man from Girard, Crawford County, Kansas, for the charge of rape. It happened on July 6, 1885.

I moved the flood from 1881 to 1885. There was a great flood in 1844 that came through the West Bottoms with a deafening roar and filled it bluff to bluff. It was reported that, during the night of the flood, cries were heard but the flood was too overwhelming to attempt rescue. The next day, rescuers found Louis Tromley perched in a tree, his wife in a tree a hundred yards farther on, and his son sitting on the peak of the swaying house. Later that day, onlookers saw Tromley's house floating with the current, with Tromley's favorite dog perched on its top. Tromley yelled out the dog's name, and the dog let out a mournful wail. Tromley almost plunged into the water to save it. And then, in 1881, the spring was cold and wet, and sleighs were seen in the city as late as March 19. The 1881 flood peaked on April 29. There were more large floods in 1903 and 1951.

Little things. President Cleveland did have a mistress. Sara's paste opal jewel exists, and in 2003, it was for sale by The Three Graces, Houston, Texas, for $1,380. The description of passengers getting cozy during a train wreck that is told by Moses is from Bill Nye's 1882 *Forty Lies and Other Liars*. I based the rats at the river on an account given by a man who grew up in Kansas City in the twentieth century—the 1960s, I think. The description of the packing factories owes a lot to Sinclair Lewis's *The Jungle*. On September 15, 1885, Jumbo the elephant was crushed by a train in Saint Thomas, Ontario, Canada. Thomas's Tsististas are the Cheyenne, and the words from the Cheyenne language is from the Dull Knife College web site, but their spelling is my own.

I thought a lot about the story's dialog. Who knows how people talked in 1885? The past is another country. Just like today, what was written was probably much different than what was said. But I also wanted it to sound to the reader like real people talking. To compromise, I wrote the dialog as I would any other, and then I tweaked it and took out the words that either weren't contemporary or don't "feel" historical and then put in words that do feel historical. For me, communication and clarity rank above "truth" (as if there is only one truth).

In a few places, I tip my hat to particular images or turns of phrase from writers I admire. I think of them as grace notes. When James first goes into the bowels of the packing factory, Joseph says hello to Jurgis—Jurgis is the main character in Sinclair Lewis's *The Jungle*. When the moon rises in KC "like a fired pine knot," it's a small homage to Jean Toomer and

"Blood Burning Moon." There were many more, but they were taken out in revision. Imitation as the sincerest form of flattery.

When I wrote the first draft of *Earth's Imagined Corners*, I had not visited Kansas City. And so it was a surreal experience to drive through the West Bottoms for the first time after I had so fully imagined it. It was the same but not the same. Today, overpasses lace between buildings that Sara and James would have seen out the cable car window. A wastewater treatment plant and a Fedex warehouse lie next to narrow empty streets crowded with abandoned nineteenth century buildings, their lower windows shattered and their elaborately painted signs still visible behind graffiti. Driving through them, even in broad daylight, feels a little like one of those horror movies where no one's around and you're just waiting for something nasty to pop out from an alley.

To this day, I can't help thinking of all those people who lived and worked in those giant husks, people who felt itchy in wool and got sunburned and loved that early morning splash of water on the face. People like Sara and James, like Frank and Ellen Strong. I look forward to continuing their journey in the next book.

– Tamara Linse, Laramie, Wyoming, 2015

Discussion Questions

1. The title of *Earth's Imagined Corners* comes from John Donne's "Holy Sonnet VII." Why might the author have chosen a line from this poem as her title? How does the poem relate to the novel's action, characters, or themes?

2. The novel is set in small-town Iowa and then the metropolis of Kansas City. How are these settings characterized? Do these settings support or detract from the action and themes of the novel?

3. Historical fiction is often set during well-known events in history such as the Civil War. However, *Earth's Imagined Corners* is not. Does it add or detract from the action of the story?

4. Historical fiction is said more to reflect the time in which it is written than the actual historical time period in which it is set. Which aspects of *Earth's Imagined Corners* are a reflection of 1885 and which reflect present-day sensibilities?

5. Writers of historical fiction are faced with both remaining true to the historical period yet making the actions of the characters relatable by updating certain things. For example, in *Earth's Imagined Corners*, the dialog has the flavor of the time but does not strictly represent how people talked in that time. What do you think about this? Where should the line be?

6. There are echoes of the legacy of large forces—such as the Civil War, racism, and waves of immigration—throughout the book. Where do you see these echoes? Is there a larger message about the historical, societal forces that shape us?

7. Certain events in *Earth's Imagined Corners* are based on

real events. For example, the hanging of Moses is based on newspaper reports of a similar event at the time. Also, the rats coming out of the ground near the offal pipe is based on an incident in the 1960s in Kansas City. What are a fiction writer's responsibilities to history? What are her or his responsibilities to the readers' experiences?

8. One of the themes of *Earth's Imagined Corners* is poverty. How does Sara's experience of money change over the course of the book? James's experience of money? Do you think it's an accurate representation?

9. Another theme is romantic love versus married love, as well as the difference between courting in the 1880s versus courting today. Social pressures were much more "Victorian" in the 1880s. How does the author try to convey the differences between then and now? Does she do it effectively? How does Sara and James's relationship change over the course of the narrative?

10. Women had few rights in the 1880s. They could not vote at this time, and they had just gained the right to own property and earn their own money in the U.S. Does the author effectively convey the danger in which Sara places herself with her decision to elope with James?

11. Both Sara and James have had challenges in their upbringings—Sara's father was very controlling, and James experienced severe poverty and unsettled circumstances. How do these upbringings manifest themselves in their adult lives and what does it bring to their marriage?

12. How is race represented in *Earth's Imagined Corners*? Does this representation tread new ground, or does it seem to rehash things you've read before? What are a writer's responsibilities when it comes to race? Should an author write about people of a different race?

13. One of the pitfalls of writing about race is to stereotype minorities as evil. Another is to stereotype minorities as good. How does *Earth's Imagined Corners* walk this delicate line?

14. This time period saw "a cult of death," with the deaths of prominent citizens reported in gruesome and salacious detail in the newspapers. There were many rituals around death. Today, we have largely swept death under the rug. Which is the healthier approach? Why the differences in approaches then versus now?

15. James has a hard time finding work. Do you think this accurately reflects the time period? What forces, both historical and personal, cause these challenges? What might James have done differently?

16. James is severely injured and in a coma for days. Discuss medical science at the time versus medical science today. What are the differences? How does this trauma effect James? Do you think James is to blame for his later actions, or is it due to the head trauma?

17. What is the dog Opal's function in the book? Introducing a vulnerable character such as Opal or a child into a story is dangerous. It can tug at your heartstrings, but then it can seem gratuitous if that character is killed off. Does the author effectively walk that line?

18. The flood is reminiscent of the flood in Zora Neale Hurston's *Their Eyes Were Watching God*. If you have read this classic, how do the floods compare? In general, what narrative purpose do natural disasters such as floods serve? Does it seem natural to the story (i.e., did the author prepare you well enough?) or does it seem out of left field (i.e., *deus ex machina*)?

19. Did you like Sara? James? Does a female character need to

be "likable"? Does a male character?

20. The novel could be considered a *bildungsroman*, or coming-of-age novel. What other bildungsromans have you read, and how does *Earth's Imagined Corners* compare? Why do we keep returning to this type of story?

21. Does Sara's story end in triumph, despair, or a mixture of both? Are you satisfied with the ending? Would you have liked more closure? Or do you like an ending to be looser and less tied into a nice bow?

22. Did you like the book? If so, why? If not, why not?

455

The Round Earth Series

Book 1 – *Earth's Imagined Corners*

In 1885 Iowa, Sara Moore is a dutiful daughter, but when her father tries to force her to marry his younger partner, she must choose between the partner—a man who treats her like property—and James Youngblood—a kind man she hardly knows who has a troubled past. When she confronts her father, he beats her and turns her out of the house, breaking all ties, so she decides to elope with James to Kansas City with hardly a penny to their names. In the tradition of Willa Cather's *O Pioneers!* and Zora Neale Hurston's *Their Eyes Were Watching God, Earth's Imagined Corners* is a novel that comprehends the great kindnesses and violences we do to each other.

Book 2 – *Numberless Infinities*
Coming in January 2016

In 1890 Kansas City, Sara and James Youngblood have built a life for themselves, but then James's yearning for the West gets the better of him. He accepts a contract to supply ties for the burgeoning railroad, and off they go across Nebraska and the Dakotas. Life on the road is hard, and Sara cooks for the crew, but then she discovers she's pregnant—she lost a baby before and almost died. The crooked railroad boss refuses to pay, and James's crew revolts, and so they are stranded on Indian lands with the rising tide of the Ghost Dance religion. *Numberless Infinities* may remind you of Jane Kirkpatrick's *All Together in One Place* and Thomas Berger's *Little Big Man*.

Book 3 – *This Lowly Ground*
Coming in January 2017

In 1894, Sara and James Youngblood are exhausted by life on the wagon road, and so when their son Jake has his hand taken off in a gun accident, they decide to homestead in northern Wyoming. James teams with a local rancher to build an irrigation system, and soon a town grows up—one that all agree should be called Youngblood. Years pass. A straggling band of Mormons pushing handcarts from Salt Lake City show up in the middle of a snow storm, and the town pulls together to help them settle. Soon, though, conflicts erupt in the running of the town, and when the town's livelihood, a brick and tile factory, mysteriously burns down, Sara and James's son Jake is blamed. *This Lowly Ground* is in the tradition of Willa Cather and Carson McCullers.

About the Author

Tamara Linse grew up on a ranch in northern Wyoming with her farmer/rancher rock-hound ex-GI father, her artistic musician mother from small-town middle America, and her four sisters and two brothers. She jokes that she was raised in the 1880s because they did things old-style—she learned how to bake bread, break horses, irrigate, change tires, and be alone, skills she's been thankful for ever since. The ranch was a partnership between her father and her uncle, and in the 80s and 90s the two families had a Hatfields and McCoys-style feud.

She worked her way through the University of Wyoming as a bartender, waitress, and editor. At UW, she was officially in almost every college on campus until she settled on English and after 15 years earned her bachelor's and master's in English. While there, she taught writing, including a course called Literature and the Land, where students read Wordsworth and Donner Party diaries during the week and hiked in the mountains on weekends. She also worked as a technical editor for an environmental consulting firm.

She still lives in Laramie, Wyoming, with her husband Steve and their twin son and daughter. She writes fiction around her job as an editor for a foundation. She is also a photographer, and when she can she posts a photo a day for a Project 365.

Please stop by Tamara's website, www.tamaralinse.com, and her blog, Writer, Cogitator, Recovering Ranch Girl, at tamara-linse.blogspot.com. You can find an extended bio there with lots of juicy details. Also friend her on Facebook and follow her on Twitter, and if you see her in person, please say hi.

Find Tamara Linse on the web:

www.tamaralinse.com
tamara-linse.blogspot.com
@tamaralinse
fb.com/tlinse

Your Turn

If you enjoyed *Earth's Imagined Corners*, it would be tremendously helpful if you would spread the word—stop by your favorite online book site and review it! It's the one thing you can do to really help an author. It doesn't have to be anything elaborate, just a sentence or two if that's all you're up for.

Here are some sites you might visit to leave a review:
- Amazon
- Barnes and Noble
- Goodreads
- Booklikes
- LibraryThing
- Shelfari

You can also visit www.tamaralinse.com/writing_earths_ imagined_corners_review.html for direct links to these sites.

If you'd like to sign up for Tamara's newsletter, stop by her website (www.tamaralinse.com). There you'll also find some freebie content as an incentive.

And, if you liked *Earth's Imagined Corners*, there will be two more coming in the series—*Numberless Infinities* and *This Lowly Ground*. You might also enjoy other previously published works by Tamara Linse—a short story collection called *How to Be a Man* and a novel called *Deep Down Things*. They are available online at Amazon, Barnes and Noble, iBooks, IndieBound, and possibly a bookstore or library near you—you can always order them through you favorite bookstore.

How to Be a Man
a short story collection

"Never acknowledge the fact that you're a girl, and take pride when your guy friends say, 'You're one of the guys.' Tell yourself, 'I am one of the guys,' even though, in the back of your mind, a little voice says, 'But you've got girl parts.'" – Birdie, in "How to Be a Man"

A girl whose self-worth revolves around masculinity, a bartender who loses her sense of safety, a woman who compares men to plants, and a boy who shoots his cranked-out father. These are a few of the hard-scrabble characters in Tamara Linse's debut short story collection, *How to Be a Man*. Set in contemporary Wyoming—the myth of the West taking its toll—these stories reveal the lives of tough-minded girls and boys, self-reliant women and men, struggling to break out of their lonely lives and the emotional havoc of their families to make a connection, to build a life despite the odds. *How to Be a Man* falls within the traditions of Maile Meloy, Tom McGuane, and Annie Proulx.

Also available in audiobook read by P. J. Morgan.

Deep Down Things
a novel

Deep Down Things, Tamara Linse's debut novel, is the emotionally riveting story of three siblings torn apart by a charismatic bullrider-turned-writer and the love that triumphs despite tragedy.

From the death of her parents at sixteen, Maggie Jordan yearns for lost family, while sister CJ drowns in alcohol and brother Tibs withdraws. When Maggie and an idealistic young writer named Jackdaw fall in love, she is certain that she's found what she's looking for. As she helps him write a novel, she gets pregnant, and they marry. But after Maggie gives birth to a darling boy, Jes, she struggles to cope with Jes's severe birth defect, while Jackdaw struggles to overcome writer's block brought on by memories of his abusive father.

Ambitious, but never seeming so, *Deep Down Things* may remind you of Kent Haruf's *Plainsong* and Jodi Picoult's *My Sister's Keeper*.

Soon available in audiobook read by P. J. Morgan.

Made in the USA
Middletown, DE
27 July 2018